AGAINST ALL ADVICE

J.S. EADES

Eades, J.S.
Against All Advice / J.S. Eades
ISBN: 978-0-9939582-1-2

Website: www.jseades.com
Facebook: AuthorJSEades
Twitter: @JS_Eades
Instagram: @jseadesauthor

Editorial Assistance: Colleen Ferrier, Dina Bielby, Lara Krebs, and Samantha Flower
Cover Design: Heather D. Murray

Edition: Amazon Paperback June 2023

Massive thanks to: Eva, Heather, Colleen, Sam, Lara, Dina, Mara, Kate, and of course my husband and son. All their help and encouragement to keep pushing ahead with this story has been very much appreciated.

Chapter 1

Evie Colville has a secret identity.

She may be a lot of things to a lot of people—dutiful daughter, loyal friend, hard-working waitress at her father's coffee shop just to name a few—but one thing she absolutely *isn't* is even remotely qualified to write her weekly 'Miss Lonely Love' column for *The Sutterton Herald*.

At least she doesn't think so.

Luckily, no one but her editor, her dad, and her best friend, Grace Bryant, know Evie's secret. The byline of her column is credited to Shara Strong, Evie's carefully crafted fictional alter-ego. Shara is basically Evie's opposite. She's definitely *not* an eighteen year-old senior at Sutterton High. She's a Grown Up. And she had plenty of dating experience before she married the Man of Her Dreams. The regular readers of 'Miss Lonely Love' know Shara is neither a Miss nor Lonely; in her column she often mentions her handsome, perfect husband. Evie assumes, correctly, that if her readers believe she's been so successful in love, they'll be more inclined to trust her advice with their own problems.

Which is ironic really, because Evie is nothing of the sort. She's never been in love. She's not even dating. She *has* had a boyfriend. Once. But it wasn't serious. Evie's not ready for a relationship. In fact, over the past year, she's barely thought about boys. Concentrating on her school work and her two jobs, not to mention taking care of her father and brother and squeezing in occasional time with friends—well, it doesn't leave much room for dating.

She doesn't mind, though. She needs to graduate at the top of her class to win a scholarship to a good college and escape this tiny town. Falling in love would only complicate things. And she doesn't want complications.

This evening Evie sits at the counter of Colville's Coffee Clutch, mug of hot chocolate in hand, polishing her column for Friday's paper. She's just finished advising a teenage girl, whom she suspects might be her brother Dylan's friend Charlie Lancaster, to stand up for herself to her controlling boyfriend.

Once Evie's happy with her replies, she emails the document to her editor. A glance toward the clock over the door shows she still has ten minutes until she can close up.

Sometimes, if she reads a message she feels deserves a response but she's already finished her column, she takes a few moments to send a personal reply. So tonight, with passing curiosity, she pulls the top letter from the bundle in her knapsack.

The writing is small and cramped, with jagged, crow-scratch vertical lines.

Dear Miss LL,

I've got a messed up situation for you. What do you do when you find out the love of your life has been sleeping with your brother behind your back? You thank your lucky stars you're free of her, right?

My problem is I can't stop thinking about her. She stabbed me through the heart, and I left town and haven't looked back. But the sad truth is, much as I hate myself for it, I'm still in love with her. And I'm terrified that if she apologized and groveled, I just might give in and take her back.

Now I'm not dumb enough to think that's ever going to happen.

2

As far as I know, she's still with my brother, and I really don't
want to see either of them again.
So, my question for you is, how do I get over her?
Just Another Idiot

Evie frowns as she re-reads the letter. She's answered
questions about cheating before, but never cheating involving
sleeping with two brothers at the same time, then swapping to
date the other. She agrees with the writer—that's pretty
messed up.

Tapping her fingernails against the countertop, she
contemplates how to reply. She tries to imagine how she might
feel if she found herself in a similar situation, and how she'd
want to deal with it. Tearing out a fresh sheet of paper from her
notebook, she picks up her pen and starts writing.

Dear JAI,
Even though I can't include your letter in this week's column, I
wanted to send you a personal reply.
First of all, I'm so sorry you went through that.
Second, you're absolutely right. You should probably get down
on your knees and thank God that you're free of her and get on
with your life, but I know it's not that easy. Love isn't something
you can flick off like a switch. It burrows deep inside and
becomes a part of you. The only thing that might help lessen
its grip is time, but I think you probably already know that.
Good on you for leaving town, though. Time and space away
from them is just what you need right now. I recommend you
get out and meet some people. It might surprise you how new
friends can distract from old problems. Although you may not
be ready yet, I also suggest you consider maybe starting to
date again, even if it's just casual.
Be strong. Someday you'll look back on this and see that it
pointed you toward the path you were meant to be on.
Best of luck!
Miss LL

Evie reads her reply over, then tucks it into an envelope and prints the local post office box return address across the front. She glances up at the clock again, and with relief sees it's time to head home.

She packs up her things, pulls on her heavy winter coat and hat, and dims the lights. The welcome bell over the door tinkles its goodbye as she steps out and locks up.

Sutterton in mid-January after midnight is cold and still. The silence is so overwhelming Evie's eardrums interpret it as a low roar, a crowd cheering off in the distance, a jet plane passing overhead at six hundred miles an hour. The emptiness feels absolute, with only the fading echo of the bell to ground her in reality.

White clouds of breath mar the frigid air in front of her and her boots squeak on the hard packed snow. She looks up at the night sky above the jagged black silhouette of the distant mountains. The stars seem to shine brighter than ever tonight, too frigid to even twinkle.

The buildings are dark, the snow is light, and the few streetlights cast long shadows. The vivid blue of the mailbox on the corner pops out of all that monochrome. When Evie reaches it, she pulls the letter from her pocket and slips it inside.

She takes a deep breath, her lungs filling with ice before hurrying along the frozen sidewalk, anxious to reach the warmth of home.

Friday morning's alarm is always unwelcome. On Thursday nights Evie has to close the coffee shop late, and the resulting lack of sleep tends to make her grouchy. The thump of her phone hitting the floor as her flailing hand knocks it off the nightstand only jolts her further from dreamland.

With a groan, she pushes back the covers, reluctantly emerging from her cozy cocoon. She trudges to the bathroom half-awake, pounding on her brother's door to rouse him as she passes. An annoyed groan is her only response.

Her father left nearly two hours ago to open for the before-work crowd in need of their morning fix. Every morning but Sunday it's just Evie and Dylan, fighting for the bathroom, scrounging up breakfast, and then scrambling out to the corner to catch the school bus.

This morning they manage to end up at the kitchen table at the same time, Evie with jam on toast in one hand and a mug of hot chocolate in the other, Dylan digging into an enormous bowl of half Raisin Bran, half Fruit Loops. He claims that since he's a point guard on the school basketball team, it gives him the energy he needs for the day. Evie just rolls her eyes.

Her phone beeps with a message from her editor, and it reminds her of the final letter she'd included in her column last night.

"Hey Dyl?"

With barely a glance her way, he shoves another heaping spoonful into his mouth. "Mmm?"

"Is Charlie still dating Cameron Wheeler?" She tucks a loose strand of long, dirty blonde hair behind her ear.

Her brother's face twists. "Yeah. Why?" It's clear he doesn't approve.

"No reason. I was just curious."

Now she's more suspicious than ever that the email might have come from Charlie. Cam is the captain of the football and basketball teams and is, in Evie's opinion, a complete alpha-male douchebag. His ego is nearly as big as his father's. Martin Wheeler is Sutterton's mayor. The Wheelers were one of the original families to settle in this area. So were the Colvilles, but that might be the only thing the two families have in common. Tom Colville is content to live a quiet life, and though his coffee shop is moderately successful, Evie knows that some months they barely scrape by. The Wheelers have money and power—plenty of it. They live in the largest of the riverfront mansions along Route Ten, and are famous for hosting lavish parties. Since founding families are a mandatory presence at such events, Evie has had to endure every one of them.

She glances at the digital clock on the microwave. *Crap!* "The bus is gonna be here any minute!" Jumping to her feet, she dumps the remains of her chocolate into the sink and dashes for her coat.

As usual, Dylan heads straight to the back of the bus, while Evie sits near the middle with Grace. She notes her brother has taken the empty spot beside Charlie. Cam drives himself to school, so if he *is* still dating Charlie, he didn't bother giving her a lift today.

Evie chats with her friend until the bus approaches the gray stone and brick castle that is Sutterton High. Her eyes are drawn to the corner turrets whose upper windows have an awesome view of the park and river bend across the way

The high school was built in 1915 at the height of the architectural castle craze that swept across America. Now its hulking edifice seems out of place: an embarrassment to be ridiculed by the students, a point of pride to the mayor and town council, and a roadside attraction to outsiders.

Evie thinks it's beautiful. She's loved this building since she was small—years before she'd ever stepped foot inside its hallowed halls. When she's having a crappy day, she needs only to make her way to the highest tower and look out at the view to instantly feel a bit better. It's like something clicks inside and, even if only for a moment, she understands her place in the world. Like she finally feels she's where she belongs.

After Math class, she has a free period. Normally, she spends this time doing homework in the library, but today she has an appointment with her guidance counselor.

"Good morning, Evie. What can I do for you today?" Mrs. Ziegler asks once Evie takes a seat. She's an older woman with thick red hair streaked with grey that she piles into a messy bun. Evie likes Mrs. Ziegler. She treats Evie like an adult.

Evie sits with her spine straight, her legs crossed, and her hands clasped on her thighs. "Good morning. I was wondering when I should start applying for college scholarships? Are they all online now, or do any still do paper?"

Mrs. Ziegler shifts some files off a stack on her desk. "I got some paper ones for Syracuse last week. I know for Cornell, Columbia, and S.U.N.Y, you can submit online, but I don't think they're reviewing for this fall yet. It's still a bit early, as your final grades aren't locked down for a few more months. Try applying in another month, around the end of February."

"I'll take the Syracuse application then, please."

Mrs. Ziegler hands the forms over. "You can fill out most of it now, and then attach a copy of your mid-term report card once you get it. They may want recommendations from some of your teachers as well."

"That won't be a problem," Evie tells her with a self-conscious smile. She knows her teachers will have good things to say. She usually gets straight As, and the only time her grades ever dipped below a B+ was in the months following her mom's death. Otherwise, she's always been a model student.

She gets up to leave, but Mrs. Ziegler stops her. "You're only considering in-state colleges, right?"

Evie sighs softly. "For now, yes. I'll let you know if I need any out-of-state information."

Mrs. Ziegler nods, and Evie walks back into the hall. She'd love to apply to out-of-state colleges, but the thought of living far away from her father and brother worries her. She wants to get out of Sutterton, that's a definite, but she also doesn't want to be too far away. Her father might still need her to work weekend shifts at the Clutch.

There's also the fact that they have no money to pay for flights or living expenses beyond the bare minimum. This limits Evie's choices, but she'll just have to do the best she can with what they can afford. And if she doesn't earn a full scholarship, she won't be going anywhere.

It's been a busy evening, but The Clutch is finally starting to empty as people head up the street to Henry's Grill for a drink, or home, or wherever else they need to be on a frigid Saturday night. As Evie wipes the counter, she glances back at the slim boy sitting in the corner. Well…he isn't really a boy, is he? He's tall and pale, with dark hair mostly hidden under a black Greek fisherman's cap. He wears tinted glasses and, as usual, has his nose buried in a book. As usual because, although Evie has no idea who he is, she knows he's been in her shop before. More than once. Always when she's been too busy to really pay him much notice. She remembers noting his cap and glasses, as well as the thick, black pea coat he wears. And that he only orders coffee, also black, which he has her pour into his own travel cup instead of a red Colville's Coffee Clutch mug.

"Excuse me, Evie?"

With a start, she turns to the elderly woman at a side table with her husband, where they sit almost every Saturday evening.

"Yes, Mrs. Clancy? Can I top you up?"

"No, thank you. It's time for us to head on home. I just wanted to say you look lovely in that shade of blue. It matches your eyes."

Mr. Clancy nods in agreement. A few weeks ago, they had told Evie they'd been married for forty-eight years. He slides a few bills onto the table, then gets to his feet to help his wife stand and ease her arms into her coat. They have matching down jackets with fur-trimmed hoods, perfect for a chilly January night.

"Aw, that's so sweet of you. You guys take care on those icy sidewalks," Evie advises.

Not long after they leave, her history teacher, Mr. Wright, also heads out. Now there's only Evie and the reading stranger.

She takes a breath, straightens her spine, and walks back to him.

"Warm you up?" she asks, holding out the coffee pot.

8

He looks up at her and lowers his glasses.

Evie's breath catches in her throat as she stares into the most brilliant green eyes she's ever seen. In the harsh fluorescent light of the shop they shine like emeralds— emeralds framed by thick, black lashes. And right now those mesmerizing eyes are watching her with amusement.

"-in mind?"

Crap. She missed most of that. Heat floods her face. "P-pardon?"

"I said depends what you have in mind," he repeats, one side of his mouth curving into a lopsided grin.

She flushes deeper as she realizes the double entendre of her words. *Warm you up. Oh God.*

"More c-coffee?" she stutters. *Holy cow. Get a grip, loser. You left yourself wide open for that one.*

"No, thanks." He flashes a real smile this time. "I should probably go. Aren't you about ready to close?"

His smile is as striking as the rest of him, and it eases Evie's embarrassment a little. She wonders how old he is. She's sure she'd remember if she'd seen him at school. No, he is definitely not a teenager. But not by a lot.

"We're open 'til midnight Thursday to Saturday," she says with a bit more assurance. "I have to stay, even if there's no one here."

"That sucks. Don't you get bored?"

She shakes her head. "Nah. If it's dead I just do homework or clean or read. There's always something that needs doing."

He looks her up and down and her temperature spikes again. "You're in high school…" Pausing, he checks her nametag. "Evie?"

"For a few more months," she admits.

One dark brow arches thoughtfully. "Huh. I pegged you for older."

"I'm eighteen. Why? How old are you?"

He looks at her for a second, his face going neutral. Then that easy grin returns. "Twenty-two. Just moved here a few weeks ago."

"Welcome to Sutterton. What brings you to our quiet little town? Certainly not the weather." She sits down opposite him. Why not? There are no other customers to serve.

He sighs, so softly she almost doesn't hear it. "That's a long story I'd rather not relive right now. My uncle owns a house on Route Ten just outside town. Used to be a bed and breakfast. I'm staying with him at the moment."

Evie's eyes light up. "Oh! Your uncle is Max Sterling! My dad knows him. He comes in here pretty often."

"Yep." His eyes shift down to the book in his hands.

Following his gaze, she asks, "What're you reading?"

He flips it over so she can see the cover.

A bright smile of recognition lights Evie's face. "*The Great Gatsby*? Cool. I'm reading that right now for English. Well, I actually got so into it I couldn't put it down and finished it in two days, but I'm re-reading at the pace we're supposed to. Have you read it before?"

He presses his lips together self-consciously. "Nine times," he confesses.

Evie's eyebrows fly up. "Woah! Maybe I should get you to help me with the five-thousand word essay I have to write on it," she laughs.

"Maybe," he mumbles, shifting around on his chair. Tucking his book inside his coat, he abruptly stands. "Hey, so, I gotta bounce. Thanks for the coffee and conversation."

Evie wonders if she's said something wrong. They seemed to be getting along fine, but now he looks like he'd rather be anywhere than here. Scrambling to her feet as well, she clarifies, "You don't actually have to help. I was just kidding."

Their eyes meet as he adjusts his cap, for a moment revealing more of that messy dark hair. A waft of fresh, light cologne hits her as they stand in close proximity, and much to her surprise, hot desire clenches low in her belly.

"I don't mind looking over your essay. As you might've guessed, it's one of my favorite novels. Maybe I'll see you in here next week. Enjoy the rest of your night, Evie."

She doesn't reply at first, frozen in thought as she watches him walk away. Just as he reaches the door she calls, "Wait!"

He pauses and looks back at her.

"I don't even know your name." Her voice comes out sounding much younger than her eighteen years.

With a small smile, he replies, "It's Alistair."

Then he slips out into the night.

Chapter 2

When Max hands him the letter as he sits in the library reading, Alistair Sterling's surprised, to say the least. He can't even remember the last time he got an actual letter. It might have been back in high school when that weird chick had a huge crush on him and would sometimes mail him stuff in pointless and increasingly desperate attempts to be noticed.

This envelope, however, is not decorated with hearts and kisses. It's plain white and is addressed to *JAI* at Max's post office box. The loops and swirls of the handwriting are decidedly feminine.

"How'd you know it was for me?" he asks as his uncle pokes at the dying embers in the fireplace. The house is huge, rambling, and like pretty much every other building around here, old. It's next to impossible to keep warm, so at this time of year it's necessary to keep a fire burning in any room in which you want to spend time.

"Sure not meant for me," Max states flatly, straightening to hang the iron poker on its hook. He turns back to Alistair. "Talk to your dad yet?"

Stiffening, Alistair mutters, "Nope."

"Paul?"

"Nope."

Max sighs. "Well, at least they know you're here and didn't run off and do anything stupid. Any idea how long you might stay?"

Their eyes meet. Alistair's irises are stony. "Does it matter? Let me know when you're sick of me and I'll split."

Another sigh. "You're my brother's kid. I'm not going to kick you to the curb. You're welcome here as long as you like."

There's a long pause. "I don't know yet. But you'll be the first to know when I'm moving on."

His uncle snorts. "Thanks for that much, I guess. Hey, I'm heading to Henry's to pick up hot wings. You want?"

"Sounds good," Alistair replies absently, his attention returned to the letter in his hand. He hears Max's footsteps cross the hardwood and leave.

Alistair tears open the envelope and slides out the page. Reading it over quickly, random phrases pop out at him:

you're absolutely right.
I know it's not that easy.
burrows deep inside and becomes a part of you
time and space away from them is just what you need right now.
consider maybe starting to date again.

Alistair crushes the page into a jagged white ball. With a sigh he stands, meaning to toss it into the fireplace.

Dating? Yeah, right. Like I want to throw myself into that volcano again. Not gonna happen.

None of her advice is of any use to him. But then again, why did he even think it would be? It's pointless. His question is the most inane, the most unanswerable question in the world. How do you stop loving someone? Ridiculous. Like he'd asked himself at least fifty times before he dropped the letter in the mailbox—why is he even bothering?

He stares at it for a moment. Instead of fueling the fire, he sits back down and pulls the reply open again, flattening it on the side table with his hand. The formerly smooth surface is now crinkled below his palm. It brings to mind a phrase from a book he read long ago: *A heart is like a piece of paper—once it's crumpled or torn, it can never return to its former purity.*

So the bitch left permanent scars? So what? What did it fucking matter? She's happy back home with his brother, and he's sitting here miserable in Sutterton. How is that fair?

Then Alistair's eyes land on something else Miss Lonely Love had advised.

It might surprise you how new friends can distract from old problems.

An image of the cute blonde with the expressive blue eyes from the coffee shop pops into his head and a small smile surfaces. Maybe later he'll brave the cold in search of a caffeine fix.

School buses always seem to emit a pungent blend of diesel exhaust, old vinyl, and stale sweat. It's a universally accepted fact. Today's potpourri of unpleasantness also includes a vague hint of weed wafting from the back and the rancid, sickly sweet odor of a decaying apple rolling around beneath the seats. Evie tries to remember to breathe through her mouth.

As the bus trundles along, she darts what she hopes are surreptitious glances over her shoulder at Charlie Lancaster. Charlie is sitting in the very back with Dylan again, whispering and giggling, their heads close together. Evie wonders what Cam would think if he could see them. She assumes he wouldn't be impressed—he's known to be possessive with his 'toys.'

Snow-shrouded houses slide past her window as she forces herself to look outside instead. Her mind is troubled. Evie had been the first one inside the girls' locker room before Gym this afternoon, as third period History had been dismissed a few minutes early for once. As she came around a wall of lockers, she startled a half-dressed Charlie, the last straggler of the juniors from the previous class.

Although the other girl was quick to pull up her jeans and throw on her hoodie, it wasn't fast enough to prevent Evie from noticing the bruises on the inside of her upper arm. Small, round ones—the kind that could have been left by squeezing fingers.

Evie stopped in her tracks, too shocked to speak.

Charlie avoided meeting Evie's eyes, just muttering, "Hey" and scrambling past her for the door.

Those bruises have been weighing on Evie's mind ever since. Did Charlie write that letter to Miss Lonely Love last week? Could Cam be getting rough with her behind closed doors? Evie isn't sure, but her gut keeps insisting something isn't right.

She stares through the glass, but doesn't notice the bus nearing her stop. She keeps seeing that ugly, purplish-yellow row of spots on Charlie's arm. And, even more concerning, the larger bruises she'd glimpsed on the younger girl's inner thighs.

The late afternoon sunlight is starting to fade as Evie sits on her bed with Grace discussing the themes of *The Great Gatsby*. Though Grace hasn't finished the book yet, they both agree that Gatsby is so fixated on the idea of Daisy as 'the one who got away' that it dooms him to repeat the mistakes of his past.

Once they put their English homework aside, Evie leans back against her pillow.

"Hey, did you read my column this weekend?"

"Of course. Why?"

"Remember the letter from the girl about her douchey boyfriend?"

Wrinkling her forehead, Grace says, "Um, I think so. He was super controlling, right?"

"Yep. So, this might sound weird but…I've been wondering whether it could've been Charlie Lancaster."

Grace arches a brow. "She's still seeing Cameron, isn't she?"

Evie nods.

"Hmm. Could be. I heard he treated Amber pretty shitty last year." Graces pauses. "Yeah, I could see that."

Though there's no one else in the house to overhear, Evie lowers her voice. "I ran into Charlie in the change room before gym today and she had bruises on her arm. It might be nothing, but…"

"But it might be something," Grace finishes, her eyes narrowing.

Evie doesn't mention the other bruises she saw, the darker, uglier ones lower down. For all she knows, maybe Charlie likes things a little rough in bed. And if so, that's no one's business but her and her partner's.

"Yeah," Evie sighs.

Grace starts gathering up her school books. It's almost dark, and her grandmother will be expecting her home for dinner. As she gets to her feet, she turns back to Evie. "What about telling Dylan what you saw? They're friends—he may know how she hurt her arm."

It's a good idea, but Evie is beginning to wonder if her brother has a thing for Charlie. If he finds out she's been hurt, he might confront Cam about it, which could end up getting ugly. Evie isn't ready to escalate things unless she finds more evidence to support her fears.

"True. But I don't think I'll mention the bruises. I'll just ask if she said anything about her arm. Maybe she fell or something? It could be no big deal. But if I tell him my suspicions, and he says something to Charlie or Cam, and it turns out I'm wrong…well that would make things uncomfortable for all of us."

"But if Cam's hurting her, it has to stop."

"I totally agree, but I think we need more information before we go jumping to any conclusions. Let me see if I can find out what Dyl knows first."

"I really hope it's nothing."

"Me, too."

Tuesday nights are never very busy at the shop, and this cold, blustery Tuesday is even quieter than usual. Evie finished all her cleaning a while ago, and now sits behind the counter sipping hot chocolate and reading tonight's assigned chapter.

The bells over the door jingle, jarring her from the lavish room at the Plaza where Gatsby and Tom are embroiled in their tense confrontation. She glances up in annoyance, hoping whoever it is just wants a coffee to go.

When she sees the familiar black cap and coat, her eyes flare and a smile chases away her irritation. Alistair. She's surprised to see him back so soon; it's only been three nights since they talked. The thought that he might have come just to see her this time makes her pulse quicken.

"Oh hey," she greets him, bookmarking her page and standing as he approaches the counter. Tonight his face is glasses-free, and his green eyes stand out like neon signs. Those eyes are dangerous as hell—and they probably melt the panties off every woman he meets.

Pull yourself together, loser, she mentally scolds. As professionally as possible, she says, "Dark roast, black, right?"

He chuckles. "I'm impressed you remember."

In an attempt to hide her red face, Evie turns to the row of coffee machines behind her, lifting the only remaining pot to the light and examining it dubiously. As she swirls it around, the black liquid oozes viscous fingers down the inside of the glass.

"I'll have to make a fresh pot. This stuff's sludge." Looking over her shoulder at him, she adds, "Hope you're not in a rush." What she really hopes is that he'll stay and keep her company. She still has another hour to go.

"No problem. I'd prefer fresh anyway."

She rinses out the pot, then measures coffee grounds into the top of the machine, setting the switch to brew. When she turns back to him, Alistair is perched on a stool across from her, her novel in one hand. His cap sits on the counter beside her mug of cooling chocolate, and he's combing his fingers through his hair to unflatten it. Evie has a strange urge to reach over and mess it up further. She can't help wondering if that thick hair would feel as soft as it looks.

He opens her book to where she left off and scans the page. "Ah," he observes with a quirk of his lips. "Things're starting to heat up."

"That scene is so tense!"

Alistair chuckles, tucking her bookmark back inside. "So when's your essay due?"

"A week from Friday. We have to finish the last two chapters this week, then pick a theme and write about it." She raises her mug to her lips. Lukewarm chocolate is still miles better than no chocolate at all.

When she sets it back down, he picks it up and takes a sniff. "No wonder the coffee is old. Even you're not drinking it!"

Self-consciously brushing a strand of hair behind her ear, she admits, "Actually…weird I know, but…I don't drink coffee."

Both eyebrows fly up. "You work in a coffee shop and you don't drink coffee?" He begins to laugh.

"I work in my *dad's* coffee shop and I don't drink coffee," she clarifies, laughing along with him.

"That explains why you're here all the time. No choice."

Evie's laughter stutters to a halt. *No choice.* It's true. Sort of. But he doesn't know the whole of it, and she doesn't intend to tell him. She wants to be here. She wants to pitch in any way she can.

"Well, my brother helps out sometimes. And if we're really stuck, my friend Grace will fill in. But Dad mostly tries to keep things in the family. It's simpler." She deliberately leaves out that she doesn't get paid for these shifts, that she does whatever she can to help make ends meet since her mom passed away. The Colville's financial struggles are nobody's business but their own.

"Family business. I get that. My dad has a law firm in New York and I was expected to go to law school." Alistair rolls his eyes. "My brother's at Columbia following in the old man's footsteps. And I'm...well...here. Letting dear old Pops down, as usual."

A *ping* behind her startles Evie before she can respond, letting her know the fresh pot of coffee is ready. She reaches for a clean mug from the shelf.

"No need," Alistair reminds her. "Just pour it in here. One less dish to wash that way." He sets his travel cup on the counter beside his hat and twists off the lid.

Her cheeks grow warm again. *Right.* He brings his own cup. "Sorry, I forgot," she mumbles, picking up the bubbling carafe. *Now, what had we been talking about? Oh yeah.*

"So, you don't want to be a lawyer. So what? Most lawyers are egotistical, manipulative jackasses." That earns her a small smile. Encouraged, she continues. "Did you go to college?"

"Not yet." Alistair blows on the surface of the steaming liquid before taking a tentative sip. "I might apply at some point. Once I straighten my head out enough to get my life back on track."

Evie takes another swig of her chocolate. It's cold now. She tilts the cup and swallows the last of it. "Your dad doesn't approve of you taking a timeout in Sutterton?"

He shrugs. "No clue. I haven't spoken to him since I left. Doubt it."

"What about your mom? Does she support you?"

Alistair goes still, dropping his gaze to a spot on the countertop. For a moment she thinks he isn't going to answer. Then he murmurs, "She would, if she were around. She died when I was twelve."

Empathy floods through Evie. She remembers far too well her own mother's final months, days, moments. Sometimes she wishes she could forget. Her reply is little more than a whisper. "So did mine. Two years ago."

Those intense green eyes lift to hers, full of understanding. "I'm sorry."

She waves his words away, pretending it's no big deal, trying to brush it off like she always does when people offer sympathy. Then she stops herself. Maybe this time she doesn't need to pretend. Alistair gets it, after all.

"Cancer," she states with a small sigh.

"Ah. That sucks."

He doesn't offer his own mother's cause of death and she doesn't ask. She just says, "Yeah."

They sit in silence for a bit. It isn't an awkward silence though; it's companionable. Easy, even. Evie has never talked about her mom's death with anyone who's lost their own mother. She finds herself feeling suddenly closer to Alistair—which is crazy, because she doesn't even know him. But she realizes she wants to.

For the last thirty minutes of her shift they discuss their favorite books. No further mention is made of disappointed fathers or dead mothers. He waits until she wipes down the coffee machines and dims the lights, then follows her to the door.

The snow is falling harder than ever; gusts of wind off the mountains billow white clouds up the street. Evie shivers as she locks up, pulling her scarf tighter.

"Well, goodnight then," she says, turning back to Alistair. Snowflakes are melting on his cheeks.

He tugs the brim of his cap down. "How're you getting home?"

She glances down the blustery street in the direction of home. "Uh, I walk. It's not that far."

One eyebrow arches as he takes another look around them. The light from the nearest streetlight casts no more than an otherworldly halo in the blowing snow. "It's not a fit night out for man or beast. Let me give you a lift."

She hesitates. And she knows he sees her reluctance.

"C'mon. I promise I'm not a serial killer. Would you seriously rather walk home in this than get into a vehicle with me?"

20

Alistair adds a wink and a smile, determined to disarm her fears.

Evie can't help laughing. "Wouldn't a serial killer say exactly that to charm me into his car?"

"Probably. But I don't drive a car. I drive a Jeep. Which is parked over there under about half a foot of snow." He gestures toward a white-shrouded vehicle across the street. "How handy are you with a snow brush?"

She snorts. "I've spent eighteen winters in Sutterton. I think I can handle it."

"Great," he grins. "Let's go."

Alistair pushes the snow off the driver's door with gloved hands and opens it. Reaching behind the seat, he retrieves two long brushes with red bristles on one side and plastic scrapers at the other end.

"As it turns out, I just happen to have a spare. Catch!" He tosses a snow brush her way.

She reaches to grab it, but is too slow; it flies over her shoulder and lands in the slushy street behind. Embarrassed, she scrambles to retrieve it.

"Nice reflexes," he teases, leaning inside the Jeep to start the engine. "Actually, why don't you climb on in and I'll take care of the de-entombing?"

Evie goes around to the passenger side and pulls open the door. But instead of getting inside, she tosses her knapsack on the seat. She isn't some fragile girly-girl, and she doesn't want Alistair to think she isn't willing to do her share.

With the first sweep of her brush along the roof, she accidentally flicks snow into his face. Her eyes flare, mortified. Before she can apologize, she hears him laugh.

"Two can play at that game," he warns, and a volley of cold and wet flies her way. She has just enough time to duck. Most of it lands on her hat, although a few icy bits sprinkle her temple.

The resulting chaos, hereafter called the First Great Snow War of 2018, ends with a mostly cleaned Jeep and two damp, snow-covered, and laughing occupants. Alistair at last calls a ceasefire, and as Evie is quick to point out, it looks like he's taken the brunt of it. Snow sticks to almost every inch of his thick wool coat and hat.

"Just admit I won," she challenges, lifting her brush high in triumph.

He shakes his head, sending bits of snow flying, and chuckles softly. "Fine! You win. Get inside. It's plenty warm now. Let me just put a blanket down so my seats don't get soaked." He pulls a tartan blanket from the backseat and spreads it across the front ones.

Once they're both inside, Alistair turns to her, one brow raised in question. "So?"

"So what?"

He shakes his head, grinning. "All that snow freeze your brain? Where do you live?"

Luckily, she knows her cheeks are already red from exertion. "Oh, right. Maple Street. Just turn left at the corner there onto Pine, then go down two blocks and take another left and that's Maple. It's really not far. I walk home every night."

Though the streets aren't yet plowed, the Jeep has four-wheel drive and makes it to her place with little problem. The Colville home is a small white bungalow, its outline barely visible through all the snow, but Dylan's bedroom window glows and the light is on over the front door.

"Thanks for the lift," Evie says, grabbing her knapsack from the floor.

"Don't mention it."

She reaches for the door handle. "Well, see ya."

"We didn't talk about your Gatsby essay," he reminds her.

Pausing, she looks back at him. "Oh, right. It's fine. You don't have to—"

"I'll drop by the shop again soon, and if you're not too busy we can discuss it then." Alistair's voice is firm.

"Um, okay. Sounds good. Drive safe."

As she steps out into the ankle-deep snow, she glances at him once more. He's still watching her. That quivering sensation in her chest starts up again.

"Goodnight, Evie," he says softly.

"Night."

When Alistair returns to his uncle's, he feels antsy. Instead of heading up to his room, he goes down the hallway to the small gym in the back and jumps on the treadmill. It takes him a while to figure out where all this energy is coming from. Then it hits him: he's happy. *Happy.* He snorts, shaking his head in amazement. How fucking long has it been since he's felt happy? So long it seems almost foreign.

Apparently a chat about dead moms and a snow fight with a cute girl has done the trick, though. Who would've thought? Oh, wait. Miss Lonely Love, that's who.

He hasn't laughed so much since…well, since Michelle, back when things were still good.

After a quick shower, he stretches across his bed with the letter he'd received earlier, once again smoothing the crinkles beneath his palm. The fire crackles and spits behind the grate, sounds that warm him just in hearing them. He enjoyed spending time with Evie, and he recalls how stoked he felt when he came in, at least before memories of Michelle elbowed their way back in.

Hanging out with Evie, goofing around with her—he'd felt so much lighter, even if it only lasted a few hours. It seems Miss Lonely Love had been right about the benefits of a new friend. Evie is a great distraction. And it doesn't hurt that when she smiles at him he feels compelled to smile back.

On impulse, Alistair grabs his silver Cross pen—a gift from his father when he'd graduated high school, no doubt intended to flourish his signature on countless wealth-producing official documents—and his journal, pressing it open to a fresh page. He begins to write.

Dear Miss LL,
Thanks for taking the time to reply. It's appreciated.
Although I was initially skeptical of your advice to get out and

meet new people, tonight I decided to give it a shot. And much to my surprise, you were actually right. I met a girl. We talked, we laughed, and truthfully…I had fun. I haven't had fun in a very long time.

As for your suggestion that I consider dating again, that's where I have to draw the line. No more relationships. No more emotional attachments. To anyone. My ex was the last. I refuse to put myself through that any more. It's just not worth it. I'm not writing this to ask for more advice. I have no more questions for you. I only wanted to say thanks.
JAI

Alistair reads it over, hopes she can decipher his even-messier-than-usual scrawl, and then tears out the page. He'll mail it in the morning. A rare feeling of calm descends, and although he usually stays up late reading, tonight he slides under the blankets and turns off the lamp.

Contrary to most nights these days, he falls into an easy sleep. His dreams are haunted by two beautiful, yet very different women, one the bewitching she-devil who ripped out his heart, the other, a smiling, blonde angel with snow dusting her lashes.

Chapter 3

Ten Years Ago

"Ali!"

He pauses with his fingers on the door handle and turns to her. She looks tired, but her shoulders are straight and she holds herself tall.

"Don't forget to stop at the pharmacy on your way home." Her voice is low and rough. She stifles a cough against her shirtsleeve.

He nods. "I won't, Mom."

A groan is heard from upstairs. "Mommy! I neeeeed you!"

"Just a minute, baby. I'll be right there," she calls. Her shiny black hair glows in a beam of sunlight through the window. As she turns back to her older son, her narrow form is backlit, giving her an otherworldly halo. "I can't go myself 'cause your brother's sick, and your father will be in court all day." She puts a hand on his shoulder. Her eyes, green as a four-leaf clover, smile warmly down at him. Even in her current frail state, she is beautiful, he thinks.

"I need you to be a good boy and pick up my inhaler for me."

"I promise," he assures her, pushing his glasses up on his nose and giving her a bright grin.

She drops a kiss to his cheek and presses him out the door into the bright May morning. Her lips are rough and dry, like sandpaper on his skin.

He has no idea it is the last time he will feel her touch.

Alistair runs most of the way to school, nearly the entire eight blocks. He runs partly because he knows he was a few minutes late leaving, but mostly because he's hoping to make it inside the school doors before he is spotted by *them*.

The big boys. The Three Stooges, as he calls them in his head (he and his mom used to sometimes watch old movies in the afternoons when a young Paul was napping.) Their real names are Mike, Scotty and Connor. They are in the eighth grade, two years older and several sizes bigger than Alistair, who is scrawny for his twelve years.

He's not sure why he is their current target. Maybe it's because his clothes are nicer than theirs. Maybe it's because he wears glasses and spends more time in the library than on the baseball diamond. Who knows? His father says bullies prey on the weak. And they have decided he is weak, and therefore deserves their abuse.

It started about a month ago. Mike Rainier was leaning against the brick wall when Alistair came out a side door of the school—the door nearest the library, of course. He'd stayed a bit late to help the librarian catalogue and shelve all the new paperbacks that just came in. It also didn't hurt that Miss French has pale blonde hair, a cheerful smile, and smells like strawberries. Whenever she needs a hand he is always quick to volunteer.

As he stepped outside, something hit him hard in the shin and he fell face-first onto the asphalt, scraping his chin in the process. He heard laughter and looked up into Mike's beady brown eyes. The larger boy's mouth may have been laughing, but the rest of his face scowled.

"Doofus," Mike sneered, glaring down at him, silently challenging him to try to retaliate.

Alistair's chin hurt like crazy and when he swiped at it, a smear of red came away on his dirt-encrusted fingers. His throat knotted up dreadfully at the sight of the blood, and baby tears rose. Scrambling to his feet, he tried to hold them in. Crying would only make things a hundred times worse.

When he had tripped, his knapsack had flown nearly ten feet across the pavement. Mike walked over to it and gave it a kick, sending it skittering off to rest against the fence. Without looking back, he stuffed his hands in his pockets and sauntered away. Alistair slowly got up and collected his bag. He pressed a tissue to his bloody chin and stumbled home, shameful teardrops burning his cheeks.

Then Mike and his friends started to follow him home some nights. If Alistair wasn't fast enough or smart enough and they caught him, the results were always humiliating. And painful. He'd come home with bruised ribs, aching shoulder blades, sometimes torn out knees in his jeans. If they caught even a glimmer of a tear, the abuse would ratchet up about five notches.

"Boo hoo hoo. The baby's gonna cry," Connor would tease.

Next Scotty would chime in. "Hey Four Eyes, you gonna blubber? Maybe my fist in your face would shut you up."

"Don't wet your pants, Sissy Boy. Your momma might get mad."

Then they would kick and punch and shove.

They are smart enough to not leave visible marks though, save for the scab on his chin after the first time Mike tripped him. And they know Alistair has never squealed. He is well aware of what happens to kids who tattle. Terrible things. Much worse things than he has endured so far. He has heard the stories, and he is young, so he believes them.

Alistair swears to himself that if he just makes it through the remaining weeks of sixth grade alive, he's going to sign up for karate lessons this summer. Maybe Jiu-Jitsu, too. Anything to help defend himself come fall. Sure, those three thugs will have hopefully graduated to high school by then, but who knows which other bullies might take their place? Paul might even want to take a martial arts class with him. Though he's three years younger, it could be a fun thing for the two of them to do together, and some day his baby brother might find himself in a similar situation. Alistair shudders at the thought— Paul is even scrawnier than he is, and his lungs suck for running. He makes a mental note to ask Mom about it when he gets home.

At lunch he gobbles down his sandwich, then heads straight for the library to pass the rest of recess. The Stooges never set foot inside the library unless they absolutely have to, so he considers it his safe place.

Miss French is up on the sliding ladder putting away books on one of the higher shelves. She is wearing a blue and white dress that stops just above her knees. Seeing the long muscles on the backs of her calves flexing on that ladder makes Alistair feel tingles and twitches in certain places. Since she hasn't noticed him yet, he hurries to the other side of the library, grabs a book at random and drops into a chair, pulling himself up to the table so the evidence of his discomfort is hidden. His cheeks are hot, his palms damp, as he looks down at the book he has taken. It is *The Giving Tree*. He sighs. *Great*, he thinks. *Real appropriate for a twelve year-old who's read over half the books in this library*. He reads it anyway.

When the final buzzer goes at three, Alistair takes his time packing his knapsack. At last he shoulders it and steps outside, glancing around fearfully for any signs of trouble. The coast seems clear. He breathes a tentative sigh of relief as he leaves the schoolyard.

After a block he turns left on Washington Street instead of continuing straight, heading for the drug store. His mom has asthma, and this spring her allergies have been making her attacks more frequent. About a month ago, she was even hospitalized for a few days. Paul has inherited it from her, but his is nowhere near as severe—at least not at this point in his young life. Mostly he just uses his inhaler when he has an allergy attack, or when he runs around too much and his lungs rebel.

Alistair isn't hurrying. Now that he's away from school and off his usual route, he walks at a leisurely pace. His thoughts drift to Miss French's flexing calves as she stretches to place a book on a high shelf. In his mind he sees the hem of her dress flutter against the smooth skin above the backs of her knees. He realizes his jeans feel too tight again, but this time he doesn't mind all that much. It's happened before, and he isn't embarrassed about it if he is alone.

He is too caught up in daydreaming about the school librarian's fascinating legs to realize there are voices behind him until it's too late.

"Sissy Boy's not going home today."

A mocking laugh sends a shiver up Alistair's spine.

"Maybe he's headed to his boyfriend's house?"

This is followed by raucous laughter.

Alistair looks over his shoulder and is frustrated but unsurprised to find the Stooges less than thirty feet behind him, and gaining. He shoves his other arm into the empty knapsack strap and breaks into a run, knowing if they catch him this time it will be bad. Not just bad—awful.

The boys may be big, but they can move fast when they want to. And right now they are definitely motivated. Alistair hears the pounding of three pairs of sneakers on the pavement as they try to close the distance. He pushes himself harder, diving between vehicles when he reaches the intersection at Marshall, dodging around a red truck whose horn blast echoes through his skull as he narrowly avoids being crushed into the back end of the Volvo paused at the stop sign. Up over the curb he jumps, flying past the pharmacy with its blue neon sign, past the tantalizing smells wafting from the burger place next door, past the hair salon, and coffee shop. He spots a break in the cars moving parallel to him on Washington and shoots through it, feeling the rush of displaced air from a passing van push him forward as he leaps onto the opposite sidewalk.

Sweat trickles down his spine as he slows, risking a glance behind him. About half a block back he spots Connor pointing his way, hears him shout something at the others, clearly looking for an opening to cross traffic.

Adrenaline surges through him and Alistair resumes pelting down the pavement. There are more pedestrians on this side of the street. Old ladies with huge handbags block his path as they peruse the racks of clothing on the sidewalk in front of The Dress Den. The hard corner of a purse jabs him in the bicep as he passes.

At last he spots the narrow laneway dividing the store from the laundromat next door. Without a single thought, he darts down it. It's lucky Alistair is so slim, because the way is not exactly clear. Old, splintered crates are stacked along one side. Garbage cans, a couple of abandoned mattresses, and a smelly black dumpster sit further down against the other wall.

As he dodges to avoid stepping on an old board on the ground—the rusty nails poking up from it look sharp and are probably teaming with tetanus—one of his sneakers skids in a puddle of who knows what, and he goes down on one knee, tearing a hole in both his new American Eagle jeans and the skin beneath. The muck now coating his leg and shoes is rancid, but that's the least of his concerns. He checks frantically behind him again to see if the Stooges have caught up, if they have spotted his latest detour. With relief he sees only the open-topped rectangle of sunlight, its glow barely penetrating the alley.

Alistair drags himself to his feet and limps further into the gloom, making his way around the end of the dumpster before slumping to the ground on a discarded blanket. It smells of piss and likely belongs to some homeless guy, but right now there is no one else in sight. He sits there, one knee (the cleaner one) pulled up to his chest with his arms wrapped around it, and gasps for breath as the sweat drips off his brow and into his eyes. He pushes up his glasses and swipes it away, but tears of pain and fear threaten to dampen them again.

His knee is bleeding. Not only does it smell like rotting garbage, but it also hurts like hell. It's lucky he didn't land on a nail, but who knows what bacteria are swimming in that sludge? He hopes the scrape doesn't get infected; he's heard horror stories of what can happen to body parts if they get infected. Visions of hobbling to school on a crutch with a prosthetic lower leg pop into his mind. Would that be worse than what the Stooges will do to him if they catch him? Possibly.

But possibly not.

In the distance he hears someone yelling, "I think he went this way!"

Damn it, he thinks with a sigh. Why must they be so persistent in their desire to beat the crap out of him today? Just call it a day and scram already.

I just want to go home. He scrunches tighter against the concrete and prays they don't decide to explore this particular smelly passageway.

Then Alistair's stomach drops as he hears the low scuffle of someone entering the alley. With every ounce of strength he has, he pushes himself into the thin space between the crumbling bricks and the back of the dumpster. It's not much of a hiding spot—if they look behind the dumpster they will still spot him—but it's the best he can do.

Man, it reeks back here! Gorge rises in his throat, but he fights it back down. He takes shallow breaths through his mouth.

"Any sign of him?" That sounds like Mike.

"Nope." Definitely Connor now. "I swear he vanished before the Suds 'n Save though."

"I think you need specs, too," Mike snarks. "There's nothin' down here but rats and roaches. He's too chickenshit to go this way."

"Maybe he's hidin'?" Scotty's higher pitched voice this time. Puberty has not yet deepened his tone, but it squawks through every now and then.

The rough brick digs into Alistair's back, dirtying and probably tearing holes in his shirt, but he can't let himself care right now. He hears shuffling steps coming closer and he stops breathing altogether.

"It's kinda dark, but I don't think he's back here. Probably saw a rat and took off."

A sharp bark of a laugh, Mike's for sure. Then silence.

Alistair doesn't breathe; he doesn't move; he doesn't even blink. He begs his racing heart to shut up. The silence stretches out and he understands they are right in front of the dumpster, looking and listening like the predators they are.

Just at the exact moment he has no choice but to draw in some putrid air, Mike speaks up again, masking the faint sound of his desperate inhalation. "Little faggot's not here. It smells like shit. C'mon, let's go. He probably ran straight out the other end and is halfway to his boyfriend's by now."

For the life of him, Alistair can't understand why the Stooges equate slim, bespectacled, and smart to gay. It puzzles him, but it doesn't offend him. Even at age twelve, he is confident in his sexuality, so their insults don't hurt. Their fists, knees, and feet on the other hand…

Once the sounds of the boys leaving the alleyway fade, he squeezes out from behind the dumpster and squats on the filthy blanket again. Frustrated, he knows he has to stay here a while longer to give them time to get on their way to wherever they've decided to head next. Maybe they are tracing the route back to his house, still looking for him.

With a sigh he realizes that is probably exactly what they're doing. Mike is the smartest of the three, and the most determined to make Alistair's life miserable. He is sure Mike will be leading them toward his place. In fact, they will probably lie in wait for him a block or two away. Especially now that they are pissed off he's avoided them.

His injured knee is throbbing, but he knows he has to wait them out. For how long he has no clue. Checking the silver watch on his wrist that his dad gave him for Christmas, he sees it is already after four.

Alistair sits on that pissy, ripped up blanket, presses his face between his knees and closes his eyes. He curses the three bigger boys for their infernal need to terrorize the weak. He knows it's just the way it is, but the way it is sucks, frankly, for kids like him.

When the big hand finally gets close to the six, he thinks maybe, just maybe, it's been long enough. He edges his back up the wall until he's standing and tentatively peeks around the side of the dumpster. The alleyway and sunny sidewalk beyond are empty.

A scurrying sound from underneath the dumpster, however, says otherwise. Recalling Mike's comment about rats, he finds he's able to move fast after all. He heads for the opposite end of the laneway out to Cherry Avenue, just in case.

By the time he turns onto his own street, Alistair is tired, dirty, bloody, and wants nothing more than a hot shower. About a block away, he stops in surprise when he sees an ambulance in front of his house. At first, he doesn't notice his father's black Cadillac along the curb behind it.

As he watches, the big double front doors swing open and paramedics carry out a shrouded stretcher, his father following closely. Then he sees something he's never seen before. And never wants to see again.

His dad's face streams with tears.

Alistair blames himself of course. He is pretty sure his dad blames him, too. He was the one who was supposed to bring her the inhaler, after all. If only he'd made it to the pharmacy and back home when he was supposed to. If only the Stooges hadn't picked today of all days to be strolling down Washington Street and catch him daydreaming. If only Paul wasn't sick, and Mom could have gone to pick it up herself earlier in the day. If only…well, he could list a million 'if onlys' but none of them will change a damn thing. He loved her, and now she's gone.

She collapsed just before four, and somehow his little brother managed to remember to dial 911. The paramedics got there in thirteen minutes, and his father arrived home in fourteen. But by then, it was already too late. They tried unsuccessfully to revive her for another ten minutes, and then called time of death at 4:24. Alistair trudged up the walkway in a daze to his weeping father eleven minutes after that, understanding what happened without being told.

They bury her four days later. Standing there on the grass with his father and brother, all the rest of the mourners behind them, Alistair feels like he is having an out-of-body experience, like he is nothing more than a spectre looking in; seeing, yet unseen. He inhales the dank smell of recently overturned earth mixed with the tang of sickeningly sweet flowers. It is a combination that will always remind him of death.

He wears a stiff black suit that makes his arms and legs itch everywhere it touches bare skin. Paul clings to his hand like a lifeline and blubbers, snot coating his trembling upper lip. Handing him a tissue, Alistair looks away. He looks not at the rose-draped gleaming mahogany coffin, but over the trees to the fluffy cumulus clouds scattered across the blue sky. Just like the opening credits on 'The Simpsons', he thinks idly. A perfect spring day. All the rest of the world is probably outside enjoying this beautiful Saturday, oblivious to the man and two boys who have had their entire world ripped apart. It's hardly fair, really. It should be raining—thunder-storming, even. Bolts of lightning crashing down like the wrath of God himself. How dare the sun shine while they put his mother in the ground?

Alistair feels many things acutely right now: guilt and anger, isolation and sorrow. These emotions stab into him like needles. Yet his face is blank, unreadable, as if he feels nothing at all.

He does not cry.

Chapter 4

The next morning is bright and sunny. The plows have been out since before dawn clearing away the foot and a half of snow that fell during the night, and the school buses are all running more or less on schedule. Evie's pleased to find Dylan already at the table when she comes into the kitchen.

"G'morning."

He mumbles something unintelligible through a mouthful of cereal. It may or may not have been "Morning."

She pops some bread into the toaster and turns to him, leaning back against the counter. A flash of red catches her eye. There's a card stuck on the fridge. Curious, she tugs it out from under a Dumbo magnet. It's an invitation to the Wheelers' annual Valentine's Day party a week from Saturday. Formal dress required. Since the Colvilles are a founding family, so is their presence. Evie makes a mental note to ask Grace if she can fill in at the Clutch that night.

Returning her attention to her brother, she rubs her bicep through her sweater and fake-winces. "I bruised my arm up pretty good last night. Stumbled and fell into the edge of the counter as I was mopping."

Dylan's eyes lift to hers. "You okay?"

"Yeah, fine. Just a klutz." The toaster pops up, and Evie spreads jam on her toast and sits across from him. He's almost finished breakfast. Since he hasn't said anything else since she mentioned her 'injury,' she decides to press on.

"So I ran into Charlie in the change room yesterday. She seemed to be favoring the same arm I hurt. Did she tell you what she did to it?"

He looks up at her again, clearly confused. "No. Why would she?"

"Oh you know…you guys seem pretty tight these days. I thought she might've said something."

His brows narrow with suspicion. "Why're you asking me this?"

With a shrug, she says, "I just wondered." She takes bite of toast and picks up her phone, trying to appear nonchalant. As she looks through her messages, she thinks of last night and wishes she'd asked Alistair for his number so she could text to ensure he got home safely. Maybe she'll be brave enough to ask for it next time she sees him.

"You sure? You sure her arm was sore?" Her brother looks worried now, and it further confirms her suspicions that he has feelings for Charlie.

While Evie might leave out some details, she isn't going to lie to him. "Yes, I'm very sure."

"That asshole better not have…" Dylan says it low, almost to himself, his eyes fixed on the bottom of his cereal bowl. Though most of the time she'd rather not know exactly what her brother's thinking, at the moment Evie wishes she could read his mind.

"Dyl?" His eyes lift to hers again. "Do you think Cam would do that? Get rough with a girl? Has it happened before?"

Pushing his chair back, Dylan stands with a sigh. "Maybe." He shrugs. "I dunno. I've heard a few things. Can't see Char putting up with that shit, though. She'd tell him to fuck right off if he ever tried."

"Okay." Evie lets the matter drop. She isn't going to push this topic right now and risk riling her brother up further. He's already given her something to go on. Cameron has left a slew of cast-offs in his three and a half years at Sutterton High, and the next person Evie thinks might be worth talking to had been his only serious relationship that she's aware of—his ex, Melody.

A senior like Evie, Grace, and Cam, Melody Monroe is a bubbly redhead. She is also very popular. Evie knows her well enough to say 'hey', but they don't exactly have the same friend squad. The rich kids mostly hang with other rich kids, and Evie and her friends sure don't fit in that category. Melody is also the head cheerleader for the second year in a row, which had made her the perfect match for the football team captain. Melody and Cam had dated for most of eleventh grade, but split up some time over the previous summer. Evie has no idea why; she's never had reason to care one way or the other, so had never asked. Now she suspects it might be worthwhile to find out.

When Evie boards the bus, she recounts her breakfast conversation with Dylan to Grace in a rapid whisper, and asks her friend what she thinks about finding out more about Melody's relationship with Cameron.

Grace agrees it can't hurt to ask around. She also decides to see what she can unearth about the rumors that Cam had gotten rough with Amber prior to dating Charlie. Although he's the school's Golden Boy, they figure if there is a nasty side to him someone would have let something slip at some point.

Evie has English with Melody second period, but they don't sit near each other. When the lunch bell rings and the other students surge for the door, Evie lingers, falling into step beside the taller girl near the back of the throng.

Melody glances at her curiously. "Hey Evie. How's things?"

"Things are…interesting."

"Oh yeah? Why's that?"

Evie feels her cheeks flush. She decides to just start. "Are you going to the Valentine's party at Cam's next weekend?" Of course she already knows Melody will be there, but it's as good an opening as any.

This brings a smile and an eye roll. "Of course. I have to, same as you."

Hoping to capitalize on the 'we're both stuck doing this' camaraderie, Evie drops her voice. "Would you skip it if you could? Cause I sure would."

The other girl's grin falters. "Spending a Saturday night forced to watch my ex cozy up with his new girlfriend isn't exactly my idea of a fabulous time. I'd much rather be at the movies with Jack. But I'll drag him along for an hour or two to put in my appearance and then we'll split. It won't be so bad if I have my own arm candy." She pauses, examining Evie closer. "You really hate these things, don't you?"

The corner of Evie's mouth curves up. "So much." She looks around to see if anyone is near enough to overhear. The coast looks clear, so she tilts her head close to Melody's. "Look, I know we're not exactly BFFs, but can I ask you something?"

One sculpted brow arches, but Melody nods.

"Was your breakup with Cam…uh…amicable? Or…?"

"Amicable? You mean, like, are we still friends?"

"I mean was it…did it get…um…ugly? At the time?" Evie gulps, dropping her eyes to her binder. "I'm sorry, Mel. I know it's none of my business. I just heard some rumors…"

Melody grabs Evie by the shoulder and drags her into a corner by a row of lockers. Still holding on, she looks Evie straight in the eyes, her expression serious. "You heard rumors? About things getting ugly between me and Cam? Who told you that?" Her deep blue eyes flash, but Evie can't read the emotion behind them.

Evie's face is burning again. "No. Well, yes, but not about you and Cam. I heard he sometimes has a temper. With other girls. Your name never came up, honest. But you were the only one I felt like I could ask."

Whoever coined the phrase 'flattery will get you nowhere' has obviously never met Melody Monroe. At that last sentence, her smile resurfaces and she drops her hand from Evie's sleeve.

She shrugs. "I don't know about those other skanks who've been throwing themselves at him, but between us? Sure, he's got a temper, but he never got handsy with me. I've got a temper too, and Cam knows better than to ever lay a finger on me…if I didn't want him to, that is. Our fights were rare, but explosive—and always ended in amazing make-up sex. So I wasn't complaining."

The expression on Melody's face has morphed into one of fond remembrance, and Evie grows more uncomfortable. She's just about to make an excuse and head down for lunch when Melody asks, "So who was it? Who said he got rough with them? Was it that little bitch Amber?"

Evie tucks a strand of hair behind one ear and pulls her binder to her chest. "I don't know. It's just some stupid rumor. Probably started by someone who was jealous of either Cam or the girl he was with."

Melody's laugh bursts out like a mini-explosion in the nearly empty hallway and she claps a hand over her mouth.

"Probably," she agrees. With that, she waggles her fingers at Evie and heads for the stairwell.

When Evie opens her locker to retrieve her bagged lunch, she realizes she never once said she'd heard Cameron had gotten rough with a girl, but Melody had jumped to that interesting and possibly telling conclusion anyway.

It's another quiet night at the Coffee Clutch. On dark winter evenings, the residents of Sutterton tend to hibernate in their homes, not that Evie blames them. By 8:30 she is alone, with another hour and a half stretching out in front of her until she can close. Deciding to get some work done, she pulls out the bundle of envelopes she'd picked up from her editor on her way over.

There are only four letters, plus an additional three emails waiting in her Miss Lonely Love Gmail inbox—a slow week for sure. Evie reads them over one by one. She has selected two emails and one letter for her column, and another she'll respond to privately, when she comes to the last envelope in the stack. The jagged handwriting across the front looks familiar, but there's no return address in the upper left corner. Curious, she tears it open.

Evie scans the page, realizing with surprise that it's from the same guy who'd written before, the one whose girlfriend cheated on him with his brother. While she does sometimes get email replies to her personal responses, most of them also thanking her like this one, it's pretty rare to get a handwritten letter back, especially from a guy. Re-reading it, she smiles, then folds it back into its envelope and tucks it into her bag.

She spends the next hour writing replies and formatting her column, then reading it over and revising some sentences, before finally forwarding it to her editor. When it's at last time to go home, she feels accomplished, although the sound of the wind gusting against the front windows brings a pang of interminable loneliness. She's been half wishing Alistair might make an appearance tonight, and a part of her she isn't sure she's comfortable with is disappointed he hasn't.

Later, when she's in her flannel jammies and snug in bed, Evie starts re-reading the final chapter of *The Great Gatsby.* Before she gets two pages in, JAI's second letter pops into her head, and she sets the book down mid-sentence. With a soft sigh, she gets up and rummages around in the bottom drawer of her dresser until she finds the first letter. Then she retrieves his most recent one from her knapsack, sits cross-legged on the floor, and reads them both over.

Normally she doesn't keep Miss Lonely Love queries after answering them—she has neither the space nor the inclination. But something about JAI's letters is different, although she can't say exactly what. She has no plans to reply to the second one, but she doesn't want to toss them out either. Instead she tucks them both into the back of an old, but well-loved novel on her bookshelf and returns to bed.

The persistent wind rattles the small window in her room, and she drags the blankets up tighter. As much as she tries to immerse her mind in the tragic conclusion of *Gatsby*, she can't concentrate. Though her father is in the next room, though her best friend is only a text away, Evie feels very alone.

Alistair is day-drinking. He knows it isn't the smartest idea in the world, but the fire raging behind the grate in the library isn't warming him, and he has no inclination to leave the house today. So he pours another two fingers of bourbon and listens to the wind gust under the eaves as the flames crackle.

His phone buzzes on the table beside him, and he glares at it, willing it with his mind to shut the fuck up. He doesn't even pick it up to see who the text is from. He already knows.

Paul. It's always Paul. And the words are almost always the same.

I'm so sorry. I hope you can forgive me.

I'm worried about you.

Please reply. I need to talk to you.

It's continually one variation of these or another. Alistair never acknowledges them, but he doesn't block his brother's number either. Paul's a persistent little bugger—he'll just use someone else's phone if he has to. Probably *hers*. And frankly, Alistair can't be bothered to make the effort.

When the buzzing stops, he grabs his glass from beside the annoying phone and downs the liquid within, relishing the silky burn as it coats his throat. He slams the tumbler back onto the oak with a sigh.

"Careful with the crystal, dude. That glass is older than you are."

He looks up as his uncle enters the room carrying a cordless phone. Alistair eyes it with suspicion. He hadn't even heard the land line. Max walks over and holds it out to him wordlessly. It's either his brother or his father on the other end, and since Alistair's cell just went off a minute ago, all his money is on Paul. Frowning, he shakes his head. They've played this game

41

before. His uncle is well aware that he doesn't want to talk to either of them, but this time he stands there insistently, the phone a few inches from Alistair's fingers.

For a few long moments they lock eyes in a silent challenge. Finally, with another put-upon sigh, Alistair sets his book beside his now-empty glass and, grimacing, takes the receiver. He doesn't put it to his ear, just clutches it tightly. The plastic casing is warm—to Alistair unpleasantly so.

Max arches a brow, still staring at him. "You gonna talk to him?"

Alistair's shoulders shift in the smallest of shrugs.

His uncle offers a tight smile. "You can't avoid it forever. You're brothers; someday you'll have to talk again. Today might as well be that day."

Alistair's frown is his only response. Max gives him an encouraging nod and leaves the room.

He stares at that damn hunk of plastic and wires in his hand for a while longer. Then, mentally bracing himself, he puts it to his ear. He is nowhere near drunk enough for this.

"Yeah?" he mutters, taking off his glasses and setting them atop his book.

"Ali?"

He rubs his forehead. He can feel a tension headache building behind his temples. "In the flesh," he replies.

"I've been trying to reach you for weeks! How *are* you?"

"Alive." And far too sober for this conversation.

"Good to know." He hears his brother blow out a puff of air. "Why wouldn't ya at least text me back? Tell me you're okay? Tell me to fuck off? Anything, really. I was worried about you."

Alistair doesn't reply. He leans over and pours more bourbon into his glass.

There's a sigh from the other end of the phone. "Okay, okay. I guess I know the answer to that. Glad you finally decided to talk to me."

"Not sure I have." He presses his fingers to his forehead again and squeezes his eyes shut.

"Ah. Well, maybe you'll just listen then. I know I fucked up, and there aren't enough words to express how sorry I am about that. I never meant to hurt you."

Alistair snorts. "Right."

"It's true—just hear me out. It never should've happened the way it did, and I'll regret that bit for the rest of my life, but I don't...I can't...I can't regret being with her, Ali. I just...I fell in love. Even though she was with you, and I knew you loved her, and that she was off-limits, I...I fell for her. I feel incredibly guilty for acting on something I knew would cause you so much pain, but..."

"You fell in *love*? Was that before or after you started fucking her behind my back?"

The wind gusts again, nearly drowning out another sigh from Paul. "I deserve that."

Alistair takes a sip of bourbon and rolls his eyes. "*So* not what you deserve."

"It was before. We fell in love before we ever touched each other. Once it started, we agreed she needed to end things with you before we could continue. She promised she would, but she knew that conversation would be painful, so she avoided it. And we just couldn't stay away from each other. And everything just got so goddamn complicated, because we both love you, and didn't want to hurt you, but knew it was inevitable."

His fingers tighten around the glass, and Alistair must force himself to take a deep breath and relax them. Putting it to his lips, he swallows the rest of the liquor in one gulp, savoring the burn all the way to the pit of his stomach. It's duller than before, now that his blood-alcohol level has risen a bit. Nowhere near enough, though.

"Are you done?" he asks tersely.

A third sigh. Alistair can just picture his brother's brow all furrowed with frustration. Paul is only nineteen, but he can brood like no one's business. As if he has any right or reason to.

"I'm done. I just needed to tell you again how sorry I am."

43

"Let me sum up, just to make sure I've got this straight. You called to tell me you're sorry, but not all *that* sorry, because you and Michelle are in *looove* and intend to ride off into the sunset together?" Acid drips from every word.

Paul sighs yet again. This conversation obviously isn't going the way he'd hoped. Maybe he'd thought Alistair would say, 'Oh, you're in love with the love of my life? Oh, well that changes everything! In that case, I forgive you for stabbing me in the back and wish you a lifetime of happiness together.'

Not fucking likely.

"Alright. No need to be an asshole. You're not quite ready for forgiveness yet—I get that."

"Do you? 'Cause I *really* don't think you do."

"I *do* love her, more than I ever thought possible. And we're happy together. And I hope someday you can find it in yourself to be happy for me, just because I'm your brother and, whether you're willing to admit it or not, I know you still care."

Alistair chuckles, low and completely mirthless. "Uh huh. Thanks for calling."

"Don't—"

He hangs up without waiting to hear more, fury boiling through every vein and artery. Without a single thought, he whips the phone across the room. Luckily, his aim is true and it lands on a chair near the windows instead of shattering on the hardwood. His uncle would be pissed if he broke the phone in a fit of rage.

Alistair's gaze falls on the half-empty bottle of Maker's Mark on the table, the firelight sending glimmers dancing along the beveled glass. It beckons to him mercilessly. He reaches for it, then stops, his fingers frozen in mid-air for a few long moments. At last he lets his hand drop. In the mood he's in, he knows it isn't the smartest idea to get shitfaced. Max wouldn't want his tumblers—or anything else in here, including his nephew—smashed to bits.

Instead, Alistair leaves his phone and book on the table and goes down to the gym. The red punching bag in the corner taunts him, and he pictures his brother's face on the side. As he pounds it, Paul's features morph into Michelle's and his fists slam the leather even harder. He beats the crap out of it until his knuckles, wrists, and shoulders are sore and sweat runs in rivulets down his face. When he can barely stand on his own feet any longer, he drags himself up to his room to shower, his body now nearly as numb as his mind.

Evie moves with speed yet grace as she navigates her way through the Friday night rush, topping up mugs, delivering pastries, and ringing up orders. The hours slip away unnoticed and before she realizes, it's after 10:30.

She has her back turned as Mr. Donnelly leaves, so she doesn't notice someone entering at the same time until she hears footsteps approaching the counter. Whirling, she finds herself face to face with a grinning Alistair, his glasses fogged over from the sudden change in temperature.

He takes them off and cleans them on his scarf tail as he greets her. "How's your night been? Seems I picked the right time to pop in."

A thin layer of untended scruff covers his cheeks and chin, obscuring the boyishness from his features. As he looks her over, she gets those warm tingles again. Alistair isn't like any of the other guys in Sutterton, that's for sure. He's so charming, and seems confident, but Evie senses he carries a weary weight within.

She returns his smile. "Busy, but good. Glad the rush is over. Coffee?"

Retrieving his cup from his pocket, he sets it on the counter for her to fill, then removes his coat and folds it over a stool. She's happy it looks like he intends to stay for a bit.

Taking a seat beside him, she asks, "So, how's your week been?"

His forehead creases in a momentary frown. "Shit, mostly. You?"

"Busy with the usual: school and work and schoolwork." She doesn't mention the Charlie thing. Alistair doesn't know the people involved, but it still feels too personal—not to mention as yet unsubstantiated—to share with others. "Why was your week shit? If you don't mind me asking."

He sighs. "Got into a…heated…discussion with my brother last night. Let's just say he and I don't exactly see eye to eye."

Evie can tell by his expression that there's more to it than just a random argument. She and Dylan get into spats all the time, but they rarely ruin her day, let alone several of them. "You said he's at Columbia?"

"Yeah. We're from Albany, but he's in New York 'til the end of April. He's following in the footsteps of our father. Same alma mater."

"Right, okay. So you won't see him until Spring Break next month?"

Alistair shakes his head with a derisive grin. "Nope. Not even then. We're not close. Not anymore."

"Ah. Is that why you left?" She knows she shouldn't pry, but the words spill out of her mouth.

He raises his eyes, looking at her over the top of his dark glasses frames, and her breath catches. At first, Evie doesn't think he'll answer, that instead he'll just stare her down until she retracts the question.

"Partially," Alistair says at last. He doesn't offer anything more and she decides not to push it. They're still getting to know one another. And it isn't like she's blurted out all her family secrets to him already, either. But she does find herself hoping he might someday feel comfortable enough to speak of his past. There's clearly some deep unpleasantness from which he's attempting to distance himself.

Instead, she changes the topic to her English essay. Evie works on her outline as they discuss how Gatsby's obsession with his overly idealized mental image of the Daisy from his past makes him blind to the Daisy of the present and who she truly is. Alistair drops a couple of sarcastic remarks about an ex-girlfriend here and there, but Evie doesn't ask about her, either. If he decides he's ready to share this stuff at some point, he will. Right now, she knows it's none of her business.

He stays until close, and once again offers to drive her home. This time she accepts without hesitation. The night is clear and frigid, and other than scraping a layer of frost from the windshield, no snow clearing is needed, so there is no repeat of their snow fight. Alistair still seems tense; he doesn't chat much on the short drive. Evie finds herself missing his playfulness and the way his eyes light up when he smiles.

When they arrive at her house, she remembers something. Grabbing her phone, she holds it out.

He looks at it curiously. "Thanks, but I've already got one," he says with a straight face.

Evie can't help laughing. "Obviously. Can you put your number into mine? That way I can text you to make sure you got home safely. I wanted to the other night during the snowstorm, but couldn't."

A smile breaks through. It brightens Alistair's entire countenance, and Evie relaxes at the sight. His fingers brush hers as he takes her phone and taps the screen a few times before handing it back.

"Thanks. I'll text you when I get inside so you have mine, too."

He just nods, staring at her with an indecipherable expression.

Evie's gaze drops to his lips. They are full, and look soft. She can't help wondering what kissing him would be like. Would he be gentle and sweet? Or intense and passionate? If she were a betting woman, she'd put her money on the latter, but truthfully she figures it could go either way. Maybe someday she'll find out.

Nope. Let's put a stop to that train of thought right now, Evie chastises herself. She has to focus on her studies and her family duties for the next five months, and then hopefully in August she'll be moving away for college. Getting involved with someone would just add complications. Complications she doesn't need.

"Goodnight," she tells him, pushing open the door and stepping onto the hard-packed snow.

Before she shuts it behind her, she hears Alistair mumble, "Night" back, but it's soft and distracted, as if his mind is far away. Considering his general demeanor this evening, she supposes it probably is. Because of the conversation with his brother? She has no clue.

Evie gives him a wave and heads inside.

Sea-green eyes are all she can see; they fill her up, take her over. They're so beautiful, yet so dangerous. She knows she could drown in them if she isn't careful.

She feels him place her phone into her hand, but she doesn't look down at it. She can't look down, even if she wanted to. Her eyes are locked—no, trapped—in his, like a cornered mouse, frozen in fear, waiting for the cat to pounce.

Only…that's not quite right, is it? She's not a mouse; he's not a cat. But she's terrified he'll eat her alive anyway. Body, mind, and soul.

God, those eyes…

She finally breaks their connection and her gaze falls lower, to his lips. They're so, so plump. And pink. She wants to nibble them like an apple. She bets they'd taste just as sweet.

Lifting her eyes to his again, she feels his intensity radiating toward her, crossing the scant few inches still separating them. He's just filled with so much life! She wants to touch him, to share in some of that vitality. She needs it, even. Her eyelids flutter closed. She presses forward just a little...

And then, just like that, she's…no, wait…he's…they're …kissing. His lips are even softer than she had imagined. Soft, yet insistent; gentle, yet demanding. She feels his warm fingers slide up her neck to tangle in the back of her hair, tilting her head so he can angle his mouth over hers and deepen the kiss.

With a gasp Evie wakes in the dark. It takes a few long seconds for awareness to sink in, to realize she's lying in bed bunched up in her sheets and not wrapped in Alistair's arms in his Jeep. Disappointment and frustration surge through her. She can still feel his mouth on hers, and as she presses her fingers to her lips, she's overcome by an acute sense of loss.

Reluctantly pushing the covers back, she gets up to go to the bathroom. When she returns to the comfort of her bed, she tries to recall the dream, but most of it has already faded, as dreams so often do.

Before falling back to sleep, she touches her lips again and tries to remember what kissing him had felt like. She can't quite get there, though. All that comes is an impression of comfort and safety. And then emptiness. Loneliness.

Once the cold light of tomorrow arrives, she knows she'll undoubtedly feel different, but right now, in this dream-muddled fog of hazy half-awareness that only occurs in the wee hours before dawn, she wishes desperately that Alistair was lying beside her.

Chapter 5

Over the weekend, Evie spends her rare free moments trying hard not to think about Friday night's dream. Which works fine when there are distractions, but while she lies in bed in the middle of the night with her eyes squeezed shut, unable to sleep though every muscle in her body is exhausted, visions of Alistair's intense eyes—and even more intense lips—refuse to go away, insisting on distracting her no matter how hard she tries to focus on other things.

After church with her dad on Sunday, she spends the afternoon doing homework and filling out scholarship applications online. There hasn't been any new information about Charlie and Cameron, so she pushes that issue to the back of her mind and concentrates on more pressing matters.

Most of Monday is hectic. Evie does nothing but rush from the time she drags herself from bed to the time she gets to work. Walking into the Clutch at 5:25 and giving her dad a hug before he heads home feels like a massive relief. Now all she has to do is finish the last thousand words of her *Gatsby* essay, and maybe, just maybe, she can end the day feeling like she at least accomplished something worthwhile.

There are several customers hanging out, and a few more come in for take-out on their way home from work, but by the time 7:30 rolls around, it's just Evie and the town postmaster, Bart Kimble, chatting at the counter. And he's sipping the last of his coffee and getting ready to go.

The bell over the door tinkles and she glances up, blushing and smiling simultaneously as she sees who's come in. Outside it's snowing, and as Alistair steps into the warmth, he removes his cap and shakes it off, sending a flurry of snowflakes drifting to the floor. He looks to her, echoing her grin right back before walking over. Evie has the coffee pot in hand before he even has a chance to pull out his cup.

"Is it fresh tonight?" he teases.

"Oh, you want fresh? I think this's from this morning." Evie swirls the liquid against the glass and examines it skeptically. Glancing back at Alistair, she winks as she sees the incredulous expression on his face. "Kidding!" she assures him, pulling the top from his cup and filling it.

He laughs, and she realizes she hasn't heard him laugh since their snow fight a week ago. She's glad he's in a better mood tonight.

As Alistair takes a stool, Mr. Kimble stands and wishes them both a good evening.

Now that it's just the two of them, Evie's nerves are all aflutter. *Relax, loser! Just don't think about the dream. Or look at his lips.*

She opens her laptop to the outline of her essay they'd worked on together last week. It gives her something to focus on other than him. Trying to act normal, she asks, "How was your weekend?"

Alistair shrugs. "I got through two books."

"Really? Did you do anything besides read?"

"Watched a few movies. Worked out. Played chess with my uncle. Nothing too eventful." As he takes a sip of coffee, steam fogs his glasses. He removes them and sets them on the counter, then looks at her through long, dark lashes. "How 'bout you?"

"Worked. Studied. In case you haven't already noticed by now, my life is pretty boring." Then Evie remembers something. Without even thinking, she blurts, "Hey, are you free this Saturday night?"

Brows arched in curiosity, he regards her for a moment. "I'm always free these days. Why? What did you have in mind?"

Inside, Evie chastises herself. This is probably a very stupid idea. Or maybe it's a great one? God knows having him with her would make the event much more appealing. She decides to just go for it. "Wanna come with me to the Wheelers' Valentine's party?"

Alistair's eyes flare. This is clearly not what he'd been expecting.

"Who're the Wheelers?"

She explains about the mayor's many events, and how Sutterton founding families are expected to attend if they're capable of walking upright. "I hate these things, but I have to go. It'd be a lot less boring if you came along."

"So you want me to keep you entertained?" He chuckles. "Would I have to dress up?"

With a playful grin, she says, "Yep and yep. That okay?"

Alistair frowns, turning his head to study the falling snow outside the plate-glass windows. Evie senses he isn't fully comfortable with the idea, and gets a sudden urge to retract the invitation, but she doesn't know how to do it without making things awkward.

"Just as friends, of course," she adds, wondering if she's going to regret asking.

He looks back at her, and for a moment she's again lost in a field of green. One side of his mouth quirks up. "Well, it's not like I have anything else going on."

A spark of warm hope blooms in Evie's chest. "Is that a yes, then?"

"Sure, why not? Could be fun. Open bar?"

She nods, smiling.

"Cool. You can point out any interesting people and fill me in on the gossip."

Evie flinches at the word *gossip*, but he doesn't seem to notice. She reminds herself he has no idea how many of the town's secrets she actually knows.

Alistair stays until close again. When she's busy with customers or cleaning, he reads his book, and when she has time to sit and do homework or chat, he keeps her company. It doesn't take long for her to return to feeling at ease with him. After she locks up, she walks with him to his Jeep, this time not waiting for him to offer a ride. It's coated in an inch of snow.

They look at the vehicle, then back at one another, sporting matching grins. Before she can react, Alistair dashes over to it, slides a gloved hand up the windshield and throws a wad of snow at her.

Evie gasps as cold clumps slide down her cheeks. Then she starts to giggle. "Dude, you're in *so* much trouble!" she shouts, scooping up her own handful and lobbing it his way. He dodges, and it misses him. This is how the Second Great Snow War of 2018 begins.

Running around to the other side of the Jeep, Alistair uses it for cover as he pushes an armful of snow off the roof and sends it toward her in a spray. Evie hears a loud laugh as she whips around so it hits her back instead of her face. She swears—and delivers—revenge, but can't contain the wide smile stretching her cheeks.

By the time they pause for a breath, she's laughing so hard tears have risen to the corners of her eyes. Her face, hat, and gloves are soaked, and both of them are covered with blotches of white, although the windows of the Jeep are far from clear.

Alistair reaches over to swipe a finger across the top of her cheek. "You have a little something on your face," he tells her, still grinning.

"Oh yeah? Cause you look like the Abominable-frickin-Snowman!"

The glow from the streetlight overhead reflects off all the white and makes his eyes twinkle. "Well, we *are* in the mountains. Or nearly, anyway. I should fit right in." He grabs his cap and shakes it off for the second time that night, his glasses spotted with droplets of melting snow.

"Guess we'll have to lay the blanket down again," Evie says, tugging open the passenger door. Grabbing it from the backseat, she spreads it across the front ones, like Alistair did last week, and he hands her his keys so she can start the engine. Her fingers are numb. She peels off her wet gloves and rubs her hands together in front of the vent, but it's far too soon for it to be blowing warm air. It doesn't matter, though. She's cold, but she's happy. So happy her cheeks ache from smiling so much.

Alistair climbs inside a minute later. "Brrr," he mutters as they pull away from the curb. "I'll need to buy a parka if I'm gonna stick around here for the rest of the winter."

Evie turns to him in surprise, some of her happiness evaporating. "You're thinking of leaving?"

He shoots her a glance before returning his focus to the road ahead. Shrugging, he replies, "Let's just say I'm keeping my options open."

She sits on her fingers to try to warm them up, staying silent until they've stopped in front of her house. Shivers wrack her small frame from the damp cold. She can't wait to be in her cozy pajamas and even cozier bed.

Before she gets out, she pauses. "Can I ask you something?"

"You just did."

Ignoring his smartass reply, Evie continues, "When you decide to move on to bigger and better things, would you let me know? So I don't worry if you stop coming by the shop?"

Alistair's eyes flare. He turns away and begins fiddling with his gloves. "Sure," he mumbles.

There he goes again. His moods are so changeable! Once more, she wishes she could peek inside his head. "But you'll come to the party?"

He lifts his head to look at her with a small smile. "I said I would, and I'm a man of my word. Besides, it might be fun. And you do make pretty good company."

Evie's face grows hot, which is a welcome respite from the chill that still permeates the interior of the Jeep. The short drive to her house hasn't given the engine time to warm up much. "You're not so bad yourself."

He stares at her, but the emotions swirling behind his eyes are unreadable. Lifting her knapsack from the floor, she grabs the door handle. "Thanks for the lift. Please text when you get in."

"Goodnight," he says softly.

The Jeep's door crunches closed behind her, and she forces herself to not look back as she hurries up the walkway. Once she unlocks her door, she hears him pull away from the curb, as always waiting to make sure she gets safely inside before leaving.

Her dad sits on the couch in their small living room watching the news. Paperwork and file folders are strewn across the coffee table. Instead of heading to her room, Evie comes in and sits with him for a few minutes, telling him about her day. When she mentions she has a date for the upcoming Valentine's party, he turns to face her, eyebrows raised. "That his car you just got out of?"

"Yes, Alistair comes into the shop some nights and keeps me company. He's given me a lift home a few times."

"Thought you said you didn't want a boyfriend?" He smiles at his daughter, casual teasing on the surface, all concerned father underneath.

"I still don't. It's not *that* kind of a date," she assures him. "He's just a friend. Max Sterling's nephew—have you met him yet?"

Tom shakes his head. "Guess I'll meet him Saturday."

"Guess you will. If he doesn't back out on me, that is," she adds, thinking of Alistair's mood swings.

"No boy in their right mind would leave *you* high and dry, sweetie."

Evie laughs. "Thanks, Daddy. We'll see on Saturday, I guess. Goodnight." She gives him a kiss on the cheek and heads down the hallway.

Once she's in bed, she opens her laptop and finishes typing out the final few paragraphs for her English essay. Tomorrow evening she'llread it over and revise as needed.

Satisfied, Evie tucks the computer into her knapsack and turns out the light. As she lies there, she thinks of her request to him as she'd said goodnight. She reaches out blindly and fumbles for her phone on the nightstand.

There is one new text: *Home safe & sound. You left your gloves in my Jeep. Want me to bring them over in the AM?*

Though the idea of him showing up at her door before school—not to mention the possibility of him offering her a ride, and her friends seeing a sexy stranger drop her off—sends excited thrills through her and makes her want to take him up on the offer, she forces herself to reply: *That's ok. I've got another pair. Get them from you later.*

In less than a minute another text arrives: *How formal is this party? Tux? Jacket & tie? Button-up & dress pants?*

She smiles. The image of Alistair in a tuxedo is definitely appealing, but she assumes he'd have to rent one and there's really no need.

The last one is fine. See you Sat. Can you pick me up at 7? Or just meet there?

I'll be over at 7. Night.

Evie returns her phone to the dresser and rolls onto her back. Her body feels tired, but her brain refuses to shut off. The rest of the house is quiet—so quiet she can hear the tick of the clock on the mantle out in the living room and the soft chug of the refrigerator.

She tosses and turns, knowing full well why she's so restless. She has a date Saturday night with the hottest guy she's ever met, a guy who, under different circumstances, might be actual boyfriend material, yet she can't even let herself be excited about it. There's no hope of a future there. He's clearly not interested in her in that way. And even if by some miracle he *is*, she absolutely does not want a relationship right now.

56

It's easy to keep telling herself this and easy to say aloud to others, but in the silent dark when she's alone with only her overactive mind to keep her company, it's getting more and more difficult to believe.

After school a few days later, Evie's bopping around her room listening to music and getting ready for work, wondering if Alistair might come in tonight, when she hears a knock on her door.

It opens and her brother's head pokes around the edge. "Hey, can I come in for a sec?"

"Sure." She beckons him forward.

He only takes a step inside, clearly not intending to stay long. Running his fingers through his hair, he looks at her with uncertainty. "So I was talking to Charlie on the bus home…"

"As usual," Evie says with a smile, examining her reflection in the mirror as she brushes her hair into a ponytail.

"Yeah. Anyway, she was in a real bitch today. Said she and Cam got into a massive fight last night."

Evie turns to him, suddenly more interested. "Oh, yeah? Did they split?"

Dylan snorts, shaking his head. "Not yet. Hope she dumps his ass soon though. She says he can be a real dick when he's pissed off."

"Did she say anything else?" Evie asks, frowning. She can't help wondering if Charlie has any new bruises. Not that she has any way to find out, short of asking the other girl directly, which she isn't about to do.

"Nope." Her brother turns to leave.

"Dyl, wait."

He looks back at her, dark brows raised in curiosity.

"You're going to the Valentine's party Saturday, right?"

"Unless I can convincingly fake the flu." Dylan smiles ruefully. They both know neither of them would set foot inside the Wheeler mansion if they didn't have to.

"Good luck with that," Evie laughs. "I was thinking maybe we should keep our eyes and ears peeled while we're there."

"For what, exactly?"

She shrugs. "I don't know…we could keep tabs on Cam and Charlie?"

"You still think he hurt her?" Dylan is obviously reluctant to believe it without proof, but the thought it could be true bugs him.

"I don't know. I hope not. And I know it's technically none of our business even if he does, if she refuses to put a stop to it. But…I just hate the idea of any guy thinking he has the right to control or abuse a woman." Evie pauses, looking her brother right in the eyes, ensuring he's paying attention. "I want to make sure that's not what's going on here. And if it is, we need to help Charlie end it."

"Couldn't agree more," he states firmly before walking out the door.

Once the coffee shop quiets on Thursday night, Evie takes advantage of the lull, and by the last hour of her shift, she's put the finishing touches on her English essay and emailed it to her teacher. A sense of pleasure always comes from a job well done and she knows she's written a great essay, hopefully even an A+ one.

Turning her attention to her column, she clicks open her inbox to check this week's inquiries. She finds two messages she'll answer in the paper, one she'll reply to privately, and this:

Dear Miss Lonely Love,
My issue is pretty personal, but my BFF says you sometimes answer questions privately, so I figure it doesn't hurt to ask. I know I can Google it, but we only have one computer and my whole family shares it. I don't want them finding out I'm researching this stuff. I'm too embarrassed to ask my friends or they'll think I'm even more of a loser than they already do. So

I'm asking you.

Wow. This is hard. Ok, here goes: I recently started having sex with my boyfriend. I knew it would hurt at first (and it totally did!) but we've done it four times now, and it hasn't gotten any better. It's uncomfortable for me, still kind of painful, and I don't really get much out of it. All my friends who've done it say it's supposed to feel good and be oh-so-amazing and stuff, but for me it's not. Luckily it doesn't last very long, and my boyfriend seems to really like it, so I keep trying for him.

So what am I doing wrong? How can I make it better? (oh yeah and I'm 16.)

Thanks.

Sex Advice Desired

Evie heaves a deep sigh. She really wishes she could give some useful advice to SAD, but she just can't. This isn't the first time someone has written to Miss Lonely Love asking questions about sex. Most of the time Evie just ignores them, however in SAD's case she feels she needs to at least say *something.* Evie dashes off a quick reply telling the girl that, although Miss Lonely Love can't help her, SAD needs to go use the internet at the library or talk to her doctor about what she's experiencing. Evie feels guilty over not being able to help SAD more, but there's not much else she can do.

The problem is, Evie doesn't consider herself the least bit qualified to offer guidance about anything sex-related. She's only done it once, over a year ago, back when she'd been dating Jason Lancaster, Charlie's older brother, who is off at Syracuse University now. They hadn't ever been anything serious, but Evie had been depressed about her mother's death, and one afternoon went to him and told him she didn't want to be a virgin anymore. Unsurprisingly, he'd been more than happy to help her out. The whole thing had left her decidedly underwhelmed. She'd put an end to their relationship not long after, and they'd had no problem remaining friends. And although she'd gone on a few dates since, she hadn't had any urge to try sex again.

It's funny, really, how she'd even come about writing a love advice column in the first place, since she has so little experience. The editor of the *Herald,* Sheila Masters, used to be a regular at the Clutch, although she drops in less often these days. One quiet weekday evening, she and Evie had been sitting at the counter chatting when Sheila had mentioned her idea of a new advice column. She'd explained that she wanted something juicy that would intrigue local readers. Evie had suggested it be about dating, and the next thing she knew, she'd been asked to write it. Their conversation had gone something like this:

"But I don't know much about love or relationships!"

"Do you read books about love relationships?"

"Yes."

"Have you watched movies and TV shows that depict love relationships?"

"Yes."

"Then you're qualified enough for this."

"But..."

"Look, I don't need Ann Landers. Just answer the letters you can, and ignore the rest. It'll all be anonymous anyway. You *can* keep a secret, can't you?"

"Sure, but—"

"Great. You're hired. I'll post an ad saying we're accepting letters from the lovelorn. Can you start next week?"

And although it had seemed crazy, since Evie loved a challenge, enjoyed helping others, and most of all really needed the extra cash, she'd agreed.

Taking a sip of hot chocolate, she works on her answers to the other questions and tries to forget about SAD. The rapid click of her fingers dashing across the keyboard fills her ears, and before she knows it, it's time to go home.

It's another brutally cold night.

The Colville house is still as Evie lies in her bed, shivering and staring into the dark. She wears her thickest flannel pajamas and has layered an extra blanket over her comforter, but she still can't seem to get warm enough.

There's no wind tonight, but the icy temperature seems to permeate everything. Her father salted the front step and walkway of both their home and the Clutch, but there are still plenty of slippery areas on the town's sidewalks. She'd nearly fallen twice on her way home, eventually opting to walk in the road for better traction.

Now Evie huddles under three blankets and wonders, not for the first time, if her dad was late paying the heating bill this month. She makes a mental note to check in the morning to be sure.

Instead of changing position for the umpteenth time and getting more frustrated with her wakefulness, Evie switches on the lamp. Pushing back the covers, she gets out and kneels on the floor in front of her bookshelf. A chill seeps through the floorboards, the thin rug, and the fabric of her pajamas. As her eyes grudgingly adjust to the light, she scans the spines, blinking, until she finds the book she wants. She plucks it out and dives back into the relative warmth of her bed.

Letting the pages fall open to the two envelopes tucked within, she re-reads both letters from JAI. She isn't quite sure why they crossed her mind, but once they did, she just had to dig them out. There isn't much to the second one; he isn't asking for any advice, just thanking her. There's no valid reason for her to feel compelled to reply. None at all.

Grabbing a pen and notepad from her nightstand, she props it against the back of the book and starts to write.

Dear JAI,

I have to ask: why are you swearing off any more relationships? I don't know how old you are, but that vow seems a bit premature. I know you've been badly hurt and betrayed, and I get that your trust has been shattered, but is it really worth becoming a hermit forever? Negating any hope of future happiness?

You say you met a girl and you had fun. Was there a

connection by any chance? Will you see her again? Forget the idea of dating for a moment—do you think you two could be friends?

My point is that you didn't do anything wrong to cause the horrible situation you went through with your ex (that I know of), so why should you be punished for the rest of your life because of it? Something to think about.

If you need someone to talk to, you are welcome to continue writing to me. Sometimes it's easier to share our true feelings with anonymous strangers.

Have a good week,

Miss LL

Evie yawns and sets the book, letters, and pen on the floor beside her bed before switching off the lamp. She pulls the blankets up to her chin, rolls onto her side and closes her eyes, at last sleepy. The tap drips in the bathroom down the hall. Her brother snores in the room next to hers. And sleep, blessed sleep, finally comes.

Chapter 6

Alistair moves from room to room, sliding books from shelves, glancing at them, putting them back. His fingers trail along various surfaces as he passes, and he examines the gathered dust with apathy. As he rambles, his eyes dart around, looking for a distraction, not finding one.

The Valentine's party is tonight and he's due to pick up Evie in a few hours. Since he arrived in Sutterton, he's been trying to keep a low profile. Other than her, his uncle, and a few random cashiers, he hasn't really talked to anyone. Though he's been to many parties, both formal and casual, the idea of attending this one, for no logical reason he can pinpoint, makes him antsy.

Max is reading in front of the fire in the study, and he looks up as Alistair enters. "Another letter came for JAI," he says, indicating the table by his nephew's elbow. "Who the hell is JAI?"

Surprised, Alistair grabs the envelope and stuffs it in his back pocket. "Long story," he mumbles, turning to go.

"Wait." Max sets down the newspaper. "Your dad called this morning.

Alistair stops, his spine stiffening, and turns back. "Oh yeah?"

"He wants to know when you're coming home."

"What did you tell him?"

"That I didn't know if you were."

Not fucking likely, Alistair thinks. Out loud he asks, "How'd he take that?"

"He's worried about you. He's worried you're throwing your life away 'cause some girl broke your heart."

Some girl? Not just some girl—THE girl. And if she stays with Paul and they get married someday, Alistair would always have to see the two of them at family gatherings and remember their betrayal. Ergo, no more family gatherings. He's never been close to his father anyway; surely Alistair's presence won't be missed.

With a snort, he replies, "That's what he told you? Bullshit. He's worried about looking bad in front of his rich asshole friends if they find out he has a loser for a son."

Max sighs. "I know things haven't been easy between you two since your mom passed away. But he loves you. He may not show it very well, but trust me, he does. My brother's never been one to share feelings, and he hasn't been the same since he lost Jean."

At the mention of his mother's name, Alistair's throat constricts. Even ten years in, thinking of her hurts. He supposes it always will. Applying the same logic to the other woman who broke his heart—this time deliberately—he knows he'll never be able to go home again.

"Uh huh," he mutters.

His uncle's eyes hold no judgment, only sympathy. "Hope one of these days you'll consider speaking to him when he calls. If you're still here next time he calls, that is."

Alistair recalls Evie's request to tell her if he decides to leave town so she won't worry. He thinks of the cheery smile she always greets him with at the coffee shop. It isn't so bad in Sutterton. Maybe he'll stick around for a while.

"Don't hold your breath on that one," he says.

64

"Which? You talking to your dad, or you still being here?"

"The former."

"Good," Max grins. "To tell the truth, I kinda like having you around."

Alistair snorts, shaking his head. "You'll probably live to regret that admission."

His uncle's grin grows wider. "I'm sure I will."

Alistair goes upstairs to his room and stretches across the bed. He tears off the end of the envelope with his teeth and slides out the folded note, reading it over quickly.

Grabbing a pad of paper from his desk drawer, he starts to scrawl a reply.

Becoming a hermit sounds pretty good to me right now.

He stares at it for a moment then scratches it out.

You're right. I do feel hurt and betrayed. Wouldn't you?

With a small sigh he crosses that out, too.

Spinning his pen in his fingers, he thinks harder. He rips out the messed-up page and tosses it toward the trash. *Slam-dunk!* One fist pumps the air for the invisible cheering crowd. With an clean sheet in front of him, he presses his lips together and begins writing.

Dear Miss LL,

You want to correspond? Sure. Anonymity means no judgment, and that's a concept I can get behind.

I met my ex when I was 19 and she was 17, in her final year of high school. I wasn't in college; I was taking a year to "find myself" or whatever, that's the crap I told my family anyway. Basically, I was a deadbeat, living at home, spending my father's cash, and hooking up with nearly every hot girl I saw. Until I met her. She was different from the others. The word hot simply didn't do her justice. She was beautiful—top-shelf beautiful. Tall, fit, and put together in all the right ways. She looked like a supermodel, and she sometimes acted like one, too.

She wasn't into high school boys. I don't think she ever had been, even when she was just a starry-eyed freshman. She told me she always went for college guys and bad boys. I was neither. Sure, I liked to have a drink sometimes, and getting laid had never been any major challenge, but I wasn't a true bad boy. No tattoos, no motorcycle, no cigarette dangling from my lower lip like some James Dean wannabe. I was just a lazy-ass rich kid, wasting his life away.

I didn't know what she saw in me, but I didn't much care either. The only thing that mattered was that she saw something. She wanted me, when a girl who looked like that could have had anyone. I never stood a chance in hell of resisting her charms. Not that I wanted to resist. I think I fell head over heels in love with her the first night we spent together.

More fool me, as it turns out.

I'd never been in love before. I didn't know how I was supposed to act, or what constituted smothering, or too much pressure. I treated her like a queen. Flowers, fancy dinners, shopping trips, PDAs—as you can tell, I was a smitten kitten. And one memorable night she told me she loved me, too, and like the lovelorn idiot I was, I believed her.

We were together for two years. You already know how it ended.

Your turn.

JAI

Alistair tears the sheet from the pad and folds it up. He'll mail it downtown on his way to pick up Evie. Which reminds him, it's time to get ready.

"What's he look like?"

Evie raises her shoulder and tilts her head to hold the phone in place and free her hands to rummage the floor of her closet for her black heels. "He's...hold on." Finding the elusive shoes at last, she holds them up and examines them skeptically.

"Um...he's tall and slim. He wears glasses and has shaggy dark hair. And he has the most incredible green eyes you ever saw!"

66

"So he's cute?" Evie can hear the smile in Grace's voice.

"Very. But like I told you: this is *not* a date." She pulls open a drawer and digs out a crumpled pair of black pantyhose. Her mouth screws up in distaste as she glares at them. *God, I hate pantyhose!*

"If you say so," Grace chuckles

"It's not! We're just friends. You know how I feel about getting involved with anyone right now."

"Yeah, I know. But August is still a long way off. You're only a senior once. You should have some fun."

Evie sighs. "I only own three pairs of Jeans, yet two formal dresses hang in my closet. How is that fair? Couldn't I just trade them in for more jeans? Also: black and white floral strapless or red satin?" She does not mention the black dress tucked in the back that she wore only once, to her mother's funeral.

"It's a Valentine's party! Definitely red satin—you look fierce in that one. I wanna see pics!"

Pulling the dress from its hanger, Evie tosses it on the bed. "I'll get my dad to take a few before we leave," she replies distractedly, eyeing the fabric for stains from last time she wore it.

"Including Alistair."

She sighs again. "Fine. Including Alistair. If he's willing." She hears the sound of bells.

"Okay, I'm walking into the Clutch," her friend says. "Talk to you tomorrow. Have a blast tonight! Live on the edge and kiss a boy, will ya?"

"Grace! That's not—"

"Later!"

Evie stares at her phone for a moment, her face growing warm as an image from her dream about Alistair flashes through her mind. Setting it on her dresser, she drags off her sweater and jeans and shimmies into the party dress.

By the time she hears her dad's car in the driveway, she's checking herself out in the mirror with a doubtful expression. The dark red fabric clings to her body. Is it her imagination or does it fit a bit snugger than last year? Has she put on weight? She doesn't think so, but maybe her curves are a little fuller now? Is it too tight? Is it too slutty? The last thing she wants is for Alistair to think she looks cheap.

In sudden inspiration, she dashes across the hall to the master bedroom, slides open the closet door, and gropes around on the shelf above the rod of dust-speckled clothing. Her fingers close around something soft, and she pulls down her mother's favorite black shawl. Evie's heart twinges as memories flood in of Mom sitting on the couch muttering to herself, knitting needles a blur as she reworks a section of the complicated pattern. She knows if her mother were here right now she'd let Evie borrow it for the party, no doubt adding the caveat that it must be returned undamaged.

With that thought in mind, she goes back to her room and closes the door, draping the lacey knit over her shoulders and re-examining her reflection. Much better. And she'll be warmer now, too, as the dress's inch-wide shoulder straps don't do much more than hide her bra.

She's startled by a knock on her bedroom door. It opens a few inches. "Evie?" Her father's face pokes through the crack. He looks tired, but then again, of course he'd be tired—he's been at the shop for over eleven hours. "Sweetie, you look lovely." He doesn't mention the shawl, but she's sure he recognizes it.

With a smile she says, "Thanks, Daddy."

"This boy of yours will be here in a half hour?"

Evie nods. "Yes. And he's not *my* boy. Please don't say that in front of him."

"Never," her father promises, winking. "You and your brother get some dinner?"

"Just sandwiches. You know there's always enough food to feed all of Sutterton at these things. It's totally excessive!" She picks up her curling iron and begins to twist sections of hair around the barrel. "I'll be ready. I still have plenty of time."

Her dad laughs. "Sure you will. You're just like your mother, always fussing with this or that until you're running late."

"So I'm a perfectionist. You say that like it's a bad thing!"

Tom just shakes his head and smiles. "Think about it this way: do you *really* want me and Dylan to have to entertain your boy while he waits for you?"

Evie grimaces, rolling her eyes at his reflection in the mirror. "Point taken. Now go have a quick shower and change before he gets here!"

At nearly seven o'clock on the nose she hears the doorbell ring, just as she's finishing applying lip gloss. Dropping it into her handbag, she dashes for the door, elbowing her brother out of the way as he's about to open it. She pulls it wide to find Alistair on her front step.

"Hey," Evie greets him, smiling. "Come in for a minute." She gestures inward.

For a moment he seems to hesitate. Then he steps onto the mat and stomps snow from his boots, unbuttoning the top two buttons on his coat and loosening his scarf as she shuts the door behind him. His glasses are nowhere to be seen, and Evie makes a mental note to ask if he wears contacts.

She follows the path of his eyes as they move from his boots to her heels, gliding up her calves and over her knees, rising along the shiny fabric of her dress to her bare upper chest. Her skin seems to sear beneath his gaze. When at last his eyes met hers, she grins shyly, sure her face is as red as her clothing.

His Adam's apple bobs as he stares, eyes wide and glazed. At last he speaks. "You look…" He swallows and tries again. "You look incredible."

Before she can respond, her dad comes down the hallway. Tom now wears his favorite plaid sport jacket over a pair of charcoal gray trousers. Earlier, Evie had mended the cuffs of that old jacket for him.

Her father smiles as he takes in Alistair in his black felt pea coat and stunned expression. "You must be Alistair," he says, extending his hand.

Alistair's eyes refocus. He flashes Tom a grin as he shakes his hand. "Pleased to meet you. You know my uncle Max, I think?"

"Yes, Max's been coming into my shop for years. He's a good guy. A bit of a hermit, though, huh? Keeps to himself mostly."

Alistair shrugs. "He went through a rough divorce before he moved up here. I think he just prefers the peace and quiet, although I suppose I've put a bit of a crimp in that lately."

"Ah. And what brings *you* to Sutterton?"

Knowing Alistair's reluctance to discuss that particular subject, Evie jumps in. "Dad, we've gotta get going. We'll see you and Dyl at the party."

Pulling her coat from the front closet, she's startled when Alistair takes it from her and holds it out so she can slip her arms into it. She notices her dad watching them, his eyes shining with approval.

Evie slips off her heels and crams her feet into her scuffed old boots as Alistair politely says goodbye to Tom. Her brother disappeared into his room as soon as Alistair arrived, so she'll have to introduce them later.

As she steps outside, she feels Alistair's hand brush the small of her back before he shuts the door behind them. A shiver passes through her that has nothing to do with the chill in the air.

As they come around a bend in the long driveway, the big colonial mansion looms into view. Tiny twinkling lights adorn the columns and façade; they seem to echo the stars, glowing pinpoints in the frozen black sky. Evie can tell the clear weather won't last, though. On the way over, she'd noted thick white clouds building up on the mountains, and knew they'd soon descend to dump their burden of snow.

Alistair drives slowly, looking for a spot to park among all the vehicles along both sides of the lane. Once he finds one, he insists Evie stay put until he comes around to open her door for her. For a moment, she looks down at his extended hand. Then she smiles shyly and slips her gloved fingers into his. She can't help a flutter of disappointment when he drops it once she has both feet on the ground.

The first scattered snowflakes begin to pirouette in the air as they walk up the front steps to a tuxedoed young man holding open the door for them. Alistair helps Evie remove her coat, then shrugs off his own, handing them both to the valet as she switches from boots to heels.

Just as she gets herself organized, Cameron's mother sweeps into the entranceway. "Evie Colville. So nice to see you. Will your father and brother also be joining us?"

"Hi Mrs. Wheeler. I'm sure they'll be here any minute."

The older woman's eyes glide past her to land on Alistair, and her smile magnifies, all white teeth and red lipstick. "And who is this handsome young man with you?" Before Evie can respond, Mrs. Wheeler extends her bejeweled fingers to him. "I'm Yvonne Wheeler. Welcome to our annual Valentine's party. Can I get you a drink?" With her other hand, she snaps her fingers beside her head and, as if by magic, another guy in a tux appears with a tray of wine glasses.

Alistair clears his throat, glancing sideways at Evie.

"This is Alistair Sterling," Evie tells Yvonne. "Max Sterling's nephew. He's new in town." It occurs to her that Mrs. Wheeler probably has no idea who Max even is.

Alistair takes the proffered hand and gives it a quick pump. "Pleased to meet you, Mrs. Wheeler. You have a beautiful home. I'm glad Evie invited me to join her tonight."

Yvonne glances between them with clear curiosity, and Evie wonders if she's trying to determine if they are a couple. Turning her full attention back to Alistair, she says, "Welcome to Sutterton, Alistair. I'm sure you'll love our beautiful little town, especially once it warms up a bit." She plucks two glasses of wine from the waiter's tray and puts them in their hands. "Please make yourself at home. I'm sure Evie can give you the grand tour." She pauses, looking Alistair up and down.

"Or, if you'd like, I'd be happy to take time to show you around myself."

"Thank you. I'm sure Evie will take care of me tonight," he says politely.

Yvonne smiles, dropping a less than subtle wink at Evie. "I'm sure she will." She grabs a glass of wine from the tray, takes a sip, and then saunters off to join the guests in the adjacent room. Blushing from the older woman's implication, Evie can't help remembering her dream.

As they start down the hallway, Alistair leans close to her ear. "She seems like a piece of work."

Evie rolls her eyes. "That's one way of putting it. If you see her even once without a drink in her hand tonight, your coffee's on me for a week."

That earns a snicker. "Lush?"

"Pretty much." Evie raises her glass to her lips. The wine is tart, but has a nice fruity aftertaste. She takes a second sip.

Alistair arches a brow. "Underage drinking tonight, are we? What will your father say about that? And will I get blamed?"

"Don't worry about Dad," she laughs, taking another mouthful. She swishes it around and swallows it as she holds his bemused gaze.

His eyes widen for a moment, then he laughs, too. "Planning on tying one on tonight? Is that why you invited me? To carry you out of here later?"

Evie snorts and shakes her head.

Alistair has a sip from his own glass and grimaces. "First stop on our little tour: show me the bar. I need a real drink."

Already starting to feel a slight buzz, Evie takes advantage of its accompanying courage and takes his elbow to guide him into the large front room. She hears a familiar laugh as they approach the bar along the back. Craning her neck to see around the tall man in front of her, she spots Melody at the bar sipping something fruity and chatting with her date.

Jack Dunbar is on the basketball team with Dylan and Cam, but he doesn't really hang out with either of them. He's a good foot taller than Melody, with close cropped dark hair and high cheekbones. At the moment she's in full flirt mode, with one hand on his arm as she stretches up on tiptoes to whisper something in his ear.

Evie decides now is a good time to get the necessary hellos out of the way. She tugs Alistair toward the bar.

"Hey Mel," she says as they approach the couple. Melody wears a pale pink strapless sheath that showcases every curve—and she has plenty. Jack can barely keep his eyes off her cleavage.

Melody turns to her and smiles. "Hey Evie." Then her gaze shifts over Evie's shoulder and lands on Alistair, and her dark eyes flare. She leans in close to Evie's ear and whispers. "Who's your date?"

Evie feels her cheeks reddening again. She releases Alistair's arm and turns to look at him. "He's uh...he's not—"

"Alistair," he cuts in, giving the redhead a polite grin. "Great to meetcha."

"Oh...um..." For once in her life, Melody seems to be at a loss for words. "You, too," she replies, at last flashing a dazzling smile.

Evie introduces both Melody and Jack, and then the guys turn to their attention to the bartender to order drinks. Melody stares at Evie with blatant admiration.

"He's hot!" she mouths, darting her eyes in Alistair's direction in case Evie's too dumb to understand who she means.

"I know," Evie mouths back, feigning nonchalance as she leans her back against the bar. Let Melody think Alistair is her date. Why not? It might be beneficial if the girls at school think she has a hot older boyfriend. Even if it isn't true.

Once Melody and Jack wander off to greet some new arrivals, Alistair slides over until his upper arm brushes Evie's shoulder. He holds a lowball of amber liquid. "She a friend of yours?"

"Who? Melody? Sort of. Not really. I mean, we know each other, but..."

"You're not close," Alistair finishes, taking a sip from his glass as his eyes wander over the huddles of people. It seems like more are coming in every minute.

"Not especially, no."

Dylan picks this moment to enter the room. He scans the crowd until his eyes connect with his sister.

"My brother's here," she tells Alistair.

"Where?"

There's no need to point him out; he's striding over to them. "Hey. You seen Charlie around?" he asks Evie, sparing only a casual glance at Alistair.

"Not yet. I haven't seen Cam either."

"Okay." Dylan turns to go, presumably to continue searching for his friend, but Evie calls him back.

"What?" He looks irritated.

She motions beside her. "This is Alistair."

Dylan gives him a brief once-over. "Okay."

"Dylan! Don't be rude." Turning to Alistair, she says, "This is my obnoxious little brother."

Alistair chuckles. "I've got one of those, too." He sticks a hand out to Dylan. "Nice to meetcha, dude."

They hold eye contact for a moment; it looks to Evie like they're sizing each other up, challenging each other…for what? She has no idea. Then her brother breaks into a smile, and any tension there'd been—if it wasn't her imagination—dissipates.

"You, too. Catch you guys later." Dylan heads off toward the dining room, leaving a somewhat bewildered Evie. *That was weird*. Her brother hasn't seen her with a guy since she and Jason split, so maybe his overprotective sibling instincts had kicked in for a moment. She makes a mental note to set him straight on her continued singleness later.

Evie looks up at Alistair at the same time he's looking down at her. "Feel like continuing my tour?"

She shows him the rest of the main floor. He's most impressed with the modern and well-equipped kitchen. It's swarming with caterers and waiters, so they don't linger, but she notices the covetous admiration on his face as he checks out the high-tech appliances.

"You cook?" she asks, trying to hide the note of surprise in her voice. Her father and brother aren't capable of much more than grilled cheese or bacon and eggs.

"My mom taught me some stuff when I was a kid, and when I got older our housekeeper showed me more. Sometimes she had to shoo me out of the kitchen when I got in her way too much."

Evie smiles, trying to imagine what Alistair had looked like as a child, but she just can't do it. All she can picture is the man in front of her, but smaller.

Her brother appears at her side, beer in hand. Before he can say anything, her brows rise. "You're drinking?"

Dylan rolls his eyes. "So're you. How else are we supposed to make it through this thing?"

"Does Dad know?"

He winks. "If he asks, I'll just say I'm holding it for Alistair."

Now it's Evie's turn for an eye roll. "Did you find Charlie?"

With a sigh, Dylan says, "Yeah. Last I saw she was dancing with Cam." He gestures toward the living room where space has been cleared in the middle to make a temporary dance floor. A few couples are dancing, but there's no sign of Cam or Charlie. Most people just stand around the edges, drinking and making small talk. More alcohol will need to flow before the floor will fill up.

Dylan wanders off toward the study, and Evie turns to Alistair and sees him set his empty glass on the counter. "Which way to the washroom?" he whispers.

She shows him to the one near the entrance, but it's occupied. "C'mon," she says, pointing to the curved wooden staircase.

Raising an eyebrow, Alistair grins devilishly. "Taking me upstairs? What would your father say?" He adds a wink to ensure she knows he's teasing.

Evie smiles back. "You have to pee or not?"

She starts up the steps, and he obediently follows. Once up, they turn right and go down the hall until she pauses in front of an open door. "In there," she motions. "I'll wait at the top of the stairs." Alistair disappears inside.

The general cacophony of chatter and music from the party drifts up to Evie as she leans on the balcony rail, arms crossed, looking down at the people milling about in the entranceway. Being the unseen observer instead of the participant is much more her style; she prefers a bit of distance between herself and all the action.

"I said, stop!"

Jolted from her thoughts, she swivels in the direction of the yell. The voice is female. And familiar. Evie takes a few cautious steps down the hall away from the bathroom.

She hears a low rumbling reply that sounds male, but she can't make out the words. Then the girl shouts again. "Get your hands off me!"

Evie's eyes flare. Is that Charlie? Fighting with Cameron? She tiptoes closer. The voices are coming from behind a closed bedroom door.

"What's your deal tonight? One minute you're all hot, the next a total Ice Queen. I don't get it." That's definitely Cam.

Charlie's tone softens. "There's nothing for you to get. I just changed my mind—I wanna go back downstairs."

After a long pause, Evie hears Cam grumble, "No one's gonna miss us for a few minutes."

She hears movement within and hurries back to the balcony in case one of them comes out and sees her. Her heart is pounding. Where is Dylan? Leaning over the rail, she tries to see if she can spot him.

"Hey."

She jumps back in surprise, but it's only Alistair.

"Who're you looking for?"

At the creak of a door opening down the hall, she grabs his arm in a panic and drags him down the stairs.

"Whoa, what's your rush?" he asks as they reach the bottom.

Evie releases Alistair's sleeve and glances up to see Cam stride past the railing. He looks annoyed.

"It's nothing," she mutters. Sighing, she looks around for Dylan. The party is now in full swing. More waiters are circulating, offering guests trays of chocolates and champagne. The music has slowed to romantic ballads, and the dance floor is filling up. She finally spots Dylan dancing awkwardly with Melody's mother by the front windows.

On impulse, Evie turns to Alistair. "Can you dance?"

At first he looks startled, then bemused. "Sure," he replies.

Evie grabs his hand and pulls him into the midst of the couples on the floor. Just then the song changes to Chris DeBurgh's "Lady in Red", and Alistair can't help smiling at the appropriateness. He slides an arm around her waist and holds her fingers up near their shoulders with the other.

Evie stares into his eyes as they begin to dance. Her feet know all the moves from years of parties like these, and they fall into step with his lead. Thoughts of Charlie and Cam flee her mind; all she can focus on is how close Alistair's body is to hers. The fresh scent of his cologne envelopes her, and as she breathes it in she feels a tightening low in her belly. Her pulse, which had just returned to normal, speeds up again.

Alistair's eyes narrow as he looks down at her. "Something wrong?" he whispers.

She knows her cheeks are once again flaming. "No, I'm fine." It's a total lie.

"Red is definitely your color," he says with a small nod. She knows he probably means her dress, but all she can think is that her face must match the fabric.

"Thank you," she mumbles.

A faraway voice in her head reminds her she wants to tell Dylan what she'd overheard, and that she should be steering them toward her brother so she can switch partners and speak with him. That voice seems small and unimportant.

Their eyes remain locked as they dance, moving in synch, for the first time truly connected. Alistair's smile is genuine, his usual walls temporarily lowered. Evie echoes it right back at him, no longer feeling like an outsider looking in, but for once somewhere she truly wants to be.

Chapter 7

All too soon, the song comes to an end. Alistair drops her hand and steps back, sending a wash of disappointment through Evie. She brushes it off, reminding herself she needs to talk to Dylan, who is currently heading toward the kitchen.

"Excuse me for a sec," she tells Alistair, then hurries after her brother.

"Dyl, hold up."

He turns to face her. "What?"

Evie grabs his sleeve and tugs him into the study. It isn't empty, but it's quieter than the big room.

"I overheard Charlie and Cam upstairs earlier," she whispers, leaning in close. When he just raises an eyebrow, she adds, "Fighting."

Dylan's eyes widen. "About what?"

She explains what she can, but unfortunately she hadn't caught all that much of the argument. Her brother looks displeased, but not angry. "So it sounded like it was about sex?"

"I don't know. Maybe." She shrugs. "Probably."

He frowns. "I wish I could ask her what's up, but she'd just say it's none of my business. Which it probably isn't, but…it still bugs me."

"I know. I wish you could ask, too. She's a strong girl, Dyl. I hope she can take care of herself."

"Yeah. Hope so. Thanks for telling me. If I find out anything else, I'll let you know." He heads back toward the bar.

Before Evie can return to Alistair, her father enters the room. Spotting her, he smiles and walks over. "There you are. Been wondering where you'd gotten to."

"Hey Dad. Just needed to escape the crowd for a minute."

Glancing around the room, he asks, "Where's your boy?"

Evie rolls her eyes, but she can't help grinning. "I *told* you, he's not my boy. We're just friends. Honest!"

"So you say. But I saw how you looked at each other earlier. He's a good looking fella, Evie. And college isn't for months yet."

Heat floods her cheeks yet again. "Are you saying you'd be cool with me dating Alistair? *Really*?"

Tom laughs. "I'm your father—I don't know if I'll ever be," he pauses to add finger-quotes, "*cool* with you dating anyone. But I know Max, and he says Alistair's a good kid. I just want you to be happy and have a bit of fun. It's been so long since—"

"It's okay, Dad, you don't need to—"

"Since I've seen you happy," he finishes.

Her throat tightens. Her father's right; she hasn't allowed herself much happiness since her mother died. None of them have.

"I know," she whispers, tugging the shawl up around her shoulders. "I'm just trying to focus all my energy on earning a full scholarship, like you and Mom wanted."

Understanding fills his eyes as he puts a hand on her arm. "What I want—what your mother and I wanted—is for you to study hard and get good grades, of course, but to still find time to enjoy life. You're only young once. You work so hard all the time…and I'm so proud of you for it…but if you decide you want to do something a little selfish once in a while, something just for yourself that would make you happy, I'd be all for it. You know?"

Evie nods, looking down as she exhales a small laugh. "Don't make me cry—I'll mess up my makeup!"

"Sorry. This probably isn't the right time or place for that little speech."

"No, it's fine." She swipes the pads of her fingers under both eyes, whisking away the moisture. "I think we're gonna take off soon though, so I'll see you at home later, okay?"

"Okay. Have a good rest of your night, sweetie." Tom pats her shoulder and wanders off toward the kitchen, leaving Evie to try to regain her composure. A passing waiter stops to offer her a glass of wine, and she gratefully accepts, drinking deep.

When she feels like she can again breathe without her chest aching, she returns to the big room. The dance floor is filled with elegant couples slowly spinning to Nat King Cole's classic "Unforgettable." Love feels like it really is in the air; it seems to radiate from the faces of everyone she sees. Cam and Charlie are dancing close together in one corner, eyes only for each other, whatever they'd been arguing about forgotten for now.

For a moment, she's jealous of all the starry-eyed couples, wishing she, too, had someone who would look at her that way. Jason had liked her, had thought she was cute, but he'd never stared at her with such devotion. With a pang of longing, she thinks, *If only Alistair…*

Evie stops that thought, commanding herself to snap out of it. After college she'll have the rest of her life to find the man of her dreams, as Miss Lonely Love would surely advise her—if she were real, that is.

She makes her way around the perimeter of the room until she spots Alistair leaning against the high back of a chair, arms folded, gazing out the window at the falling snow. His features are set in an alluring, yet implacable mask.

Approaching him, she asks, "Whatcha staring at?"

He starts. "Oh, sorry. Nothing, really. Where'd you get off to?"

81

"Sorry for ditching you. I had to tell my brother something. Then my dad showed up, and we ended up talking about my mom." She gives a little shrug. "I needed a few minutes to myself after that."

Alistair narrows his eyes, examining her closely. "You okay?"

"Yeah." She sighs, glancing at the dancers again. "I think I've done my time for tonight. Feel like getting out of here?"

He straightens up with a grin. "Sounds good."

"Great. I already said bye to Dad. Let's go thank Mrs. Wheeler and get our coats."

They weave through the crowd until they spot Yvonne chatting with Marcus Sutter at the bar. Marcus is a councilman who works with her husband, the mayor. Evie has always felt the men on the town council look down their noses at her father, so she ignores him.

"Hello, Evie," Yvonne says before once again shifting her attention to Alistair. "And…Alistair, isn't it?"

"Yes. We're just heading out and we wanted to thank you for inviting us into your beautiful home." Evie smiles at her and hopes it looked genuine.

"Leaving so soon? The party's just getting started!" Again, her gaze darts to Alistair.

Evie has to stop herself from rolling her eyes, wondering if Mrs. Wheeler realizes Alistair's only a few years older than her own son.

"I want to get Evie home safely," Alistair tells Mrs. Wheeler. "Looks like the roads are getting messy out there."

Yvonne seems surprised. "Are they? I hadn't noticed. Maybe that's why Melody Monroe and her date left already."

Evie holds back a knowing grin. She knows exactly why Melody and Jack slipped out early, and it wasn't because of the road conditions.

They say their goodbyes and move into the entranceway to ask a valet to retrieve their jackets. As they wait, Dylan passes through carrying another beer. He stops when he sees them. "You guys taking off?"

"Yeah. I'm pretty much done," Evie replies.

"Dad wants to stick around a bit longer. He's over there talking sidewalk de-icing with one of the council dudes. I'll see ya later."

Before her brother can walk away, Evie remembers Grace's request for a photo of Alistair and herself all dressed up nice. "Dyl, wait." She rummages in her purse for her phone.

"What?"

"Can you...hold on." She sighs, looking back up at him. "I was gonna ask you to take a pic of us, but I can't find my phone." With a frown she adds, "I think I must've left it on my dresser." From the corner of her eye, she sees Alistair glance at her in surprise.

Dylan's brows shoot up comically. "You? Forget your phone? That's like you forgetting a finger!"

Evie rolls her eyes. "Ha ha. You have yours?"

"Course."

"Can you take it please?"

Still chuckling, her brother says, "Sure." He holds his phone up, examining the image on the small screen. "Snuggle close, you two."

Again, her cheeks heat up—no, check that—this time her entire body heats up as Alistair slides an arm around her waist and pulls her against him.

As she's tucking a loose strand of hair behind her ear, the flash goes off. "Take another one. I wasn't ready!" she exclaims with a note of irritation.

Dylan sighs. "Fine. Now smile pretty. Three, two, go."

Alistair and Evie both grin as he takes another shot. Dylan then holds his phone out for his sister's approval.

Evie scrutinizes the photo. Alistair's hand is on the side of her lower rib cage and his head leans close to hers, looking for all the world like cuddling up to her is something he does every day. He's grinning, his eyes crinkling at the corners. The flash was bright enough that she can even see their particular shade of intense green. He looks sinfully delicious, but then again, he always does. Turning her attention to herself, she thinks she seems…young. And kind of tired. But her smile is genuine. It'll have to do.

"Thanks, Dyl. Can you send it to me?"

"Will do. Later." He disappears down the hallway.

Seconds later, the valet rounds the corner with their coats. Alistair takes them both and tucks a folded bill into the guy's hand, earning a grateful smile. Turning to Evie, he again holds her coat out for her. She wonders if his mother taught him such good manners or if he'd just picked them up on his own. None of the guys she knows act like this.

When they step outside, Evie's surprised to see how much snow has accumulated in the two and a half hours since they arrived. Every car, every hedge, every branch of every tree is coated in a thick shroud of white. Fat snowflakes fill the air, making even seeing across the driveway difficult.

"Wait here," Alistair tells her. "I'll go clean off the Jeep and bring it up for you."

"Thanks. I guess we'll have to forgo another snow fight tonight, huh?"

He grins. "I'm up for it if you are. With you hampered by that party dress, I might even have the advantage for once."

Laughing, she says, "True. But I think I'd better pass this time, if you don't mind too much." As he starts to turn away, she adds, "I'll go easy on you next time to make up for it."

"Go easy on me?" He looks at her incredulously. "I don't think so. Next time I'll kick your ass fair and square." Before she can protest, he adds, "Be right back." He trots down the steps and trudges through the snow to where the Jeep is parked under a thick white blanket. Evie can barely see it through the snowflakes.

In the time it takes to clean it off, two older couples Evie knows also leave, pausing to say goodbye to her as they pass. She shivers under her woolen coat as she waits. At long last, he pulls up in front of the steps, jumps out, and comes around to open her door, holding out a hand to help her climb inside.

"I'm sure the main road will be better," he says as the Jeep crawls down the driveway. They turn onto Route Ten, heading back toward town. Tire tracks split the layer of white on the pavement, but it's clear no plows have been along yet.

Alistair is silent, focused on driving. His headlights reflect off the falling snow. The rhythmic thump and swish of the windshield wipers fills the interior; they have their work cut out for them tonight.

They've only been driving for five minutes when two spots of red glow through the swirling white in front of them: a road block. Evie's hands clench into worried fists as she realizes there must be an accident up ahead. She hopes there aren't any serious injuries, and is relieved she knows her father and brother are safe at the Wheelers.

Pumping the brakes a few times so he doesn't lose control on the slippery surface, Alistair pulls over to the shoulder. "Guess we'll have to find another way," he says, frowning. "Or should we return to the party and hope the plows clean things up in a few more hours?"

"No," Evie says without hesitation. "I know a way. About a half mile back we passed a road on the left. I can get us to town that way."

"You really don't want to go back, huh?"

"I really don't."

Alistair makes a three-point turn—which ends up being more of a five-point turn to keep them out of the ditch—and heads back the way they came. He drives carefully, keeping an eye on the left side of the highway for a side road. The poor visibility doesn't help.

"There it is," Evie blurts, pointing.

He's almost past it when he spots the narrow road, and he hits the brakes harder than he intended. The Jeep starts to fish-tail, so Alistair steers into the skid to bring them around the corner.

Evie has been in her dad's car in conditions like these many times, and although it makes her a little nervous, after eighteen winters she's pretty used to it. She knows Alistair is a good driver, and she trusts him to keep her safe.

"Okay, so we take this road for a couple miles and then there'll be another turn on the left. It winds a bit, but will eventually bring us out on the back side of town." She reaches over and switches the radio on, but the storm has made the local signal too full of static to decipher. Alistair hits the CD button instead and the thumping of the wiper blades fades behind melodious piano notes accompanied by a gentle male voice.

"Who's this? I like it."

Alistair spares a glance her way. "Father John Misty. Formerly of Fleet Foxes. Heard of them?"

She shakes her head.

"They're from Seattle. Indie rock. I saw them play live in Brooklyn a couple years ago and they were amazing."

"Huh. Believe it or not, I've never been to a concert."

"Really?" His eyes dart to her again. "Evie, have you ever left Sutterton?"

"Of course! Well, do school trips to a museum in Albany, and to see play in Utica count?"

"Uh, not really." He chuckles. "That's just—"

"Sad. I know," she finishes.

"I wasn't going to say *sad*," he protests.

Evie laughs. "Sure you were. I know I have no life. But I'll be getting out of here for college at the end of summer. Though it sure feels like it right now, it's really not that far away."

He's just about to speak again, maybe to clarify what he meant to say, when she shouts, "Crap! There's the turn!"

Too late. The Jeep sails right past it. Alistair comes to a careful stop and puts it in reverse, backing up slowly until he can make the turn. This road is in even worse shape than the last. He suspects there's now gravel instead of pavement underneath the layer of snow.

The driving snowflakes reflect the glow from his headlights back at them. Evie attempts to make out their surroundings, but it's nearly impossible.

Alistair tries to stay in what he assumes is the middle of the road, away from the edges where they could get stuck. When it bends to the right, he hears Evie mutter, "Hmm."

"What?"

"Nothing. Just…that didn't seem right. But I haven't been on this road since last summer."

They head up an incline. It grows steeper and then bends left.

"Huh. I don't know. I'm starting to think we might be on the wrong road."

"Should I turn around?" He nudges the brakes.

Evie leans forward, squinting through the windshield into the gloom. "Maybe?"

Alistair brings the Jeep to a halt on the slope. As he shifts into reverse again, Evie notices how tight he's gripping the steering wheel, and how white his fingers look against the black leather.

They begin to edge backward, curving to the right as he attempts to make another three-point turn. Suddenly, the nose swings higher and they slide downhill. Fast.

"Fuck!" Alistair exclaims, as with a crunching sound, the rear of the vehicle jolts to an abrupt stop. Against a snow bank. In the ditch.

Father John still sings his sweet song and the headlights illuminate nothing but swirling clouds of white.

Evie gasps, unable to speak.

"Are you okay?" Alistair asks anxiously.

Inhaling another deep breath, she takes mental inventory of herself. "Think so," she manages. "You?"

"I'm fine. But I don't think I can get us out of this."

She tries to lean forward to see their position, but gravity makes it difficult. "We're in the ditch?"

"Yeah. I'm a *total* dumbass. Your dad's gonna *kill* me." He silences the stereo, then turns back to her. "You don't happen to have the number for the nearest tow truck in your phone, do you?"

Evie pats the leather beside her, then reaches down to rummage on the floor for her clutch, at last finding it wedged beneath her seat. She gropes around inside, but doesn't locate her phone. At first she's confused. Then: "Crap. I forgot I left it at home. Can I use yours to call my brother?"

Alistair pulls his phone from inside his jacket and hands it over

"Thanks." Her fingers hover over the numbers, but her mind is blank, still in shock maybe. It takes her a moment to realize she doesn't actually know his number. It's programmed into her phone, but she doesn't have it memorized. She stares down at the keypad, trying to make her brain work, trying to just *think*.

Finally she hands it back to Alistair with a sigh. "I'm sorry. I don't remember Dylan's number. Can you call Max? Ask him to please look up Mayor Wheeler's number for us?"

"Don't be sorry. I'm the one who got us stuck." He taps at his phone. After what seems like a very long time, his uncle answers. Alistair explains the situation and then waits while Max goes to get the town directory. A couple minutes later, he punches in the Wheelers' number and hands the phone back to Evie. "Better make it quick," he whispers. "My battery's getting low."

Her eyes widen as she holds it to her ear. Very soon they'll be without a way to communicate. And that could become a serious problem.

"'Lo?" a male voice answers.

"Hi, this is Evie Colville. Could you please find my dad, Tom Colville, and put him on? It's kind of an emergency."

"Hold on." She hears the clunk of the receiver hitting a hard surface and then only the faint sound of music and people talking. The wait feels like an eternity as she eyes Alistair with worry. What if his phone dies before she can tell her father what happened?

Pick up, please just pick up already!

"Evie?" It's Tom. He sounds alarmed. "What's going on? You guys alright?"

Exhaling a relieved sigh, she says, "Yes Daddy, we're fine, but we're stuck in a ditch on one of the back roads. Can you call us a tow truck?"

She describes the route they took, and he assures her he'll call Dougie Washburn, who owns Sutterton's only tow truck, to come pull them out as soon as he hangs up. He's off the line before she can tell him the only phone they have is about to lose power.

Handlng it back to Alistair, Evie pulls her coat tighter around her. "He's calling the tow truck. Hopefully we won't be stuck out here for long."

Alistair's lips are a tight line. He looks away.

"What?"

"I hope it's not too long." With a sigh, he turns back to her. "Because that's not our only shitty luck tonight. I'm almost out of gas."

Evie sucks in a sharp breath. "Are you *kidding* me?"

"I would *not* kid about something like this. I meant to fill up before I picked you up and was running short on time, so I just figured I'd do it later." He shakes his head, smacking the steering wheel with the palms of his hands. "I'm *such* an idiot!"

"How much is there?"

He leans forward and examines the gauge again. "Not much. We should probably shut it off to conserve what's left, in case we get too cold waiting and need to turn the heat back on."

"Oh." Her brain still feels thick. She assumes it must be from the wine.

With clear reluctance, Alistair kills the engine, then stretches an arm behind her seat and grabs the blanket. "This should help you keep warm," he says, unfolding it and spreading it across her lap.

"What about you?"

He pulls his gloves from his pocket and drags them on. "I'll be fine," he replies grimly.

With the motor off, all light from the dash and headlights go out. They sit in the dark for a few minutes, just listening to the wind gust around the sides of the Jeep and pepper snow pellets against the glass.

Evie isn't dressed to be outdoors in weather like this, but she tries to conceal her growing chills. Eventually, her eyes adjust to the sparse light reflected into the vehicle from the white outside. Looking at Alistair's profile as he stares into space, she swears she sees him shivering.

"You're cold."

He glances at her. "I'm okay."

"Are you sure?"

"Yeah, don't worry. Someone will come and pull us out soon."

She thinks about the accident out on Route Ten, and the road conditions, and the people who will be driving on them as they leave the Valentine's party, and the strong possibility they aren't the only ones in need of help tonight. "It could be a while," she says doubtfully.

Alistair's quiet for a few moments. Then he turns to her. "You want to play a game to pass the time?"

"Uh, sure. What did you have in mind?"

Flashing a mischievous smile, he asks, "Have you ever played *Never Have I Ever*?"

Evie's brows fly up. "No, but I know what it is. Isn't that a drinking game?"

"Usually. But we can play it without doing shots."

"So instead of drinking, we just admit if we haven't…done stuff?"

He chuckles softly. "Something like that. It's up to you, but I'm game if you are. What d'ya say?"

With her mind still kind of fuzzy, Evie's not sure a game where you confess your life inexperience is a great idea. On the other hand, it might be a good opportunity to get to know Alistair better, and it *would* help keep them amused while they wait. She shrugs. "Okay. You first."

He thinks for a moment. "Never have I ever...worked in a coffee shop."

She laughs. "Well you already know I do, so that one doesn't really count. Hmm. Never have I ever...smoked a cigarette."

In the dim light she sees one of his eyebrows arch. "I bet you think I have to take an invisible shot now. But you'd be wrong."

"Really?"

"Really. My mom had asthma, and my brother has it, too. Smoking was always verboten, and I never had any urge to try it."

"Huh. Okay, your turn."

"Never have I ever...shot up heroin."

Evie snorts. "That's good to know. Obviously I haven't either."

"Hey, you might have! I don't know what you're like when I'm not around. Maybe you're a party girl."

She tucks the blanket tighter around her. "Never have I ever been a party girl. Like you ever once thought I was!"

"Me, neither. Although I've been to my fair share of parties." He gets quiet as he tries to think of something good. A smirk twists his lips. "Never have I ever...had a three-way."

Clapping a hand to her mouth, Evie stifles a laugh. "Um...never have I—"

"Hold on, you didn't answer my Never!"

Her cheeks are hot; they're the only part of her that is right now. "No! Of course I haven't! I've barely..." She stops. Is she really prepared to talk about sex with him? The fog over her mind has begun to clear, but only a little. She exhales a small sigh and mutters, "I've barely done anything, let alone something OTT like that."

"Touchy subject?"

Evie isn't looking at him, but she can hear the smile in his voice. "No, it's okay." She stares out the window, but can see nothing but shadows and snow. "Who knows how long we'll be stuck for?" Turning back to him, she adds, "I trust that whatever we admit during this little game will be kept in strictest confidence?"

"Of course. Cross my heart." He makes the shape of an X in front of his chest.

"Fine." She takes a deep breath. "Never have I ever done…uh…oral."

Alistair's eyes flare. She holds her breath, waiting for the laugh, waiting for the teasing remark. She gets neither.

"Truth?"

"Truth."

"You got me on that one," he says, raising his fist toward his mouth and pretend-downing a shot. He stares at her for a few moments. Then his voice softens. "Evie, are you a virgin?"

She looks away again, pursing her lips. "That's a bit personal, isn't it?"

"Sure. But this whole game is personal. We're getting to know one another, right? And I promised I'd never reveal your secrets."

Her mind flashes to Charlie and Cam's earlier argument. *You don't know the half of my secrets,* she thinks.

"Since you didn't start it with 'Never have I ever,' I don't think I have to answer that." With resignation, she adds, "But I will anyway, just because. No. I'm not."

"Ah."

Her eyes dart back to his. "Surprised?"

"No, not really. Are you embarrassed to talk about this stuff?"

She starts to shiver. Rearranging the blanket over her lap, she hopes he hasn't noticed. "It's fine." Another quiet sigh. "Your turn."

Alistair frowns. "You're freezing." He turns the engine back on, and air starts blowing from the vents, making her shake harder. She wants to tell him he should save what gas is left, but the thought of heat is just too appealing.

They play for a while longer, each now trying to keep the subjects light. Evie learns that Alistair has never played football, eaten at IHOP, or seen *The Bachelor*. Alistair learns that Evie has never sung karaoke, seen the ocean, or flown in an airplane. By the time the engine sputters and stops, he's imagining taking her down to Miami so they can swim in the sea during the day and get drunk in karaoke bars at night. Just as friends, of course. Although she *is* incredibly sexy in that tight, red dress that shows off her curves. Just as he's mentally reprimanding himself for such thoughts, the gas runs out.

"Don't worry," he blurts. "The tow truck'll be here any minute, and I'll pay him to take you home first and then drop the Jeep at the gas station. Everything will be fine."

"D-do I seem worried?"

He looks at her with concern. "You seem cold. I might have another blanket in the back. Let me look." Twisting around, he clambers over the center console into the backseat and feels around in the storage space behind. After a minute, he sighs. "Nope. Sorry. I guess there's just the one."

Evie swivels to look at him, eyes wide in the dark. "You're just as cold as I am. What if it's hours before they find us? It's still snowing like crazy, and I'm not even sure which side road we're on. We could be stuck here all night."

He's quiet for a few moments. Then: "Don't freak out."

"I'm not." She shifts onto her knees. "Stay right there." There's no easy way to do it, but she tries to keep the blanket around her lower half for modesty's sake as she inelegantly climbs into the back and lands on the seat beside Alistair.

Unwrapping herself, she shifts until her thigh is against his and tucks the thick wool around both of them. "We need to conserve as much heat as we can."

The moment her body touches his, Alistair goes still. Evie isn't sure if she's crossed some invisible boundary, but right now she also isn't sure she cares. Luckily, she doesn't have to worry about it for long. A few seconds later, he lifts an arm and wraps it around her shoulders, pulling her to his side.

"Is that better?" she whispers after several moments of...not exactly awkward, but not totally comfortable silence.

He doesn't answer right away. Then he murmurs, "Yes. Thank you."

Evie has an idea to help break this new tension between them. "D'you wanna play some other game while we wait?"

"Sure. Which one?"

"Um, well, along the same lines as the other one, how about *Truth or Dare*?"

Alistair chuckles. "*That* could get real interesting real fast, considering our very limited position at the moment."

With a grin, she replies, "I'll kept that in mind. You go first."

He shifts until he's facing her, the sides of their heads against the seatback. The arm that had been around her shoulders now rests against her waist. They lock eyes. "Truth or dare?"

"Truth."

Alistair is silent for a moment. Then he says, "I'll make the first one easy. What perfume are you wearing?"

"It's…" She stops herself with a small laugh. "You're gonna think it's weird, but it's actually just an essential oil I rubbed on my wrists. My mom used to use it. It's geranium oil."

"It smells fantastic."

"Thanks." Evie smiles as she feels his fingers rub lightly over her coat. "My turn. Truth or dare?"

He shrugs. "I'll go with truth, too."

"Do you wear contacts?"

"Yes, sometimes. I usually can't be bothered though. Okay, enough with the easy ones. Time to amp this up. Truth or dare?"

Laughing softly, she replies, "I'm sticking with truth."

"Hmm." Evie thinks she sees a ghost of a smile in the dim light. "I've got one. Have you ever been in love?"

"Nope," she answers without a single second's hesitation. "That wasn't hard at all. My turn again. Truth or dare?"

"Let's live on the edge a little. Dare."

Evie stares into his eyes and remembers her dream. The wine buzz has made her feel brave, made her feel like just once trying to be someone else, someone who takes risks. Grace's parting words from earlier pop into her mind. *Kiss a boy, will ya?* So she decides maybe now is a good time to take a leap. What's the worst that can happen, right?

She takes a deep breath. "I dare you to kiss me."

Chapter 8

Alistair's eyes flare and his jaw drops, making Evie instantly regret her dare. After a moment, he whispers, "You sure?"

With a gulp, she nods. Just a small nod, but it's enough.

At first he does nothing, says nothing; he simply stares at her. He looks like he's waging an internal battle. And she has no idea which way it's going to go.

Then he exhales a sigh, so quiet Evie almost misses it. He shifts the hand on her waist up to cup her jaw. The buttery leather of his glove is cool against her skin. She holds her breath as his face moves closer, stopping when their noses are maybe an inch apart. She isn't sure he can see her eyes in the gloom, but she can tell he's trying.

Evie's throat is dry. Her heart gallops within its cage, like it wants to escape. She wonders if he can hear it. She waits for him to make a move, to kiss her, to pull away, anything, really. But he stays still, just looking at her. At last she can't stand it a second longer. She leans forward just a little and their lips touch.

That's all it takes. Alistair kisses her. He's tentative, careful, and she can tell he still isn't sure this is a good idea. But he doesn't back off. He doesn't try to deepen the kiss, but he doesn't stop either.

A rush of need unfurls inside her. She wants more. Evie brings her hand to his shoulder and tries to tug him closer, parting her lips against his. She feels him hesitate, feels him freeze, and with chagrin knows he's about to retreat. For an excruciatingly long moment neither of them moves. She doesn't even breathe, lest it tip their precarious balance and chase him away. Her pulse throbs in her ears as she waits to see what he'll do.

All at once, she feels a shift in the energy between them. The tip of Alistair's tongue traces her lower lip and his fingers splay into her hair. As Evie tilts her head for a better angle, their noses bump. She smiles against his lips, has to hold back a nervous giggle in fact, but he doesn't pull away. She's forgotten all about the cold—right now her internal temperature is rising fast. Their tongues touch, and she hears a soft moan.

Was that me? Oh God, the wine has made me wild tonight!

It's like something has come unlocked within them, and everything is different now. Everything has changed. They both know it, but neither is ready to put a stop to it. Not yet. Her fingers drift from his shoulder up to his neck. Alistair sighs against her mouth and slides his tongue along hers. He tastes of bourbon and coffee and she just can't get enough. She shifts her knee up over his leg, straddling his thigh, the hem of her dress forced up to her hips.

Evie grows braver still. Her thumb strokes circles on the side of his neck. She runs her fingers into his hair at the same time as his hand slips below the blanket to grasp the back of her thigh, pulling her closer, opening her up further. Their kisses deepen, and she presses herself wantonly against him, searching for some release from the pressure building within.

Just then, headlights illuminate the inside of the vehicle. Like two magnets of matching polarity, they shoot apart. Evie nearly groans in disappointment at the sight of their suddenly not-so-welcome rescuer.

If only he'd been delayed just a few more minutes.

Wiping his lips, Alistair scrambles over the center console and arranges himself back into the driver's seat. Evie fixes her skirt and runs her fingers over her hair, trying to refocus her mind, calm her heartbeat, even her breathing.

Oh my God!

Did she really just climb into Alistair's lap, rubbing herself against him like a cat in heat? What the hell is *wrong* with her? Her face burns with embarrassment as she tucks the blanket around her legs again, pushing her back against the seat and inhaling deep breaths of frosty air as the tow truck stops in front of them.

Without a word, Alistair gets out, wrenches open the rear door, and offers his hand to help her climb outside. The snow in the ditch is deep—it's almost up to his knees—and he lifts her with seeming ease over the bank and onto the edge of the road. As Evie watches him clamber over the snow to greet their new arrival, she glances nervously at Dougie Washburn, wondering if he noticed she'd emerged from the back instead of the front. She's pretty sure he didn't. He's too busy hooking the Jeep up to his tow truck.

Before long, they're squished into the warm cab of the truck and on their way into Sutterton. It's a tight fit. Their thighs and shoulders press together, and Alistair's left arm rests along the back of the seat behind Evie. He makes small talk with Dougie a little, but otherwise the drive is quiet

When they pull up in front of her house, Alistair helps Evie down from the high seat, but once on the ground, drops her hand, walking beside her to the door.

"Alistair…" she starts, wanting to break past the weirdness that's settled between them.

"I'll talk to you tomorrow," he cuts in firmly. "Not too early though."

"Thanks for being my date. I had a great night."

He snorts. "I got us stuck in a ditch in a snowstorm. Not sure that qualifies as a great night."

Stifling a yawn, she says, "It wasn't so bad. If I had to be stuck with someone, I'm glad it was you. And it all worked out."

"Yeah," he sighs. "You should go in and get some sleep. I'll text you when I get home. Goodnight."

She wishes he'd lean in and kiss her again, but she knows he won't. Because no matter what happened at the end of it, it had *not* been a date. Instead, she just offers a small and sleepy smile. "G'night."

A hard winter sun pierces the cracks in her blinds and casts too-bright lines across her bed, rousing Evie from a restless sleep. Her first thought is that she's thirsty. Her second is that getting up seems like too much effort and she'd rather just go back to sleep. She turns over, squinting at the clock on her nightstand through bleary eyes. With a surprised groan, she realizes it's almost eleven. Then her eyes fly wide as a third much more alarming thought kicks in. Rolling onto her back, she stares at the ceiling, her fingers unconsciously pressing her lips as she recalls last night's events.

"Oh God." She claps a hand over her eyes as memories of being with Alistair in the back of his Jeep flood over her. What had she done?

Groping for her phone, she checks her messages. He'd texted her at 2:38 in the morning: *Home at last. Talk to you tomorrow.*

It's now tomorrow. Will he bring up their kiss? Or will they just pretend it never happened and try to act normal? And, more importantly, which would she prefer?

Evie sighs, setting the phone back on the nightstand. Her head drops hard against her pillow. If only she could just fall back into oblivious sleep, but unfortunately that's not an option. She knows if she stays in bed, she'll end up agonizing over every detail of last night.

She drags herself from the warm blankets and with half-lidded eyes stumbles down the hall to the bathroom. A shower will help clear her head. She needs to figure out what she'll say to Alistair if he mentions the kiss. Because as mind-blowing as it was, it can't happen again. It wouldn't be fair to either of them if they start something she'll have to break off in a few months. That would just cause unnecessary pain, and she refuses to do that to him. Or to herself.

After Evie's shower, her stomach grumbles so she heads to the kitchen to make some breakfast. She assumes Dad and Dylan are at church and is grateful they let her sleep in today.

As she sits down with some toast, her phone buzzes in her pocket. It's Alistair: *Morning. How're you feeling?*

I'm fine. You?

She's rinsing off her plate and planning to start her homework when another text arrives: *Okay if I pop by?*

Evie frowns. She does want to talk to him. It won't be an easy conversation, but it needs to get out of the way so they can return to being friends—if he even still wants to be her friend after hearing what she has to say. She tries to ignore how happy she feels at the thought of seeing him. If they're going to be able to maintain a successful friendship, she needs to get a better handle on her attraction to him.

Somehow she misses the sound of her father's car pulling into the driveway. The front door opens and her family enters, letting in a blast of arctic air as they stomp snow from their boots.

"Good afternoon, Sleeping Beauty!" Her father greets her with a smile.

She returns his grin. "Thanks for not waking me for church today."

"I figured you deserved to sleep after last night. But don't ever scare me like that again, okay?"

"I won't." Then she remembers Alistair's text. Having a private and important conversation with her family in the next room will be difficult. "Can I borrow the car for an hour? I want to go check in on Alistair."

Her dad's smile widens and he tosses her his keys. "It's all yours. Don't take any back roads, though."

"Not a chance. Thanks Dad."

Evie picks up her phone and texts back: *How about I come there instead? When works?*

A minute later he replies: *Sure. I'll be here all day.*

As she heads to her bedroom to change into something a bit more presentable, she types, *See you in 20.*

The laneway leading up to the Sterling house is nearly as long as the Wheelers'. Although it's been plowed since the storm last night, Evie drives carefully. Sunlight glints off the fresh snow blanketing the wide front lawn; it glimmers like a field of diamonds.

She pulls up in front of the big house and parks beside Alistair's Jeep. There are a few scratches in the paint on the back, and the bumper is a little twisted, but she's relieved to see it doesn't seem to have otherwise sustained much damage.

Her boots crunch on the walkway's hard packed snow as she approaches the big front door. In the middle of it is a tarnished iron door knocker shaped like a lion's head. Evie scrutinizes it for a moment before lifting the heavy ring and banging it against the metal.

For a few moments she waits, shifting her weight from foot to foot, her cheeks rosy from the cold. At last the old hinges creak as the door is pulled wide. Alistair stands framed within, squinting against the glare.

"Hey. Come on in."

Evie steps into the gloom of the entranceway, and the door closes behind her with a resounding thud. Temporarily blinded, she reaches for the wall to steady herself as her eyes adjust.

"Better leave your coat on for now. This old place doesn't hold heat very well."

Alistair leads her into a cavernous room with a high, vaulted ceiling. She looks up to see a polished oak railing along an upper floor hallway. The entire room is paneled in dark wood, with paintings of local landscapes on the walls. Strategically placed high-backed leather chairs bracket a large fieldstone fireplace. It's clearly meant to look rustic and welcoming, but in Evie's opinion is far too spacious to be cozy.

"You want the full tour?" he asks.

To be polite, she nods. Truthfully, she just wants to get the conversation they need to have over with so she can return to feeling comfortable around him instead of this crazy tension that grips her every time she glances his way.

The house is far too large for two people. She can't imagine how Max must've rambled about alone before Alistair moved in. Just as he'd warned, most of the rooms are chilly, and Evie's glad she kept her coat on. She stuffs her hands into her pockets as they walk through the dining room, kitchen, sitting room, and library. In the study, a fire is burning in the hearth, and Alistair's uncle is reading the *Herald* in an overstuffed armchair nearby. Max greets her politely and they chat for a moment about last night's fiasco until Alistair ushers her out to continue the tour.

At last they come to his bedroom and he holds the door open for her. She can feel her pulse race as she passes close to his body.

Much like the rest of the house, his room is furnished in dark, polished wood. Evie's happy to see the fireplace across from the foot of his bed is already aflame. The large bed itself is covered with a gray duvet, and a thick book rests on one pillow. Neat stacks of more books fill the lower shelf of the bedside table. The entire room smells enticing, a combination of burning wood and old leather, with a faint hint of Alistair's cologne mixed in. Unlike the others, this room is definitely her idea of cozy.

Evie plops down on the rug in front of the fireplace, shedding her coat and folding it over the arm of the chair. The radiating heat soon warms her. It feels so good, she's tempted to just stretch out like a cat and nap right here all afternoon.

Alistair sits on the end of his bed and looks at her. She stares back, unsure how to begin.

"Sooo..." they both start at the same time. Then they laugh.

"Sorry," he says. "Ladies first." He sweeps a hand her way, urging her to continue.

"About last night..."

"Last night. Yeah."

"Yeah," Evie sighs. "Not the getting stuck part, but the…other part."

His mouth curves into a knowing half-grin. "The other part? You mean the kissing part?"

"Um, yeah." She bites her lower lip. "That. So, the thing is—"

"I'm not looking for a girlfriend, Evie. I got out of a real rough situation a few months back, and I'm just not in the right place for anything new. I value your friendship a lot, but—"

With an amused look, she cuts in. "I thought you were gonna let me talk first?"

He flushes and nods, focusing on the flames crackling behind the grate. "Right, right. Sorry. Go on."

"It's funny you should say that, though, because I was about to tell you something similar. Not because of a previous relationship, but 'cause I'll be leaving for school in August—at least that's my plan—and I have so much to do between now and then. Between work and studying, I don't have much free time, and I have to keep my grades up so I can earn a scholarship. I promised myself I'd focus on my schoolwork until the end of senior year. And I don't want to get all attached and then have to leave. It wouldn't be fair to either of us." She's been talking rapidly, but now she takes a deep breath and falls silent.

Alistair meets her eyes and flashes a tight smile. "Okay, perfect. Friends it is then."

"So we're good?"

"Yeah. Great. I was worried that… well, I didn't want to have to disappoint you. That would've sucked if I'd wrecked our burgeoning friendship over something as silly as one little kiss." He's still smiling, but his eyes are serious.

"Yeah, I was kinda worried about that, too. But I'm glad you feel the same." She gets to her feet and picks up her coat, heading toward the door. "On that note though, I should probably get home and do some actual studying this afternoon."

Alistair walks down with her to the front door. "Next time bring your books with you. You can study here if you need some peace and quiet. I promise to not bug you too much—I'll just read and bring you hot chocolate."

She considers his suggestion for a few seconds, thinking about her brother and his friends playing noisy videogames in the living room some Sunday afternoons. "I might just take you up on that," she says. "Have a good rest of your day."

Evie gets into her dad's car and starts the engine, but she doesn't shift into Reverse right away. *Something as silly as one little kiss*, he'd said. Truthfully his words *had* stung a little, much to her annoyance. Their kiss hadn't felt silly or minor. At the time, it'd actually felt pretty major, and she'd had to work hard afterward to convince herself it was a mistake. Knowing he also thinks that hurts more than she wants to admit.

But it's for the best. Friends is all they can be. And she can do it. Sure he's hot, and she's pretty sure the attraction goes both ways—at least last night it definitely did—but it isn't like she's in love with him. She's never been in love with anyone, and she certainly isn't about to start now. Not when her very future depends on her academic success.

They're friends. And it's all good.

Dammit.

Alistair feels kind of strange after Evie leaves. He knows he should be relieved she thinks last night's kiss was no big deal, and agrees they should just be friends and nothing more. And he *is* relieved. Well, mostly. There's also a small part of him that feels a bit...disappointed.

That night he lies in bed for a long time listening to the sounds of the old house settle around him and the spits and crackles of the dying embers smoldering in the fireplace. It isn't the first time he's had trouble sleeping because all the skittering thoughts in his head won't shut up, but it's the first night in a very long time that those thoughts aren't fraught with hurt and anger over Paul and Michelle's betrayal.

To distract himself, he tries to come up with some sort of plan for his future. When that fails, he switches on the light and attempts to get immersed in his book, but he cannot focus. He even writes, then crumples, three different versions of a rambling and incoherent letter to Miss Lonely Love. Nothing helps.

Sometime in the wee hours before dawn, Alistair falls into a listless sleep. At one point he dreams he's back at the Valentine's party dancing with Evie. This time her body is pressed against his, her temple against his cheek. She smells incredible. Like strawberries. And sex.

He gulps. Every inch of him is very aware of—and very turned on by—her proximity. And she knows it. Insistent fingers tug on the hair at the nape of his neck, trying to bring his lips down to hers.

"Your dad…" he manages to mumble, doing his best to resist as oblivious strangers twirl in circles around them. But all he wants is to give in. He wants to kiss her more than anything right now. Not to mention do other, more sinful, things. She looks absolutely edible in that tight red dress that showcases her bangin' body. And those long, shapely legs…God, all he wants is those legs wrapped around him.

It's like she can read his mind. She smiles at him, a sexy, dangerous little smile full of dirty, filthy promises. Then she steps back and takes his hand, lacing her fingers through his and leading him off the dancefloor, through the front hallway, and up the stairs as fast as her high-heels can go. He finds he has no trouble keeping up.

The lights are off in the hallway upstairs, making it difficult to see where she's taking him. Evie drags him along until she stops abruptly in front of a door. His heart is pounding as she pulls it open and tugs him inside.

As soon as the door closes behind them, he takes over, pushing her against the nearest wall and attacking her lips, his fingers diving into her hair, messing her perfect curls, claiming her.

She moans into his mouth, running her hands inside his jacket and up his chest to the collar of his shirt. Instead of unbuttoning it, she grabs each side and yanks, sending buttons flying.

Alistair pulls back a few inches and stares at her with equal measures of awe and lust. He doesn't think he's ever been more turned on.

He picks her up and spins her around, bringing her down on her back on the bed, covering her body with his own. He kisses her again, hard, determined, a hand roaming over her, finally caressing those luscious curves he's been distracted by all night. He finds the hem of her dress and pushes the fabric up to her waist, running his fingers over the soft skin of her bare thigh as he goes.

She gasps into his mouth, lifting her hips as he grinds himself against her. Lord Almighty, this girl's going to kill him before this night is through. His brain goes into overdrive, filled with one thought and one thought only: he needs to be inside her; and he needs it right the fuck now. And from her urgent writhing below him and the breathy mews she's making, she needs it just as much as he does.

He slides his thumbs under the elastic sides of her panties and drags them down her legs, tossing them over his shoulder. With increasing desperation, he then reaches between them and unzips his pants. She grasps the sides and pushes them down, as eager as he is to free him from his confines.

Just as her nimble fingers find their way inside his boxer-briefs, the ringing phone in the hallway wakes him up.

He blinks, at first confused by the early morning sunshine beaming through the slit in his curtains. Pushing his head back into his pillow, he wraps an arm over his eyes and groans. It was just a dream.

But what a fucking dream!

Alistair sighs. Too bad it's never going to happen.

Dreams can be fun as hell, but they can also confuse the waking mind. He doesn't need confusion. He needs to stay focused on the promises he made himself. He needs to remember that he made them for some very good reasons.

But damn!

Hauling his reluctant ass from the warmth of his bed, he heads for the bathroom and considers a cold shower. Better yet, maybe he should just go outside and throw himself groin-first into a snowbank. That would surely clear his…um…head.

A strong cup of coffee, a bagel, an intense workout, and a shower later and Alistair at last starts to feel like his usual self. He wonders if Miss Lonely Love will get his letter today. And he finds himself hoping she'll write back.

Chapter 9

The lunch bell rings, startling Evie. Mr. Wright stops his lecture on the Salem Witch Trials mid-sentence as, in a mad cacophony, students slam their books shut and rush for the door. Grace falls into step beside Evie in the hallway en route to their lockers.

"So?"

"So what?" Evie replies, although she knows exactly what.

"*So,* how was the Valentine's party? How did your date with Alistair go?"

"I told you it wasn't a date," Evie whispers fiercely as they turn the corner and enter the stairwell.

"Yeah, you keep saying that. Well? How was it? Did you dance with him at least?"

"Yes, we danced. It was…" She trails off with a sigh.

"What? It was *what*?" Grace almost walks right into a tall boy in front of them because she's staring at Evie, trying to decipher her expression.

"Hold on." Evie detours into the library. As expected over lunch, it's deserted. Once they have some privacy, she tells

Grace what she overheard at the party between Charlie and Cameron, and then everything with Alistair afterward.

"Holy shit," Grace exclaims, her eyebrows nearly in her hairline.

"Yeah."

"I can't believe you dared him to kiss you! Where did *that* come from? The wine?"

Evie's face is hot. She studies her fingernails, nodding. "I think so. I can't believe I did either."

"Is he a good kisser? Did you get a pic of you two for me, like I asked?"

"Oh God yeah. Hella good. And yes." Evie pulls out her phone and shows her friend the photo Dylan took.

Grace sucks in a breath, raising wide eyes back to Evie. "*That's* Alistair? Jesus, girl. You lucky little shit! Please don't say you wussed out and told him you just wanted to be friends after? Don't you dare tell me that!"

"Um…"

"You didn't!"

"Sorry to disappoint. But yeah. It wasn't only me—he just wants to be friends, too. He says he's not looking for anything right now."

Grace laughs. "They always say that at first. Guys like that hate commitment. I'm sure he still wants to get in your pants, though. Are you *really* sure? Cause *damn!*"

Evie shakes her head, flushing deeper. "Just friends. And I'm totally cool with it. Honest. I don't think he hates commitment. It sounds like his ex really did a number on him, although he doesn't talk about her, and I haven't asked." Something scratches at the back of her mind, but it flees just as fast.

Grace looks doubtful. She shrugs. "If you say so."

"I do. But he *is* cute, isn't he?"

Grace takes Evie's arm and leads her back toward the library doors. "Jason is cute," she whispers, leaning close. "This dude is in a whole different stratosphere from cute. I wanna meet this hot *friend* of yours who also happens to be an amazing kisser. You need to introduce us. ASAP."

Evie giggles, agreeing as they head for the cafeteria.

Work isn't busy tonight. Evie washes mugs behind the counter as she chats with Mr. Donnelly. She'd hoped Alistair might stop by, but so far there's no sign of him. Maybe he's giving her some space after the past weekend's intense activities and conversations. If so, she doesn't blame him for staying away.

Once Mr. Donnelly heads out, she pulls the Miss Lonely Love letters from her knapsack and rifles through them. A smile surfaces when she spots the now-familiar crow-scratch handwriting.

She reads it over twice, a bit surprised by the content. This one is much more conversational than JAI's previous letters. He talks about his relationship with his ex, the one who messed around on him with his brother. It's clear from his words how deeply he'd loved her, and it makes Evie angry on his behalf. What kind of a girl could do that to their boyfriend? Not one who really loved him, or cared much about his feelings.

It ends with two simple words: *Your turn.*

Which means he wants her to share something personal with him. But what could she write about? Her mother's death? No, she's not prepared to relive that. Jason? Too boring. What has she ever even done that's interesting enough to tell him? Also, she needs to remember to maintain Miss Lonely Love's happily married persona. She can't get tripped up in any lies.

Evie thinks about it for a while, but doesn't know what to write, so she tucks the letter away to consider later. She works on her History paper for over an hour with no interruptions. Business is always slow on cold winter weeknights, but she can't help worrying about her father's cash flow. Two bills had shown up this week with the words 'Past Due' stamped in red on the envelope. And those were just the ones she'd noticed. There might've been others that her father took before she saw them. Not that late payments are unusual for them, but she

109

knows this winter things are tighter than ever. Her dad always brushes off her questions about it, though. He's a proud man, and doesn't want anyone to think he can't take care of his family. Evie isn't dumb—she knows they're barely scraping by. Even having to pay Grace to work last Saturday so they could go to the Valentine's party is an additional expense Tom doesn't need.

No other customers come in before closing. Much as she wishes Alistair's no-show didn't faze her, she feels a weird sense of melancholy as she locks up and starts her frosty walk home.

Once she's tucked into her bed, she finishes the last of her math homework, then reaches to turn off the lamp. Her fingers hesitate over the switch. Instead they stretch down to the floor, feeling around for her knapsack and pulling out JAI's letter. She reads it over again. Something about his tone makes her want to reach out to him, to connect. But what to say? She sighs, setting it on her nightstand and digging out her tattered notebook and pen from the drawer.

Evie sits up straighter against her pillow and props the book on her thighs. With no plan in mind, she begins to write.

Dear JAI,
I was pleased to receive your most recent letter. I'm so glad you decided to write me again.
To be honest, after reading it I can't help feeling like your ex-girlfriend took advantage of you. I'm sorry your first experience with love ended the way it did. I know it's probably hard to believe, but most women are nothing like her. You shouldn't write all of us off just because of one (admittedly horrible) relationship.
Are you still hanging out with the girl you mentioned in your previous letter? How's that going? Or have you got her locked up tight in the 'Just Friends' box because of your ex? And if so, are you sure that's really what you want?
Anyway, I'll drop it for now, but rest assured I'll probably keep asking you hard questions and giving you my opinion if we

continue to correspond. It's kind of what I do best.

So, my turn, you say? I've been wracking my brain trying to decide what about me might be worth sharing. Then I realized the 'worth sharing' bit is why I was struggling. We don't know each other, so therefore we can choose to write about anything we want.

In stark contrast to your own childhood, I grew up poor. Well, I didn't actually understand that we were poor until I was older. My parents both worked, and they managed to make ends meet, but we kids didn't know how tight it was for them some months. Later, after a terrible tragedy struck our family, things got even tighter. I started working as a young teen to help make sure our bills got paid and food was on the table. I didn't mind though. I wanted to do my part, and I knew my family appreciated my contributions.

When I was young, it was instilled in me that if I wanted to get anywhere in life, I'd have to work hard and not rely on others to help me. My mom and I used to have long talks about my future—not just what she wanted for me, but what I wanted, and how best to achieve it. Though we didn't have much money, they both supported my desire to go to college and better myself.

Not sure why I'm telling you all this? I guess it's just to show you that anything is possible. I hope you don't become too jaded about fixing things with your brother, or about falling in love again. Don't give up hope that one day you'll be able to live your dreams.

If I could get past the many obstacles in my way to find love, happiness, and the life I wanted, then I feel sure you can, too. I hope eventually you will let yourself be open to loving again. Loving means making yourself vulnerable to another person, and while I know you're not ready for that right now, I want it for you someday. Because you deserve it.

So, think about that girl you just met. Or some other girl, whom you maybe pass on the sidewalk, or lives up the street, or hands you your coffee on your way to work. Think about telling your pain to go take a flying leap because you're stronger than it is, and you're going to go out there and live your life however you darn well please.

I realize all this is easy to say from where I'm sitting, but difficult to actually do. But before you write me off (and stop writing to me) please just give my words some thought.

Hope to hear from you again.

Good luck!

Miss LL

Evie narrows her eyes as she reads it over, trying to decide if it comes across the way she wants. She's done her best to make it seem like it's written by a woman ten years older, one who's content with her life and has wisdom to impart. It certainly doesn't sound like how her friends talk to each other, so she figures she's probably good. Slipping it into her bag to mail in the morning, she turns off the light and rolls over.

Alistair's always kind of edgy these days, but lately he's been even more restless than usual. Over the past three days, he's spent so many hours in the gym that most of his muscle groups are staging protests. He's gotten through two fairly thick books. He's read the newspapers—both the local *Herald* and the *New York Times*, cleaned his bedroom and bathroom thoroughly, and played four intense games of chess with his uncle. Max has asked him several times why he's so antsy, but Alistair has no real explanation. His uncle, more like him than Alistair ever realized, doesn't press the issue.

Wednesday evening finds him lying on his bed, arms crossed under his head, staring at the circular patterns in the ceiling plaster and thinking about Evie. He hasn't spoken to her since she visited on Sunday and they'd agreed they both want only friendship. It isn't that he's been deliberately avoiding her. Well okay, maybe he has, but only a little. After the smokin' hot kiss they'd shared in the back of his Jeep Saturday night, and then afterward deciding it had been a mistake, well, he just doesn't want things to be awkward between them. So he's giving her a bit of space, staying away from the coffee shop for a while. But he doesn't intend to avoid her forever.

It's only been three days. How is it possible that he misses her face after only three days? Has she really become so important to him? Or is it just because he has no one else, with the exception of his uncle, to talk to these days?

With a sigh, he rolls off the bed and trots downstairs. As he passes the doorway to the study, he tells Max he's going out to get some air.

Ten minutes later, Alistair sits in his Jeep rubbing his hands together for warmth, though hot air pumps through the vents. He's parked along the curb in the dark zone between two streetlights, across the street and down a bit from Colville's Coffee Clutch. The light streaming through the windows creates canted rectangles on the snow-packed sidewalk, the hand-painted lettering on the glass making backwards shadows in the glow like coded messages.

He isn't close enough to be noticed by anyone glancing outside, but he can make out Evie pouring coffee for a couple of middle-aged guys sitting at a side table. Her hair is up in a ponytail, and she wears a dark red sweater and jeans. She looks amazing in red; it brings to mind how gorgeous she'd looked at the Valentine's party.

She smiles, then laughs at something the men have said. As she turns to walk away, one of them reaches out and pats her ass. Alistair frowns, his body going rigid. He grabs the door handle with every intention of jumping out and rushing in there to defend her honor. Evie, however, doesn't need a knight in shining armor, or black felt as the case may be, to come to her rescue—she slaps the offending hand away without even glancing back, as casually as swatting off a fly. Her smile never falters, although Alistair now doubts its veracity.

He can't help grinning, too. She's a strong-willed girl, something he really likes about her. She doesn't put up with bullshit; she knows what she wants and she goes after it. So does Michelle—he, of all people, knows that—but Evie is nothing like Michelle. Not as far as he can tell, anyway. She genuinely cares about others. She isn't the type to lie or cheat. He's sure of that much already.

A few minutes later, the guys throw their money on the table and head out. Evie clears away their mugs and wipes down the Formica. It looks like she's either talking or singing to herself as she works, and as he watches her ponytail swing back and forth, he thinks again how sexy she is.

A flash of memory skitters across his mind of her writhing below him on a strange bed: his dream from Monday morning. Or had that been Michelle? Maybe his traitorous imagination had conjured up some strange combination of the two? Doesn't matter either way. Both are terrible choices for dream partners, for very different reasons.

Alistair feels kind of guilty for watching her without her knowledge. If she spots him, he's sure she'll think it's creepy, or worse, that he's some kind of stalker. That's the last thing he wants. He isn't even sure why he came, but he certainly has no sleazy intentions. Maybe he just needed to see her face for a few minutes? She's sweeping the floor as he shifts the Jeep into gear and heads home.

On Thursday night, again there's no sign of Alistair. Once Mr. and Mrs. Clancy leave and she has the Clutch to herself, Evie pulls out her laptop, deciding to distract herself from wondering about him by writing replies for her column.

She picks out four queries and answers them as best she can. Before she closes her email, a new message pops up. Opening it, she reads it over and reddens. Another sex question. Another girl out there who needs advice—who wants *her* advice. Another girl who isn't going to get any.

The writer's boyfriend has been begging her for oral sex, and she's willing, but doesn't know how to do it right. She's read some stuff about it, but writes that none of it is super helpful, so she asks Miss Lonely Love for some tips.

This gets Evie thinking again about her own lack of sexual experience. She feels bad that she can't offer advice to these

114

girls. Heaving a frustrated sigh, she files the email away and closes her laptop. Very little bugs her more than not being able to help people in need.

Just as her thoughts turn to Charlie, the bells over the front door jingle. Evie straightens, welcoming grin plastered into place. When she sees who it is brushing the snow from his shoulders, her smile grows wide and genuine.

As Alistair approaches the counter, she glances at the clock above the door behind him. "Pushing it a little close, aren't you?" she teases.

He laughs. "Would you believe I was in the neighborhood? Saw the time and thought I'd see if you could use a lift home."

"Really?" She's skeptical, but pleased.

"I'd never lie to you." He notes her raised eyebrow. "I was picking up some stuff at the Easy Mart and figured I'd pop in. Is that okay?"

Evie nods, still smiling, secretly delighted once again at his thoughtfulness. "A ride would be great, thanks. Let me get my coat."

The night is crisp and clear as she locks up. Twinkling pinpoints of starlight speckle the black sky, Orion perpetually chasing the Pleiades to the west above the mountains' ragged silhouette. She blows out a foggy breath as they approach Alistair's Jeep. Tonight it wears no snow to clean off, and to her pleasure is still cozy warm inside. Evie can't resist a surreptitious glance into the back while climbing in. Heat blooms on her cheeks as she remembers the feel of his lips on hers...and how she'd climbed into his lap. It was all the fault of the two glasses of wine she'd drank! So embarrassing, especially in light of their conversation the next day.

"So how's your week been?" he asks, starting the engine.

"Uh. Algebra test. Salem Witch Trials paper. Collection of poems due Monday. Typical high school stuff. I'm sure you don't miss it."

He chuckles. "Not that much, no. Although I never hated school. Most of it came fairly easy to me, especially English. If you want a second set of eyes on the poetry, I'd be happy to look it over."

Depends what I write them about. Out loud she says, "Cool. I'll keep that in mind."

The drive to her house is short and they pull up against the sidewalk a few moments later. He shifts the Jeep into Park and swivels to face her, but doesn't say anything. His expression is impassive, and again, she wishes she could read his mind.

"Well...thanks for the ride." Evie holds his gaze but doesn't reach for the door handle.

"No problem." He just looks at her, still giving away nothing about what's going on behind those intense eyes.

She bites the inside of her lower lip. They had agreed they just want to be friends, so why does this feel so awkward? She really needs them to get past this weirdness.

"Is the offer to study at your place still open?" she blurts. Maybe spending more time together will help speed them back to their previous comfortable rapport. It's worth a shot.

Alistair's eyebrows lift and one side of his mouth curves up. "Sure. Mi casa es su casa."

"Huh?"

With a laugh he replies, "It just means you're always welcome. Not that you have much free time. When did you have in mind?"

"Um, this weekend? I can text you when I know better." Now she does open the door.

"Okay. Have a good night."

"G'night."

The Colville house is quiet. Not silent, but quiet. The usual subtle late-night sounds that signal all is well provide background noise to Evie's tumultuous thoughts. As she lies in bed, again shivering under multiple blankets, two very different things keep playing leap-frog over one another in her head. One is of the handsome guy to whom she just said goodnight.

The other is those letters to Miss Lonely Love that she isn't able to reply to.

She blows out a frustrated sigh, recalling the one and only time she'd had sex a year and a half ago. If she only knew more about it, she might be in a better position to give advice to these girls. To be honest, it also wouldn't hurt to be less naïve about such things when she goes off to college in the fall. She'll make new friends, possibly far more sophisticated and experienced ones, and she doesn't want to seem like some poor, ignorant country girl.

It's late, and Evie can't sleep, so she lets her mind relax and float off to places she might not normally let it wander. The way she sees it, the only way to solve this problem would be for her to do some practical research. Field research, you might call it. Like a science experiment. She'd need to have sex again in order to educate herself. But how can she go about getting the experience she wants without messing up her well-thought-out plans for the rest of senior year? She knows finding a willing guy won't be too difficult, but she doesn't want to sleep with just anyone. If she actually does this, it would have to stay a secret. She has to be able to trust him. And there needs to be no emotional strings attached for either of them.

The answer is obvious. Convincing herself it's a good idea is the hard part.

Before she can change her mind, she reaches for her phone. Alistair's *I'm home* text from a couple hours ago is the most recent message.

Her fingers tremble as she types a reply: *Is it ok if I come over Sunday afternoon?*

Evie has deliberately left herself a few days' window to think things over more, to change her mind, but at the moment, in the dead of night, all alone and cold and lonely, it seems like it could work.

To her surprise, her phone beeps less than a minute later. Someone else clearly isn't sleeping tonight either. She smiles as she reads it.

See you then.

Not long after, she has second thoughts. What if he's annoyed by her request, since he's made it very clear he just wants to be friends? Or worse, what if he's repulsed by it? *Ohmygod!* What if he tells her they can't hang out anymore?

No. I can't do it. This is a terrible, terrible idea.

Before she gets herself too freaked out, she decides she'll ask the one person she knows she can trust, the one person who already knows all of Evie's secrets and loves her like a sister. Tomorrow she'll run her idea by Grace, and if Grace gives her stamp of approval, Evie will take the risk and ask Alistair.

Chapter 10

Over lunch on Friday, Evie again drags Grace into the library stacks. She deliberately doesn't explain until they're alone.

"What's up?" Grace demands. They sit on the floor with their backs against the shelves.

Evie bites her lip. She tells Grace about the questions Miss Lonely Love gets about sex, detailing the content of the most recent one. Then she explains that she feels bad that she can't offer any advice because of her own lack of experience.

Her friend stares at her, a knowing smile on her lips. "You know, you can fix that easy enough if you want to. And please don't pretend you don't know who I mean."

Blushing, Evie says, "Well, that's kinda what I wanted to talk to you about. Do you really think that'd be a good idea? I mean, he made it pretty clear he just wants to be friends, and I told him I didn't want a boyfriend right now either, which is totally true, and—"

Grace bursts out laughing.

"What?"

"He's a guy, dude! He'll jump at the chance for no-strings-attached sex. Especially with you."

Snorting, Evie asks, "Why especially with me?"

"He's obviously at least a bit into you, since you two had a full-blown make out session when you were stuck in his car. And you're sweet, pretty, and most of all willing—there's no way he'll turn you down!"

Evie looks doubtful. "I don't know," she sighs.

Her friend lays a hand on her arm. "The only thing I'd be worried about with this little plan is that you're gonna fall for him." Grace looks her right in the eyes. "Which is valid, since, you know, you kind of already are."

"No, I'm not!" Evie shakes her head, but she can feel her face grow hot. "I value his friendship, and I don't want to lose it. That's all!"

Graces arches a skeptical brow. "If you say so."

"I do."

"So then it's decided? You're gonna ask him if he's DTF for science?" Both hands slap over her mouth to suppress her giggle.

Evie can't help it; she starts laughing, too. This whole idea is absurd. It's completely mental. But, if she can be brave enough, and manage to be adult about it, there's a good chance it might just work.

When Alistair enters the study on Saturday morning with a steaming cup of coffee in one hand and a thick novel in the other, he's pleasantly surprised to find a letter addressed to JAI on the seat of his usual chair.

Tearing the envelope open, he pulls out the page. His first reaction is annoyance. Pity and futile advice—two things he neither wants nor needs. Then he reads it a second time. And sighs.

Everyone expects him to just get over it: his father, his brother, his uncle, even Miss Lonely Love. But none of them really get it. None of them have ever gone through what he has. They all think they know what's best for him. It drives him fucking crazy.

120

He takes a sip of coffee and tries to put it out of his mind. As he's settling into the soft leather, the house phone rings. Alistair ignores it, assuming Max will pick up in another room. It keeps ringing. His uncle must be out. The answering machine will come on any second, though. After four more rings, he blows out an irritated huff, sets his mug down, and gets up, stalking to the table in the corner and grabbing the receiver.

"Hello?"

The line is quiet, but he's pretty sure he detects the sound of breathing.

"Hello? Anyone there?" If It's some sicko looking to get his rocks off, he's picked the wrong number. Just as Alistair's about to tell them to fuck off and hang up, he hears a soft female voice.

"Ali?"

He groans. He should've known better than to pick up the damn phone. "The fuck do you want?"

"You're avoiding your brother."

"No shit," he snorts. What do these people really want from him?

She sighs, loud and full of her typical Michelle put-uponness. It's one of her trademarks, although she's rarely used it on him. "He feels awful. He's depressed. He needs you to forgive him."

"Uh huh. I got that much from our last conversation."

"So can you?"

"What? Forgive him?" He pauses, taking a deep breath. "No."

"Why not? You know damn well how sorry he is. It's time to stop being such a self-righteous ass and get over it."

Jesus, now he really *is* annoyed. With a bitter laugh he says, "Yeah. *I'm* the asshole here. Typical."

"He can't stand you hating him. It's eating him up inside."

"So *that's* why you called? Not to say *you're* sorry or to ask me to forgive *you*, but to try to convince me to ease Paul's guilt? Figures. I'm hanging up now."

"Wait," she blurts. "Yes, that's why I called. I know you, and I know you still care about him. You can't punish him forever. He never meant to hurt you; neither of us did. It wasn't plotted behind your back. It just…it just happened."

"There's a faster chance of me forgiving *you*. You were just my girlfriend. He's my brother. Family. Family doesn't do shit like that to each other."

He hears another soft sigh. "Maybe not in your limited little world, Alistair, but in the real world, yes, stuff like this happens. It sucks, but it does. I would love for you to forgive me someday, but Paul is my priority right now. Will you please just talk to him?"

Gritting his teeth, he replies, "I *have*. I don't have anything more to say. Have a good rest of your life, though. You two deserve each other."

Before she can protest further, he ends the call. This time he doesn't throw the receiver across the room. He places it back on its base and returns to his chair. Gulping down the rest of his coffee, he takes the dirty mug to the kitchen and with more calm than he would have expected, heads down the hallway to the gym.

Channeling his anger into an intense workout is the best way to deal with it these days. And he doesn't want to be in too horrible a mood this weekend. Evie's coming over to study tomorrow, after all.

The sermon seems to drone on forever. Evie sits between her dad and brother, shifting around on the hard wooden pew. She's trying to concentrate on Pastor Marshall's words, but is having little success. Finally, she just gives up and lets her thoughts drift to what she should wear, what she should say, and most of all what might end up happening when she visits Alistair this afternoon. Probably not very appropriate thoughts for church, but it's hard to focus on anything else.

She's still not sure whether telling Alistair her idea is smart. Since discussing it with Grace, she's changed her mind at least ten times. But this morning she'd woken up all excited about seeing him. Blasphemous or not, she prays this afternoon will end up going the way she wants.

When church is over at last, she rushes to the car, smiling politely at the other parishioners but not stopping to chat.

Her dad gives her a knowing look as he slides into the driver's seat beside her. "You in a hurry?"

"No." She pauses. "Well, sort of. I told Alistair I'd come over about one. To study."

Tom raises his eyebrows as he moves into the line of cars leaving the parking lot.

"He's helping me with my poetry assignment," Evie adds.

"You don't need to make excuses to visit him."

"I'm not," she protests.

"Then why're your cheeks so pink?" He shoots his daughter a grin. Evie doesn't respond, but she hears Dylan chuckling in the backseat. Obviously he overheard them even with his earbuds in.

Once home, Evie goes straight to her room to change out of her church clothes. Off goes her blouse, skirt, and pantyhose. On goes…what?

What does someone wear to a potential seduction?

Evie laughs out loud at her mental choice of words. Seduction. Is *that* what she intends to do to him? It's kind of hilarious, since she has pretty much zero experience in seducing. Chances are high he'll laugh in her face. This could go wrong in *so* many ways. But…it could also go really, really right.

She's clearly no seductress and there's no point in pretending otherwise. Evie pulls on her jeans, a long-sleeved tee, and a hoodie. She smooths down her hair, dabs on a bit of mascara and lip gloss, and then, heart racing, grabs her knapsack and heads for the door.

When she gets to Alistair's, Evie sits in her dad's car for a few moments staring at herself in the visor mirror and willing her heart to descend from her throat back to its usual place, and pace, in her ribcage. Finally she takes a deep breath, shoulders her bag, and goes to the door.

She bangs the heavy knocker twice. The deep clang of metal against metal seems to reverberate right from her fingertips to the pit of her stomach.

Alistair pulls the door open and smiles, and she smiles back, and her heart calms a little.

"Follow me back to the kitchen. Kettle's already boiling."

"Actually…" She pauses to toe off her boots. "I think I'd like something…different today." Some liquid courage seems like an excellent idea. She isn't sure she can manage to ask him what she wants without it.

He looks confused. "Different how?"

"Um. Harder?"

"Harder?" he laughs. "What did you have in mind, Miss Colville? Liquor?"

She blushes. Then nods.

"Really? I have a bottle of bourbon in my bedroom. Or are you more of a vodka and juice kind of girl?" He starts walking toward the steps.

She bites her lip, following him. "Uh, bourbon's fine, I think."

Alistair glances back at her with a curious expression.

When they get to his room, Evie tosses her bag beside the chair and sits on the rug in front of the fire. She hears the clink of glass and looks up to see him turning two tumblers upright on top of his dresser. He picks up a bottle and pours a small amount of amber liquid into one. Handing it to her, he says, "Try this. See if it meets your needs."

Evie puts the glass to her nose, breathing in the strong scent of the bourbon swirling around the bottom. All the hairs on the inside of her nostrils curl, and she pulls her face away with a grimace. She knows Alistair's watching her, so she braces herself and takes a sip.

The result is instantaneous. Her eyes widen and tear up. Her throat attempts to gag, but she manages to suppress it with a cough as the bourbon burns a fiery trail to her stomach.

"Well?" he asks, grinning.

Evie blinks, trying to find her voice. She doesn't want him to realize she's never tasted hard liquor before. "It's…fine." She raises the glass again, intending to down the rest in one gulp and get it over with.

Before she can, Alistair steps forward and intercepts it. "Let me get some ice for you. It'll take the edge off a bit."

"Thanks," she says gratefully.

He goes downstairs, leaving Evie alone in his room. She grabs her bag and pulls out her English folder. Only two more poems to go. She's chosen the theme of heat; it seems fitting during the frigid depths of winter. Maybe this afternoon she'll be inspired by a whole new way to keep warm on a cold day.

Oh God! I've clearly lost my mind.

She drops her burning face to the tops of her knees, laughing softly. One sip of booze and her brain is already in the gutter. Alistair's going to wonder what the hell's gotten into her when she tells him her idea. She tries to imagine his expression when he hears it. Those incredible green eyes will widen in shock. His mouth will fall open as he wonders if she's lost her mind.

God, that mouth…

She remembers how soft his lips felt against hers. Will she ever get to kiss him again? Could it happen today? Might they even make a mess of that oh-so-neatly made bed over there?

Evie giggles again, scolding herself for such horny thoughts. But then she stops. Actually, she reminds herself, there's nothing wrong with them. Lust is fine. He's hot. And they're both consenting young adults. Lust is normal. Expected even. As long as they can trust each other, a little bit of lust might just solve her dilemma. And as long as their feelings for one another don't go beyond good friends who respect each other, everything should work out fine.

She opens her notebook and looks over her hastily scrawled ideas for the next two poems. As she's jotting down the line 'flames dancing over my sweat-dappled skin,' Alistair returns, two fat ice cubes clinking in her glass. He pours a little more bourbon over them and hands it back to her.

"See if that's any better," he instructs, filling his own glass about a quarter of the way.

Evie takes another tentative taste. The ice has done just what he said it would, taken the edge off. She has a larger sip, swirling it around her mouth before swallowing. Interesting. There's a bit of a caramel-y aftertaste. It's still strong, still burns her throat, but now it's not so bad. He's only given her a little, and she upends the glass, letting the last of it flow over the ice on its way into her mouth. She's starting to warm up; the heat radiates outward from a place deep in her belly. Most of this is from the bourbon, she knows, but some of it is also because of Alistair's proximity. The memory of their kiss won't leave her head. And she really wants to kiss him again.

She hands the empty glass back to him with a small smile.

Alistair's eyebrow quirks up again, and he chuckles softly as he returns to the dresser. "I thought you wanted to come over here to study, not get wasted. Not that I'm complaining. I'm just surprised, is all."

"I *do* want to study. This afternoon what I want is to learn. But learning comes in many forms, and not all of them involve reading or writing."

Alistair gives her a strange look as he sets her refilled glass on the table behind her. "Yes, that's very true. What sort of learning did you have in mind then? I thought you wanted me to look over your poems for you?"

"Oh, I do," Evie replies hastily, setting the folder of completed poetry on the carpet as he sits down. She takes another sip of bourbon. It seems to taste better with every swallow. Either that or she's becoming immune to the burn.

He opens the file and starts to look over the first poem. Evie's nerves shoot higher, but this time for a different reason. She hopes he likes what he reads. The thought of Alistair judging her writing and finding it lacking makes her anxious. She doesn't know why, but his approval matters to her.

To distract herself from trying to decipher his thoughts, she picks up her notebook and pencil again. Already her brain feels a bit fuzzy from the alcohol. Not a lot—just an odd sense of lightness and a difficulty focusing.

From the corner of her eye, she sees Alistair raise his glass to his lips as his eyes flick over the paper. When he comes to the end, without a word he flips the page and begins to read the next one. Evie can't help watching him; she gives up even trying to pretend she's writing.

A few moments later, he lifts his gaze to her with a self-conscious grin. "What?"

"What what?"

"Why're you staring at me?"

She flushes, dropping her eyes to her poem again. The words flicker in and out of focus. "I'm not staring," she mutters.

"Yes, you were." He chuckles, pushing the bridge of his glasses higher on his nose. Then he resumes reading.

A few more minutes pass in silence. The room seems too quiet with only the crackle of the flames in the fireplace. Evie jots down words like "smolder" and "melt" and "steam," but doesn't put any of them together into phrases. At last, she hears him clear his throat, and when she glances up, he's looking back at her again.

"Why are you staring at me?" she teases, picking up her tumbler and having another drink.

"These are really good, Evie. Your themes of heat and change come across clearly in each poem. I love the one about slowly melting ice the best. The one about the campfire could use a little more fleshing out, but it's still excellent. You write very maturely for someone your age." He looks impressed, and she can't help feeling proud.

"Th-thank you," she stammers. "I'll re-look at 'Flames to Ashes' after I finish these last two."

For a few minutes they sit in companionable silence while she tries to write a few lines of a new poem. It's still so hard to focus, and nothing very good is coming to her.

She's grateful for the interruption when he says, "You never answered my question from before."

"Which one?"

"About what kind of non-reading and writing learning you want to do today."

Evie lifts her eyes to his. Her hand gropes for the glass by her knee and she lifts it to her lips without looking. "Well…I actually have a bit of a…proposition for you." She can feel heat flooding not only her cheeks, but her entire body.

Alistair smiles. "A proposition? Do tell."

She swallows nervously. "Do you remember our word games while we were stuck last Saturday?"

"Sure. What about them?"

Her gaze darts around the room, from the door to the painting on the wall above his dresser to the notebook resting on her thighs. Any spot but his face. Or his bed. "Um. So, remember how I said I'd never done much…stuff?"

He's quiet for a few seconds. Then: "By 'stuff' you mean, like, sex?"

Evie's eyes flash to his for a second. She nods, looking down again.

"Okay," he says. "Yeah, I remember."

She takes another sip of bourbon. "Do you trust me?"

To her relief, he doesn't even hesitate. "Yes."

"Good. Because I trust you, too."

"I'm glad." He pauses, and she hears him take a drink from his own glass. "So what's up?"

OMG, how to even say this? With a deep breath, she starts in. "Okay so, like I said, I'm not a virgin. But not by much." He chuckles softly at that, but she doesn't look up. "I've had sex once, with my ex, a few months after my mom passed away. It was…less than amazing. I mean, I think it was probably fine for him. But for me, well…" She sighs. "I just don't get why everyone's so hung up on it. It wasn't horrible or anything—and he's a nice guy, don't get me wrong—but…"

"But?" Alistair asks quietly. When she doesn't reply, he says, "But you didn't get much out of it? No fireworks?"

Evie blows out a short laugh, raising her eyes to his at last. "Nope. Not one."

"I'm sorry to hear that. The first time's never that great for anyone, though. It gets better. Much, *much* better."

"So I've heard." She picks up her tumbler again and downs the last swallow. Her fingers are cold against the glass as she sets it back on the table.

Alistair exhales a soft breath. "Why are you telling me this?" His voice is soft.

The liquor is starting to work its magic. She isn't drunk, but her inhibitions are dropping by the second. Looking right at him, she flashes a nervous smile. "I think you know why."

Alistair's eyes flare as it sinks in. His mouth and brows become parallel lines. "I thought we discussed all this last weekend. Just friends, right? We both agreed. Have you changed your mind? Because—"

Feeling bolder, she reaches over and shushes him with the pad of her index finger against his lips. Lips she hopes she'll be kissing soon. "I haven't changed my mind. We're friends and I value that. But I thought maybe, as my friend, you could…you know…show me what I'm missing? Teach me. I wanna know what the big deal is." She smiles again. "No strings attached, I promise."

He pulls her hand away from his mouth, but instead of releasing it, he holds it against his thigh. In a shocked yet bemused voice he asks, "Are you seriously suggesting Friends With Benefits?"

Evie nods, her fingers trembling in his.

For a long minute he just looks at her. She can almost see the wheels turning behind his eyes as he thinks over her request, examining it from every different angle, looking for potential potholes.

She's not wrong. Alistair is completely floored, although he tries to keep his face neutral. How many different ways could this go wrong? In mere seconds, each and every one flashes across his mind. He doesn't want to hurt her. But, and if he's being honest with himself, even more importantly, he doesn't want to get hurt again.

Then his dream from the other night once more pops into his head. This smart, fun, and incredibly sexy girl is sitting right beside him, and she's been brave enough to risk her self-confidence by asking him to sleep with her. And it's not like he doesn't want to. He does. Lord knows he's hard as a rock right now just contemplating the idea.

Is there any way this could actually work and not wreck their friendship? It's risky, but it's not impossible. Maybe, if they can stay open and honest with each other, if they can be adults about it, it just might.

Finally, with a tight smile and a soft sigh, he says, "There would need to be ground rules."

Evie's heart leaps in her chest; for a second it feels like it's stopped. Then it resumes pounding even faster. Is he really going to agree?

"Definitely," she replies. "First and foremost: no emotional attachments. If either of us thinks we might be catching serious feelings, we have to tell the other, and go back to just regular friends. I mean, minus the, uh, benefits."

Alistair nods. "Agreed. No falling in love." He drags the fingers of his free hand through his hair, making it even more unruly. "Rule two: either of us can put a stop to this for any reason, no questions asked. We just have to say so." He pauses, seeming to consider something else. "Honesty is key."

"Agreed." A flash of guilt stabs through Evie as she consents. He doesn't know about her alter ego, and she has no intention of telling him. It's not that she wouldn't trust him to keep her secret; she knows he would. She just wants as few people to know as possible. At the moment there are three: her editor, her dad, and Grace. That's enough. Much as she's proud of her column, if word got around Sutterton that Miss Lonely Love is really a high school senior, she would be finished. No one would ever write in again.

"Anything else?" he asks, studying her closely.

Evie thinks about it for a moment, and then shakes her head.

"So to sum up, rule one: no messy feelings. Rule two: either of us can walk away at any time. Rule three: we have to be honest with each other. Did I leave anything out?"

She shakes her head again. Her palms are clammy and she hopes he can't feel it. His thumb strokes her knuckles absentmindedly as he speaks.

"Okay. So we have a FWB agreement." He exhales a laugh, looking a bit dazed. "Wow. Never would've guessed this is what we'd be discussing today. You surprised the shit outta me."

Giggling, she replies, "Me, too! I can't believe I even suggested it. I blame the booze."

"Speaking of, do you want a refill?"

She drops her eyes to the notebook on her lap again. "No, I'm good." No more bourbon. She wants to remember this afternoon.

They're both quiet for a bit, Evie pretending to read over her poetry notes, Alistair lost somewhere deep in thought. He still holds her fingers.

When she looks up at him, he's staring at her again. He rubs lazy circles on the back of her hand. "So..." he begins.

"So?"

"What exactly do you want me to show you?"

More blood rushes to her face. "Um. I don't know. Everything?"

"Everything?" He chuckles. "That might take a while. Do you want to start, like, *today*?"

Evie bites her lower lip. Shyly she nods. "Is that okay? Or do you want some time to think things over more?"

He shakes his head, smiling. "I have a lot of alone time, and frankly I spend far too much of it over-analyzing things. So tell me, what should your first lesson be?"

Swallowing is suddenly difficult. "It's up to you," she manages to whisper.

Please stop asking me questions and kiss me already!

Alistair grins. It's a sexy, lazy grin, and the sight of it makes her lower belly clench. His eyes twinkle in the firelight as he swallows the last of his drink. He removes his glasses and sets them aside. Then he snakes a hand under her hair, tickling the back of her neck as he pulls her to him.

Chapter 11

He hadn't kissed her goodbye.

It hadn't seemed appropriate, given the circumstances. But it weighs on Alistair's mind as he lies half-covered by rumpled sheets, sheets that still hold her scent. He flings one arm over his eyes, memories of the previous hour swirling in his head.

He hadn't kissed her goodbye.

No woman had ever left his bed in the past without at least a parting kiss. It all feels so weird. So detached. Just…wrong.

After, Evie had jumped up and collected her discarded clothes, scrambling to get dressed, and pack up her schoolwork. As she'd slipped through the door, she'd mumbled something about needing to get home to make supper. Alistair had sensed a panicky weirdness, an urge to flee. So he'd just let her go.

It isn't a huge surprise that she'd had trouble looking him in the eye as she'd hurried off, but he hopes she'll soon get over it. This FWB arrangement she'd suggested seemed like it could be asking for trouble, but she'd assured him everything would be fine. So he'd decided to ignore his reservations and just go with the flow. He knows he trusts her—at least as far as he can trust anyone anymore—and now he'll have to trust that she'll be able to deal with this. And if not, that she'll let him know she wants to revert to their old dynamic. Sighing, he wonders again if agreeing to this was a big mistake.

Alistair tells himself he'd be cool with it if she's too freaked out and wants to go back to how things were. Evie has enough stress on her without him adding to it. The last thing he wants is for her to feel pressured to continue just to save the embarrassment of admitting she's reconsidered.

And if she does, that will be two women who've changed their minds about him, not just in the recent past, but, well, ever. He decides he'll take it as a sign that maybe he's just meant to be celibate. Maybe that's his lot in life now—deserved punishment for the sins of his younger self.

Sins like throwing around his father's cash and living large and lazy, instead of going into pre-law like he was expected to.

Sins like all the pussy he'd gotten and hearts he'd broken before meeting Michelle and stupidly believing he'd finally found The One.

Sins like forgetting to pick up his mom's inhaler on the day she died.

Yeah. That's a pretty fucking big one.

The grandfather clock down the hall begins to chime six o'clock, interrupting Alistair's maudlin thoughts. With another soft sigh, he slides to the edge of the bed and, with reluctance, gets to his feet. Retrieving his discarded jeans from the floor, he drags them on over the boxer-briefs he still wears before searching for the rest of his clothes. His t-shirt and sweater are piled on the chair. One sock is balled up on the ceramic hearth, a little too close to the dying embers behind the grate for his comfort. A quick glance around the room fails to locate its twin.

Instead of going downstairs to see what his uncle wants to do for dinner, he sits on the edge of the bed and pulls out his side-table drawer, retrieving the latest letter from Miss Lonely Love. Flopping across the mattress, he braces himself on his elbows and props it and a pad of paper against his pillow. He doesn't know why writing back to the advice columnist seems more important than food right now, but it's been one of those days where he just goes with his impulses. And hopes like hell they won't lead him astray. Again.

Dear Miss LL,
My childhood wasn't as idyllic as you might assume.
When I was young, my mother died suddenly. She and I were very close, and my life was never the same after that. In his grief, my father became distant and detached. He spent most of his time working and left our housekeeper to take care of us. Because our dad was rarely around, my brother and I grew to rely on each other. I'm a few years older, so I watched out for him, protected him as best I could, and helped him when he needed help with schoolwork or just generally fitting in. We were tight. Really tight. I considered him my only real family. As we grew older, he became my closest friend, too.
In case it wasn't already obvious, I don't trust easily. Never have. But I trusted him. And, later, her as well. Never in a million years would I ever have imagined that the two people in the world I loved and trusted would end up betraying me. Everyone keeps telling me I need to get over it, that I need to forgive and forget and move on. But they don't understand. I can't forgive. I won't forget. They're both strangers to me now. In hindsight, I guess they always were.
I don't believe in second chances. As I had to learn the hard way: the only one I can rely on is myself.
So yes, I've given your advice a lot of thought. Too much, possibly. And it's true that there's now someone I might actually be willing to place a small amount of trust in. She's different from anyone else I've ever known—more real, if that makes sense. And less complicated. I don't really know what makes her special, but her friendship has grown to mean a lot to me.
So be happy, for I've actually taken your advice, at least a little. Baby steps, right? Thought you'd want to know that.
Have a great week.
JAI

Evie lies on her side, eyes closed, listening to snow pellets pepper the windows and siding. The sound makes her feel cold, and she shivers, but she doesn't crawl beneath the blankets. Her fingers drum against the top of her thigh. She's supposed to be finishing off her poetry assignment, but she still can't focus. Her thoughts swirl like the snow outside. And she can't keep still. Her insides are all tied up in knots. She's giddy; there's no other way to describe it.

Her afternoon with Alistair had been…a learning experience. Definitely. The words *earth-shattering* come to mind. So *that's* what she's read about in trashy books, overheard girls bragging about their boyfriends' skills at. She remembers Melody telling anyone within earshot in the girls' washroom last year how hard Cam had 'rocked her world.' Evie hadn't fully understood what she'd meant.

But now, for the first time in her life, she does. Alistair had rocked her world. And she knows her little world will never be the same.

If they both decide they want to continue their Friends With Benefits experiment, things are sure to get even more interesting. Because if her body reacted so intensely to what they'd done a few hours ago, how on earth will she react when…if…they have full-on sex? Evie can't even imagine. But she's imagining anyway.

The next morning, Evie's fabulous mood is still intact, and apparently it shows. The second she drops into the seat beside Grace on the bus, her friend turns to her with an arched brow. "What's with you?"

Evie blushes, attempting to suppress her grin. "What d'ya mean?"

"Something's different. You're…" Grace pauses, examining her. "You're extra smiley. What's up?" Suddenly she grabs

Evie by both shoulders, leaning in by her ear. "Did you see Alistair this weekend? You *did*, didn't you?"

Evie bites her lip and nods.

"And? You asked him? C'mon, tell me all the juicy deets." Her eyes sparkle with excitement.

Evie shifts away, looking down at her fingernails. The bus's brakes squeal as it jolts to a stop to pick up more kids. With a sigh, she mumbles, "Not here."

"No, no, no. Tell me. Right now." Grace's voice drops to a whisper. A harsh whisper, but still. "Did you two actually do it?"

Fidgeting with the buckle of her knapsack, Evie refuses to reply.

"You didn't! OMG, you did!"

"Shhh!" Evie looks up at her with wide eyes. Her face feels like it's on fire. "Sort of. Not exactly," she murmurs, just loud enough for Grace to hear. "Will you shut up about it now if I promise to tell you at lunch?"

Grace's eyes narrow. "Fine," she huffs. "I guess I can wait. Shit, you torture me, girl—you know that? Good thing I love you." She turns to look out the window, pretending to ignore Evie.

Evie laughs. "I know. That's what friends are for."

About ten seconds after the lunch bell sounds, Grace grabs Evie's arm from behind and drags her to their lockers.

"Get your coat. We're going off property today."

"It's gotta be minus five out there! Is that really necessary? Let's just go eat up in the turret."

Lunch bags in hand, they wind through the throng of students heading in the opposite direction. Past the boy's washroom, the girls slip through an unmarked door to the side staircase that leads up to the northwest tower. The stairs are old, wooden, and narrow, forcing them to climb one in front of the other. When they exit through the door at the top, they step into a sunny semi-circular room with built-in benches below tall, slim windows.

This is Evie's favorite spot in the entire school, her secret hiding place when she needs a break. Sometimes it can be chilly and damp, but today's sunshine has made it warm and cozy and perfect.

The windows are kind of grimy, but she can still see the river across the road. It's nearly frozen over, but a small rivulet of dark, rushing water splits the ice. This section has been steadily shrinking, and now looks to be only a few feet across. It wouldn't surprise Evie if the entire river freezes solid before this winter is over.

Grace takes a seat and sets her lunch beside her thigh. She doesn't open it. Patting the spot next to her, she says, "Spill. I can't wait a second longer."

Evie remains standing, bracing one hand against the wooden sill and training her eyes on the soaring speck of a hawk hunting in the distance. "Well…"

She hears Grace exhale a frustrated puff of air. "Since this is clearly difficult for you, I'll help you get started. Did you do it, or didn't you? What does 'sort of' mean? How do you 'sort of' have sex?"

"We…he…" Evie stops, sighing. Her voice falls to a whisper, though there's only the two of them. "We didn't have sex the way you're thinking, but we…" She trails off again, watching the hawk dive for something along the river's edge. She can't help hoping the creature, be it rabbit, mouse, or whatever, will escape becoming the bird's dinner.

"You what? You're not making sense, girl. You didn't have sex, but you *sort of* did? I don't get it."

Evie's eyes shoot to Grace's, narrowing in mild irritation. "You're really gonna make me say this?"

"Of course I am! Just tell me already. What? Did he go down on you? Is that what you're too embarrassed to say?"

Evie's gaze returns out the window, her posture rigid, her face now cherry red. She nods.

Grace slides closer and rubs her friend's forearm. "Was it the first time you've ever done that?"

Biting her lip, Evie nods again.

She hears Grace suck in a breath. "Oh wow. So was it good? I bet it was."

Evie's quiet for a moment. Then she mumbles, "I...um...I think I even...you know."

The other girl laughs. "Good for you!" She pauses to look closer at her friend. "Don't tell me you've never had one before?"

With a small shake of her head, Evie thinks, *Could it be any hotter up here?* She tugs at the neck of her sweater, letting some cool air on her overheated skin.

"Really?"

"Nope."

"Huh. Well I'm happy for you." Grace pauses. "And did you, you know, reciprocate?"

Evie finally turns to meet her friend's eyes. "Did I *what?*"

Now Grace's bronze cheeks have high dots of color on them, too. "You know what I mean. Did you...to him?"

"Oh! Uh, no. I sort of wondered if I should, but...I don't really know how. Maybe next time he'll show me what to do."

"Jesus, girl. You and Jase never did *that* either? I can't believe he never asked you to." She chuckles. "You poor, sheltered thing. Thank God you've finally met a guy you can experience all the good stuff with. It'd be a shame for you to graduate high school so damn innocent!"

"I agree!" Then Evie grows serious. "I really like being with him. But don't forget we're still just friends. Only now we're..."

Grace gives her a knowing smile. "Friends With Benefits. Yeah, yeah. We'll see how long that lasts."

"It has to," Evie says flatly. "We agreed. No emotional attachments. Otherwise, we end the benefits. And possibly the friendship."

"Okay. If you say so." Grace runs a hand over her dark curls, then gives Evie a saucy grin "So...when are you gonna see him again?"

Opening her lunch bag, Evie rummages around inside until she finds her apple. "It's not like we made firm plans, but hopefully soon. Maybe this weekend." She examines the waxy red and green mottled skin and takes a bite.

"Firm plans?" Grace starts to giggle. "Yeah, I bet *something* will be firm about them!"

Evie can't restrain her own laugh, spraying out tiny bits of white apple flesh into the air. She claps a hand over her mouth to stifle it.

"Ew! Control yourself, girl." Grace wrinkles her nose in disgust. "Now what was I about to say before you so rudely spit food at me? Oh yeah." She looks at her friend with concern. "So…you know I totally get why you wanna do this. And I also know I told you to go for it. But there's another part of me that's worried about you. Maybe this isn't such a smart idea. If you don't wanna fall for this guy, maybe sex needs to stay right off the table." With a smirk, she adds, "Or the bed. Or the floor. Whatever."

Evie rolls her eyes. "No need to worry. It's not like that. We talked it over and made an agreement. No strings attached. No messy feelings. Just fun. I can do fun. I deserve some fun, don't ya think?"

"You definitely do. I can't argue with that. I just think you're playing with fire. And I don't want you to get hurt." She picks up her sandwich and leans back against the window, chewing thoughtfully. A few minutes later, she turns to Evie again. "You know, I still need to meet this dude. I wanna look him over, give him my stamp of approval. That's part of my job as your best friend."

"Well, come by the shop a night or two this week and do your homework with me. Maybe he'll pop in."

Grace flashes Evie a wicked smile. "See you tonight."

The next few days pass without a word from Alistair, but Evie tries not to read anything into it. After all, it isn't like she's messaged him either. She figures she'll wait a little longer, and if she doesn't hear from him by the end of Wednesday, she'll text him a 'hey'. Evie's great mood continues, and Grace can't resist teasing her about her 'new boy-toy' every chance she gets.

Wednesday night is quiet. A few regulars sit along the side, but otherwise Evie has plenty of time to study. By the time Grace shows up around eight, the place is empty. She spreads her Algebra homework across the countertop while Evie wipes down tables. It's still too early to sweep the floor or clean out the coffee machines, so once Evie finishes, she joins Grace and opens her poetry book. This week they're reading Dylan Thomas. So far, Evie likes his poems; they have a rhythmic, catchy style.

"So, did you tell him about your column?" Grace wonders, looking up from her calculations. "You know, when you asked him about the FWB thing?"

Evie glances at her in surprise. "No."

"Why not?"

Shrugging, she replies, "I don't know. I guess I just want my secret identity to stay secret. The fewer people who know, the better."

Grace frowns.

"I might tell him someday," Evie concedes. "Just not right now."

About quarter after nine, the bells over the door tinkle. Both girls look up at the same time, and a happy grin stretches Evie's face when she sees Alistair's black coat and cap. She jumps up and rushes over.

"Hey." Her cheeks are hot again. Same old, same old, when she's around him. Or talking about him. Or thinking about him. His eyes shine, matching the smile below. He's happy to see her, and she's more than a little relieved.

"Hey," he replies softly. "Sorry I've been AWOL the past few days."

"It's okay. C'mere, I want to introduce you to someone." Evie grabs the sleeve of his jacket and guides him to the counter.

Her friend is just staring, eyes wide. From behind Alistair, Evie mouths the words: *Be cool!*

"Grace, this is my friend, Alistair." Evie tries to put subtle emphasis on the word *friend*.

"Hey," Grace says. She scans him up and down, and clearly likes what she sees.

"Alistair, this is my BFF, Grace Bryant. We've known each other since we were toddlers."

Alistair smiles at Grace. "Pleased to meet you. Any friend of Evie's...well, you know the rest."

"I hear you've been helping her, uh...study." The meaning of Grace's deliberate pause is obvious. Evie's eyes flare, and she shoots her friend a dirty look.

Alistair just laughs. "Yep. English was always one of my favorite subjects. Now, if it was French she needed help with, it would be a *completely* different story."

"Foreign languages not your thing?"

With a wicked grin, he replies, "Let's just say I've never had any problems communicating."

Grace chuckles. "I bet not."

Alistair turns to catch Evie's eye and arches an inquisitive eyebrow. She shrugs as she goes behind the counter to sit down and he slides onto a stool beside Grace. "What're you ladies studying on this God-forsakenly frigid evening?" He picks up Evie's book. "Dylan Thomas, huh? Cool. Always loved him."

"Me too, so far. It's the next part of our poetry component." Evie takes a sip of her hot chocolate before remembering she's actually working. "Oh! You want coffee?"

He pulls his mug from inside his coat and sets it on the counter. "Sure. I could use some warming up."

Grace stifles a giggle and raises amused eyes to Evie, who glares back at her.

"What about you?" he asks, returning his attention to Grace. "What're you working on tonight?"

She groans. "Algebra."

"Fun."

"Not really. But I'm almost done." After punching some numbers into her calculator, Grace jots down the results and closes her notebook, happy she doesn't have to look at any more numbers tonight. She swivels her stool to face a curious Alistair head on. "So. Evie tells me you just moved here from the city?"

"Yep. About a month ago. I'm staying with my uncle."

"Sorry, but I have to ask. Why the hell would *anyone* voluntarily move to our crappy little town? I mean, had you never been here before? Did your uncle bullshit you about what this place is like?"

Alistair chuckles. "I assure you it was completely my idea."

"Huh. Did you get too loaded on New Year's Eve and fall on your head? Suffer brain damage maybe?"

He snorts, looking over at a grinning Evie, who's watching them with amusement. "I like her," he declares.

"Good," Evie says. "I was hoping you would."

"Hold on," Grace interrupts. "I'm not done grilling him yet. The big question, Alistair—the *biggest* question, actually—is this: just how long do you plan to stay?"

He glances at Evie again, then flashes Grace a smile. "You're right, that's a very good question. And the answer is: I don't know. Until I don't feel welcome anymore, I suppose. Or until there's a good reason to move on. For now, I'm content to stick around. Not the most definitive answer, I know, but it's the best I can give you right now."

Relief floods over Evie. For now, for the next few months anyway, she intends to do her best to make sure he feels very welcome.

"On that note, I should head home before my grandma starts to worry. It's nearly time to make her tea." Grace gathers up her homework before pulling on her coat.

Evie comes around the counter to give her friend a hug. "See you in the morning," she calls as Grace heads out.

And then it's just the two of them, alone together for the first time since she'd rushed out of his bed three days ago.

Evie turns away from Alistair and begins rinsing out the coffee pots, not sure what to say. He remains quiet as she works, and their lack of conversation makes her anxious.

Maybe he's waiting for her to start? She sighs softly as she dries the glass carafes and puts them back under the machines so they're ready to go for morning.

Alistair clears his throat behind her, and she straightens to face him.

"Soooo…" He's looking right at her.

"So?"

"Can I give you a lift home tonight?"

She shrugs. "Sure."

He examines her for a moment longer, eyes narrowed. "Is this gonna be awkward now?"

"I hope not." She smiles again. "Cause awkward would pretty much suck."

"Good. Hey, I apologize again for not touching base sooner. After the way you left on Sunday, I thought maybe you needed a bit of time to think things over."

Evie nods in understanding. "Yeah, sorry about that. I guess I did kinda freak out a little. If it makes you feel better, I'm fine now. I was fine not long after, actually. Maybe I just needed some air or something." She presses her lips together, then asks the question that's worrying her. "What about you?"

"Cool as a…well as pretty much the entire world at the moment." He flashes a tight smile. "We good then?"

"Totally." She gathers her stuff, pulls on her coat and walks to the door with him, the bells jingling their goodbye as she locks up. His Jeep is nearby, and since the engine hasn't had time to get fully cold yet, by the time they pull up in front of her house, the interior is nice and toasty.

"You working 'til midnight on Saturday?" Alistair asks.

"Yeah, of course."

He hesitates for a moment before blurting, "Wanna come back to my place after?"

She looks at him in surprise. "That late?"

"I was thinking maybe you could, you know, stay over? If you want to. I don't know if your dad would go for it or not, but—"

Evie cuts in. "I think I can work it out with him."

"Yeah?"

144

With a small smile, she replies, "Yeah."

He looks pleased. Then something in his gaze shifts, becomes more intense as he stares into her eyes. For a moment, she thinks he's going to kiss her. Which would violate their Friends With Benefits rules, wouldn't it? Or would it? She's pretty sure friends wouldn't give each other goodnight kisses. Even though she wouldn't mind.

Alistair reaches over and squeezes her gloved hand. "Night, Evie."

She pulls on the door handle, knowing there will be lots of time for kissing on Saturday night if she sleeps over. "Goodnight."

Chapter 12

Thursday night brings a near-constant flow of customers into the Clutch. Evie doesn't get a chance to read the letters she picked up from the *Herald* until she's tucked into her own bed. Her homework load has been particularly heavy lately; normally she has her column completed and sent to her editor by the end of Wednesday. She's a day behind, and it needs to get done before she can sleep.

The bundle is only four letters this week, which is a relief. She starts to read and makes notes about potential responses. When she reaches the bottom envelope, she smiles, recognizing JAI's printing. His message makes her feel several different emotions: empathy over losing his mom at a young age, annoyance at how his father treated his sons afterward, frustration over how JAI's brother betrayed him, and then, to her surprise, relief that he's finally found a new friend. Evie hopes this girl is patient with him, because he's going to need a lot of understanding from anyone new in his life.

Finishing her column is her priority, so she folds his letter and tucks it inside the book with the others. She'll respond to

JAI tomorrow. For now, she begins answering the publishable letters, like the responsible girl she always tries to be.

"I've never lied to Dad before," Evie says, her forehead furrowed with worry. "What if he sees right through me?"

The bus jolts in and out of a pothole. This sunny Friday has brought a surprise end-of-February thaw, and the melting ice and snow make for a bumpy ride.

Grace pats Evie's knee. "Just tell him you're helping me with my English essay that's due Monday, and you'll be home in the morning in time to go to church. Tom'll be cool with it."

"I don't know," Evie sighs. "I really want to go to Alistair's tomorrow but...I hate having to lie. It doesn't feel right."

"Lying to your parents so you can go make out with a cute guy is, like, a teenage rite of passage. Look at it this way: it'll be a life experience. And you want more life experiences, don't you?"

Evie still looks doubtful, but she nods reluctantly. "Yeah. I guess."

"Am I seriously gonna have to talk you into sleeping over at your smokin' hot not-boyfriend's place?" Grace drops her already low voice to barely a whisper. "I think you should go fuck his brains out. And then tell me all about it, so I can live vicariously through *you* for once!"

They both erupt with laughter. The two girls in front of them swivel matching blonde heads and shoot curious looks their way. Evie claps a hand over her mouth to stifle her giggles. Once she calms, she leans close to Grace and murmurs, "I really want to."

"Then it's settled. Tell your dad tonight, and pack a bag before you leave for work tomorrow. I'm calling you at noon on Sunday though. Got it?"

Blowing out a nervous puff of air, Evie agrees.

Saturday is also unseasonably warm. Dripping icicles provide background percussion as Evie tries to avoid puddles on her way to work, her knapsack heavy on her shoulder.

It feels great to not wear gloves and a woolen hat this afternoon, and she revels in the sun's warmth on her skin. She knows this is just Spring's little tease, that Winter is still far from finished with Sutterton, but on days like this, she can't help being excited for the turning of the seasons.

Why not, right? Evie has every reason to be in a fabulous mood. Not only is the warmer weather enough to cheer anyone up, but later tonight she has a hot date with an even hotter guy. Although it isn't *really* a date, she can't help thinking of it like that.

At the Clutch, she reminds her dad she won't be home until morning as he tops up mugs at the counter. When she finally shoos him out the door, the place is packed. The next four hours zip by as she makes sandwiches, plates pastries, and brings coffee to cheerful customers. This warm spell has brought more people out and though serving them keeps her hopping, Evie's grateful.

She doesn't even notice Alistair slip in and take a seat at a table in the back until he's been there for quite a while, his travel mug sitting open on the table.

"Sorry," she tells him with a harried but genuine smile as she fills it. "I've been slammed all night."

"No problem. Can I help out?" He adjusts his glasses, returning her smile.

"Really?"

"Sure." Standing, he takes the coffeepot from her hand. "Let me top up those needing refills while you take care of the people waiting to pay."

"Sure you don't mind?"

"I've got it. Go." He waves her toward the cash register with his free hand.

As she hurries back to the counter, she hears him say to Mrs. Huxley, "Need a warm up?" Evie can't suppress an amused grin at the older women's surprised, "Oh! Yes, please!"

For the next two hours, Alistair looks after all the coffee orders and refills, while she manages the food and till. She's impressed with his ability to service customers quickly, yet still find a few moments to chat with each one. Frankly, he's a natural. They all seem to love him. Even the usual curmudgeons manage to rouse a grin when he turns his attention on them.

If only Dad was still here to see this!

It's after eleven before they can take a break. Evie's feet ache and she's exhausted. Although she's still excited about going home with Alistair, when she thinks about his big, comfortable bed, she imagines crawling into it, snuggling up to him and falling asleep in his arms. She's pretty sure that isn't all he has in mind, though. But then again, they haven't discussed any details. Since they're just friends, maybe sleeping over really means only sleeping? Oh, who is she kidding? The two of them alone in bed together for an entire night? Now that they've already crossed the friendship line not once, but twice in the recent past? The thought of what might happen later has her feeling much more awake.

"You want more coffee?" she asks Alistair, starting to rise.

"Nah, I'm good. I'm still buzzing from running around so much. Never seen it so busy in here."

"Thaw," she replies with a shrug. "It always lures people out and puts them in the mood to socialize."

"Makes sense I guess," Alistair looks up at the clock. "So, forty minutes 'til close. What do we still need to do? Sweep the floors, start the dishwasher, clean the coffee machines. Anything else?"

"Get everything ready to go for Monday morning. Balance the cash register." She looks around, chewing her lower lip. "That's about it."

He smiles. "Cool. I'll do the sweeping and washing up. You do the register and prep for Monday. Deal?"

"Oh no, you've already done more than enough to help me tonight! Just sit and relax." Evie slides off her stool and turns to finish loading the dishwasher.

She hears Alistair snort as he comes around the counter. He edges her away from the dishwasher with the side of his hip and, kneeling, pulls it open and begins filling it. Evie looks at him in surprise, then smiles to herself and sits back down. She picks up the stack of receipts to start calculating the day's totals.

Working together, they're done by quarter to midnight. Evie's body is tired, but her mind is now hyper-alert. Every time she glances at Alistair, she feels a rush of heat. Even sweeping floors, he looks good enough to lick. Pushing loose strands of hair off her face, she frowns. After all her hustling tonight, she must look a mess. It isn't fair in the slightest.

Alistair finishes up and puts the broom back into the closet. "Almost done?"

"Yep. It was a pretty good night. We made enough to make up for earlier in the week. Dad'll be happy."

"Excellent. So, what do you want to do for the last ten minutes? Another quick round of Truth or Dare?" He drops her a wink.

Evie gets up and walks to the front to look into the street. A block and a half down, a group of people are smoking on the sidewalk in front of Henry's, but no one is anywhere near the Clutch. Her brows tighten as she debates. Then, with a flick of her wrist, she flips over the Open sign and turns back to Alistair with a smile. "I think it'll be okay if we close a few minutes early tonight."

"You sure?"

Evie nods, opening the broom closet and pulling out her coat. A minute later, the shop is locked and she's following Alistair across the road to his Jeep.

They're both quiet during the drive. When a melodic male singer comes on the radio, Alistair turns it up and starts humming along. Evie barely notices, her thoughts cascading as she plays out scenario upon heat-inducing scenario of what might happen later.

The tires crunch over the gravel as they pull up in front of the garage. Evie reaches behind her seat to get her knapsack, but before she can grab the door handle, Alistair's right there pulling it open and offering her his hand. A shiver unrelated to the winter night passes through her as he touches the small of her back, guiding her toward the door

As Evie expects, it's chilly inside the house. She slips off her boots, but leaves her coat on as they head upstairs as quietly as posslble. The thought ot Max discovering she's here—not just here, but actually spending the night with his nephew—mortifies her, although she has no intention of admitting that to Alistair.

Once they step inside his room, he goes to the hearth and kneels, pushing the grate aside to poke at the remains of the fireplace embers. "My room warms up pretty fast," he assures her as he positions fresh logs.

Evie contemplates the neatly made bed. Tired as she is, she's been run off her feet for hours and knows she must reek of stale coffee and sour sweat. Sweeping her gaze around the room, her eyes land on his open bathroom door.

Alistair crumples newspaper and tucks it under the edges of the wood. He stands to grab a box off the mantle and as he pulls out a long wooden match, she says to his back, "Hey, so, it's been a pretty long day. Would you mind if I used your shower?"

His attention's focused on starting the fire, so he waves a hand in the general direction of the bathroom. "Help yourself. Towels are on the shelf on the right."

Evie sets her coat on the chair and takes her knapsack into the bathroom. After turning on the shower, she strips off her grungy clothing. Examining her face in the mirror, she thinks she looks more anxious than tired. She twists up her ponytail, securing it high on her head in a messy bun.

Steam is already rising when she pulls open the shower door. *At least one thing in this place is efficient*, she thinks. She braces her palms against the ceramic tiles and lets the water drum on her tired muscles. Her eyes squeeze shut. She hears nothing but the wet thrumming against her skin. In the darkness behind her eyelids, she feels safe inside her own protective little bubble.

At last Evie opens her eyes a fraction of an inch and fumbles for the soap. She takes her time washing and rinsing, going over every inch of skin. She's in no hurry to finish, anything to delay going to bed with Alistair.

Oh God! Going to fricking bed with him! What am I—what are we doing?

Finally, she shuts off the water and steps out into the steam, wrapping herself in a soft white towel. Her heart is hammering as she pulls on her sleep shirt and leggings, then tugs her hair loose. After brushing her teeth, she takes a deep breath and re-enters the bedroom, feeling sort of guilty about how long she's taken

Alistair is reading by the now-crackling fire. Upon seeing her, he smiles and gets to his feet. "Feel better?"

Evie nods. "Much. Thanks."

"You need anything? Something to drink?"

She shakes her head.

"Okay, my turn. Make yourself comfortable." He sets his glasses and book on the bedside table and goes into the bathroom. A minute later, she hears the shower come back on and hopes she's left him enough hot water.

Evie's eyes dart from the bed to the vacated chair, then back to the bed again, not sure where she should wait. She sits on the edge of the mattress for a moment, then pulls back the blankets and slides underneath, propping herself against the pillows. The sound of the shower brings a small smile to her lips. She can't help picturing Alistair soaping himself down. While she hadn't seen him fully naked last Sunday, what she had seen had been impressive. He's lean and toned, every muscle in his upper body taut and defined. She remembers his soft skin, and how he'd shuddered when she ran her fingers over his stomach. That slight quiver had given her a thrill, a small feeling of power. She wants to feel like that again. That, and more. So much more.

The water shuts off. Evie switches on the bedside lamp and pulls her Dylan Thomas book from her bag so it looks like she's been studying. Two minutes later, Alistair emerges, toweling off his dark hair as he saunters to the fire wearing nothing but black pajama bottoms. His smooth chest gleams in the firelight as he leans down to jab the logs with the poker. Sparks shoot into the flue. Matching ones bloom in Evie's lower belly.

Alistair straightens and steps toward her, the fire's glow creating a halo around him. She can't see his eyes clearly, but she knows they're on her. "Comfy?" he asks.

Evie nods, smiling shyly, her heart still racing as he goes to his side of the bed and pushes the covers aside.

His side? Her side? Do they have their own sides now?
Is this really happening?

Attempting to calm herself, she looks back at the poem. The words on the page blur in and out of focus. Concentration is impossible. Giving up, she closes the book, puts it away, and rolls to face him.

Alistair lies on his side with his head braced on his hand, the white blankets pulled up to his waist. The firelight makes his eyes twinkle as he watches her. "Sleepy?"

She shrugs. "I'm okay."

He grins. "Are you nervous?"

Evie exhales a soft sigh. Honesty is one of their rules. Even though she can't be as honest with him as she'd like, she made a promise and she intends to do her best to keep it—all but that one little secret anyway. "A little," she admits.

He falls onto his back and folds his arms behind his head, looking up at the ceiling instead of at her. "That's okay. It's normal. We can just go to sleep if you want."

Her gaze sweeps across his chest and along the lean muscles in his arms. She mumbles, "No, I…I don't…no."

"You don't know?" he asks, meeting her eyes again.

With a small smile, she clarifies, "No, I, um, I don't wanna sleep just yet."

They stare at each other, the crackling and spitting of the logs in the fireplace the only sounds. Evie's growing overheated. She wishes she'd brought something lighter to wear. She pushes the blankets down to her waist to allow cool air on her skin.

"Too hot? Thought you were freezing?"

She shrugs again.

"You know, you could always remove some layers." Alistair inches closer, but makes no move to touch her.

Evie bites her bottom lip. After a moments' contemplation, she slides her hands under the blankets and pushes her leggings off, dropping them over the side of the bed. "Done."

He chuckles. "Well, we're halfway there, depending, of course, on where 'there' is. I've got bottoms on and you're still wearing your shirt. Now what?"

Is he really asking me?

Evie wishes he'd just take control. Right now, she'd be more than willing to surrender it. For a long moment she doesn't reply. At last, she whispers, "Show me."

His eyes widen along with his smile. "Alright." He shifts even closer, until their faces are mere inches apart. "You need to promise to tell me if you want to stop, though. Deal?"

Evie gulps, her throat tight. She reaches behind her and switches off the lamp.

"Deal," she breathes.

Chapter 13

Alistair chuckles softly, so close Evie can feel the vibration on her skin. His fingers brush the side of her face. She holds her breath, wishing he'd just kiss her. Can she be brave enough to kiss him first? Before she can make a move, he shifts his face just the slightest bit, leaning in until his lips meet hers.

At first she tries to stay still, to let him lead. She feels his hand cup her cheek, drawing her in. Both his fingers and lips are soft and gentle, like he's testing to make sure this is really what she wants.

It is.

He tastes minty from his toothpaste, with a lingering hint of coffee underneath. Slipping her arm around his waist, Evie shifts until their bodies are pressed together. She feels him smile, and in response, he hooks a leg over hers. Their kiss deepens. As she skims her hand up his back, the muscles in his shoulder blades ripple beneath her touch.

His skin is so soft—she didn't know boys could be this soft. She'd always assumed they were rough, often hairy creatures, but Alistair isn't like that at all. He's nothing like Jason; he is like no one she's ever known.

He strokes her neck, tickling the sensitive spot behind her ear with the pad of his thumb. She gasps softly as she feels the evidence of his arousal pressing against her thigh through his pajama pants. As curious as she is, she can't bring herself to actually reach down between them and…

Nope. Not that brave, she thinks as her temperature shoots higher.

Alistair's hand is on the move again, trailing over her backside. When it reaches the hem of her t-shirt, it slides underneath, his fingers gliding up her spine. His every touch sends shivers across her overheated skin. With a sharp intake of breath she breaks away.

"Okay?" he whispers, his eyes catching hers in the dim light.

Evie nods, swallowing, tasting him still. Wanting more. She presses her lips to his again, opening her mouth wider this time, running her fingers into his hair, and their kiss quickly intensifies. His tongue strokes along hers as his fingers trace circles over her lower back. He pushes her shirt higher, and she realizes she wants to feel her bare chest pressed against his. Pulling away from him, she sits up and tugs it over her head. The firelight makes her newly exposed skin seem to glow.

Suddenly shy, she drags the blankets up, but Alistair's hand stops her. "Don't," he whispers. "Don't hide yourself. You're beautiful."

Evie doesn't know what to say. She's never considered herself beautiful. Cute, maybe, on a good day, but certainly not beautiful. Does he really think so? Or is he just being kind? She hesitates, then lets the sheets fall to her waist, but she can't bring herself to meet his gaze.

Their afternoon together last Sunday had passed in what felt like no time at all, and to be honest, she'd had her eyes closed for much of it. So, yes, he's already seen her naked once before, but tonight it feels different somehow. Like the conscious choice to spend the night together has made things between them that much more real. And intimate.

She's being silly, she knows. But it's difficult to think of herself as a sexual person, as the sort of girl who's relaxed being naked around her boyf—no. Not that. Around her partner.

He touches her shoulder, and she looks up at him. He's staring at her with admiration. And lust. That look she recognizes; she'd seen it on Jason's face the day she'd given him her virginity. And there's that to consider, too. The idea of having sex again scares her, and yet it's also exciting: two conflicting emotions that make her more nervous than she can ever remember feeling in her entire life.

Alistair pulls her into another deep kiss, his fingers sliding down her shoulder blade and coming to a rest on the side of her ribcage. His touch is light, and it tickles a little. She tries to restrain a giggle, but just as it's about to break free, the pad of his thumb slips forward and brushes over her nipple. Her laugh morphs into a sharp gasp, and she feels him smile as he does it again. And again.

He leans forward and rolls her onto her back. After a few minutes, his kisses leave her lips and start traveling across her jaw, then along the side of her throat. His mouth traces a damp path over her chest until he arrives at his destination: her left breast. She sucks in a sharp breath as his tongue flicks over her, teasing her peak until it's rigid. And she can't hold back a gasp when he latches on, his other hand tweaking her neglected nipple to attention.

Evie vaguely recalls him doing something similar last Sunday, but her memories are all obscured by what happened shortly after. The bourbon she drank probably hadn't helped her clarity. This time she vows to commit every last second to memory.

And what a memory it's going to be! Alistair squeezes and licks and sucks each breast until she thinks she'll go insane, her thighs pressing together in a fruitless attempt to alleviate the building pressure. Who knew her breasts were so sensitive? There seems to be a direct link from her nipples down to her nethers. Why hadn't she been aware of this before? This is something she probably should have known.

Evie lifts her head to look at him at the same time he raises his eyes to hers, and she thinks she sees a hint of a grin. Then he suckles her harder, and she bucks below him. She wants…no, she *needs* more. So much more. But she doesn't have the nerve to ask for it. She runs her fingers into his hair, silently urging him to continue, hoping he'll get the hint.

With a final lick, Alistair pulls away and meets her eyes again. He's definitely grinning. No doubt about it. "I take it you like that?"

She nods.

"What do you want me to do next?"

Her mouth falls open in surprise. Does he really want her to spell it out? "Um…you know," she mumbles, flushing. She feels a sudden urge to pull the sheets over her naked chest again, but forces herself not to.

"Tell me," he insists.

Evie gulps. "I...um…" She closes her eyes.

"Uh uh. No hiding. Look at me."

He tilts his head, watching her with compassion. "You need to be able to tell a guy what you want in bed. Otherwise you might not get it. So don't be shy. Just say it."

She takes a deep breath. "What you were just doing? That felt amazing."

"Glad you liked it. That's a good start. So now what? Shall we roll over and go to sleep?" He winks.

"Uh…no."

"Then what?"

"I want…I want you to…" Evie stops. Her entire body feels like it's about to burst into flames. With a soft sigh, she mumbles, "I want to…have sex."

Alistair smiles again. "Be more specific. Sex can mean a lot of different things."

That isn't good enough for him? Is he deliberately trying to torture her? "You know what I mean."

"I want to hear you to say the words."

She just stares at him.

He arches an amused eyebrow. "Is saying it really so hard? You want me to fuck you? Is that what you want?"

Evie doesn't think she can flush any deeper. Why does he need her to tell him? Why do they have to talk about it? Jason had barely talked at all. Couldn't Alistair just, you know, do it? Do her? *Ugh.* This is a bit of a mood-killer.

She closes her eyes and nods again, mortified. A large part of her brain has entered Flight Mode and she debates calling the whole thing off and just heading home.

"Say it," he instructs, his voice all husky. Her libido perks back up at the sound, and she opens her eyes to look at him again.

"I already did," she mumbles.

He's silent. And she realizes what he wants her to say. Words that have never passed her lips before. Words she never thought she'd say to anyone, ever. Because it just isn't *her*, you know? She rarely swears, she isn't vulgar, and she certainly isn't the type of girl to tell a man what she wants him to do to her.

Their stalemate drags on for a few long moments.

At last she gives in. She can do this. They're just words, after all. It isn't really that huge of a deal. Except, to her, it kind of is. Holding his gaze in hers, she whispers as confidently as she can manage, "Fuck me."

His green eyes flare as they fill with desire. Clearly this turns him on. A millisecond later his lips crash back into hers.

Their kisses are more passionate now, his mouth claiming hers, their tongues diving, sliding, thrusting, parrying. She feels his hand run down her side until it reaches the elastic of her panties. It doesn't stop, just pulls the fabric down her legs as it goes, sliding them off and tossing them who knows where.

Now she's completely bare, yet he still wears his pajama bottoms. That's hardly fair. Now feeling braver, Evie drags her mouth from his. "Now you," she murmurs, tugging at his drawstring.

Alistair chuckles. "Your wish is my command." He sits up and pushes his pants off, and she realizes he wears nothing beneath. Even in just the flickering glow from the fireplace, she can see well enough.

Evie's throat tightens. She's never seen a naked man up close before. With Jason the room had been dark, and frankly she'd averted her gaze. And last weekend Alistair had kept his boxer-briefs on. Her cheeks burn, and she doesn't know where to look. Finally she just closes her eyes again.

Another low chuckle. His hand closes over hers, lifting it and placing it on him, palm down. She hears his breath catch, feels him shudder a little at her touch.

"You're so shy," he says softly.

Evie's lips curve into a small smile, but she doesn't open her eyes.

"Shy is fine," he continues. "I have no problem with shy. But you asked me to teach you, so I'm teaching you. Watch."

With a small sigh, she eases her lids part-way open, peering down between her lashes at their joined hands. His skin there feels like satin beneath her fingers. How can anything be so soft yet so hard at the same time? He helps her gently grip him, and she watches with fascination as he starts to move their hands up and down.

"Now you take over," he says, removing his guiding hand. Immediately her fingers still. "It's okay. Just, you know, touch me. Stroke the shaft with a firm grip, but not too tight. Every once in a while rub your thumb, or even your palm, over the head." He stops with a gasp as she does as she's told. "Oh yeah. Just like that. You got this."

"It feels like velvet," she observes with quiet awe. She knows he knows she's never done this before, and he isn't judging, so she tries to relax and remember his instructions. Trying to keep an even pace, she strokes the top of him with the pad of her thumb on every upsweep. Once she thinks she's getting the hang of it, she glances at his face and realizes just how right she is. His eyes are closed and his lips are slightly parted. There's no doubt he's enjoying her novice efforts.

160

After a few minutes, Evie hears his breathing pick up speed and grow shallower. She wonders if Alistair wants her to use her mouth on him. He hadn't mentioned anything like that. Should she just try to do it? Suddenly he grabs her wrist and stops her.

She looks at him questioningly and he gives her a weak smile. "It feels really good. Too good. Time to put a stop to that before we hit my event horizon. Otherwise I'm gonna need an intermission to recharge my batteries."

She's confused. Event horizon? Recharge his batteries? She has no clue what he means, but she retracts her hand. Though he'd clearly been enjoying it, he wants her to stop. Then it clicks in and she closes her eyes, feeling stupid. *Of course!*

Alistair pulls her face to his and gives her another deep kiss. "Now…what was it you asked me to do to you before I interrupted to give you a little anatomy lesson?" His voice has roughened to that sexy rumble again, and her lower belly clenches in response. With a sly grin, he adds, "Oh yeah, I think I remember."

He dips his mouth to kiss each of her breasts in turn, licking her nipples until they tighten. One hand slides down her side and over her stomach, and Evie's flesh pebbles at his touch. As he trails a path lower, she recalls last Sunday, and parts her thighs, allowing him access. She sucks in a sharp breath as he gently taps her most sensitive spot, but then he moves on. Once he's explored her thoroughly to ensure she's ready, he inches a gentle finger inside and she exhales another gasp, spreading her legs wider. His finger curls up and hits just the right place, making her writhe for more.

Evie's own fingers dive into his hair, and though she doesn't say a word, he seems to understand. He withdraws his hand and raises his face to kiss her lips, rolling his body above her, bracing his palms on each side of her head. Instinctively she shifts her knees up and apart to cradle his hips between her thighs.

Alistair's smooth chest rests against hers, skin to skin, and it feels so good, so right, that for a moment she wishes they could always be as close as they are right now.

He pulls away a few inches to look her in the eyes. "You sure?" he whispers. "Just say the word if—"

"I'm sure."

Alistair smiles that sexy half-smile again and nips playfully at her lower lip before giving her another kiss. Rolling to one side, he pulls open a drawer, retrieves a condom, and tears the end of the package open with his teeth. Once Evie realizes what he's doing, she averts her eyes as he sits up and rolls it into place. Is this something she should ask him to show her how to do? Maybe next time. If there is a next time.

He's so focused on what he's doing that he doesn't notice she's looked away. It doesn't matter though. As he repositions himself between her legs and looks up, her eyes go right back to his again, full of anxious anticipation.

Evie's eyes flare and she exhales a soft sigh as he glides himself along her wetness. Then slowly, ever so slowly and carefully, he starts to push inside.

Oh God! She gasps louder as he fills her. This is nothing at all like what she remembers. It's so much more intense.

He stops moving and examines her face again, allowing her time to get used to him. "You okay?" he asks. There's something in his voice—it sounds different, somehow.

"Yes," she breathes.

"Am I hurting you?"

"No, I…I'm okay." God, she sounds just as naïve as she feels. She's sure Alistair is used to much more experienced women. This is probably not particularly great for him. He's just doing it to help her out, to teach her, like she'd asked. As sweet as he's being, she knows she can never live up to his expectations.

He lowers his torso back to hers and kisses her. One hand cradles the side of her face and the other runs over her hip to grip the back of her thigh as he begins to move.

Evie tries to concentrate on kissing him back, but the sensation of him inside her is too much; it's all she can focus on. Her fingers drift down his smooth back to his butt. With both hands, she grips him as he plunges his hips forward at a gentle pace.

Alistair breaks their kiss and lowers his head into the space between her shoulder and neck. "Tilt your hips up a little," he says softly, his lips by her ear. His breath against her skin makes her shiver. "That's it. Now, if you can, try to push back against me as I push forward. See if you can match my rhythm."

"Like this?" she mumbles, lifting up to meet his thrusts.

She feels the vibrations of his low chuckle tickle her throat. "Yep. Don't worry, you're fine. As we get used to each other, we'll figure out how to get in synch, and it'll all feel natural." He lifts his face to look at her again. "I promise."

Evie gives him a small smile. She hopes so.

After a few more minutes of trying her best to keep up with his lead, he whispers, "Do you want to try a different position?"

She's not sure how to respond. With Jason, they'd only done basic missionary, and it hadn't lasted very long. She has no clue about other positions, but she wants to learn, and she trusts Alistair. Swallowing nervously, she says, "Sure. Whatever you want."

"Have you ever been on top before?"

She shakes her head.

"Your ex needs a good smack," he mutters under his breath. He withdraws and rolls onto his back. "Now straddle my hips and just, you know, lower yourself onto me."

With his help, she gets into the right position. "Now you're in control," he says. "You set the pace. Do what feels good to you."

Evie experiments with raising and lowering herself, trying to find an easy rhythm again. Her forehead furrows in concentration.

"One little suggestion," Alistair says. She meets his eyes with a questioning look. "Roll your pelvis on me. It's way easier than moving your body up and down all the time. And it puts more pressure on places that'll feel good for you." Seeing her skeptical expression, he adds, "I swear!"

She rolls her pelvis. One, twice. A third time. Oh yes, that's much easier. And oh, he's right about something else, too. It feels amazing. When she tilts her hips forward, part of him brushes against her most sensitive spot, and the intensity builds each time she pushes up on it.

Sensing what's nearing, Alistair lifts his hands back to her breasts, tweaking her nipples and eliciting another sigh of pleasure. She increases her speed a little, pressing harder on her forward motions.

Just when she doesn't think she can take this a second longer, her entire body clenches up tight and a loud groan erupts from deep within. Spasms shake her and she braces her hands on the mattress on either side of his shoulders and gulps for air. Before she can collapse onto him, he sits up and pulls her against his chest, one hand stroking her hair, the other holding her in place as she rides out her release.

Clinging to him, Evie tries to catch her breath, her body still shuddering with small aftershocks.

"See why you being on top can be decidedly advantageous?" he murmurs, dropping soft kisses to the side of her throat.

Evie nods against his shoulder. "That was…" She pauses, still panting. "That was intense!"

Once her breathing returns to normal, he rolls them both onto their sides. His chest glistens with sweat. Feeling brave in the wake of her orgasm, she leans forward and licks a trail over his nipple, making him gasp with pleasure.

Her right leg is now hooked over Alistair's thigh, and as he plunges forward, she remembers through the haze of her elation that he hasn't finished yet. Leaning in, he recaptures her lips, his arms wrapping around her waist and tugging her against him. He picks up speed. She hears his breath become labored again, like before when she'd been stroking him, and she realizes he's close. Heat radiates off him. Trying to help, she pushes herself against him as he drives into her, doing her best to keep up, wanting to make this as good for him as she can.

Tearing his lips from hers, he presses his face into the curve of her neck once more. Each exhalation is like a furnace blast against her skin. He grabs her backside, pulling her to him with each frenzied thrust. Then he bucks against her, groaning low and deep and long. He clutches her to him, shuddering, sweating, panting. Evie doesn't know what to do, so she just holds him, running her fingers across his back as she waits for him to relax.

At last, Alistair pulls away a few inches so he can look at her. He wears a blissed-out, satiated smile.

For several moments neither of them speaks. Then, hesitantly, she asks, "So…was it…okay?"

His eyes widen in shock. "Are you kidding? It was great!" he says. "And it'll only get better from here." He kisses her again, as if assuring her that he means it.

"Really?"

"I wouldn't lie to you."

A stab of guilt passes through her at that, but she pushes it away. "It was great for me, too. I never knew it could be like that. I swear I couldn't even breathe at one point." She pauses, smiling shyly. "Wow."

"Wow, indeed."

They talk for a while longer, about poems and books and things, until they're both yawning too much to even get a complete sentence out without interruption. After they admit they should probably get some sleep, she rolls over to face the wall. Her mind is spinning, but she's just *so* tired. She can't keep her eyes open any longer.

Just before she drifts off, she feels his arm slide over her waist, his hand coming to rest on her stomach, his chest warm against her back. At first she's surprised, but then she lets herself relax in his arms. No one has cuddled up to her to sleep since she was small. It fills her with a sense of comfort and safety she hasn't felt in a very long time.

"Night, Evie," he whispers, giving her a little squeeze. His lips graze her shoulder, as light as the tickle of butterfly's wings.

"G'night."

Then she surrenders to blissful sleep.

Chapter 14

When Evie wakes, she's shivering. She pulls the blankets closer and tries to fall back asleep, but then she remembers where she is, and what happened last night. Her eyes fly open, and she sits upright, clutching the sheet to her bare chest as her panicky gaze sweeps the dimly lit room. Alistair isn't beside her and the bathroom is dark. Wherever he's gone, she hopes he won't be long. It's weird enough waking up in a strange house—the last thing she wants is to have to go downstairs alone. What if she runs into his uncle and has to explain why she's there? And what if that information gets back to her father?

She shudders again. The fire has gone out during the night; it's no wonder she's cold. The thick drapes are closed, but a sliver of bright sunlight slices between them. She frowns at it, hoping she hasn't slept too late.

At that moment, the door opens and the intermingled aromas of fresh coffee and chocolate hit her nose. "I brought you hot cocoa," Alistair says, smiling. He wears his black pajama bottoms and a grey sweater.

Evie lies back, pressing her head into the pillow and snuggling under the covers. Stifling a yawn, she asks, "What time is it?"

"Ten past eight." He comes around to her side and sets a steaming mug on the nightstand. The chocolaty scent makes her mouth water.

Sitting on the edge of the bed, Alistair leans in to look at her. "What time do you need to be home, sleepyhead?"

They hadn't fallen asleep until the wee hours of the morning, and Evie's mind is still groggy. She's not ready to leave yet. Once she goes home, she'll have to face her father and lie to him about where she's been, and she's not sure she can convincingly pull it off. Nor does she want to leave the comfort of Alistair's bed, and if he'd only get back in and join her, it would be even comfier.

"Um…nine, I guess." She rolls onto her side, bracing herself on one elbow as she reaches for the mug. "Mmm. Thank you."

"You're welcome. How're you feeling this morning?"

How am I feeling? Why is he…? Oh. About that. Right.

"Um…" She breaks eye contact. "Fine. Good. You?"

Alistair chuckles. "I feel great. How could I not, waking up with a hot, naked girl in my bed? Especially one who looks so damn cute when she's asleep—even when she's snoring."

Flushing, Evie protests, "I don't snore!" A self-conscious laugh slips out. "Do I?"

Smiling, he leans forward for a second, but seems to catch himself and straightens back up. She wonders if he'd been about to kiss her, and feels disappointed that he didn't.

"Just a little," he teases, going to squat in front of the fireplace. "Give me five minutes and I'll have this room warmed up nicely again."

She knows she should probably get dressed, but that would mean abandoning her warm cocoon. Instead she props her head a little higher on the pillow and drinks more cocoa as she watches Alistair re-start the fire.

Once he has the flames going, he turns back to her. "You look comfy."

168

Evie smiles. "I am." She still isn't too sure of the proper etiquette of Friends With Benefits, but if she says or does something inappropriate, she assumes he'll let her know. So, mustering her courage, she pats the mattress beside her.

Alistair's eyes flare, and he breaks into a grin. The next thing she knows, he's leapt onto the bed, landing on his side to face her. He's looking at her with *that* expression again. The one she's growing to understand means he's thinking decidedly un-platonic thoughts.

That familiar tightening down below kicks in as her pulse speeds up. She sets her mug on the table and turns to him.

"Can you spare a half hour?" he asks in a low, seductive voice.

Wow, he hadn't been kidding—the temperature really has shot up fast in here! Evie looks into those mesmerizing green eyes and realizes she could really fall for Alistair if she isn't careful. But she will be careful. She has to be.

"I think I can manage that."

He reaches out and strokes the side of her face with his thumb. Then at last he leans in and kisses her.

It's quarter after nine when Evie walks in her front door. At her request, Alistair had dropped her off a block away so her dad wouldn't spot her getting out of his Jeep. To her surprise, Alistair had leaned in and given her a quick kiss goodbye. On the cheek, not on the lips, but still.

"Morning," her father greets her from the kitchen, open paper and steaming cup of coffee in their usual spots in front of him.

"Morning, Dad." She hangs up her coat and comes into the doorway. "The Clutch was swamped last night! It's been a good week."

He looks up at her with a smile. "Wonderful! Now if only we can make that a regular occurrence."

"Fingers crossed." Evie pauses. "So, Alistair came in, and when he saw how busy I was, he took the coffee pot right out of my hand and started topping up mugs. You should've seen him! He was a natural. The customers loved him!"

Tom's eyebrows rise. "Really? That was awful nice of him." With an amused grin he asks, "Are you still insisting you two are just friends?"

Evie blushes, breaking eye contact. "Yes, of course."

They *are* still just friends. In fact, they are the very definition of Friends With Benefits now as far as she understands. Which is exactly what she wants, isn't it? So why do things between them feel like they've changed drastically now? And will this become a problem in the future? She desperately hopes not.

Her dad interrupts her internal fretting. "You should invite him over sometime. How about dinner next Sunday? Whaddya think? Feel like showing off your cooking skills?"

Evie frowns as she thinks this over. Sundays are the only days the Clutch is closed and she and Dylan get to eat meals with their father. And now that they're older, one or both of them is often off doing other things over lunch. But Sunday dinner is their family time, and she's a bit surprised her dad wants to invite Alistair to join them. He must think Alistair is important to his daughter and wants to get to know him better. She wonders if he would feel the same way if he knew what happened last night. Still, inviting Alistair to come for dinner doesn't seem like a *bad* idea. It could even end up being kind of fun.

"I'll ask him next time we talk, and let you know," she replies, grabbing her knapsack and heading to her room to get changed for church.

Alistair is carrying an armful of kindling up to his room to replenish the depleted wood-box when he hears Max call his name. After refilling the receptacle, he trots down to the library to see his uncle.

"Morning," Alistair says as he enters the room. "What's up?"

Max puts down *The Herald* and looks at his nephew. "By any chance did you have company last night?" he asks, his face carefully, deliberately serious. "Thought I heard voices earlier."

Alistair attempts a poker face. He'd thought he'd succeeded in getting Evie out of here undetected. Clearly his uncle is more aware than Alistair assumed.

"Um..." He opts for a 'guess you caught me' guilty shrug. Maybe it's best to just let Max jump to his own conclusions.

Max breaks into a wide, toothy smile. "Really? *You?* Mister self-proclaimed hermit? What happened to the whole 'I've sworn off women forever' thing?"

"Why are you assuming my company was female? And that it wasn't completely innocent?"

"Please." Max shakes his head. "I've been around the block a few times in my younger days. Plus," he adds, "I heard her laugh as you guys snuck out this morning."

Alistair wonders if Max knows the identity of his overnight guest. He guesses not, since his uncle and Tom Colville are friendly, and Max knows full well Evie is four years Alistair's junior and still in high school. Alistair is pretty sure that if Max knew it was her, he would've already heard the first of several lectures about it.

"You got me," he admits with a lazy grin. "Just blowing off some steam. No harm in that, right?"

"Depends. Does she know that's all it was?"

Alistair nods. "Yep. It's all good."

Max stands and comes over to him. "I'm happy you're finally trying to move on with your life a bit. I really am. In fact, the only thing that would make me happier would be for you to start talking to you father and brother."

Grimacing, Alistair resists the urge to roll his eyes. *Don't hold your breath*, he thinks.

His uncle keeps going as if he hasn't noticed Alistair's bitter expression. "Just promise me you'll be careful. Sutterton isn't like the city. Rumors travel pretty fast around here." He lays a hand on Alistair's shoulder and looks him right in the eyes. "Be very sure any woman you hook up with knows the score. In advance."

Alistair snorts a mirthless chuckle. Stepping away from his uncle's touch, he assures him, "Nothing to worry about. We're just friends."

Seemingly satisfied, Max returns to his paper. With a soft sigh, Alistair decides to head down to the gym to put an end to this particular topic.

He knows he doesn't have to worry about Evie falling for him. FWB was her idea, and she made it very clear what she wants from it. And what she does not want is a relationship. Which is totally fine by him. Friends, with or without benefits, is all he can handle right now. After Michelle and Paul's betrayal, the last thing he needs is another emotional attachment.

Evie is an amazing girl, and he *does* care about her, but there's no point in letting himself think of her as anything but a good friend. It won't ever be more than it is right now, which is undoubtedly for the best anyway.

As he warms up with an easy jog on the treadmill, his thoughts return to Michelle, and something jumps out at him. Before a month ago, though he'd hated himself for it, he used to dwell on her every day. Every hour of every day, in fact. She'd haunted his dreams, tormenting him with memories of happier times, then painful flashes of her cruel infidelity. But sometime over the past few weeks, his fixation on her has lessened. He realizes that something crucial inside him has shifted. No matter what the future holds, even if she shows up at his door and prostrates herself at his feet begging him for a second chance, he'd no longer even consider reconciling.

Because, Alistair realizes with a weird mixture of shock and melancholy, he's no longer in love with Michelle. He hadn't believed it possible, and now, without him even noticing, it's gone. A twinge of grief comes in knowing that her massive, important, and—whether he likes it or not—emotionally pivotal role in his life is really over for good.

Upping both his speed and incline, he starts running as fast as he can. The slight sensation of loss ebbs away like an errant breeze wafting through his mind. It's replaced by a grim sense of relief. He feels so much lighter. And freer.

Monday morning is bright, sunny, and frigidly cold. March is a fickle month; it vacillates between welcoming Spring's life-giving warmth, or remaining swaddled in Winter's icy embrace. Evie's boots squeak on the frozen ground as she walks to the bus stop.

Once aboard, Grace greets her with excitement. As warned, she'd called Evie right on the dot of noon yesterday, but due to familial ears nearby, Evie had provided only the vaguest details of her night with Alistair. It's clear from her friend's eager expression that she expects a full run-down right now.

Grace pulls her into a hug the moment Evie sits down. "My baby girl is finally a woman," she declares.

Evie reddens as she extracts herself. "Shh! And what're you even talking about? There's been no change to my...uh ...status!"

Waving her hand dismissively, Grace says, "Yeah, but your first time didn't really count. This is way different. It's for real-real now. And I need to hear all about it."

There is a sudden burst of raucous laughter from a few seats behind them, and Evie swivels her head, grateful for the interruption. Dylan is sitting at the back of the bus, goofing around with some of his basketball buddies. Charlie's nowhere to be seen. Maybe she got a ride with Cam.

Before Evie can wonder much about it, Grace drags her attention back to their conversation. "I know you're not gonna tell me anything juicy right here, but could you at least feel sorry enough for me to provide me with some 'yes or no' deets? Starting with the most important: was it good?"

Evie can't suppress a grin. She nods.

"Did he make you...you know...again?" Grace leers knowingly.

Blushing harder, she nods again.

"How many times?"

"Um…" Evie's eyes drop to her knapsack between her knees.

"Whoa."

She looks back at Grace, this time not even trying to hide her smile. Leaning close to her friend's ear, she whispers, "Once Saturday night, and once Sunday morning. I don't know what normal is, but that seems pretty good, right?"

Grace snorts, her dark eyes shining. "Yep. Especially for your first time together." She pauses, quirking up one corner of her lips. "And second." Then her face grows more serious. "I didn't the first bunch of times. But Alistair's older and more experienced than my ex. I'm sure he knows exactly what he's doing. You are one lucky bitch."

Evie just grins.

"And your little FWB thing? How's that working out? Still gonna tell me you two are just *friends*?"

"Yes," Evie replies firmly. "Just friends. I sometimes kinda wish it could be different between us, but there's just no way."

One black eyebrow arches. "Be honest. Are you catching feelings? It'd only be natural after—"

"No," Evie cut in. "Not falling for him. Can we drop this topic now, please?" She stares straight ahead at the green vinyl seat back in front of her, trying to make it clear she has no intention of discussing this further.

Grace frowns. She knows there's a huge chance Evie is probably already in over her head, whether she'll admit it or not. The more Evie stubbornly insists on the 'just friends' thing, the more Grace worries. Evie is undoubtedly going to end up getting hurt at some point between now and leaving for college, but Grace will be there for her, like she always is, to comfort her and get her through it. It's what best friends do— they have to let each other make mistakes sometimes, and then help pick up the pieces. She knows it's just a part of growing up and learning how to cope. So she does as Evie requests and shuts up about it.

For now.

That night at the shop, Evie finishes all her homework before eight o'clock. She's sitting at the counter with hot chocolate and a novel when she remembers JAI's letter.

Though it's at home tucked into the book with the others, she remembers what it said, having read it multiple times. Feeling inspired, she sets her book aside, opens her notebook to a blank page, and starts writing.

Dear JAI,
Your last letter almost has me at a loss for words. My own family life has been so different from yours. It's difficult for me to imagine those I love treating me as badly as yours have treated you. I know I'm lucky to have the family and friends I do, and your situation has made me even more grateful for them. And even more angry on your behalf.
I'm so sorry you had to go through that. It doesn't seem fair that life could hand one young man so much heartache.
You have every right to be angry and want some time alone. You have every right to need space away from them to grieve and to heal. Don't let anyone try to convince you otherwise. Take care of yourself right now.
On the plus side, the fact that you made a new friend whom you feel could be someone special makes me hopeful for a positive change in your life. Although I don't really know you, I truly believe you deserve happiness, and that you'll eventually let yourself open up to someone and learn to trust again. So I'm pleased to learn you're at least open to the possibility with this woman.
All the best,
Miss LL

Evie reads it over, decides it sounds like it could have been written by someone ten years older, and then tears it out. She has just finished tucking the letter into the front pocket of her knapsack when she hears the bells over the door.

Her heart leaps. Glancing up with a smile, she hopes to see Alistair, but is surprised to see her brother striding toward her with a worried look on his face.

Evie jumps up and comes around the counter. It's rare for Dylan to come into the shop in the evenings. From his determined expression, he needs to tell her something important. "Hey. What's up?"

"I just got a call from Leanne Lancaster. Charlie didn't come home last night."

Her brows narrow. "I noticed she wasn't on the bus today."

He drops onto one of the stools. "Nope. But I just figured she was sick or something. She told her mom yesterday she was going to Cam's for dinner, and that was the last time Leanne heard from her. She hoped I knew where Charlie was, but I haven't talked to her since Friday."

"What did Cam say?"

"He claims she left around nine. Says he hasn't been in touch with her since." Dylan frowns at his sister. "Her phone's off. I don't like this."

Evie presses her lips together. A knot of worry has formed in her chest. "Me, neither. You think he's lying?"

Dylan swipes a hand over his eyes and through his hair. "I don't know. My gut says…yeah. I think he's a lying piece of shit."

"Has Leanne called the cops?"

"She wants to wait and see if Charlie turns up tonight. If not, she's gonna report her missing first thing tomorrow. She's touching base with all Char's friends first, in case she's off sulking somewhere about some fight with Wheeler and deliberately avoiding everyone."

Grasping that idea, Evie says, "I bet that's exactly what it is. They probably got into a big blow up and she's hiding out at one of her girlfriend's. I'm sure she'll be home by tomorrow, and her mom will ground her for a week or two, and soon this will all blow over."

Dylan looks up at her again, his eyes filled with worry. "I hope you're right."

"Me, too. If you hear anything else, text me."

"I will. I've sent Char, like, twenty texts already. Hope she turns her frickin' phone on and gets back to me soon." He pauses, then adds, "And to her mom, of course."

Evie agrees, and he gets up to leave. She worries Dylan might head over to the Wheeler's and confront Cameron before the local police can speak with him first. But there's nothing she can do to stop him if he does, so she just hopes he's smart enough to stay away.

The moment her brother is out of sight, she scrabbles for her phone and calls Grace.

"Hey Little Miss Sex Kitten. What's up?"

Evie ignores her friend's teasing. "Remember that stuff I told you about Charlie Lancaster? That I'd seen bruises, and then later overheard her arguing with Cam at the Valentine's Party?"

"Of course. How could I forget? Why?"

"It might be nothing—God, I *really* hope it's nothing—but, she's gone missing. We have to make sure she's okay."

Chapter 15

Tuesday morning, much to Evie's frustration, winter still holds Sutterton in its freezing grip. Her breath sends out white billows as she boards the school bus behind her brother. She quickly scans the occupants and frowns. Still no sign of Charlie.

Dylan had called the Lancaster home after breakfast, but had gotten no answer, so they have no idea if Charlie has been found yet. Evie is growing more and more concerned. Something feels very wrong about the girl's disappearance. She hopes Charlie will turn up soon, embarrassed and ashamed about hiding maybe, but at least safe.

As soon as Evie takes her seat, Grace fills her in on the latest. Leanne Lancaster has officially reported her missing. The local police, as well as volunteers from neighboring towns, have already started a door-to-door search of Sutterton and the surrounding area.

The whole bus seems to be discussing it, and everyone has an opinion. Most of them are negative, assuming Charlie has run away with no thought at all to her worried mother. Evie overhears several people express sympathy for Cam, but not a single word of suspicion. He's a Wheeler, therefore above reproach, at least to most people in this town. She hopes the police will be thorough with their investigation.

Dylan sits alone, arms crossed over his chest as he stares out the window and tries to ignore the conversations flying around him. She knows he's worried about his friend.

It's the primary gossip on everyone's lips at school, too. Evie can't seem to escape the whispered speculations about Charlie. Her schoolmates are so distracted that Mr. Wright has to call for silence three times in History class to get everyone to pay attention. The bell signaling the end of the school day brings more relief to Evie than usual.

After the bus drops them off, Dylan says, "Cam has no clue where she is."

"You talked to him?"

He nods. "You were right though—they did get into a big fight on Sunday.He lost his shit and told her they should break up. He said Charlie stormed off, furious."

Frowning, Evie looks up at her brother. "You believe him?"

Dylan shrugs. "I don't know. He does seem worried, and says he's doing everything he can to help find her. Claims his dad is even hiring a P.I. But it could all be bullshit to cover his ass. I know everyone idolizes the guy, but c'mon. We both know he's got a violent side." Dylan sighs. "I don't like this. She'd better turn up soon."

"Agreed." Evie unlocks the front door and they both step inside. It seems her brother shares her bad feeling about all this.

It's been a productive night. Evie sits at the counter at The Clutch working on her History assignment. The few customers had picked up orders to go. Only Mr. Donnelly remains at a side table, nursing the last of his coffee as he reads the paper. He doesn't mind if she does schoolwork while he's there. In fact, he'll often help her out with more complicated math problems if she asks, as he used to be a teacher before he retired.

About an hour before close, she's pleasantly surprised when Alistair comes in. She didn't know he was dropping by tonight—they'd texted a few times since Sunday, but hadn't yet made any plans to see each other. Evie's pulse races the moment she sees him, and suddenly she's too warm. She shrugs off her cardigan, hoping he hasn't noticed how intensely she always reacts to him.

"Hey," she says, holding up the carafe to fill his mug before he's even had a chance to unscrew the top.

"Hey." He flashes that crooked grin she's come to adore. "What's up?"

Evie's own smile falls away. Should she tell him about Charlie? He doesn't know these people, so she isn't sure it's fair to unload her worries.

Before she can decide, Mr. Donnelly comes up to settle his small bill and wish her goodnight.

Now it's just the two of them. Alistair takes a sip of coffee and studies her face. "You look worried. What's up?"

Well, we're friends, and good friends confide in each other. So what the heck, right?

Evie blows out a little puff of air and then tells him about her brother's friend Charlie, her disappearance, and what Evie has seen and heard over the past few months. She even mentions the suspicious letter from the girl with the controlling boyfriend from one of Miss Lonely Love's columns in January. Alistair doesn't need to know she hadn't read it in *The Herald* like everyone else.

When she finishes, he's frowning. "You think the douchebag boyfriend had something to do with it?"

Evie sighs. "I don't know, but I'm suspicious. He's denied it, of course. And by now the police will have already questioned him. If he was a suspect, I don't think he would've been at school today."

"Good point." Alistair looks thoughtful. "Well, hopefully she'll show up tonight. Her mom must be freaking out."

180

"She is. So's Dylan, although he tries to hide it."

"He got a thing for her?"

Evie smiles. "He says not, but I'm pretty sure."

"Poor kid."

"Yeah. He's really worried." Before Alistair can say anything else, her eyes fly wide. "Oh! I nearly forgot! What're you up to on Sunday?"

A devilish look comes into his eyes. "You wanna come over and study with me again?" He winks. "Because for you, I'm totally free."

Blushing, Evie chuckles. She breaks eye contact and starts wiping the counter. "I was actually gonna ask if you wanted to come to my place for dinner. With my family," she clarifies.

With raised brows, Alistair asks, "Whose idea was that?"

"My dad's. I think he wants to get to know the new guy I've been hanging out with lately."

There's a short pause. Then: "Okay."

Evie eyes shift back to his. "You sure?"

"Why not? If you want, you could still come over for a few hours earlier in the day. I'd invite you to spend the night again, but I assume that won't fly two weekends in a row."

If only, she thinks. "Um, no. Probably not. I hated having to lie to my dad last time. But Sunday afternoon should work." She smiles. "I'll come after church. Then we'll have a few hours before we need to be at my place for cooking and awkward conversation with my father."

"You're cooking?"

Laughing, Evie says, "Yep. Better make sure the number for Poison Control is in your speed dial."

Alistair snorts, then comes around the counter to grab the broom from the closet. Next thing Evie knows, he's sweeping up, unasked. She shakes her head with a small smile and goes back to cleaning. It's too bad, really. If things were different, he seems like he'd make an awesome boyfriend.

The next day, there's still no sign of Charlie. Cameron isn't in school either, and Evie assumes he's probably busy assisting the police with the search. Everyone is called into the gymnasium for an assembly after lunch. It's rare that one of their own goes missing, and they want to ensure all the students understand the seriousness of the situation, and how important it is to come forward if anyone has any information about Charlie's disappearance.

Unfortunately, no one does.

On Thursday, *The Herald* publishes a special front page report about the investigation, including interviews with Mayor Wheeler and one of Charlie's teachers. Leanne Lancaster declined to speak with reporters, which in Evie's dad's opinion was smart.

Nonetheless, the paper has managed to glean quite a lot of personal information about Charlie's family life. The article says that the Lancaster's had an extremely volatile marriage, and that Charlie's father, with whom she'd been quite close, up and left his family when she was only ten. Although Mitch Lancaster has texted her and sent gifts once in a while, he hasn't set foot back in Sutterton since. It's rumored he's out on the West Coast somewhere, but nobody seems to know exactly where, why, or with whom. The police don't think Charlie's been in touch with her dad for a year or more. Evie already knows most of this, having dated Charlie's brother.

By the time Friday hits, Dylan's anxiety has ratcheted up several notches, and the rest of the town is also pretty worried. It's the primary topic of conversation at the Clutch, just as it has been the previous three evenings.

Dylan and Grace sit at the counter drinking coffee and talking softly, ignoring the homework spread in front of them. Evie keeps their mugs topped up, but she's busy taking care of customers until the crowd starts to thin out.

With a sigh, she at last goes behind the counter to join them. As she's making herself a hot chocolate and asking her brother yet again if he's heard anything new, she hears the bells over the door and looks up, hoping it's Alistair. She last saw him when he'd dropped her home after work on Tuesday. He hadn't kissed her goodbye that night, not even on the cheek. She couldn't help her disappointment, although she knows he's just following their agreement.

It isn't Alistair.

It is, however, someone she's also been intimate with, although not for a long time.

He's tall, with closely-cropped light brown hair and broad shoulders, and he strides into Colville's Coffee Clutch wearing a determined expression. The moment his gaze locks with Evie's, he breaks into a wide smile.

Evie eyes flare and she smiles back. "Jase!" she exclaims, hurrying over and throwing her arms around him. "It's so good to see you! Although I wish it were under better circumstances. Have you guys heard anything new?"

His grin falls away. "Not yet. Mom's going mental. I figured I should get my ass home and support her. The cops have zilch. Nada. And they can't locate Dad, so he doesn't even know she's missing yet."

With a small frown, Evie asks, "Is there any chance she could be with him?"

"That's what I was wondering," Dylan says, coming to stand with them.

Jason's eyes dart between the siblings. "I highly doubt it. He doesn't give a shit about us. We don't even know how to reach him. And anyways, Char would never go anywhere with him without telling Mom."

"I wouldn't have thought so, either," Dylan says. Charlie rarely mentioned her father, but when she had, it was with bitterness. He suspects her cynical attitude is just a coping skill, and that she misses him more than she'll admit. "What about Wheeler Junior? You buy that he hasn't heard from her since she left his place on Sunday?"

Jason shrugs. "No idea. Haven't talked to him. I've only been in town a couple hours."

A few more customers leave, and Evie pours coffee for Jason as the four of them move to an empty table. They discuss Charlie at length, pooling all the information about their ideas and suspicions. Jason listens to them with growing concern. Every once in a while he glances over at Evie. Each time, his face brightens and he shoots her a little grin.

Dylan and Grace have just said they need to head home when the bells chime again. Evie glances toward the front and sees the familiar black fisherman's cap she'd been hoping for earlier.

Smiling, she beckons Alistair over to join them. He pulls out a chair from the table behind theirs and straddles it, dragging it toward the space between Evie and Jason. Jason, clearly a bit surprised, shuffles over to make room.

Alistair greets Grace and Dylan with a perfunctory nod and smile. That leaves Jason, who is looking at the new arrival with curiosity.

"Jase, this is my…uh…friend, Alistair." Evie turns to Alistair. "This is an old friend of mine, Jason Lancaster. He just got back in town." As an afterthought, she adds, "He goes to S.U."

"Hey," Jason says politely.

Alistair studies him for a moment, brows drawn in, before replying, "Hey." Then he returns his attention to Evie, leaning in close to her but speaking loud enough that the others can hear. "Sorry I'm so late. I meant to get here sooner and give you a hand, but my uncle needed help shoveling out the driveway. Was it nuts in here?"

Evie stares at him in surprise. He hadn't said he was dropping by tonight, yet he's talking like she'd been expecting him and he'd been running late. Had she maybe missed a text? With a small shrug, she replies, "That's okay. It was busy, but I can handle it."

"I know you can. But we've proven we make a great team. I'll be here by six tomorrow night. Promise."

Before Evie can respond, Grace interjects, "On that note, I'd better get going." She flares her eyes at Evie, presumably in reaction to Alistair's bizarre comments.

"Yeah, me too," Dylan says, standing up. He's oblivious to any weirdness in the room; all he can think about is Charlie.

184

They say their goodnights and head for the door. The last customers leave money on their table and shuffle out behind them.

Now that it's just the three of them, Alistair edges his seat closer to Evie's and casually slides an arm along the back of her chair. He looks at Jason. "So you're Charlie's big brother?"

"You know my sister?"

"Not really. I only met her once, at the Wheeler's Valentine's party last month. She was with her boyfriend. What was his name? Carter?" He looks back to Evie for confirmation.

"Cameron," she corrects.

"Right, Cameron." Alistair gives her shoulder a rub. "Thanks. You introduced me to so many people that night. It's a bit hard to remember them all." He chuckles softly.

Jason's eyebrows fly up as he looks between them. "So I take it you two…?"

Evie flushes. "No! No." She shifts her back a few inches away from the chair and Alistair's lingering forearm. "We're just friends."

Jason snorts at her facial expression. He glances at Alistair again. Then he smiles. "Cool. Well in that case, can I walk you home after you close? It'll give us a chance to catch up. It's been too long."

Her gaze darts to Alistair. He isn't looking at her now. He seems to be searching for dirt under his fingernails. Bright spots of color have flared high on each cheekbone. Maybe it's from the cold air he's just come in from? She tries to recall if he always gets those red patches on cold nights. Then she remembers that Jason is waiting for her response.

"Actually," she starts, intending to tell him she already has a lift home tonight. But before she can get the rest of the words out, the metal legs of Alistair's chair groan as they are shoved backward over the linoleum.

He stands abruptly. "I gotta bounce, too. Just wanted to pop in and say hi. Great to meet you…uh…Jason, right? Catch you later, Evie." Grabbing his coat from the table behind him, he heads for the door.

Evie's shocked by Alistair's strange behavior. So much so that she doesn't even say goodbye. A gust of cold air swirls inside as the door swings shut behind him. Is it just her, or did the air get chillier in here even before he'd opened it?

She turns back to Jason. "Um, sure, company on my walk home would be nice. I'll just balance the cash and wash up these mugs, if you don't mind waiting."

Alistair's sudden departure is disappointing. His unexpected appearance had pleased her, and she'd been hoping for some alone time on the drive home he always offered. His whole demeanor seemed weird tonight, and she isn't sure why. If it had been anyone but Alistair, she'd probably think…no. It's not like he could be jealous of Jason. Could he? She pushes that thought away, chuckling to herself at the sheer ridiculousness of it.

Alistair slams the front door behind him harder than he'd intended. It's just past one in the morning and his uncle will be sound asleep. He stops and listens for any sign of movement in the large house. Other than the tick of the grandfather clock in the next room, all is silent. Which is good. He isn't in the mood to talk to anyone right now. He knows damn fucking well he has no right to be pissed off. But he just is.

Something about that Jason guy—the way he kept ogling Evie, the way he'd insidiously worked his way into walking her home the very second she'd explained that she and Alistair weren't a couple—just makes him want to punch something. Well, *someone*, if he's being honest.

But he couldn't say a word, couldn't even react around them. Because Evie's right—they *are* just friends. Friends who'd recently seen each other naked, sure, but just friends nonetheless.

So he'd scooted out of the coffee shop like his ass was on fire, jumped into his Jeep, and drove off without any destination in mind. For over an hour, he'd just roamed around Sutterton and the back roads surrounding it. He had avoided her street, though. It wouldn't do to be noticed by Evie and end up looking like some kind of stalker. And, honestly, he really had no urge to come across the two of them walking together.

This isn't jealousy. Alistair is *not* the jealous type. Never was, not even with Michelle. He has always been quite confident in both himself and whomever he was dating. He's never felt threatened by other guys, never worried that the woman at his side might up and leave him for someone else. It had always been Alistair who'd done the leaving, after all. Well, before the whole Michelle and Paul debacle, that is.

Is *that* what this is about? Have those two assholes turned him into some kind of wussy ball of fucking insecurity? This thought makes Alistair so livid he can almost feel steam rising from his ears.

Insecure, my ass, he fumes, stomping up the first riser of stairs and taking a left toward the library instead of continuing up to his room. Max had obviously been reading in here before he'd gone to bed—the embers in the fireplace still glow and the room hasn't yet lost all its warmth.

Alistair pours two fingers of bourbon into one of his uncle's precious crystal lowballs and drops into the chair by the dying fire. The alcohol burns its way down his throat and creates a hot little ball in the pit of his stomach that slowly spreads outward. He stares out the tall windows on the other side of the room. The crescent moon glows through the skeletal branches of the big oak just outside. It looks peaceful, and a little bit eerie. He takes a deep breath and exhales it slowly, letting the molasses-y notes of the liquor linger on his tongue.

Michelle was his past. Evie is his present, at least sort of. Temporarily, anyway. He has no idea who, if anyone, will be his future, should he be so lucky as to have one. If he's learned anything, it's that the most important thing is to focus on the right here and right now. Here and now. Which means Evie. Screw Jason—the loser hadn't even given her a good first time in the sack. She'd needed Alistair to show her how pleasurable sex can really be, something he's confident he'd succeeded at. And he's hoping they'll have another round on Sunday afternoon before he has dinner with her family. So there's no need to be wary of her newly returned ex-boyfriend. It's Alistair whom she wants to spend what little free time she has with. And anyway, she doesn't want a boyfriend. She couldn't have been more clear about that. Therefore, there's nothing to worry about.

Is there?

Dude, you've got *to rein this insecurity shit in,* he chastises himself. It's either that or leave town, and he doesn't think he's ready to put Sutterton behind him quite yet.

Maybe he'll just have to show Jason that Evie is currently off the market. Not without her permission, of course. He'll mention the idea to her tomorrow evening after she finishes work, see what she thinks about maybe upping the ante of their public relationship a little bit.

Unless she ends up going home with Jason again.

At this thought, Alistair downs the rest of his drink. It sears a blazing path the entire way to his stomach. Instead of going up to his room, he trots back down the steps and heads to the gym. Maybe getting in a round on the punching bag before bed will help burn off this excess energy. He seems to have an abundance of it lately.

It won't be his brother's or his ex's face he'll be picturing on the bag tonight, though.

Chapter 16

Evie wakes to a warm patch of sunlight across her quilt. Rolling over to check the clock, she sees it's nearly ten. Since it's Saturday and she doesn't need to be anywhere for a few hours, she snuggles back under her blankets.

Jason had walked her home last night, and they'd had a good chat. Since Syracuse is one of the universities she's considering, she'd deluged him with questions about college life. He'd seemed pleased at the idea that she might be on campus with him this fall.

Before he'd said goodnight, he'd invited her to drop by his mom's this afternoon, saying he'd be grateful for a break from his mother's tension and intermittent breakdowns. Evie told him she had a lot of homework this weekend and she'd have to let him know.

Her phone pings. Curious, she reaches for it.

It's a text from Alistair. *Good morning*

She smiles. Maybe he doesn't have a bug up his butt about Jason after all. That hadn't made sense to her, but jealousy was the only thing she'd been able to come up with to justify his strange behavior.

A little wary after the way he acted last night, she texts back: *Morning.*

Soon there's another ping. *What are you up to today?*

Evie purses her lips as she debates her reply. But they'd promised honesty, so she types: *Homework, then if there's time I might go see Jason and his mom before work.* She hits Send and hopes Alistair won't get all weird about it. Jason is a friend, and anyway, he'll be heading back to school in a few days. Alistair has no reason to be jealous.

She's up and dressed by the time he replies. *Have a great afternoon. See you around 6.*

Relief floods her. At least that's one less thing to worry about.

Dylan heads to basketball practice after lunch, and her father is at work, so Evie has the house to herself. The quiet lets her focus and she completes all of her homework by three-thirty. Her English paper can wait until tomorrow—it's the perfect thing to bring to Alistair's after church.

Since she has a little over an hour before she needs to relieve her dad, she decides pop over to Jason's after all. Charlie's disappearance is never far from her thoughts and she wants to find out if there's any news.

Her dad walked to the Clutch this morning, so his car is still in the driveway. She grabs the extra keys off the hook in the kitchen, figuring he won't mind if she borrows it for a quick visit.

The Lancasters live on the west side of town. Their street is comprised of small wartime bungalows, most in various states of disrepair. The house where Jason and Charlie grew up is one of the nicer ones, but it still needs of a fresh coat of paint, a new roof, and a fair amount of exterior maintenance, none of which will likely happen anytime soon. Leanne is a receptionist for Dr. Carditt, but her salary barely makes ends meet, something Evie understands all too well. Jason had been lucky enough to win a full football scholarship to Syracuse the previous year, but as far as Evie knows, Charlie's grades are mediocre at best. Chances of her being able to attend college after graduation are minimal. Evie wonders if Charlie felt trapped in Sutterton, stuck in a dead-end little town in the middle of nowhere. If Cam really did dump her, maybe she'd decided to run off and make a new life somewhere else. It's unfathomably cruel to disappear without telling her mother, but Evie suspects Charlie wasn't thinking straight. Teenage girls' raging hormones sometimes make them irrational and selfish—something else Evie gets, although she's so far kept a handle on her own.

She parks along the curb and carefully steps her way through the footprints in the snow along the uncleared path.

When Jason wrenches open the front door, his tense expression morphs into a wide smile. "Hey Evie. Didn't think you'd show."

"I had a bit of time, so I thought I'd check in. How're you guys doing?" She steps inside and toes off her boots. "Anything new?"

His grin falls away. "Nope. Nada."

"How's your mom?" she whispers, in case Leanne's within earshot.

"Not great. The not knowing is driving her nuts imagining the worst. I made her take a sedative about an hour ago. She's finally asleep."

"Poor Leanne. I can't even imagine. The entire town's freaked out. My dad has given Dyl and me more hugs this week than when we were little." Evie perches on the edge of the overstuffed couch in their small living room. Moving some papers out of the way, Jason sits beside her. There are dark circles below his eyes and she wonders if he's gotten any sleep himself.

Touching the back of his hand, she asks, "What about you? How're you holding up?"

He sighs. "I've had some bad moments, but mostly I'm okay. I have to be, for Mom. She needs me."

"Yeah, I get that. Don't forget to take care of yourself, too, though."

He gives her a small smile. "Well, I gotta admit, seeing you again has been great. Sorry I kinda fell outta touch after I moved."

Evie tilts her head, a little perplexed. It's not like she'd expected him to stay in regular contact. Sure they were friends, casual friends, but they'd never been super close, especially after they split up. "That's okay. I'm glad I can help take your mind off things. Temporarily, anyway."

At that, Jason's face grows serious, and he looks intently into her eyes. Taking her hand, he sandwiches it between his larger ones. "We were good once," he says, in the tone of someone who has just recalled some long forgotten pleasant memory. "Remember that? Remember when we were good?"

Mutely, she nods. She debates retrieving her hand, but doesn't.

His voice grows softer, huskier. "We could be good again. I know we could. If you were open to maybe giving us another try…"

Jason inches his face closer. With deepening chagrin, Evie realizes he's about to kiss her. *Oh God, no!* Adrenaline floods her as her body shifts into Panic Mode. She pulls away and jumps to her feet. "I'm sorry, Jase, but I can't."

He goes beet red. "Don't apologize. I'm the one who's sorry. I shouldn't have. I just thought maybe…"

"It's okay. You're under a lot of stress right now. It's understandable."

He follows her to the front door. "It's that Alistair guy, isn't it? I saw the way you looked at each other last night. You said you were just friends, but c'mon. We both know that's bullshit."

Evie stares at him, debating her reply. Finally she exhales in submission and nods.

"Thought so. Why the secrecy? Why not just admit it and save us both this afternoon's embarrassment?"

"Um…" She shoves her feet into her boots. "It's…it's just sort of…complicated. We aren't really…"

"Let me guess. You haven't defined your status yet, right? And you didn't want to freak him out by telling me he was your boyfriend in front of him?"

Not exactly, but it'll do, Evie thinks. With a relieved smile, she nods. "Something like that, yeah."

"I'm really sorry for, you know, earlier. I just thought maybe… Well, anyway. Can we just forget that ever happened? Whaddya say?"

"It's already forgotten." She stands on her tiptoes and gives him a quick hug and kiss on the cheek. "I really hope you guys hear from Charlie soon."

Jason sighs again. It has an echoing regretful sound to it. "Me, too."

On the short drive home, Evie recalls the moment when he tried to kiss her. Jason is sweet, and she likes him, but she's no longer attracted to him. The only guy she wants to kiss is Alistair. Her feelings for him are…intense. And growing stronger every day.

As she pulls into her driveway, she worries her lower lip between her teeth, a deep frown marring her forehead. Not falling in love with Alistair might prove to be a lot harder than she'd anticipated.

But Evie Colville is a very determined young woman. And it's not like there's any choice in the matter. She'll just have to make sure that doesn't happen.

True to his word, Alistair walks in right at six. Like the previous Saturday, the Clutch is packed, the bells over the door providing background music to the buzz of dozens of conversations. A line-up extends from the counter all the way to the entrance. Some are opting for take-out, but most of the patrons are content just to hang out and socialize.

Alistair takes one look at the crowd and works his way through until he joins Evie behind the counter. The moment his coat is off, he grabs a coffee pot and an order pad and goes to serve the customers at tables. The grateful smile Evie flashes him is all the thanks he needs.

They're both sweaty and tired by the time it quiets, which tonight is well past eleven. Evie grabs a damp cloth to wipe the tables, but before she can start, he touches her arm. "Sit for a few minutes. We deserve a break."

"I can't thank you enough," she says, slumping onto her stool. "But you really don't have to—"

"Stop. I'm helping you clean and that's final. If I wasn't here, I'd just be bored at home. Consider it a favor for keeping me entertained."

She rolls her eyes. "I'd much rather be bored. At the very least we should be paying you."

He waves her off. "I wouldn't accept it even if you tried. And anyway, it's not like I need the money. But I do need to keep busy."

Bracing her elbows on the counter, Evie looks at him like she's debating something. Just as he's about to say "out with it," she sighs. "So, I have to tell you something. I went over to Jason's this afternoon."

His body tenses, but he tries to keep his voice casual. "Yeah?"

"He, uh…" She fidgets with her bracelet. "He tried to kiss me."

Alistair exhales a hard little chuckle. "Can't say I'm surprised."

"It's not like I let him," she clarifies. "I pulled away, said I wasn't into it."

He's silent for a few moments. Adjusting his glasses, he says, "Um…why are you telling me this?"

"I just wanted you to know. That I wasn't interested. In Jason."

"I know that. You've been pretty clear about what you don't want in your life right now. Hence our little arrangement." He pauses, meeting her eyes. "Unless…have you changed your mind about that?"

Frowning, she shakes her head. "No. It's not that. I just—"

194

"I have a thought," he interrupts. "Not sure you're going to like it, though."

"What's that?"

"Wellll…maybe we could show him that you're off the market right now? Up the PDA a little bit when he's around? Just so he gets the hint. I mean, if you want?"

Evie's face brightens as she thinks it over. "That's not a bad idea. And it might save me getting hit on if people around here think I have a boyfriend." She pauses. "But then we'd have to tell everyone that we're…you know…dating. Even if it's just for show."

A smile curves Alistair's lips. "Well, it's not like it's that much of a stretch. We *are* sort of dating—in a no-strings-attached kind of way. I mean, I'd be happy to take you out on dates, if this town had anywhere for us to really go."

She laughs. "There's a drive-in theater on Side Road 12, but it's closed until June. Not much to do in the winter except go to Henry's or hang out at people's houses."

"I could take you to Lake Placid for lunch next Sunday. Go to a movie afterward and have you home by dinner. How's that for a real date?"

Evie bats her lashes at him. "Are you asking me out, Mr. Sterling?"

Alistair chuckles. He stands and pretends to doff an invisible hat, sweeping it in front of him as he bows theatrically. "If you'll have me, Miss Colville."

Through her giggles she manages to answer, "It'd be my pleasure."

Laughing, he takes his seat. "Are you sure you're cool with telling people we're a couple? And acting like it in public? I mean, I know your priorities are school and work and stuff. I don't want to be a distraction from any of that."

"You help me here at work. You help me with my homework if I need it, and give me a quiet place to study if I don't. What more could a girl ask for in a guy?"

Alistair gets to his feet again. This time he goes around the counter, coming close enough to rest his hands on her waist.

He leans down, his lips almost to hers, and whispers with a smirk, "Don't forget the orgasms. I think I help out just a little bit with those, too."

Heat floods Evie's entire body. "Oh yes. Those, too," she murmurs.

Then, in the spirit of their new arrangement, she lifts her face the scant two inches between them and kisses him.

"What time is it?" Evie asks sleepily, rolling over in Alistair's arms to reach for her phone. She shoots up with a start. "Oh crap! It's nearly four-thirty! I need to get home and start dinner."

It had been a lazy Sunday afternoon. After church, she'd gotten her dad to drop her off at Alistair's. Alistair had read while she'd studied for an hour, then they'd spent the remaining time rolling around in his bed. She'd ended up falling asleep curled up against him, so relaxed she'd almost been purring.

His hand clutches the bare skin of her hip, pulling her back to the warmth of his body. "*Nearly* four-thirty. Which means it's *nearly* time to get up." He sits up and plants a kiss on her shoulder. "But not quite yet."

Evie sighs, but her lips curve upward. "Much as I wish we could, there's no way we have time to—"

Her words are cut off by his lips. He runs his fingers into her hair and falls back to the pillow, pulling her down with him. Their kisses are sweet and gentle, with no sense of urgency to them. Evie loves moments like this; she feels like she could just keep kissing him for hours. If only they had time to stay wrapped in each other's arms.

Reluctantly, she pulls away. "I wish I could stay, but I really do have to get home. I can call Dad to come pick me up if you want to sleep for a bit longer?"

Alistair throws off the blankets and slides out of bed, retrieving his boxer-briefs from the floor. "Not a chance. I was planning to help you cook dinner, not just show up and eat it."

196

He looks up at her in time to notice a bemused expression as she drags on her jeans. "What? I can cook! I told you the women in my household taught me well."

"I know. I just…I kinda wanted to show off for you, that's all," Evie admits. "To prove I had at least *some* valuable life skills."

"Ah. Well in that case, there's basketball on that I could watch with your dad while you slave away for us menfolk." He winks.

"Yeah, Dyl isn't missing any of the college games right now. Ten bucks says they're in front of the TV this very moment, not even aware I'm not home yet. You can hang with them, and if you need a change of scenery, feel free to come into the kitchen and I'll put you to work."

Alistair pulls on a sweater and looks at her with a twinkle in his eyes. "Change of scenery? You clearly haven't noticed my domestic side. I'd be more than happy to help. If you want me, I'm all yours."

They arrive at the Colville's small house just before five. As Alistair comes around to open her door and help her out, Evie hopes her father will glance out the window and notice how gentlemanly Alistair treats his daughter.

Inside, they are greeted by the sounds of the basketball game from the living room. "Told you," Evie whispers.

Her dad looks over his shoulder at them and waves. "Hi guys. Hope you got all your homework done." He gives his daughter a smile before turning to her companion. "Alistair, do you follow college ball?"

"Absolutely," he replies with a grin. "What's the score?"

"Orange's up by nine," Dylan pipes up, glancing at them. "Thompson just nailed a three-pointer."

"Cool." Alistair touches Evie's elbow, leaning down to her ear. In a low voice he says, "I'll watch the game with them for a bit, then I'll come be your personal slave. Deal?"

Evie smiles and gives him a little push toward the couch. His eyes linger on hers for a few seconds before he joins her family.

She dumps her knapsack in her bedroom, washes up, and starts dinner. She hasn't planned anything complicated, and they don't have any fancy ingredients anyway, so she mixes up batter for the chicken. Once the pieces are coated, she arranges them on a baking sheet and puts them in the oven.

Next she peels potatoes. Intermittent cheering from the other room tells her S.U. is still leading. She wonders if Jason is watching it, too. He hadn't played basketball in high school, but Evie figures he probably supports his school's teams. Thinking of Jason reminds her of her conversation with Alistair about taking their relationship public. What if he assumes she wants to start immediately, tonight, with her family? What if he's openly affectionate with her right in front of them? She isn't sure she's ready for that. Just last weekend, she'd once again assured her dad that they were just friends. What if he thinks she's been lying to him all along?

Just as Evie starts slicing the carrots, Alistair comes in. "Do I hear chopping? Sounds like someone needs a sous-chef." He comes up behind her, trailing his hand across the small of her back before plucking the knife from her fingers. Nudging her aside with his hip, he takes over.

"I'm fine," she protests. "Go back to the game. I've got it all under control."

Alistair tilts his head toward her and drops his voice. "I already told your dad I was going to give you a hand. Don't make me look like a lazy ass in front of him. Plus, I'm a pretty good carrot chopper. You won't even notice the little bits of my fingers in them."

Bursting out laughing, Evie gives him a smack on the arm that isn't holding the knife. "Fine. Can I at least get you a beer while you work?"

"Nah. Your dad already offered."

"Coke?"

"Just water is fine."

She pours him a glass of water before starting to set the table. Every now and then her eyes dart to his jeans-clad backside. He really does have a nice butt.

Once the veggies are in the pot, she begins making the gravy. Alistair stays and talks with her while she stirs, and before long dinner is ready.

They gather around the table. There's only room for four, but instead of seating Alistair in her mother's chair, Evie sits there and points him to her usual spot. Her dad gives her an odd look when he notices the change in seating, but doesn't mention it.

"So, Alistair," Tom says. "I'm not sure how you're used to doing things, but in this house we say grace before our Sunday meal."

Alistair flashes an agreeable grin. "No problem. My mom was always big on giving thanks before meals, too."

"Glad to hear it. She clearly raised you well. In that case, everyone please bow your heads."

Before Evie drops her gaze, she shoots a quick glance at Alistair. His eyes are closed, chin down in supplication, but his cheeks have those high spots of red again. She's sure they weren't there a moment ago, and wonders if the mention of his mother still stresses him out after all these years. She supposes it probably does; her own mom's missing presence certainly still affects her, hence the change in seating arrangements tonight. Maybe that overwhelming rush of sadness that engulfs her every time she pictures her mother's face will never go away. She's thankful Alistair understands.

Dinner is quieter than usual, with everyone on their best behavior. The most conversation comes after Evie asks who won the game, and since the Orange trounced the Blue Devils in a spectacular fashion, the guys all agree their favorable spot in March Madness is a sure thing.

After a few moments of silent chewing, Tom turns to Alistair. "So, what brought you out here to the middle of nowhere to live with your uncle? I don't recall Evie or Max ever telling me."

Evie glances nervously at Alistair, aware this is not his favorite topic.

A few strained seconds pass before he answers. "Bad breakup. Needed some space to get my head straight, and Max offered."

Tom nods with a wry grin. "Ah. Women trouble. I get it."

Dylan snorts, and his father looks at him in surprise.

"I won't deny it's been a long time, but I did date other girls before I met your mother, you know."

Lifting one hand palm forward in protest, Dylan says, "Okay, Dad. I don't really wanna hear any details."

Everyone chuckles, and Evie shoots her brother a grateful look.

Turning back to Alistair again, Tom asks, "So, how do you like Sutterton so far? Think you might stay awhile?"

Alistair eyes dart to Evie's. Reaching across the table corner, he sets his hand on top of hers and gives her fingers a squeeze. Right in front of her family. She feels her face flush bright red.

Without shifting his gaze away from hers, he replies, "It's been so much better than I ever thought it would be. Thanks to meeting your beautiful and remarkable daughter, I have every intention of sticking around."

"Alistair…" Evie whispers. She wants to tell him to please shut up, but his words are so sweet. She can't look away.

The sound of Dylan clearing his throat brings her back to reality. "Um, hello?" he says. "Other people in the room, you know."

Alistair retrieves his hand and turns back to her father. "I'm sorry, I just mean that getting to know her and having her friendship has been absolutely invaluable the past couple months."

Dylan stands and collects some dirty dishes to take to the sink. He's clearly had enough of this particular conversation. Neither the basketball game nor their dinner guest can take his mind off the fact that Charlie is still missing.

As Alistair rises to help clear the table, Tom says, "The two of you come in the living room with me for a minute, would ya?"

Evie and Alistair exchange glances before following him. They sit together on the couch and Tom takes the chair, angling it toward them.

He looks between them before focusing on his daughter. "Evie, you've been telling me for weeks that you two're just friends. But that's a big ole lie now, isn't it?" His voice is soft and serious.

Oh crap. She's been dreading this conversation. She sucks in a sharp breath. "Daddy, no! It's not like that. When I said we were friends, I meant it."

Her father frowns. He gaze shifts between them again. "I don't disapprove of him, honey. You know I just want you to be happy. But what I won't abide is my teenage daughter sneakin' around and lying to me. Tell me the truth about what's going on between you two."

"Sir…" Alistair starts.

"We're dating," Evie cuts in. "Now. But we *were* just friends. Honest. We always intended to be just friends, even once we realized we were, uh, kinda into each other. On account of me having such a heavy load of schoolwork right now, and working so many hours at the Clutch. And, of course, going off to college soon. I didn't want a boyfriend to distract me."

"Which I totally get," Alistair adds. "And I had no intention of finding another girlfriend after the last one screwed me over. But—"

"But somehow things changed." She glances at Alistair and smiles. "Alistair doesn't keep me from the important things I need to do—he helps me out and I get them done faster. And we finally talked about stuff the other night, and realized we did want more after all. So yeah, we're…um…together now, I guess."

Alistair reaches for her hand and laces his fingers through hers. They look at her father, united.

Tom's face remains impassive for a long moment and Evie worries he's still not happy. Then he breaks into a wide smile.

"Glad to hear it. My girl needs all the happiness she can get. As long as you don't distract her from her education, or break her heart, you two dating is fine by me."

"I would never hurt her," Alistair proclaims solemnly, giving her hand a squeeze as his other one comes up to rest palm down over his heart. Evie has to restrain a giggle at his theatrics.

"See that you don't. And on that note, I have some paperwork I need to finish, so I'm going to retire to my room." Tom stands and wishes them goodnight.

Alistair and Evie look at each other. She pulls her hand from his and rolls her eyes. "Well that was completely not what I expected. And weird. And awkward. Although I'm glad he's fine with it. But my heart was beating a mile a minute for a bit there! You're a pretty good actor. Maybe you have a future in Hollywood someday."

Alistair laughs. "Maybe. But I just told him the truth, same as you did. No acting required."

"It was the *way* you acted though! Holding my hand, looking deep into my eyes—I think you almost made Dyl puke up his dinner! So, you know, good show, I guess. I'm sure Jason and everyone else will buy the whole thing."

His brows narrow a fraction. "I'm glad you liked it. And as a good fake boyfriend should do, I'm going to head home and leave you to finish the rest of your English assignment." He stands and goes to the door, grabbing his coat from its peg.

"You can't stay a little longer? We could watch some TV or something?"

"Nah, I'd better run. You'll get sick of me if I stick around. Thanks for dinner."

She tries to keep her face deliberately relaxed. "Okay. Well, thanks for…keeping me company all day."

"Goodnight."

At that, he walks out the door. Without a kiss or even a hug. Which disappoints her. Rather a lot. She puts her hand on the doorknob to call him back for a proper goodbye, but then changes her mind and lets her fingers fall away.

No one is watching. And they aren't in bed. So no kisses or touches required. Right? Is that the way this is going to be now?

With a sigh, she tells herself this is what she wants, after all. What she needs.

Even if some of it kind of sucks.

Chapter 17

The following week is busy, with lots of assignments due and general rushing around as both students and teachers prepare for Spring Break. There's still been no news about Charlie, and people around town have begun assuming the worst.

Jason drops by the Clutch on Monday night to let Evie know he's returning to school. His mom told him there is nothing more he can do here, and she doesn't want him to miss finals, so he's leaving in the morning. Evie says she hopes he'll have a happy reason to come home soon, and asks him to text her when they learn anything new.

She stares at the door for a moment after he's gone. The shop is empty, her homework is done, and she feels a little lonely with an hour left until close. She's hoping to see Alistair, but after the way they left things last night, she isn't sure he'll drop in. He'd acted kind of weird right before he left. Maybe he hadn't been comfortable with lying.

It's kind of ironic that their main reason for going public about their 'relationship' is about to leave town, but it's too late now. Her father and Dylan know, so everything is already out in the open. Unless they stage a break-up. The thought sends panicky tendrils twisting through Evie's chest. She hopes it won't come to that. At least not anytime soon, although she supposes it's inevitable at some point over the next few months.

Sighing, she pulls out her phone and checks for new messages. There are none.

The rattle of the chain connecting the punching bag to the ceiling echoes through his head, drowning out his tumultuous thoughts as Alistair pummels the oblong leather sack.

His uncle's dry voice interrupts his workout. "You're gonna break that thing right off if you keep up that kind of assault."

Alistair's fists fall to his sides, his chest heaving, his face dripping as he turns toward the door. Grabbing his water bottle, he downs a few gulps before answering. "Just trying to blow off some excess energy. Sorry. I'll try to be more gentle with her." Giving the bag an affectionate pat, he grins at Max.

His uncle frowns. "Is all this pent-up frustration still about Paul and your ex? Or has something else got you all hot under the collar now?"

Evie's face flashes into his mind, but he shoves her image away. Everything between them is fine, just the way they both want it. So that can't be it. "No idea. I think maybe I'm just ready for spring to finally get here so I can get outside more."

"I think we're *all* feeling that way," Max laughs. "Good news on that front though—it's supposed to warm up this weekend. They say we could hit the high sixties."

A genuine smile spreads across Alistair's face. "Great! I'm taking Evie up to Lake Placid on Sunday, so some nice weather would be ideal."

His uncle's eyes narrow. "Evie Colville?"

Shit. Alistair should've realized news of them dating hadn't spread as far as Max's ears yet. If it had, Alistair surely would've heard about it. Evie's dad seems to be fine with them, so his uncle will just have to be as well. And if not, Alistair will just tell him the truth: that they're just friends pretending to be a couple to keep Evie's ex from trying to get back into her pants. He decides to keep his answer simple and see where the conversation goes. "Yep."

Max frowns. "Isn't she a little young for you?"

Sighing, Alistair says, "If you're wondering if her dad's gonna storm over here and raise hell, you can rest easy. He knows. And he's cool with it." He throws a towel over his shoulder. "And it's nothing serious. We're mostly just hanging out. It's actually been kind of nice to have someone to talk to in this crappy little town. Present company excluded, of course."

This earns him a shake of the head and small smile.

"I've been helping her with her homework and stuff. She's leaving for college in a few months anyway, so she's not looking for a relationship—and you know damn well I'm not, either."

Max gives him a long look. He opens his mouth, then closes it again. Finally he says, "Just remember what I told you a few weeks ago. Make sure she knows the score. I'd hate for either of you to end up getting hurt."

"You've got nothing to worry about," Alistair assures him as he brushes past his uncle to head upstairs to shower.

He just hopes that assertion is true, because lately a few nagging little whispers of doubt have begun to creep in.

At eleven-thirty on Sunday morning, Alistair pulls up in front the Colville's house with his elbow cocked out the open window. For once the weather forecasters are right—it's a beautiful day. Sunshine through the windshield has warmed his Jeep so much he's tossed his coat in the back. The entire outdoors seems to be wet and dripping as the snow and ice release their stronghold on the world, finally surrendering to the sun's welcome dominance.

Before he can knock on the door, Evie pulls it open and greets him with a wide smile. She's wearing heels and a black and white floral dress that skims the tops of her knees, presumably her church outfit. Alistair hasn't seen her dressed up since the Valentine's party, when she'd ended the night lip-locked and straddling him in the backseat of his Jeep. His jeans seem to grow tighter just remembering it

"Hey," she says. "Just give me two minutes to change, and I'll be right out."

"Don't."

"Don't what?"

"Don't change," Alistair tells her, grabbing her wrist and leaning in to give her a quick kiss. They're in public, after all, so she can't very well protest. Not that he thinks she would, exactly, but after her comments before he left last Sunday, he's decided once they're out of town it might be best to just to act like friends.

Evie looks down at her outfit doubtfully. "Aren't I a bit over-dressed for lunch and a movie?"

He shakes his head and smiles. "You look great. And it's warm today, so just grab a coat and we'll head out. I promise I'll have you back before the sun goes down and it gets cold again."

'Okay," she agrees, stepping back inside to get her jacket. Alistair hears her dad call to her to have a great day. "Will I be home by dinner?" she whispers to Alistair. After he promises she will, she closes the door and they get on their way.

They've barely rounded the corner onto Main Street when Evie turns to him. "You don't have to do this, you know."

Alistair shoots her glance. "Do what?"

"Drive all the way to Lake Placid today. Take me out and stuff. We could just go back to your place instead. No one would need to know we didn't go."

He snorts. "Is this your not-so-subtle way of telling me you'd rather spend the afternoon in my bed than out enjoying my company in public?"

"No! Well, I mean, yeah I'd be into that, too. But I just meant you could save the cost of gas and food and stuff if we stayed here. We could tell everyone we had a fun time and leave it at that."

With a small frown, Alistair says, "My uncle might notice you being in my bedroom all day instead of where I told him we were going." They pass the Clutch and turn onto Route Ten. "I can't believe I'm saying this, but…I don't want to spend all day in bed. I *want* to take you on a real date. I've been looking forward to this all week. And money's not really an issue for me, in case you haven't noticed. So would sticking with the original plan be okay with you?" He flicks his eyes toward Evie and sees her staring at him in surprise.

"Okay."

"Okay, you're settling? Or okay, you actually want to do this?

She smiles. "I've never done anything like this before in my life, never had a guy want to take me out for anything more than a burger at Henry's. So, yeah, if you're really up for it, let's do it."

Alistair chuckles, shaking his head in amazement. "Teenage boys in this town are clearly idiots. Be prepared to have an awesome day. And if my timing's good, maybe I'll be able to get us back with an hour or so to spare so we can still go to my place for a bit. If you're not sick of me by then." He flashes her a wicked grin.

With a genuine laugh that makes his heart clench in ways he hasn't felt in a very long time, she agrees.

The drive to Lake Placid takes over an hour. When she isn't admiring the scenery, Evie fiddles with the radio station and pops CDs in and out until Alistair feels like he might lose his mind if she doesn't let at least one song play all the way through.

They wind their way through the Adirondacks, which sometimes regress into the distance, but more often hug the highway. The rock had been blasted out for road construction, and their route is frequently bracketed by cliffs of broken strata. Some of the hairpin turns have sheer drops into deep valleys below. These make Evie a little queasy, but she doesn't comment.

The Jeep navigates another bend, and at last they descend towards Lake Placid. The entire town is spread out before them, the sun reflecting off the wide blue mirror of the lake. Forests of green stripe the slopes between ski runs, but the mountaintops are snowy and cold.

Evie hums along to some pop song Alistair is unfamiliar with as they enter town. He's only been to Lake Placid a few times, but it's easy enough to follow the road to the downtown.

"So what do you feel like for lunch?" he asks. "There's lots of options along here."

Her eyes are wide as she looks out the window at the various places they pass. With a shrug, she says, "You pick."

Alistair glances over at her and sighs softly. He keeps forgetting she's rarely been out of Sutterton. Nosing the Jeep into an empty parking spot, he says, "How about we get out and stretch our legs and see what we can find?"

They stroll along the sidewalk for a while, looking in shop windows and enjoying the sunshine. He's tempted to reach for Evie's hand, but talks himself out of it, telling himself there's no one here to put on a show for. Then he recalls that she's never had a guy take her out and treat her right before. She is sweet and honest and works hard, always trying to be everything to everyone. It seems to him that, other than her schoolwork, she puts her own needs pretty low on her priority list. They may only have a temporary no-strings-attached relationship, but dammit this is a girl who deserves to know what it's like to be spoiled.

So he takes a chance. He grasps her hand, lacing his fingers through hers as they walk. Evie looks up at him in surprise, and he's sure she's about to make an excuse to pull away. But she doesn't. She just flashes him that cute little smile and goes back to window shopping. It dawns on him how much he's come to adore that smile.

"How about here?" he suggests, gesturing with his free hand toward a brightly painted Mexican restaurant that's sandwiched between an antique shop and an ice cream parlor.

Evie pauses to read the menu posted by the door. A small frown creases her forehead. "I've never had real Mexican food before. Just nachos from Henry's. And my mom used to make tacos once in a while."

"Well then it's settled," Alistair tells her, opening the lime green door. "C'mon."

The interior is also decorated in garish, yet cheerful colors. He pulls out a yellow chair for her at a bright red table by the front window so they can people-watch as they eat.

She isn't sure what to get, so Alistair takes the liberty of ordering chicken fajitas for both of them. He thinks she'll like how the chicken arrives on a sizzling platter with all the toppings in little side bowls, and she can load up her fajitas just how she likes them.

After the waitress leaves, Evie raises her eyes to his and gives him that shy smile again.

"What?"

"I just want to thank you."

He's confused. "For what?"

"For taking me out today. You really didn't have to."

"I wanted to." He places a hand over hers on the table. "Evie, I need you to do me a favor today, please."

"What's that?"

"I want you to stop thanking me. Stop feeling guilty, or like you're taking advantage of me somehow. I wouldn't have offered if I didn't want to. It doesn't matter if we're," he pauses, "a *real* couple, or just Friends With Benefits. Face it, I like spending time with you." He grins at her.

Thankfully she smiles back, a little wider this time, but equally as shy. His heart does a weird little double-thump against his chest when he sees it.

"I like spending time with you, too. In case you haven't already noticed," she confesses quietly.

"Good. So is it okay if we just relax and have fun today? No more worrying. Deal?"

"Deal."

210

The waitress returns with their drinks and a basket of homemade chips and salsa. Evie's eyes light up when she tastes the dip. "It's *so* good!"

Alistair agrees. He tells her about an authentic Mexican place he used to frequent in New York until it closed a few years back, and before long their fajitas arrive. Evie seems to enjoy them, too, and pretty soon her plate is empty.

She pushes it away, groaning and rubbing her distended belly. "I'm stuffed! Now I'll have to walk around with a food baby all afternoon!"

He bursts out laughing. "I think I have a matching one. We can pretend we're expecting twins."

At that, Evie giggles, and a strange sensation spreads through him. Had Michelle's laughter ever made his chest tighten like this, ever made him feel so carefree? Right now, he honestly can't remember.

They scroll through a list of movie options on Alistair's phone, settling on a screwball comedy. He looks up directions to the theater, and since it's not far, they decide to walk. The Palace is in a historic building, and further along the street is a park by the lake with a spectacular view of the water and the mountains behind. As they have about forty minutes to kill before the movie, they go for a walk.

Alistair takes Evie's hand, and she smiles as he intertwines their fingers once more. She's surprised at how natural holding hands with him feels.

A red-tailed hawk swoops low over the water, then soars up to perch on the peaked rooftop of a nearby building, and she points it out to him. As they near the park, she grows quiet.

"Penny for your thoughts? Well, with inflation it's probably more like a buck."

Evie looks up at him. "I was just thinking about my mom. She went to college not far from here, in Saranac Lake."

"Really? What did she study?"

"She majored in English Lit, with a minor in Creative Writing. She actually got offered a job at the college after she graduated, but she turned it down to return to Sutterton and marry my dad."

"Huh. Did she ever do anything with her degree?"

"No. She stayed home with us when we were small, then worked in the mayor's office once we were old enough to come home from school to an empty house. But that only lasted for a few years before she got sick."

Alistair frowns. "It's okay. You don't have to talk about it if you don't want to."

Evie drops his hand and turns her back to him. "It's been two years. I'd thought it would have started to get easier by now." She wipes away the moisture gathering in the corners of her eyes. "Does it ever get any easier?"

He sighs, rubbing her shoulders gently. "Honestly? Not really. It's been ten years since my mom passed away, and not a day goes by that I don't still miss her."

Evie spins to face him, wrapping her arms around his waist and resting her cheek on his shoulder. He strokes her back, but doesn't comment. She tells herself she will not full-on cry, and after minute or two succeeds. "Thanks," she whispers.

"Welcome." His lips brush the top of her head.

They begin walking again. At first, they stroll around the park in companionable silence, just admiring the view. Evie feels so comfortable with him. It's nice to have someone to walk hand in hand with. It makes her feel like an adult, almost.

Just as she's about to ask how much time they have before they need to go back, Alistair breaks the quiet. "I told you my mom died when I was twelve, right?"

"Yes," Evie says. He hadn't told her anything else about it and she hadn't asked, knowing how uncomfortable that topic always makes her feel.

Taking a deep breath, he says, "She had asthma. It was the end of May, and unseasonably humid that year. She'd been having a bad few weeks, and her inhaler was almost empty.

My brother was home sick that day, so she couldn't leave him to go fill her prescription herself."

Alistair stops walking and looks down at Evie. His face is drawn and tight. "She asked me to stop at the pharmacy and pick it up for her on my way home from school."

Evie's eyes widen. "Oh no! Did you forget?"

He shakes his head, a bitter smile surfacing. "When I left school, I remembered. But..." He pauses, sighing. "I was a scrawny little bugger back then. Thick glasses, spent more time in the library than on the baseball diamond. I was a prime target for bullies—they'd often follow me home, chase me, beat on me."

She frowns, squeezing his fingers as she waits for him to continue. She has trouble picturing Alistair as a nerdy, vulnerable little kid.

"Because I had to go the pharmacy, I took a different route that day, and at first I thought I'd managed to avoid them. But I was wrong. Once they saw me, they chased me for blocks. Luckily I was faster, and I managed to sneak down a grimy alleyway and hide. I had to wait them out for a long time before they gave up and left. Afterward, I was pretty freaked out and I forgot all about the inhaler. And by the time I got home..." He trails off. Evie hears the hitch in his voice and understands what he'd returned to.

"Oh God, Alistair. I'm so sorry."

He doesn't reply. He's no longer looking at her; his eyes are directed across the lake, but they are empty. She knows it isn't the mountains he's seeing.

"It was all my fault," he whispers.

"No." Evie moves in front of him and takes his other hand so she holds both of them in hers. She forces him to meet her eyes. "It was *not* your fault. You were just a kid! And those bullies...if you're gonna blame anyone, blame them!"

Instead of replying, he pulls her against him again, holding her close and burying his face in her hair. He doesn't reply, but she knows he will always blame himself no matter what she or anyone else says. Some things can never be washed away, no matter how much time or distance you scrub them with.

For a few minutes they just stand in the park, holding each other, supporting each other. Then he steps back and gives her a small smile. "Time to go or we'll miss the beginning of the movie."

Alistair seems to return to his cheerful self as they walk back and head inside the theater. True to its promise, the film is quite funny. Once their popcorn is finished, he takes Evie's hand again.

By the time they're back on the highway heading home, their former melancholy has ebbed away. Alistair puts on a band called Spoon, and their upbeat guitar sounds fill the Jeep. Evie has never heard of them, but she likes them.

They talk about music, and Charlie, and Evie's next English assignment, until at last they turn onto Route Ten. "Do you want to go straight home or…?" he asks, smiling as he raises a brow her way.

"I think we have time to stop by your place for a bit. If you still want to?"

He looks incredulous. "You kidding? Of course I want to!"

They both laugh, and instead of continuing toward town, Alistair turns into the driveway of his uncle's house, whistling along to the music.

Two hours later, Alistair is once again making his way down Max's driveway after dropping Evie at home. He'd declined her invitation to join them for Sunday dinner a second week in a row, saying he didn't want to make her sick of him. Honestly, he isn't sure he feels up to putting on a show in front of her family tonight. It's not that it's a chore to be affectionate with her around others. It isn't. Far from it, in fact, it's becoming way too easy. But something about the way she refers to it as 'acting' makes him uncomfortable. Because, the truth is that he isn't acting at all. He's just doing what feels natural. Evie's easy to be affectionate with, to want to touch, to want to kiss, to

214

want to do the things they did in his bed earlier. Which is a little disconcerting. If he actually lets himself fall for this girl, it's guaranteed to not end well. And he doesn't know if he can handle another broken heart. After last time, the thought of going through all that again—well, he isn't sure he'd survive it.

When Alistair comes around the bend and the big house looms into view, he slams on the brakes. An unmistakable bright yellow Corvette is parked in front of the garage. Paul's car.

Shit.

Chapter 18

Six Months Ago

"Hi Alistair," Mary, his dad's buxom blonde secretary, greets him as he steps off the elevator into the offices of Sterling and Sons, LLP. "Please have a seat. Your father will see you in a few minutes. Can I get you a coffee while you wait?"

"No, I'm good. Thanks." Alistair flops onto one of the leather chairs. The room is decorated in cool blacks, whites, and grays, with stainless steel accents. A visitor's eye can't help being drawn to the only colors—they pop from a large Jackson Pollock on the wall behind the reception desk. He suspects it's probably the real deal, too. After all, his dad has a thing for collecting abstract expressionism. A Newman, a Kline, and another Pollock all reside in their home, displayed in strategic and highly visible positions of honor.

Picking up the latest copy of *Forbes* from the table, he leafs through it idly, wondering why he's been called to his dad's downtown office to meet instead of just talking on the phone or at home. Something is obviously up. But what? He shrugs it off. Probably just another lecture. He's had enough of them over the years.

He cools his heels for another ten minutes before Mary tells him he can go in. Straightening his glasses, he opens his father's office door.

Wentworth Sterling nods, but doesn't rise from his chair when Alistair enters. He's impeccably dressed in a charcoal gray bespoke three-piece suit. His only color is a blood-red tie, and it demands attention. *He* demands attention; his very presence—the straight rod of his spine, his flashing dark eyes, the deep, commanding voice—makes everyone around him feel an inescapable need to stop what they're doing and listen.

"Alistair," he greets his oldest son evenly.

Alistair is very used to that tone. He removes his jacket and takes a seat across from the large desk, crossing a leg over his knee as he flashes his most relaxed grin. "Dad. What can I do for you today?"

His father tents his fingers below his chin, staring at Alistair. He's silent for a few long seconds. Then: "I'm a patient man, as you're well aware."

Alistair snorts softly, just loud enough to ensure his father hears. It's the same little non-verbal game they always play. He's ignored, as expected.

"You're twenty-two, son. Twenty-two. High school was— what? Five years ago? And now yet another birthday has slipped past and still you show no sign of wanting to pursue any sort of..." Here he pauses, his tongue darting from the corner of his mouth just a little, peeking out from between his thin lips for a quick taste of the thickening air in the room. "Higher education," he finishes.

Alistair sighs. "Ah. This again." He rolls his eyes, more non-verbal sparring. "This was so important you had to drag me downtown? We could have just replayed this same old conversation at home, don't you think?" Though he tries to mask it, exasperation permeates his words. "I don't want to be a lawyer. I don't know how many more times I can say it before it sinks in."

"Yes." His father punctuates the word with an acknowledging nod. "I'm aware. But the question remains: what *do* you want to be? Other than a drain on your trust fund, that is."

Alistair gives him a long, contemplative look. He's trying to decide whether it's in his best interests to be honest. Finally he replies, "I know it isn't exactly the future you've always envisioned for me, but I've been thinking about getting my English degree and teaching."

One of Wentworth's thick eyebrows twitches. It doesn't fly up—he's an excellent attorney and adept at guarding his reactions—but it tremors just enough that Alistair notices. This is not information his dad is pleased to hear, not a profession he would wish for his offspring. The name Sterling should be attached to prestige, like a lawyer, or a surgeon, or possibly even a politician. Not something so lowbrow as teaching.

Alistair waits for a verbal response, but he gets none. Just that piercing stare. He hates that stare. It makes him feel like his father is picking apart his deepest thoughts, looking for the dirty, nasty, hidden truths so he can use them to his own advantage, just like he does in court.

Wentworth exhales a small sigh. Barely audible, but of course Alistair hears it. It's an all-too-familiar sound.

His dad's tented fingers ball into joined fists and drop to his leather desk blotter. The sudden thump makes Alistair jerk in his seat. "It's high time you made some important decisions about your future. As you're fully aware, your trust fund explicitly states that you need to complete some sort of pre-approved higher education, or I can cut it off anytime I see fit. Since this year is soon drawing to a close, I've decided you have until next autumn to enroll in college—at this point, *any* college—if you expect me to pay for it, which means you'll need to get your applications out this spring." He pauses, his eyes turning icy. "If not, goodbye trust fund. Goodbye cushy life. You'll be out on your ass serving macchiatos at Starbucks to the kind of hard-working professionals you could have been, had you had even a single shred of ambition."

Whether Alistair is willing to admit it or not, he has inherited a lot of his father's temperament. His own face matches Wentworth's stony expression. Rising to his feet, he grabs his jacket. "Message received," he mutters as he heads for the door.

Alistair is not in a good mood. Not at all. His dad thinks he's lazy and useless, that he'll never amount to anything, nothing but a drain on his inheritance. The most annoying part is that Alistair isn't so sure he's not right.

Right now all he wants is a stiff drink and Michelle. He needs to look into her flashing gray eyes, smell the rich scent of her skin, feel her soothing caress. He almost needs her more than air. Only she can ease his frustrations. She always does.

He drives home too fast, screeching his tires around corners, blasting past shocked pedestrians. Normally he's a much more careful driver, but today he can think of nothing but getting home. To her.

Although he still lives in his father's house, Wentworth is rarely there, and Paul is off at school. His brother comes home most weekends, but during the week Alistair and Michelle usually have the place to themselves. While she doesn't officially live with him, she might as well. She sleeps in his bed almost every night, has clothes in his closet, a toothbrush by his sink, a box of tampons stashed below. Alistair loves being able to come home to find her waiting for him. He loves waking up beside her, nuzzling his face into her hair right where it meets that sensitive spot behind her ear. He even loves cleaning up all the escaped strands of that long hair that end up in his bathtub and on his floor. Because it's just more proof that she's with him, that she's chosen him. When he's with Michelle, he knows he's the luckiest man alive. For some inexplicable reason, she loves him. And he is just over the goddamn moon for her.

So much so that some days he has to stop and force himself to take a breath, suddenly overwhelmed by how happy he is, how happy she makes him. He's never felt that way about anyone before. He thinks he'd give her the entire world if she asked for it.

These thoughts ease the stress from the conversation with his father. All Alistair needs to clear his head is her.

As he turns onto his street, now slowed to just over the speed limit, he takes one hand off the wheel and reaches inside his jacket to finger the small box hiding in the pocket. He smiles as he pictures what's inside.

He'd been impulsive, he knows. It's not like they'd ever talked about marriage. They're both far too young for that. But…he'd been walking past a jewelry store a few weeks ago and he'd seen a ring in the window that he just *knew* she'd adore. And an image popped into his head of her wearing that sparkling diamond on the fourth finger of her left hand, how it would proclaim to everyone she meets that she intends to spend her life with him. That she loves him. And that he's worthy of her love. So he'd just taken a leap. He'd gone inside and bought it.

He's been carrying it around in his jacket ever since, waiting for the right moment. And now he realizes he's not going to wait for Thanksgiving, or Christmas, or her birthday; he's going to ask her as soon as he sees her. He can't wait any longer to see the expression on Michelle's face when he drops to one knee and presents that little velvet box.

Alistair's heart pounds with excitement as he pulls up in front of the triple garage. His father's ultimatum now gone from his mind, he comes in the front door with a smile, leaps up the stairs two at a time, intending to turn right and head straight to his bedroom in the east wing.

As he reaches the top, he's surprised to hear noises from the other side of the house. Curious, he changes direction, treading softly on the plush carpet, moving in silence down the hall. Following the sounds, he turns a corner and realizes voices are coming from behind his brother's bedroom door. He frowns. Paul didn't tell him he was coming home a day early. And, more importantly, is that a woman in there with him?

Alistair swells with pride at the thought. To the best of his knowledge, Paul hasn't had a girlfriend since high school. The last one was at least two years ago. He's been hoping his brother will meet someone at university, but Paul continually tells him he isn't looking, that he prefers to focus all his attention on his studies. Their father, of course, insists he's smart to avoid unnecessary distractions.

Alistair moves a little closer to the door. Paul's definitely not alone. He begins to back away, to give them their privacy. Before he can leave, a lush laugh reaches his ears, all full of throaty amusement. It's a laugh he knows all too well.

He goes numb.

His body parts seem to have minds of their own, because his stunned brain surely didn't tell his hand to twist open the door, didn't command his feet to enter his brother's bedroom.

The sight that greets him will be emblazoned across his mind forever.

Michelle.

And Paul.

Naked.

His voice doesn't seem to be working any better than his brain, because although his mouth falls open, no words come out. His throat is bone dry. He can hardly breathe. Still as a statue, he gapes at them, entwined on his brother's bed.

Paul is the first to notice. Michelle's straddling him, and he grabs her hair—she does like it rough—and sits up. When he sees his brother standing in the doorway, his eyes bulge. His jaw drops. One word comes out, one single strangled word, and it puts an end to everything. *Everything.*

"Ali?"

Michelle whips around, her dark hair flying out like a fan, her eyes wide. She grabs the sheet and covers herself, but wisely keeps her mouth shut.

All three of them stare at each other in stunned silence. For what feels like a long time, no one moves. The room is so quiet. Dead quiet. The lack of sound stretches out so far and so long it's nearly deafening.

Paul looks like he's about to try to speak again, and seeing his brother's face contort in distress like that is the catalyst Alistair needs. He spins around and leaves, slamming the bedroom door behind him and running down the hall.

At the top of the stairs, his only plan getting to his car and heading God knows where just as long as it's got a bottle at the end of it, he forces himself to stop in his tracks. Yes, he needs to get away from them. But Alistair Sterling is not a coward. And this is his home. He's not just going to flee. There *will* be a bottle in his near future, but it's going to be emptied in his own room, not in some seedy bar. Not tonight, anyway.

So he keeps walking. Once inside his bedroom, he locks the door and pulls a cardboard box from the floor of his closet, upending it. Old clothes he'd planned to give to Goodwill land in a heap. One sneaker rolls into a corner. He doesn't even notice.

Alistair rips Michelle's clothing from the hangers and unceremoniously tosses it into the empty box. He rifles through every drawer, looks under his bed, pulls items from the bathroom cabinet until everything of hers is gone.

Just as he's folding the flaps of the box closed, he hears footsteps approaching his door. There's a pause and then a soft knock. He ignores it.

"Ali?" Paul calls in a voice choked with remorse. "I know you're in there. And I know you don't wanna talk to me right now, but would you please just—"

He cuts off his brother's planned speech, or apology, or groveling, or whatever the fuck it was going to turn into, by opening the door. Relief starts to rearrange Paul's frown, but Alistair just shoves the box into his arms.

"Guess she's your problem now."

Then he shuts the door—shuts, not slams, although it takes all his willpower not to—firmly in his brother's stunned face.

That's the last time Alistair opens his bedroom door for three days. No amount of pleading, or crying, or yelling from the other side has any effect on him. He drinks a lot, sleeps a little, stumbles to the bathroom from time to time, but he doesn't talk. He shuts his phone off, but not before deleting more than fifty photos. He's not hungry, although his stomach is definitely not impressed with the lack of respect he's been showing it. It rumbles almost constantly.

At one point, Paul tells him through the door that Michelle has left. She didn't come to grovel for forgiveness through the wood like his brother has done over and over, but then again, he didn't really think she would. It's not in Michelle's nature to grovel.

Paul tells Alistair he never meant for any of this to happen, but that it's been going on for a while now. He says they're in love, and that he's sorry, so, so very sorry for all the pain he's caused.

Alistair does not respond.

On the third day, his father's fist rattles the door and Wentworth's resonant voice commands his son to stop being such a goddamn child and grow a pair. Then, almost as an afterthought, he mentions that Uncle Max wants him to call.

Alistair thinks on that a while. His uncle lives about three hours north, in a small town lost somewhere in the foothills of the Adirondacks. They visited once, quite a few years ago, but he doesn't really remember much about Sutterton. It's pretty much a blink-and-you'll-miss-it kind of place.

With a sigh, he turns his phone back on. Fourteen voice-mail messages, twenty-three texts, five emails, three tweets, and nine new Facebook messages await him. He'd lay odds that the majority of those are from his brother. And that none are from Michelle. But he doesn't bother to check. He scrolls through his address book until he finds Max's number and, with a glimmer of curiosity if nothing else, calls him.

"Hello?" Max answers after the fifth ring, sounding breathless. Alistair recalls how large the former bed and breakfast is, and wonders if his uncle had to run for the phone.

"It's me." His voice is somewhat hoarse from disuse and he hopes Max will recognize him.

"Oh, Alistair! Thanks for calling back. I wasn't sure if you would." He pauses, presumably to catch his breath. "Your dad told me what happened, at least his interpretation of it, as I'm sure you've guessed."

"I did."

"I'm not gonna try to make you talk about it or anything. I know you just want your space right now. That's actually why I called." Max pauses again, and Alistair is even more curious about where this is headed. He's startled by his uncle's next words.

"I'd like you to consider coming up and staying with me for a while. A few days, a few weeks, a few months—whatever you need."

"I don't know," Alistair starts, but Max doesn't let him finish.

"Look, I'm not sure if you remember, but when I moved up here, I was pretty messed up myself. I know better than most that sometimes you just need to get away from your problems for a while, to get some time and distance to screw your head back on straight. That's what I'm offering. Time and distance. Plus, I know I'd like some company. You're welcome here. If you want."

A tight lump has formed in Alistair's throat. He's unable to respond.

"Just...at least say you'll think about it?"

Finding his voice at last, Alistair mutters, "I'll, uh, I'll let you know." He disconnects and falls back onto his pillow. The house around him is silent and empty, the only sound the furnace blowing warm air through the vents. It's funny how sometimes you just know you're alone.

Tomorrow is Thanksgiving. Not so many days ago, he'd assumed it would be his happiest Thanksgiving since his mom passed away, as he'd be spending it with the woman he loved—his fiancée—at his side. Now all that has been shot to hell. Maybe his father and brother will still spend the day with her, but this year Alistair won't be joining them.

And just like that, a decision is made. He gets up, hauls his suitcase from his closet, and starts to pack. Once it's full, he loads up a large duffel bag as well.

The little velvet box that's been hidden inside his jacket for over two weeks is left on his bedside table. They will probably find it and surmise its intent, but so what if they do? It doesn't make a single shred of difference now. And Alistair no longer gives a fuck what any of them think.

Unlocking his bedroom door at last, he steps into the hallway, listening closely for any sign of life. As expected, all is quiet.

He goes downstairs but stops in front of the large oak double doors. Setting down his bags, he makes a detour into the adjacent room. His mother's photo sits on the mantel over the fireplace, as it has for the past ten years. Alistair picks it up and examines it thoughtfully.

She was too young. That lump rises in his throat again as he takes in her dark hair and expressive green eyes so much like his own. Her cheekbones are high and a little drawn. Her skin is pale, and she looks a bit unwell. But then again, she often did in the last few years before she died. She looks just like how he remembers her the last time he saw her.

All at once, he's that twelve year-old boy again, standing in the entranceway looking up at her smiling face. He feels her dry lips on his forehead as she kisses him goodbye, her hand on his shoulder as she guides him out the door. His eyes, which have so far remained miraculously dry throughout this whole hellish ordeal, itch at the corners, and his throat grows tighter still.

Not caring in the least what his father will say, Alistair takes the portrait with him.

He doesn't head straight to Sutterton. Much as he doesn't want to worry his uncle, he's nowhere near in the right headspace to spend Thanksgiving with anyone he knows.

Instead, he drives to a cheap-ass motel just over the Connecticut border and checks in. There's a shabby roadhouse across the way and he has every intention of drowning the clawing demons in his head with bourbon. Or tequila. Or vodka. Or rubbing alcohol, if he has to.

On Thanksgiving Day, Alistair wakes with thin motel sheets twisted around his legs, a bulldozer of a hangover doing its level best to cave in his skull, and what feels like a month-old dead skunk trying to tear its way out of his belly via his throat.

After an unpleasant few minutes bowed before the porcelain throne, he rinses out his mouth, brushes his teeth, and has a long, although not particularly hot, shower. Eyes closed, he braces his hands against the tile and lets the water drum on his back, wanting to cleanse himself not only of his sins, but also his memories.

Of her.

Of them.

Of his own failings.

Of everything.

It doesn't work. And booze only allows him a temporary reprieve. There must be *some* way to abolish all these unwanted feelings. But he has no idea how.

Then Alistair remembers his uncle.

Once he's clean and dressed, he sits on the edge of the bed. The cheap mattress springs groan as he reaches to the nightstand to retrieve his glasses and phone. His stomach grumbles—or perhaps snarls would be better way to describe it. He has no idea if he ate anything at the bar last night. Some peanuts maybe? Which means he hasn't eaten a proper meal in four days. No wonder he feels so damn shaky and weak. Hard liquor does not offer much in the way of nutrition. So, first he orders delivery from the pizza place up the street. Then he calls Max's number.

When his uncle answers, all he says is, "I'll see you tomorrow."

Chapter 19

Alistair sits in his Jeep clenching his fists on the steering wheel as he glares at his brother's car through the windshield.

What the hell is Paul doing here?

Scratch that, he knows *exactly* why the little shit is here. To give him those big puppy-dog eyes and grovel for the two-hundredth time. To try to pressure Alistair into forgiving him, so he can alleviate his guilt over being with *her.*

Blowing out an ex he can alleviate his guilt over asperated puff, Alistair contemplates his options. He could just restart the engine, go back into town, and grab a drink at Henry's. If he drinks it slow enough, and goes for a long, aimless drive afterward, maybe his brother will be gone when he returns.

Oh, who am I kidding? There's no chance in hell he'll leave until he talks to me.

Alistair knows his brother well enough to know that. Paul is as stubborn as he is, and as their father, when he really wants something. And he *really* wants Alistair to ease the crippling weight of his guilty conscience. So unless Alistair's prepared to hightail it out of town for good—which he most definitely is not—he's just going to have to go inside and deal with it.

Shit. So not what I need right now.

All he wants is to go up to his room, put on some music, lie across his bed (which probably still smells like Evie—a thought that causes the hard line of his mouth to curve into a grin), and mull over the events of the day. Since that clearly isn't about to happen anytime soon, at least not until he faces his brother, Alistair gets out of his Jeep. His boots crunch on the newly-exposed gravel as he walks to the door.

When he enters the front hall, he hears Max and Paul talking in the living room. His eyes roll to the ceiling, thanking Fate or whatever higher power there is that Michelle didn't tag along. Not that he thinks she would. But still. Small blessings.

They must have heard him come in, because their conversation comes to an abrupt halt. A moment later, his uncle appears in the doorway wearing a concerned expression. "Your brother's here."

Alistair nods. "I noticed."

"You want me to stay? Or leave you two to hash things out? *Peacefully*," Max stresses.

Alistair tries to force his keyed-up body to relax. "I'm good," he mutters. "This won't take long." He walks past Max and into the large room.

Paul is sitting in Alistair's usual spot near the fireplace. His elbows are propped on his knees, fingers laced into a fist below his chin as he stares morosely into the flames.

When he hears his brother's footsteps, he looks over. "Alistair," he greets him. His voice is small, young-sounding. It reminds Alistair of when they were kids and Paul did something bad and came to him for help, always so terrified of their father finding out.

"Paul," Alistair replies tersely, moving behind the bar along the side wall to pour himself a double shot of bourbon. He lifts his glass and tilts it so the amber liquid sloshes in his brother's direction. "Libation?"

Paul's brows bounce up, then resume their usual frown. He shakes his head. "I'm good, thanks."

228

Alistair shrugs. Taking a deep swig, he perches on the arm of the couch. "What can I do for you then?"

"I just..." Paul stops, sighing. "I had to..." Another sigh.

"Spit it out, dude. I haven't got all night. Bottles to empty, beautiful women to seduce—you know how busy my schedule is these days."

Is that a hint of a smile Alistair sees fluttering at the edges of Paul's lips?

"You're actually gonna let me talk this time? I half-expected you to shove me out the door the second you saw me."

With a wry grin, Alistair lifts his glass toward his brother again. "I won't say it didn't cross my mind. But you drove all this way. The least I can do is offer you a drink before you leave."

Long furrows crease Paul's forehead. "Mighty big of ya," he mutters.

Alistair keeps talking as if he hasn't heard. "Since you declined, however..."

"Will you just shut up and listen to me? Like *really* listen?"

Miming dragging a zipper across his mouth, Alistair regards his brother with serious eyes.

For a few moments, Paul is silent. He looks like he's trying to figure out how to start. Alistair had assumed he'd practiced his speech the entire drive here, but maybe he's wrong. Or maybe Paul has decided to trash the planned apology.

"I hate that my actions hurt you," he starts. "If I could go back and change some of my choices, I would. In a heartbeat.

"But I can't. I can't rewind time to fix all this. All I can do is try to make things right with you, and hope that someday maybe you'll forgive me. I know you might never be able to. Hell, I'll never forgive myself. But Ali, you're my big brother. And I miss you."

Alistair is silent. He's no longer looking at Paul; he stares at the bourbon swirling in the bottom of the glass.

He hears Paul take a deep breath. "This isn't easy for me, you know."

A harsh laugh flies from Alistair's mouth, punctuated by an eye roll. "It isn't easy for *you*? Yeah, right. Because clearly this is all about *you*."

His brother ignores his outburst. "It wasn't easy for me to come up here today, knowing full well it was pointless, that you'd just push me away yet again. Knowing you're never going to forgive me, but having to keep trying anyway, because I just can't seem to stop." His breath hitches in his throat. "What I did to you was beyond horrible. And you *should* hate me for it. I deserve your hate. But I just—"

"I don't hate you."

Paul's eyes flare as he realizes Alistair is looking back at him again. "What?"

Alistair sighs, tossing back the rest of his drink. "You heard me. And you're right—I *should* probably hate you. I *wanted* to hate you. Convinced myself I did for a long time, actually. But the truth is…I don't."

It's Paul's turn to stare. He holds his breath, afraid any little movement or sound might shatter this fragile armistice into a thousand jagged fragments, each cutting deeper than the last.

At last he asks in a hesitant voice, "Does this mean…?"

Alistair flicks his shoulder in a small shrug, then rises and returns behind the bar. "I don't know what it means. Sure you don't want that drink?"

Paul sighs. "Maybe just one."

Reaching for a second lowball, Alistair fills it with bourbon to match his own. Before he can deliver it, Paul comes over. He picks up the glass and drains it in two huge gulps. Then he looks his brother right in the eyes. "I'm *so* sorry, Ali."

"I know."

Alistair refills Paul's glass and they resume their seats, this time opposite each other with the oak coffee table between them. Alistair put his feet up on the wood, crossing his ankles and leaning back against the soft leather. "So, how's law school? Top of your class, I assume?"

Max pops his head into the room a few minutes later, and once he realizes his nephews are at least attempting to converse like normal adults instead of about to cause each other physical harm, he exhales a relieved sigh and joins them.

Alistair does his best to relax, and to his surprise finds it isn't all that difficult. Though he'd tried to push the thoughts away, he'd often wondered how his brother was. Not speaking to him for so long left a pretty huge hole in his life, and he only now realizes how much he's missed their talks.

Paul avoids the subject of Michelle—and neither Alistair nor Max mention her—right up until around two in the morning when Alistair is showing him to a spare bedroom for the night. As he wishes Paul goodnight and turns away, his brother calls him back.

"Forgive me, but I need to ask." Paul draws a deep breath. "Do you still love her?"

Alistair's brows fly up. *Seriously?* His expression softens, and he grins that same wry grin from before. "Nope."

"Really? I mean, you even had an engagement ring."

"Really. And I'm not just saying that because I know it's what you want to hear. I've given the matter a lot of thought. Too much, probably. For a long time, the truth was that I still did, no matter how much I wished it wasn't so. But not anymore. The anger is still there, but the love, the desire...it's all just...I don't know. Evaporated. I never would've believed it possible, but somehow it has.

"Don't get me wrong. I don't plan on rushing back into the ole' family fold anytime soon. Spending time with the three of you is still pretty low on my list of things I'd like to do. But..." He pauses to clear the emotion tightening his throat. "I just...lame as it probably sounds at this particular juncture, I really do want you to be happy. And if your happiness lies with her, then...well, so be it."

Paul examines his face, looking, Alistair presumes, for some sign his words are fiction, that this is what he wishes were true instead of the actual truth. At last his brother smiles. There's more relief in that smile than Alistair would have thought possible. Paul claps a hand to his shoulder and looks at him with glistening eyes. "Thank you," he murmurs.

For a moment Alistair thinks his baby brother is about to pull him into a hug. He sees the hesitation in his eyes, the worry that it's too big a risk, that he'll surely be rejected. Alistair knows him probably better than anyone, and he can read him all too well. So he makes the move himself—he puts his arms around a surprised Paul and claps him on the back. As he steps back, he smiles. "'Night, brother."

When he gets to his own room, he opts to skip the music and flops across his bed. But instead of reminiscing about his afternoon with Evie—that can, and will, come later—his mind replays his conversation with Paul.

No, Alistair isn't ready to return home yet. At some point, he knows he'll have to go back, but it still feels like that moment is a long way in the future. And there's his father's ultimatum to consider, too. It's nearly halfway through March. If he doesn't want to kiss his trust fund goodbye, he needs to get his ass in gear with his college applications. He wonders where Evie has applied. She mentioned Syracuse, but he isn't sure where else.

He snorts, chiding himself for the silliness of that thought. What do her choices matter to him? They will no longer be a part of each other's lives by the time summer is over, if not sooner, so why even contemplate things like where she'll be going to school?

Alistair decides he'll start working on his applications in the morning. He can no longer delay this, and it feels a lot more important now than it had before.

He starts to rise to brush his teeth, but sudden inspiration has him sitting back down again and reaching into the drawer to rummage around until he finds the letters from Miss Lonely Love.

Thinking about his recent self-realizations, Alistair flattens out her most recent letter and rereads it. Then he grabs his pad of paper and a pen and props them up on his pillow. It's been a while, but tonight he feels like writing to the advice columnist once again.

Dear Miss LL,

Sorry it's been so long since my last letter. Life has gotten more interesting in the meantime, that's for sure. I want to thank you for your kind wishes. I think I deserve happiness as well. I'm just not sure how exactly I'm going to get there.

But! I have come to a couple of pretty important (and surprising) discoveries about myself recently.

Drum roll, please…

You may be surprised to hear that I'm no longer in love with my ex. Believe me, it was a shock for me, too. But the more I think about it, the more I'm sure it's true. There's nothing in the world that could make me take her back now. So, that must mean something pretty major about my ability to move past all this someday, don't you think? There might just be hope for me yet.

Second, and probably more important, I'm considering forgiving my brother. My anger towards him isn't totally gone or anything, but it has lessened. I'm trying my best to understand why he did what he did. Which, frankly, I still don't. But I'm trying. He's my brother, after all. And the thought of cutting him out of my life forever, never speaking to him again, just seems sort of ridiculous now. He's the only brother I've got. He's the only one who really understands me in so many ways, because he was there, growing up alongside me. We went through a lot of good times, and even more horrible times together. And right now he's beating himself up about this enough for both of us. He needs me. So I'm going to try my best to forgive him. The truth is I need to just as much as he needs me to.

So, yeah. Two important changes in my thinking recently, so I wanted to share with you.

It's not much, but it's something. Baby steps, right?

Have a good one,

JAI

Alistair doesn't even bother reading it over; he folds it and tucks it into a blank envelope, scrawling Miss Lonely Love's

P.O. Box across the front. He'll mail it when he goes into town to visit Evie at the Clutch tomorrow night.

Monday morning, Evie sleeps late. When she jolts awake and sees the little red numbers on her clock read nine-fifteen, at first she panics. But then she smiles, pulling the covers back over her head as she remembers that it's Spring Break, and she's not late for school.

She hauls herself out of bed thirty minutes later and pads, yawning, to the kitchen to make breakfast. Her dad left for the Clutch hours ago, and the faint snores coming from Dylan's bedroom assure her she won't be seeing her brother's face anytime soon.

After a short text conversation with Grace, Evie learns her friend is busy running errands with her grandma all afternoon, but she promises she'll come by the coffee shop tonight for a study session. They both have piles of homework; for some reason their teachers don't seem to get the 'break' part of Spring Break.

By the time it's full dark, Grace is perched at the counter across from her. They aren't chatting much tonight—both have their heads down, trying to make a dent in their assignments. Their plan is to get it all finished early so they can have the end of the week to relax and have some fun. Mr. and Mrs. Clancy are sitting at a nearby table finishing their coffees, but the shop is typical Monday-evening quiet.

Grace sets down her highlighter and looks at her friend. "Have they found out anything about Charlie?"

"Not that I've heard." Worry creases the skin between Evie's eyebrows. "I can't stop wondering where she is. It's hard to focus on homework, because my thoughts keep jumping back to her." *And to Alistair.*

The bells ring, and Evie glances up with a smile as the very person she'd been thinking of walks in. She beckons him to the empty stool beside Grace.

"We were just talking about Charlie," she says as she fills his mug.

"Any news?"

"The police still can't find her dad."

Alistair frowns. "He isn't online? Email or Facebook or Twitter or something? No one has his phone number?" The girls shake their heads. "Nothing? In the age of the Internet? Then he deliberately doesn't want to be found. Which seems a little shady, if you ask me."

Evie clears her throat, dropping her voice so the Clancys won't overhear. "He, uh, apparently lives a pretty *free* lifestyle, if you know what I mean. Jason says he moves around a lot, doesn't tend to keep a phone number for long. He told me his dad has a bit of a weakness for...pharmaceuticals."

"Ah. Hippy type? Or just a drifter?"

"A little of both, I think."

"So he just up and buggered off on his wife and kids? Class act."

"Yep," Grace says, rolling her eyes. "Makes my own dad, who sees me maybe once a month, look like Father of the Year."

Alistair nods sympathetically.

Mr. Clancy shuffles up to the counter to pay and wish Evie goodnight. Grace goes back to reviewing her History notes, and Evie starts telling Alistair her idea for her big English assignment that's due at the end of term. Before she can finish, the bells chime again as the door is thrown open. Her brother hurries toward them looking anxious.

Evie frowns and comes around the counter. "What's up?"

"I just got a message from her!" Dylan exclaims. He's nearly breathless, and she wonders if he ran all the way here.

"Who? *Charlie*?" All three of them stare at Dylan.

He nods, dragging a chair from one of the tables and dropping onto it. "She finally replied. You won't believe this, but she's out in L.A. with her dad. Says she's fine and not to worry." He pauses, his eyes dropping to his twisting hands. "She also said she's not coming back."

"Oh my God." Evie takes a seat across from him. "Did you tell Leanne?"

"Char asked me not to. Don't worry though, I will. I wanted to tell you first." Dylan lifts his gaze to his sister's again, worry radiating off him. "Mitch Lancaster's a total stoner. Won't be long before he gets bored of her tagging along and ditches her again. He'll take off while she's sleeping or something. Maybe even dump her on some street corner." Dylan takes a deep breath. "She *needs* to come home."

"I know. What did you say to her?"

"That she needs to call her mom. Doubt she will, though. Said she lost her phone. I don't even know how she got online. Maybe she borrowed someone's."

"We have to tell Jase." Evie grabs her laptop. She takes it to the table by her brother, pulls her phone from her pocket, and starts tapping away. "I'm texting to see if he can come on Skype right now," she explains without looking up.

Alistair's brows draw together at the mention of Jason, but he stays silent.

A minute later, Evie's phone buzzes against the table and she snatches it up. "Okay, he's logging on right now." She opens Skype and clicks on his name to call him, then angles her screen so the others can see. Alistair comes and stands behind her, bracing his hands on the back of her chair. His fingertips brush the top of her shoulder and she glances up at him with a small smile.

"You two Skype often?" he asks her in a low voice, adding a grin to assure her he's teasing.

Evie snorts. "Barely. I think we did once not long after he left."

With a ping, Jason's face pops into view, and she turns her attention back to the computer. Jason looks tired. Evie wonders if he is still having trouble sleeping. Between exams and his family problems, he's probably pretty stressed.

"Hey Evie," he says.

"Hey. Grace, Dylan, and Alistair are here, too." Evie moves the laptop around so he can see them. Her brother and Grace wave at the screen. "We need to talk to you, and thought a group chat might be easiest."

"Oh yeah? What's up?"

"I heard from Charlie," Dylan tells him.

Relief floods Jason's face, and he perks right up. "You did? When? Where is she? Does Mom know?"

As Dylan explains Charlie's message, Jason's eyes grow wide.

"Do you have any idea how to get in touch with your dad?" Evie asks, although she already knows the answer.

Jason shakes his head with a grimace. "Nope. Last time I spoke to him was…last spring I think. Right around graduation. He didn't call to congratulate me, though. He was just fishing around to see if I could send him money."

"Did you?" Grace asks.

"I couldn't spare any. And even if I could, I've got no interest in funding his habits."

"Yeah," Dylan says. "Don't blame ya. Charlie told me all about that stuff. Why the hell would she take off to L.A. to see him without telling anyone, though? That's the part I don't get."

"Me neither," Jason says. "Look, I'm done the last of my exams this week. I'm gonna see if I can scrape up enough for a ticket to L.A. If I can, I'll go out and try to find her this weekend." He runs his fingers over his hair. "She clearly needs someone to talk some sense into her."

For the first time Alistair speaks. "That's exactly what I was thinking."

Evie twists her head to look up at him. "What?"

"We should go to L.A. and find her. All of us."

"You're kidding, right?" Dylan's looking at Alistair incredulously. "How the *hell* would we afford to do that?"

"Don't worry about the cost. I'll cover it. And it's Spring Break, so it's not like you'll be missing school."

"You can't do that," Evie protests. "And even if you did, my dad would never let us go. He needs our help here."

"Just listen: we could leave on Friday, home by Sunday night. Jason, is there any way you can meet us at Hancock airport early Friday?"

Jason frowns. "Uh, my last exam is Wednesday, so yeah, that's doable. But why would you pay for us to go to California? You barely know us."

Evie turns to Alistair again. "I appreciate your intentions, but you know I can't go. Please just take Dyl and Jason and go get her."

"Charlie doesn't even know Alistair," Dylan says. "It should just be me and Jase."

"Evie, I can cover your shifts for you," Grace pipes up. "Your dad might let you guys go if Alistair and Jason are with you, since they're older and all. And he knows he can trust you."

Jason sighs. "Fine, I'm in. But I'm paying you back, Alistair. And if you're going, I'd honestly prefer if Evie came, too."

Evie looks doubtful. "Dad *might* go for it," she says. "It wouldn't hurt to at least ask. I still don't know, though. Four round-trip tickets to L.A. is a *lot* of money."

"I've got nothing else to do with it." Alistair rubs her shoulders again.

Evie still doesn't like the idea of him paying for them all, but she can talk to him about that later, once they are alone.

"So you guys talk to Mr. Colville and let me know," Jason says. "As soon as I hear from you and we've got a plan, I'll tell Mom what we're up to. I'm pretty sure she'll be all for it. She knows I have a way better shot at getting through to Charlie than some strange cop would."

Evie glances over at Dylan. Jason might not realize it, but she'd bet her brother has as good a chance at convincing Charlie to come home as he does. Maybe better.

"Okay, 'night Jase. I'll text you tomorrow as soon as I know what's up."

"Great. Thanks for the good news, Dyl. Talk soon." He blinks out of sight.

Evie closes her laptop and puts it in her knapsack. The girls begin packing up their schoolwork.

238

"I'm heading home," Dylan says, pulling his jacket back on. He turns to Alistair. "Thanks, dude."

"We'll find her," Alistair says.

"Yeah." Her brother's face is more hopeful than Evie's seen it since Charlie disappeared. The bells ring out his departure, and Grace follows shortly after, assuring Evie as she leaves that it's no problem covering her shifts this weekend.

Alistair takes a sip of his lukewarm coffee. "It's no big deal, you know."

"It is to me." Evie puts down the carafe she's rinsing and turns to him.

"I know. But my trust fund is just sitting there. And it would be nice to see some of it go toward something meaningful, for once."

"I wish I could promise to pay you back, but—"

"Stop." His voice softens. "While I do want your friend to return home safe, I'll admit, I have a minor ulterior motive." He comes around the counter and sets his hands on her hips so he can look her in the eyes. "You've never been out of state. Hell, you've never even seen the ocean. I wanna take you out to California and spoil you a little. Will you please let me do that?"

Evie can't help smiling as she stares into those mesmerizing green eyes. He looks so earnest, and she knows he means it. Her heart's suddenly beating too fast. "If my dad says it's okay," she says softly, "then yes. I'll come."

Instead of replying, Alistair pulls her to him and lets her know just how pleased he is by kissing her soundly.

Chapter 20

Evie spends Tuesday studying. She's determined to get all her homework done so Dad won't be able to use that as an excuse to not let her go to California. Alistair is supposed to meet her at the coffee shop tonight, and once they return to her place, they're going to join forces with Dylan to discuss their plan with her father.

She hopes he'll still be up at ten-fifteen. He often goes to bed early, since he needs to wake at the crack of dawn for work. If he's already in bed, they'll be stuck waiting until tomorrow to try and squeeze in a free moment to speak with him at the Clutch, which will be cutting things close for ticket buying and hotel reserving.

True to his word, Alistair comes to keep her company while she finishes her English assignment. A few customers pop in, but most don't linger. The night is clear and not particularly cold, and the citizens of Sutterton have more important places to be.

Not that Evie minds. She has too many other things vying for her attention tonight.

Alistair uses her laptop to research hotels while she re-reads a section of *The Great Gatsby*. "What about this place?" he asks, turning it so she can see.

The screen shows an elegant gray, black, and white palace. It's a luxury hotel called Shutters on the Beach. Evie frowns, her eyes sweeping over the extravagant facade. "It's beautiful. But it looks crazy expensive."

"It's right on the beach and a short walk from the Santa Monica Pier. It's a little pricey, but it's in an awesome location."

She shrugs. "Maybe you'd better keep looking. I highly doubt Charlie and her dad are holed up anywhere near there."

"Probably true. But how cool would it be to stay there? Maybe next time."

Evie glances up at him again. Next time? What's he talking about? There's never going to be a next time, at least not with her. He must have meant next time he goes to Los Angeles with someone else. She frowns at the thought.

Alistair resumes tapping away on the keyboard while she tries to re-focus on what she was reading. It's hard to concentrate on Nick, Gatsby, Daisy, and Tom when her thoughts keep drifting away to far-off coasts.

"Hmm," he mutters.

Evie looks up. "What?"

"I think I found the perfect place."

"Let me see."

As she reaches for her laptop, he clicks the mouse, and when she sees the screen it's just her desktop background. "Hey! What were you just 'hmming' at? Why'd you hide it?"

"You'll just have to wait and see, won't you, Miss Nosy?"

"Thought you wanted me to come with you?" she huffs.

"I do. And you will be, once we convince your dad that not only is this little adventure for a worthwhile cause, it'll also be a fabulous experience for his kids to see some of this great country we live in. At no cost to him. How can he say no?"

Evie rolls her eyes. "He's more than capable of saying no. We'll find out soon enough. But you still didn't answer me. Why can't I see this perfect hotel you've found?"

Alistair slides off his stool and leans over the counter to kiss her. She doesn't retreat, but she doesn't kiss him back either.

"Because I want to surprise you," he whispers, pulling away and staring into her wide eyes.

She can't help grinning.

Ten o'clock seems to take forever to arrive. Evie grows so impatient she jumps up and locks the front door at seven minutes before the hour. "Close enough," she tells Alistair, noticing his questioning look as she grabs her jacket. "Time to get this over with."

They're quiet on the short drive back to her house, both mentally preparing for their conversation with her father. Alistair pulls up along the curb and turns to her. "Nervous?"

"Very. But the more I think about it, the more I think we might be able to pull this off."

He nods. "Hope so."

"C'mon. We've gotta grab Dad before he goes to bed."

When they get inside, they find Tom and Dylan in the living room watching the local news. The anchor is telling viewers they have no new information on the disappearance of Charlie Lancaster, and that authorities on the West Coast are still trying to locate her father.

"Good timing," Dylan says, turning to the new arrivals.

"Did you tell him?" Evie asks her brother.

Tom's eyebrows bounce up, and he glances between his children. "Tell me what?"

"We have something we need to talk to you about, Dad," Evie says, tugging Alistair by the elbow into the living room. They take a seat on the couch beside Dylan.

Her father turns to Alistair. "Hello Alistair. I take it you're a part of this, too?"

With a tight smile, Alistair replies, "Yes, sir."

Tom regards the three of them facing him in a row wearing matching serious expressions. Chuckling softly, he says, "Well, which of you's gonna start? It's nearly my bedtime, y'know."

Evie opens her mouth to speak, but her brother beats her to it. "I heard from Charlie last night. She's out in L.A with her dad."

At first, Tom looks pleased. "Wonderful! Leanne must be *so* relieved." Then his smile falls away and his forehead furrows. "She say when she's coming home?"

"She said she's not. And you know how her dad is. You know he ditched them. It's only a matter of time 'til he up and disappears again."

"I've heard some unsavory stories about Mitch, yes." Tom sighs. "But no matter how much you care about your friend, Dylan, this really isn't any of our business. It's between Charlie and her parents. So I don't really get what you need from me."

Evie and Alistair look back and forth between the elder and younger Colville. This is Dylan's fight more than theirs, and they intend to let him have his say.

"Charlie needs to get her, ah, herself back home before something nasty happens. She has nobody out there but a dude who—from what she's said—cares more about scoring his next high than his own kids. Sooner or later he's gonna get bored of playing Daddy and leave her again. She might not believe it, but he will." Dylan pauses to take deep breath. "We wanna go to L.A. and find her. And talk her into coming home with us."

Tom frowns, again looking at each of them in turn before his gaze lands back on his son. "First of all, who's *we*? And more importantly, you *do* know that's completely out of the question, right?" His eyes widen to emphasize his point. "For a variety of reasons."

"Just hear us out, Dad," Evie pleads.

He turns to her with a stern expression. "This is police business and Lancaster business. Not Colville business. End of discussion."

Frustrated, Dylan rakes his fingers through his hair "You don't get it! Charlie won't listen to cops or her mom. She's stubborn as hell! I'm not even too sure she'd listen to Jase, although he wants to come with us. But I think I can get through to her. If I could just talk to her face to face, I think she might listen to me."

"He's right," Evie says. "Dylan and Jason are the best chance we've got to convince her to come home. And Grace already agreed to cover my shifts this weekend if—"

"Hold up—what? *This* weekend? And why do *you* need to go? Or Alistair, for that matter?"

Alistair clears his throat. "Mr. Colville, I've offered to pay for the trip. Jason told us he was going to go alone, but we know there'd be a better shot at getting through to her if Dylan goes, too. Jason said if Dylan and I were going, he'd be more comfortable if Evie came as well. Frankly, so would I. It's just for three days, and you don't have to worry about the money. I've got way more than I need, and I want to help out."

Tom's eyebrows draw in tight. "Jason's cool with this half-cocked plan? Is Leanne?"

"He's gonna tell his mom once I let him know if you agree to let us go," Evie says. "He's just waiting for my text. You're welcome to call Leanne tomorrow and discuss it with her if it'll make you feel better." She bites her lip, looking at her father pleadingly. "I know Dyl and I have never been on a trip before, but Alistair will be with us, and he's traveled loads. He'll take good care of us."

Alistair takes her hand, silently assuring both Evie and her father that she speaks the truth.

"It's not that…" Tom starts.

Evie doesn't wait for him to put forth more arguments; she straightens her spine, looks her dad in the eyes, and says, "You trust me, right? I think I've proven I'm responsible. I'm sure between the four of us we can keep tabs on each other and stay out of trouble."

Her dad's tight lips finally curl into a small smile. "That's the bit I'm less sure about. But yes, of course I trust you. And I know Max trusts Alistair, which means I'm willing to trust him, too."

Hope blossoms through Evie. "We'll be home on Sunday, so we won't miss any school. And we promise to have all our homework done before we go. Pretty please say yes, Daddy?"

"I can talk her into coming back with us. I know I can!" Dylan says.

With a sigh, Tom relents. "You'll check in with me twice a day, Evie? And I want Alistair's and Jason's phone numbers, and for the four of you to make sure you keep your phones charged at all times." Turning to Alistair, he says, "And hotel and flight information as soon as possible."

"Yes, sir. I'll have the details to you tomorrow morning, as soon as I get everything booked."

"See that you do."

Evie pulls her hand from Alistair's and stands, crossing the floor to give her father a hug. "Thank you, Dad. I knew you'd understand."

He pats her back. "You're welcome. Please don't make me regret it."

"We won't."

All three of them thank Tom and wish him goodnight. Dylan disappears into his room as well, and Evie walks Alistair to the door.

"Thank you for this," she whispers, standing on her tiptoes to press her lips to his.

"No problem. I can't wait to show you Venice Beach, and the Santa Monica Pier, and the craziness of Hollywood Boulevard. It's gonna be a blast!"

"I thought we were going out there to find Charlie, not to be all touristy?" Evie laughs.

He chuckles, bending his head to kiss the tip of her nose. "I'm pretty sure we can do both."

Evie tidies up the living room before heading to her room to change into pajamas. On the way to the bathroom to brush her teeth, she sees the light is still on in her father's bedroom. On impulse she knocks lightly. "Dad? You still up?"

"C'mon in."

Pushing open the door, she steps inside. He's sitting up in bed with one of his big accounting notebooks balanced across his thighs going over the recent numbers for the Clutch. She perches on the edge of the mattress. "I just want to thank you again. It means a lot to me that you trust me enough to let us go."

"I do trust you, honey. You know I do. And it's clear you trust Alistair."

"Very much," she admits.

Tom breaks eye contact to look back down at the page before him. He clears his throat. "I'm glad you came in here, actually, because there's something I need to ask you."

"What's that?"

He closes the ledger and sets it aside, then looks at her with a small frown. "Times like these I wish your mom was around to do this. I mean, I *always* wish she was around, but…this is more of a mother-daughter kind of…conversation."

Evie notices her father's face is flushed. For a moment she's confused, but suddenly she realizes just what he's about to ask. Heat floods her own body, and she knows her cheeks have turned as red as his. "Uh, Dad, you don't have to—"

"Like it or not, I do. Even if I don't *really* wanna know the answer."

She goes still, bracing herself.

Her dad draws in a deep breath. "Are you two, uh," he starts, then stops, exhaling all the air out in a rush, "you know…are you being *careful*? Can you please just assure me of that much?"

Face burning, she looks down at her fingers, which have scrunched up the blanket. "I, uh…we, um…" She sighs and nods. "You don't have to worry, I swear."

"I'm your father—I can't help worrying no matter how much I trust you. You'll always be my baby girl. But Alistair seems like a good guy, and I think this is the happiest I've seen you since before your mom got sick."

"He *is* a good guy. And yeah, I'm pretty happy." She can't suppress a grin.

"So does this mean you'll be sharing a hotel room with him? Or with your brother?"

Evie mashes her lips together to restrain the giggle threatening to erupt. Not because her father's question is funny, but because she just got a mental picture of the expressions on Alistair and Jason's faces if she were to tell them they have to bunk together.

"Um, I have no idea. Does it matter?"

Tom smiles. "No, I suppose it doesn't. Just—as I said—be careful. And make sure you keep your grades up. I'd hate for you to lose out on that scholarship you want so bad and screw up your college plans just 'cause you're distracted by the throes of young love."

Chuckling, Evie says, "That isn't gonna happen. You know college is my top priority. All my homework will be done before I go, and if there's any reading left, I'll bring it with me."

"That's my girl."

"And as for the young love bit," she adds, "that's not an issue, either. As I told you before, we're keeping things casual."

He pats her hand. "Love isn't a bad thing, Evie. In fact, it's kind of wonderful. You'll know when you're ready to open up your heart and let someone in. I knew it on my first date with your mother."

"You did?"

"Yep. I had no doubt she was the right one for me. I just had to work a little to convince *her* of that." He yawns, covering his mouth with the back of one hand. "On that note, it's way past my bedtime. Sleep well, sweetie."

"Night Dad."

Evie lies on her side with her history reading assignment open on the mattress, but she can't focus on the sociological ramifications of the American Revolution tonight. Her mind keeps slipping back to her father's advice.

She's read books about true love, seen it portrayed in the movies, heard girls at school gush about how much they love their boyfriends, but she's never experienced it herself. She'd always assumed it would happen when she was older and had more time for such frivolities. But, much as she doesn't want to admit it, she knows things have changed. Now she has Alistair. And although they've promised to only be Friends With Benefits, and that emotions won't be allowed to complicate things, no matter how hard she tries she can't seem to curb her ever-growing feelings for him.

Being around Alistair makes her happy. He has the strangest ability to cause her to let go of all her worries, at least temporarily. Not that she ignores her studies when she's with him—far from it. They both make sure her homework is finished before moving on to other, more pleasurable activities. And after, curled up together in his bed, his warm arms holding her close, her cheek against his chest, she always gets this incredible feeling of calm and contentment, like she could stay this way, with him, for the rest of her life.

The way he makes her feel—it's just so…*intense*. She knows she cares about Alistair more than she's ever cared about any guy before. If she's being honest, he rarely leaves her mind these days. Even when she's supposed to be thinking other things, random memories of the rich tenor of his voice when he says her name, or flashes of those incredible green eyes gazing so intently at her, like he almost always does right after kissing her, will pop into her head. Warmth floods her body and she shivers, remembering the feel of his fingers sliding over her skin.

Evie swallows thickly, closing the heavy textbook and putting it on the floor, her eyes wide as she stares at the ceiling

Could this be love? Is this what real love feels like?

"Oh my God. It *is*, isn't it?" she whispers. She squeezes her eyes closed in shock, but the flimsy barriers of her eyelids can't block it out, won't let her unknow what she's just understood.

She groans, low and filled with dread. This is bad. Very bad. They'd promised that if their feelings intensified, they'd let the other know right away. And this admission, as far as she understands it, will mean an immediate end to their fake-couple status. At that thought, her chest tightens, her ribcage suddenly too small to contain her pounding heart.

This is *not* how it's supposed to go. She's supposed to be excited to go off to school in August, a bit sad, sure, but overall okay with saying goodbye to Alistair, with letting him go when the time comes—not all pathetic and heartbroken. Her clammy palms clutch at the sheets, her breath puffing out in shallow little gasps.

Now what's she supposed to do? Does she have to tell him about this right away? They're going away together in a few days, and she's been looking *so* forward to it. The last thing she wants to do is to create awkwardness between them and ruin their trip.

Maybe it can wait until they return home? Maybe it will be okay for now to just kind of…bask in their time together? Enjoy being with him to the fullest before having to admit how she really feels? Or… maybe she doesn't really need to tell him at all?

No, she made him a promise, and she intends to keep it. She will tell him, and she will just have to put on her big-girl panties and deal with the fallout.

But not until they get back.

With a sigh, Alistair wrenches his eyes open and stumbles half-awake to the bathroom. Once he takes care of business, he splashes cold water on his face and returns to pull open his curtains and let the rising sun flood his room. Putting on his glasses, he picks up his laptop and stretches out on the bed. The big house is still. Only the soft clicks of his keyboard break the early morning quiet.

When he got back from Evie's last night, he jumped online straight away and tried to book their plane tickets, but to his frustration found that the only flight to L.A. departing Friday morning from Syracuse was already sold out. He's hoping there have been overnight cancellations, because otherwise, they're going to have to leave a day late or a day early, and he isn't sure if taking off as soon as tomorrow morning will work for the others.

Alistair checks the Friday flight. *Shit*. Still full. Sighing, he looks at the Saturday morning option. It's sold out, too. With a deepening frown, he clicks on tomorrow morning's departure. There are only six seats left. And if they want this flight, they'll need four of them. He grabs his cell phone and calls Evie.

"Hey," she answers. He knows she was sleeping, but instead of sounding annoyed, he can hear a smile in her voice. It brings one to his own face knowing she's happy to hear from him.

"Morning. Sorry to wake you. You hear from Jason yet?"

"Hold on, let me check my texts." A few seconds pass, then she comes back. "Yep." She pauses with a yawn. "He talked to his mom. He's good to go."

"Great. But I've already hit a potential snag. The flight to L.A. Friday morning is sold out. So's the one Saturday. Tomorrow morning isn't, but there's only six seats left. I'll need to book our tickets ASAP if you guys are cool with leaving a day earlier than planned."

After a short pause she replies. "Well, I'm fine with it, and my brother won't care, but I'll need to check with Jason, Grace, and my dad. I'll call you back in a few minutes, okay?"

"No problem."

He ends the call and gets up to pull on a sweater. Even with the welcome warmer temperatures, it is still chilly in the house in the mornings. Instead of taking the time to stoke the embers in the fireplace, he pockets his phone and goes downstairs to make coffee.

The main floor is silent. Max must still be asleep. As Alistair settles into his favorite chair in the library and sips his coffee, he feels his phone buzz in his pocket.

"Jason's cool with leaving a day early," Evie says immediately. "And Grace is fine to take my Thursday night shift, too. Dad frowned his frowniest face, but he couldn't come up with any real reason not to let us go tomorrow. So we're all in."

"Excellent." Alistair gets to his feet, one hand pressing his phone to his ear, the other holding his steaming mug, and heads back up to his room. "I'm going to book our tickets right now."

"And the hotel?"

"That too. I'm still not going to name it for you, but I'll give all the info to your dad once I've got it confirmed."

"Fine."

Alistair can almost hear her thinking. "What's up?"

"I'm just trying to make a mental list of everything I need to get done this afternoon before I go to work. Organize, pack, get everything ready. I don't even own a suitcase!"

"Just bring your knapsack. You can pack light—it'll be pretty warm in L.A. this time of year."

"Yeah?"

"Definitely. Just bring t-shirts, shorts, a swimsuit, sandals. Wear a hoodie and jeans on the plane, and you won't need to pack much more."

"Okay, sounds good. Anything else? Will I need anything dressier?"

"Maybe a skirt or dress to wear to dinner, but it's not really necessary. I think shorts will be fine anywhere you want to go."

Evie is silent for a few moments. Then: "I can't believe I'm going away with you."

Alistair chuckles. "And your brother. And your ex. It's not exactly a romantic holiday for two." *Although it'd be cool if it were*, he thinks. He's already decided he is going to make it as memorable for her as possible.

"So...my dad asked me last night after you left if we'd be sharing a hotel room."

"Did he?" Alistair laughs out loud. "*Awkward*. What did you say?"

He hears her exhale a puff of air. "I was *totally* mortified. I just told him I had no idea. At least he let it drop, thank God."

"You think he'd mind if we did?"

She sighs. "My dad's pretty open-minded, and he trusts me to make good choices. I think he already assumes we…you know."

Alistair presses his lips together, not sure whether he likes the idea of Evie's father thinking they're already sleeping together. Even if he's right. "Okay, well…it's great he trusts you so much. Hope he trusts me, too."

"He does."

Knowing Tom trusts him with his daughter gives him a peculiar rush of pride and pleasure. It's a nearly unfamiliar emotion, as his own dad has never once made him feel worthy of such confidence. Shaking off these thoughts, he replies, "I'm glad. So then are you cool with it?"

"With what?"

"Sharing a room with me."

Evie snickers. "I was kind of counting on it."

"Good. Me, too."

"Okay, well I'd better go find Mom's suitcase and start packing. Are you gonna come by the Clutch tonight?"

"Yep, I can do that. See you later."

"Later." She disconnects.

Alistair quickly books their flights, hotel rooms—making a request in the system for the two rooms to be on different floors, if possible—and a rental car. He texts the flight info to Evie, and then grabs a towel and goes downstairs to the gym. There's no point in starting to pack yet; he knows from experience it will only take him about five minutes. His mood has soared; he cannot wait to show Evie everything Los Angeles has to offer.

By the time Evie has carefully squeezed all the items she's spread across her bed into her knapsack, it's nearing four-thirty. She buckles it closed, runs a brush through her hair, grabs her jacket, and rushes out the door.

Ten minutes later, she's standing on the sidewalk in front of *The Herald* looking curiously at the elastic-wrapped stack of letters she's just picked up. Across the envelope on top of the pile is the black jagged writing she's become so familiar with.

Colville's Coffee Clutch is only a short walk down the street, but Evie can't wait to read it. She leans against a tree at the corner of Main and Spruce and pulls the envelope from the pile, shoving the rest of the letters into her bag.

As she reads, her smile grows wider and wider. This letter has a completely different tone from the previous ones, and she can actually feel the hope radiating from JAI's words. At last he seems to be looking forward to his future again. She can't help feeling proud of him for taking the difficult and emotional steps he's just pushed himself through.

Evie knows she won't have time to craft a reply until later tonight once she's back home—too many potentially curious eyes will be around in the meantime—but she has a sudden inspiration of what she wants to write. And she feels giddy at the thought of how honest she plans to be this time.

Chapter 21

The ping of Evie's phone alarm jolts her from an uneasy sleep. The house is dark and silent. Her grogginess falls away as she remembers what today is, and she bolts upright, shoving off the covers to dart into the hallway and pound on her brother's door.

"Dylan! Time to wake up!" she calls, her heart racing with excitement.

She turns as her dad's bedroom door creaks open and his head pokes out, his face still doughy with sleep. "Morning, sweetie. I'll make sure he gets up. You better jump in the shower quick while it's free."

She smiles. "Thanks, Dad."

Thirty minutes later, Evie is clean, dressed, has her hair in a neat ponytail, toast in her belly, and is waiting by the front door. Her toe taps out a rapid rhythm against the scuffed linoleum as she watches the street through the small window. At last she spots Alistair's Jeep and erupts into a wide grin. "He's here!" she calls. "C'mon!"

Dylan hurries into the entranceway a few moments later lugging a half-unzipped duffel bag. As he crams his feet into his sneakers, Alistair knocks on the door.

Evie pulls it open. "Morning! You didn't have to come in. We were just on our way out."

Alistair leans in to greet her with a quick kiss. "Morning." His eyes sweep over the siblings, taking in Dylan yanking fruitlessly on his bag's stuck zipper. One of Alistair's brows quirks. "You guys ready to go?"

With a sigh, Dylan gives up on the stubborn zipper. He gets to his feet and pulls on his jean jacket. "Yep. Let's hit the road."

"Morning, Alistair." Tom emerges from the kitchen, blowing across the top of a steaming mug. "I trust you've got everything under control?"

"Good morning, sir. Yes, we're all set."

Dylan hoists his duffel and turns to his father, who claps a hand on his shoulder. "Hope you find Charlie, I really do, but even if things don't end up going the way you want, try to have some fun."

"I will, Dad."

"One more thing: I know you're almost seventeen, but I want you to promise me you'll listen to your sister. You're still a minor, so she's in charge this weekend. Okay?"

Dylan rolls his eyes. "Whatever."

Evie steps forward to give her dad a hug. "Thanks again, Dad. Don't worry, we'll be fine. I'll call as soon as we land."

"See that you do." Tom's voice sounds a little uneven. This will be the first time he'll be alone for any length of time since before the kids were born, and Evie knows he won't feel right until they're both back in their own beds.

Alistair picks up Evie's knapsack and holds the door open for them. Once their bags are stowed in the back of the Jeep and everyone is buckled in, coffee and hot chocolate-filled travel mugs in hand, they wave goodbye to Tom and get on their way.

The drive to Syracuse takes about two hours. Dylan wears his earbuds and dozes in the back most of the way. Evie, on the other hand, chats happily, peppering Alistair with questions about airports and airplanes and hotels and L.A. and the ocean. He's more than happy to answer as best he can and each time he explains something she thinks is cool, Evie's smile seems to grow impossibly wider. Her excitement rubs off on him and before long his side of the conversation becomes nearly as animated as hers.

At last they arrive at Hancock International Airport. They have no trouble finding Jason—he's waiting for them just inside the main doors and looks relieved when he spots them.

"Finally!" he exclaims, hoisting his backpack to his shoulder. "C'mon, I've already scoped out where we need to go. The check-in line's over here." He points to his right.

They join the end of the lineup for the Delta domestic flights counter. After they've waited for about five minutes, shuffling forward in minute increments, Evie remembers the letter to JAI that she'd tucked into her bag. Standing on her toes and craning her neck, she spots a blue U.S. Post box next to the restrooms along the far wall. "I need to use the washroom. Be right back," she whispers to Alistair, pointing toward her destination.

Evie ducks under the divider. She's surprised the airport is so busy. More and more people seem to be arriving every minute. Babies cry in their mother's arms, while stressed out fathers drag luggage behind them. In front of her, a couple is loudly arguing about whose fault it is they'd missed their flight. The cacophony of noises blends into a dull roar as she hurries toward the post box.

Once she reaches it, she glances over her shoulder to see if any of her friends are watching. Jason and Dylan appear to be chatting, and Alistair's eyes are fixed on the screens above the counter displaying continually changing departure information. None of them are looking her way, so she pulls out the envelope and slides it into the box. Before heading back, she goes into the ladies' room; it had been a long drive, after all.

When she re-joins the others, who have made their way around a couple of switchbacks and are approaching the counter, Alistair casually slides an arm around her waist and pulls her close as he talks to Dylan about basketball. He doesn't even pause his sentence, and she can't help grinning. *If only we could always be this comfortable with each other*, she thinks with a strange sense of yearning. She dreads admitting her changing feelings to Alistair, and having to face the presumable consequences. At least she has a few days to enjoy this before that conversation has to happen.

He doesn't seem to notice her sudden melancholy and excitement overtakes her again a few minutes later when it's finally their turn to check-in. They all walk up together, but the others stand back and let Alistair do most of the talking. Before long they have their seats confirmed and their boarding passes in hand.

Next is the security line-up. Evie sighs when she sees all the people waiting in front of them. This queue appears even longer than the previous one.

"Don't worry," Alistair murmurs, leaning close. He gestures toward the big digital clock on the far wall. "We won't miss our flight. We've still got plenty of time." His breath tickles her earlobe and she shivers, looking up at him with a small, grateful smile.

It takes a while to navigate this line, and the general mood of their fellow travelers seems more of frustration than anticipation, but eventually they make it past the security check without any hassles.

They spend the next forty minutes hanging out in the departure lounge by their gate. Evie's restlessness grows more obvious; she gets up and crosses over to the large floor-to-ceiling windows, studies the planes lined up on the tarmac outside, then returns to sit beside Alistair for a few more minutes, crosses and uncrosses her legs, and fidgets with her magazine before rising to do it all over again. He's amused by her impatience and tries his best to get her to relax, but it's no use. She's far too keyed up right now to focus on anything for long.

Finally, after what feels like several lifetimes to Evie, boarding for their flight is announced. They shoulder their bags and line up once more. Their boarding passes are again checked, and they make their way down the gradual slope of the jet bridge and board the aircraft. Evie and Alistair's seats are near the back of the cabin, behind Jason and Dylan. Alistair insists she take the one by the window.

She flashes him a wobbly smile, but her eyes still dart around, trying to take in everything. When the 'Fasten Seat Belts' sign on the ceiling lights, and the flight attendant stands in the aisle and calls for their attention before going over what to do in case of an emergency, Evie reaches for Alistair's hand. Then the plane begins trundling down the runway to the take-off position. Her heart is pounding, as relentless as native drums in those old black and white movies she sometimes watches with her dad on Sunday afternoons. She grips Alistair's fingers.

He leans in close. "Nervous?" he whispers. His breath sways loose strands of hair that have escaped her ponytail, and it tickles a bit.

"A little." She gives his hand a squeeze.

"The take-off's the worst bit. Then we'll even out and it'll all be fine. You'll be able to see Syracuse getting smaller and smaller below us."

Evie gulps, staring at the nubby blue fabric on the back of her brother's seat. *People do this all the time. It's really no big deal*, she attempts to convince herself. She can overhear Dylan and Jason talking about Los Angeles. Neither of them has ever flown before either, yet they don't seem to be freaking out. She takes a few deep breaths and tries to force herself to relax like everyone else seems to be. But her body is having none of it.

The entire plane starts to vibrate. The drone of the engines swells to a low roar as they rev. With her free hand she clutches the armrest, her teeth clenched, her spine rigid against the seat back.

"Okay, this is it. We're about to take off," Alistair says softly. His thumb rubs reassuring circles over the back of her hand.

The airplane speeds down the runway, moving faster than Evie would have thought possible. She stares out the window as the blurred buildings and grass and tarmac whip by. Her pulse throbs in her throat, her ears. She no longer hears the other passengers; the only sound is her heart's incessant drumming: *Thump Thump. Thump Thump. Thump Thump.*

Just before true panic sets in, before she can leap to her feet and attempt to escape, the scenery tilts as the wheels leave the ground. Evie squeezes Alistair's hand again as she sucks in a sharp breath. Negative g-force pushes her body firmly back into her seat. So much for escaping.

"Evie?"

She turns her head to the left a little, just enough to look at Alistair. It seems to take a lot more effort than usual.

"Breathe," he tells her.

Realizing she has yet to exhale, she blows it out in a long sigh. He smiles at her reassuringly, leaning close to whisper. "You're fine. We're flying. Now please try to relax, okay? We've got several hours to go before we get there. Can't have my girl passing out before we even hit cruising altitude."

At his words, she feels the ball of tension loosen. Did he just call her his girl? Warmth spreads across her chest as she draws another deep breath. She likes being Alistair's girl. Likes it more than he knows, more than is probably safe for her emotional well-being. She turns to look out the window again, distracting herself by marveling at the city falling away below them as they rise. The cars are little more than colored dots on a dark thread. They don't even seem real.

Evie spends a good part of the journey with her forehead pressed against the window watching the landscape flowing by. The cloud cover comes and goes, but it breaks up enough for her to see the Mississippi river, winding like a fat, silver snake through deep green forests and miniature towns. Further on, the Great Plains looks like a tiny yellow and green checkerboard stretching away as far as her eyes can see. And at last they fly over the landscape she's been looking most forward to: the majestic Rockies. Though she's lived her entire life in the shadows of mountains, these are not *her* mountains. They jut from the earth like some alien landscape, all jagged dark precipices and snowy tips, with dark valleys slashing through their midst. Clouds obscure many of the mountain tops and soon block her view once more. It's the strangest feeling, looking down on all that fluffy white from above. For all she knows, she could be passing over a whole different country, a whole different planet even.

When the clouds next break apart enough for Evie to see the earth, her brows draw tight in confusion. In the distance she can see a huge reddish brown cataract, a slashing chasm in the desert. "What *is* that?" she asks Alistair as they get closer, pointing out the window and leaning back so he can see past her.

He takes a look outside and then turns to her with a grin. "That's the Grand Canyon. Pretty awesome from up here, huh?"

"No way!" she gasps.

"Yep."

Her voice is tinged with wonder. "Holy cow. I had no idea it was so…"

"Massive?" he laughs, settling back into his seat so she can resume her vigil.

She nods, pressing her forehead back to the window to examine it more carefully. "It looks like a big crack in the Earth's crust, like the kind of thing you see on those science shows about how the planet was formed. How long is it?"

"Um, I think about 300 miles. Maybe a bit less. I'll Google it for you once we land. My parents took us when we were little. My brother was too scared to go anywhere near the edge, but I walked right up to the fence with my dad. It was breathtaking. You can't tell from up here, but there are hundreds of different variations of color in the strata. It's incredibly beautiful."

Evie sits back and looks at him. "You're *so* lucky."

Alistair can think of quite a few reasons why he disagrees, but sitting here with her is not one of them. "Why's that?"

"You've gotten to travel so much. I've never been anywhere."

"Well, we're in the process of changing that, aren't we? Maybe someday I'll take you to the Grand Canyon. It's only a few hours from Vegas. We could make a weekend of it." He chuckles. "Although it'd probably be a lot more fun for you once you're twenty-one."

Evie smiles. She likes hearing him speak of future plans like he thinks they might really do these things together. She doesn't know why he says stuff like this—stuff that will never actually happen—but it makes her feel all fuzzy inside. Not that she'll let any real hope blossom. Living in denial is a dangerous indulgence. But, just for this weekend, she's allowing herself the luxury of pretending they're a real couple. She isn't going to deal with reality until they are back in Sutterton. Even if it's only delaying the inevitable, she thinks she deserves a few more days of happiness.

So she leans over and kisses him softly. "I'd love that."

The flight to Los Angeles takes about five hours. Much as Alistair has been enjoying watching Evie's delight over the entire experience—once she got past her initial nerves, that is—he's relieved when the wheels touch the tarmac at LAX. As they disembark, he reminds the others to adjust the time on their phones back three hours. It's only 12:45 Pacific time, which means they still have most of the day to get settled and start searching for Charlie.

They head out onto the hot, sunny pavement. Alistair scans the line of vehicles waiting at the curb until he spots the bright yellow Hertz shuttle bus that will take them to the rental office.

Once they're onboard, Dylan pulls out his phone and announces he's telling Charlie he's in town and wants to see her. This reminds Evie that she promised to check in with her dad as soon as they land, so she gives him a quick call as the bus swerves its way through the busy airport traffic.

The shuttle jerks to a halt in front of the Hertz building a few minutes later. As Evie eagerly gets to her feet, Alistair takes her hand to help her disembark. She's hyper aware of every little touch, trying to memorize each detail so she can file them away in her 'happier times' memory bank.

"Wait here," he tells them when they go inside, gesturing toward a row of plastic chairs before joining the line for the counter.

A few minutes later, Alistair glances back. Jason is chatting with Evie, while Dylan ignores them, his eyes glued to his phone. Alistair wonders if Dylan has heard back from Charlie yet and hopes this will end up being easier than he expects. Maybe Charlie will actually be willing to meet up with them and save them trying to track her down. But, as he knows all too well, life rarely offers the easy path.

In less than ten minutes, Alistair has the keys to a red Toyota Prius and soon they set out for their hotel.

"Check it out," Alistair exclaims, pointing out the windshield as they round a corner. A block ahead is a squat, flat-roofed building with a gigantic pale brown ring mounted on the roof. "Randy's Donuts." he tells them.

"Wow!" Evie says. "That's one huge doughnut!"

Noticing her incredulous expression, Alistair adds, "It's a famous L.A. landmark."

She gives him a bemused smile and shrugs. "Never heard of it. Are we stopping there?"

Alistair laughs. "Maybe on the way home." He takes a left, then a quick right onto the on ramp for Highway 495.

"Charlie just replied," Dylan announces from the backseat.

Evie twists to look at him. Before she can react, Jason says. "*And*? What did she say? Did you tell her I'm with you?"

Dylan tears his eyes from his phone, glancing sideways at Jason with irritation. "Not yet. I'm trying not to freak her out. If she knows why we're all here, she might go silent again. She didn't say where she was, just that she'd message me tomorrow and maybe we could meet up."

Evie sighs with relief. "That's great!"

"It's a good start," Jason agrees. "But if you think you're gonna go meet her without me, you can think again."

With a sigh and an eye roll, Dylan mutters, "Yeah, yeah."

Once Alistair exits the highway, they begin working their way through traffic along Sunset Boulevard. Before long, he spots the eye-catching baby blue and white façade of the Palladian Hotel coming up on the right and turns into the curved driveway in front of the entrance.

Evie gasps, grabbing his wrist and squeezing. "This is it? We're staying *here*?"

Alistair just smiles at her and gets out to speak with the approaching valet. After handing over the keys, he takes Evie's hand and leads her through the glass doors into the lobby, Jason and Dylan trailing close behind.

They stride across the gleaming black and white checked floor to the reception desk. Evie's head twists and turns as she tries to take in all the details of the elaborate Art Deco lobby. Watching her from the corner of his eye, he tugs her deftly aside to prevent her from walking right into a tall potted palm.

The Palladian was built in 1927, two years before the stock market's most famous plunge, and the hotel is a monument to Roaring Twenties palatial excess. A narrow sixteen-storey tower rises above the wider first and second floor. The ground floor and mezzanine house not only the lobby, but the bar, a five-star restaurant, and several spacious meeting rooms.

High above the open-ceilinged lobby hangs a massive chandelier. Thousands of dangling cut crystals reflect multicolored dapples of light down on them from the stained glass windows around the perimeter of the second floor ceiling. Alistair hears Evie suck in her breath when she notices it.

Grinning to himself, he releases her hand and lets her ogle, sauntering up to the polished black counter. The word RECEPTION is mounted on the wall behind it in large golden letters. A perky blonde greets him with a smile.

He checks the name-tag pinned to her lapel and mirrors her smile. "Good afternoon, Lydia. I'd like to check in, please."

She looks him over, her ultra-white teeth gleaming. She seems to like what she sees. "Welcome to the Palladian, Mr....?"

"Sterling," Alistair tells her. "I have reservations for the next three nights."

After clicking away at her keyboard for a moment, Lydia looks back up at him. "Here it is. Two double rooms?"

"One double and one single with a king bed." He glances over his shoulder at Evie. She's sitting on a circular couch upholstered in rich maroon velvet talking animatedly with Dylan and Jason. "On different floors if possible," Alistair adds, turning back and flashing Lydia another charming grin.

"Everything looks good, Mr. Sterling. I'll just need your credit card, please."

Alistair hands over his card, again turning to watch Evie. When the check in is complete, he signs, gets their keys, and rejoins the others.

"You guys ready? We've got rooms 507 and 701" He hands Jason a key, picks up his and Evie's bags, and starts toward the elevator bank in the back of the lobby.

Each set of elevator doors has symmetrical swooping arches and fans in shades of taupe, maroon, and chocolate brown with gold filigree detailing. "Wow," Evie says, running her fingertips over the shiny enamel as they wait for a car. "This hotel is gorgeous!"

"It's all original Art Deco from the Twenties," Alistair tells her. He has an urge to touch her, to rub the small of her back, but he's carrying their bags. Instead he leans close to her ear and whispers, "I *thought* you might like this place. It's very Gatsby-esque."

"I love it." She turns to grin happily at him. Stepping closer, she looks like she's about to kiss him.

"I'm starving," Dylan interrupts with an eye roll. "You guys think we could go eat soon?"

With a ping, the elevator doors slide open and they step onboard. Alistair set their suitcases down and punches the floor buttons. They glow orange on the brass control panel.

264

"I'm gonna grab a quick shower and change before we head out. We'll meet you down in the lobby in, uh…" Alistair glances at his watch. "How about thirty minutes?"

When the doors open on the fifth floor, Dylan looks at his sister. "Are you bunking with me or…?" He gives her a teasing grin.

Evie feels her face go red. "Um…" Her forehead creases as her eyes dart, panic-stricken, to Alistalr for help.

Dylan laughs. "Don't freak out. I'm just hasslin' ya. C'mon Jase. We'll see you guys downstairs."

Jason and Dylan disembark, both still chuckling, and Alistair and Evie continue up to the seventh floor.

Before Alistair can grab it, Evie picks up her knapsack and steps into the hallway. "Which room are we in again?"

"701." After a quick look around, he points left. "This way." He stops at the end of the red-carpeted hallway and unlocks the door. Pushing it open with one arm, he holds it so Evie can pass in front of him.

Their room has a geometric-patterned parquet floor, with a plush black rug in the space between two queen-sized beds. Alistair's brows narrow when he sees them.

"Dammit," he sighs, "I specifically requested one king." He drops his bag to the floor and strides over to the black retro-style phone on the nightstand. "Sorry. I'll have to call down and get our room switched."

"Don't."

He looks at Evie in surprise, the hand holding the receiver paused midway to his ear.

"This room is amazing. I don't wanna move. So what if we have an extra bed?" She tosses her bag into the middle of it. "We can spread our stuff out on it and steal the pillows if we need more."

Evie's happy grin settles it. He hangs up the phone and goes to her, sliding his hands around her waist. Gazing down into those pretty blue eyes, he says, "You sure? I just want this to be perfect."

She stands on her tiptoes and presses her lips to his. "It *is* perfect. I've never stayed in a hotel before, and this one is incredible."

Alistair kisses the tip of her nose. "I'm glad you like it." He turns around and pulls off his t-shirt, tossing it carelessly onto the bed. When he turns back to her, he catches her staring. He grins, recognizing the look in her eyes. With a glance at the clock on the nightstand, he moves in close again. "I'm jumping in the shower to wash all the travel-grime off." He waggles his eyebrows. "Care to join me?"

Another adorable flush spreads over Evie's face. "Oh…um…" She seems surprised by his suggestion. "I think I'm okay for now," she mumbles, turning her back to him and unzipping her bag.

"Suit yourself," he says. "There's a Jacuzzi tub, so maybe we can try that out later."

She whirls back to him, excitement once more overtaking her. "There is?"

Before he can reply, she races to the bathroom. "Holy cow! This bathroom is twice the size of ours at home! The tub is massive! And is that shower curtain real velvet?"

Alistair comes in to find her rubbing the black and white shower curtain between two fingers, wearing an astonished look. Her clear delight at everything makes him feel all warm and tingly inside. And he keeps looking for new ways to surprise her, to please her, to be the source of that expression, over and over. Every time she smiles, an immense wave of pleasure rushes through him. His eyes land on the fancy miniature toiletries on a silver tray beside the sink. "See those?" He tilts his chin in their direction.

Evie's attention shifts to the little bottles and wrapped packages. She picks them up one by one. "Luxurious Oleander shampoo. Intense Moisturizing conditioner. Invigorating Oleander shower gel. Nourishing Oleander body lotion. French-milled bath bar, face bar, shower cap. Oh my God— there's even a little sewing kit and shoe polish!"

"You can keep all that stuff," he tells her. "The housekeeping staff will replace them every day anyway. Take whatever you want."

He turns on the water in the shower and unzips his fly, glancing over his shoulder as he hears the door close. She's decided to give him privacy. He's slightly disappointed, but with one glance at the tub, he starts thinking of ways they can enjoy it together later, when they aren't in any hurry.

Of course, such thoughts during his shower keep his mind decidedly distracted, and when he emerges from the bathroom several minutes later wearing nothing but a fluffy black towel, he's pleased to note they still have almost fifteen minutes before they need to head downstairs.

Evie's propped against the pillows on the closest bed, flipping through the Guide to Los Angeles she found on the desk. She's still wearing her jeans and t-shirt, although her purple hoodie is now draped over a chair.

"You haven't changed yet," he observes, stretching out across the bed beside her and giving her a lazy smile.

She sets the book on the bedside table and looks at him, one eyebrow arched. "Neither have you."

"True." Alistair reaches for the hem of her t-shirt and fiddles with it. "Guess you'd better take this off then." He tugs it up over her head, exposing her beige bra. It's utilitarian, nothing fancy, but the sight of all that creamy flesh surrounding it, not to mention her nipples poking against the cotton, makes him even harder than he'd been in the shower. With a wicked smile, he lowers his lips to one fabric-covered peak.

She sucks in a breath. "We don't have time to..."

His eyes rise to hers. "Trust me," he whispers. "This lesson is what's known as a 'quickie.'"

Evie's cheeks are flushed and her hair is still a bit disheveled as she hurries across the lobby toward Dylan and Jason, who are waiting in red high-backed chairs near the doors. Alistair trails a few feet behind her.

Dylan takes one look at them and snorts, shaking his head. "*Really*?" he hisses. "You two couldn't even wait a few more hours?"

Her face grows even hotter. Leave it to her brother to notice and comment on anything he thinks will make her uncomfortable. "What? We're here. C'mon, let's go."

She hears Alistair chuckle behind her. He doesn't say a word, just slides his fingers through hers and tugs her toward the entrance as the guys get up and follow.

Alistair hails a cab and asks to be taken to Hollywood Boulevard. He gets in the front with the driver, leaving the other three to squeeze into the back. It's a compact car, and the backseat is cramped. Evie finds herself sandwiched between her brother and her ex. Though the sides of their bodies are touching, she can't help noticing that Jason seems to be avoiding her gaze. When she tries to make small talk, he replies in little more than monosyllabic grunts. Evie frowns, wondering if he's upset with her, although she knows he's probably just worried about his sister.

The taxi lets them out at Vine, and they make their way along the tourist-infested sidewalk until Alistair spots a 1950's style diner that seems slightly less crowded than the other eateries they've passed. It's early afternoon, but their bodies are still on East Coast time and their stomachs are grumbling.

After lunch, they continue walking along Hollywood Boulevard, passing the Walk of Fame and the Hollywood and Highland Center, which is a huge complex containing a shopping mall, nightclubs and the Dolby Theatre where the Academy Awards are held. Further along, they stop to check out the famous hand and footprints in the cement in front of TCL Chinese Theatre. Evie tries to absorb everything, wide-eyed and delighted.

Her brother is less interested. He keeps checking his phone, impatient for a message from Charlie. To Evie's relief, Jason's reticence improves a little once he eats, but he still looks like he can think of a dozen places he'd rather be. She tries not to

268

worry about it; if he has issues with her being with Alistair, that's Jason's problem, not hers.

She and Alistair hold hands while they walk, and he keeps shooting her little smiles that make her suspect he's enjoying himself just as much as she is.

Once they're back out on the sidewalk, standing between a guy in a Spiderman costume and a woman dressed as Elsa from the movie *Frozen*, Jason turns to Alistair and Evie. "Y'know, with the time change and all, I'm actually pretty beat. You guys mind if Dyl and I head back to the hotel? We can meet you for breakfast tomorrow or whatever."

"Yeah, we wanna try to catch the basketball game," Dylan says.

"I guess that's fine. Text me so I know you got in safely," Evie tells him. "And let me know if you hear anything from Charlie."

The boys agree. A row of cabs waits along the curb, so they climb into the front one and wave goodbye.

As Evie watches their taxi speed off, she feels Alistair's hand on the small of her back. "*Now* what do you want to do?" he asks. His lips are right by her ear, and it gives her a shiver. Even though it's been over a month since they first hooked up, her body still reacts like a jolt of electricity passes between them each time he's close.

She turns to face him, looking up into those penetrating green eyes, studying him, trying to see what lies beneath the calm surface. The words 'I love you' rise unbidden to her lips, but she forces them back down. She does love him; there's no question of it now. She knows it's going to be excruciating when the time comes to admit it, and he inevitably tells her they have to put a stop to all this.

Instead of replying, she shrugs and slides her arms around his waist, rising up on her toes to kiss him. She intends to enjoy every second of this weekend with Alistair. Their future, whether together or—more likely—separate, can wait.

Chapter 22

Sunlight slices through the slit where the hotel room's heavy drapes meet, and the glowing stripe across Evie's face rouses her. She squints into the glare, rolling over in Alistair's sleeping embrace in an attempt to re-find her sweet spot, but it's no use—her bladder is insistent. Pushing back the sheets, she stumbles half-awake to the bathroom.

Last night had by far been the best night of her life. After Dylan and Jason went back to the hotel, they'd walked hand in hand for a while, just taking in the sights. Further along Hollywood Boulevard, Evie had pointed out a billboard for a movie she was curious about. The next thing she'd known, Alistair had spun them around and taken her back to the Chinese Theatre, insisting they see it. Armed with a massive box of popcorn, they'd settled into plush red seats, and once the popcorn was gone, he'd held her hand for the entire movie. Evie'd had trouble concentrating on the action on screen; all her thoughts had been on the man beside her.

After the movie, Alistair had taken her to dinner at a little Thai place. She'd never had Thai before, so he'd ordered for both of them, and they had shared some delicious, if a bit spicy, dishes. They'd walked around a while longer, then hailed a cab and gone back to the hotel.

The minute they'd stepped inside their room, Alistair had gone straight to the bathroom to fill the Jacuzzi. A few minutes later, as she'd been texting her dad to assure him everyone was fine, he'd called her.

"Ooooh Evie?" She'd heard splashing. "This would be a lot more fun if you actually joined me." He'd sung the word *joined*, making her laugh.

"Coming!" She'd gotten up and pulled open the closet to find the fluffy white robes she'd spotted earlier. Evie had quickly shed her clothes and put one of them on. It was made of the fuzziest, softest cotton she'd ever felt against her skin, and made her old threadbare robe back home seem like a rag.

Steam billowed from the open bathroom door, and as she'd stepped inside, a hazy cloud had enveloped her. Biting her lower lip, Evie had slid the robe from her shoulders before turning to the foam-filled tub.

Alistair had just stared at her, one arm resting along the top of the porcelain. The water sloshed as he'd moved over and she'd gingerly stepped in, sinking into the foam beside him. When she'd been submerged to her chin beneath a thick layer of bubbles, his leg pressed against hers, she'd met his eyes and smiled. "I've never had a bath with anyone before. Well, other than Dyl when we were small, but I'm pretty sure that doesn't count."

"Yeah, sharing a tub with kid brothers is definitely *not* the same," he'd agreed. Then he'd grabbed the soap. "Turn around."

Evie had carefully shifted her body until she'd been sitting between his legs with her back to him. His warm, soapy hands had slid up her back to cup her shoulders, and she'd shivered again.

"You can't possibly be chilly?"

"No...I'm just...no."

Alistair had chuckled softly as his fingers ran over her skin.

Smiling to herself as she washes her hands in the marble sink, Evie remembers how he'd oh-so-gently and carefully soaped her upper back and arms, and how she'd turned around to return the favor. He hadn't let her get very far before pulling her into a deep kiss. And not many minutes later, they'd abandoned the foam-filled tub for the bathroom counter…and then the bed. It had been well past midnight before they'd fallen asleep curled up in an exhausted, blissful tangle of sheets and limbs.

She pads back to the bed and slips in beside Alistair again. He rolls over to face her, his eyelashes fluttering open and his lips curving into a smile. "Morning," he murmurs, leaning in to kiss her.

His stubble scratches her chin, just as it had that other morning they'd woken up together so many weeks before. But she doesn't mind, in fact it's actually kind of…

The telephone on the nightstand rings. With a groan, Alistair flings an arm behind him and drags the receiver to his ear.

"Lo?" he grunts, not bothering to hide his annoyance. After listening for a few seconds, he pushes it across the pillow toward her, whispering, "It's your bro."

Evie takes the phone with a small sigh. "Morning, Dyl." Her tone is only slightly more chipper than Alistair's.

Dylan doesn't waste a single breath on greetings. "I got a reply. She wants me to meet her at the entrance to the Santa Monica Pier at noon."

"That's great!" Evie leans over until she can see the clock. "It's just past nine, so we still have lots of time. Wanna meet us downstairs for breakfast in, say, half an hour?"

There's a pause, during which she hears her brother and Jason muttering in the background.

"We just woke up. Give us forty-five." Without waiting to find out if she agrees, he hangs up.

Evie hands the receiver back to Alistair and explains that they need to head to the pier in a few hours.

"Excellent. I wanted to take you down to the beach today, anyway." He pulls her toward him and kisses her again. "Hmm. Forty-five minutes, huh? That gives us plenty of time."

Evie laughs. "For what?"

"This." He dives under the blanket and tugs it up over of both of them.

After breakfast, they climb back into the rented Prius and make their way west to Santa Monica and the beach. It's a bright, beautiful day, typical L.A. weather, according to Alistair. Evie's glad she had the forethought to pack her only pair of sunglasses.

She stares out the window at their surroundings, grateful she's in the passenger seat and not squished into the back. She's sure she's not just imaging that Jason is still acting kind of weird. He isn't ignoring her exactly, but he definitely seems distant. He's quiet and withdrawn, and when he does speak, it's mostly to Dylan. Any conversation with her or Alistair is limited to the most pressing topic: finding his sister. Evie tries not to be bothered by it, but she has to admit it stings a little. Not enough to put a damper on her high spirits, though. She's happier than she's been in years. Some of this is due to the excitement of the trip, but she knows the vast majority of it is because of the man beside her.

As it's Friday, the beach isn't swarming with people, and Alistair finds a parking spot not far from the Santa Monica Pier. Evie steps out of the car and takes it all in, amazed. The whole pier is covered with a carnival midway: huge roller coaster, loud colorful booths, smaller rides, and the crowning grace: a massive Ferris wheel so tall she's sure you can probably see the entire city of Los Angeles from the top.

"Wow," she exhales.

"You're not scared of heights, are you?" Alistair asks, standing beside her.

Evie glances up at him, smiling. "Nope. Can we go on that Ferris wheel?"

"Absolutely." Alistair turns to Dylan. "Where did she say to meet her?"

Scanning his phone again, Dylan replies, "She just said by the entrance." He looks up and glances around. "Where do ya think she means?"

Alistair points at the blue and white arched sign at the front of the pier. It reads:

SANTA MONICA
* YACHT HARBOR *
SPORT FISHING * BOATING
Cafes

"Probably under that."

They walk over to the sign and Dylan leans against one of the posts. Seagulls scream at each other as they duel over scraps on the sand below.

"It's only eleven-fifteen," Evie says, glancing at her phone. "Why don't we split up for a bit? Dyl and Jason can come back at noon and meet Charlie, and we'll find you here in about an hour. Sound good?"

"Works for me," Alistair says, sliding an arm over her shoulders.

Dylan agrees. "I'm cool with that. See you guys in an hour or so."

Jason just nods, his expression unreadable behind his sunglasses as they part ways in opposite directions.

"Jason doesn't like me much," Alistair observes once they're out of earshot. He takes Evie's hand and gives it a squeeze, smiling to show he isn't concerned about it.

Evie frowns. "That's not true. He totally appreciates you flying us out here to look for his sister. I know he does."

Alistair chuckles. "That's not what I meant and you know it. I've seen the worried glances you've been giving him. And I've also noticed how aloof he's being with you. You're not used to him giving you the cold shoulder, are you?"

274

Evie feels blood rush to her face, and breaks eye contact to gaze at the waves crashing against the sand. "I guess not," she mutters. "But I kind of understand why he's sorta weirded out being around us."

"Yeah, I get that, too. But it bothers you, doesn't it?"

"A bit," she admits.

He's silent for a few moments as they resume walking along the boardwalk that parallels the ocean. Then he says, "You think we should maybe cut down on the PDA around him?"

Darting her eyes to his, she says, "Uh…no. I'm fine with how we are. He'll get over it."

"Good." Alistair smiles.

"Good?"

"Good." He stops again and slips his arms around her, leaning in for a kiss. "Because I don't really want to."

Evie presses her body to his and rests her cheek against his shoulder. "Me neither," she whispers, staring out at the rolling sea.

When they return to the pier, Jason and Dylan are waiting below the arched sign staring at their phones.

"Any sign of her?" Evie asks.

Her brother glances up at the sound of her voice and sighs. "Not yet."

"Well, it's only twenty after. Maybe she's running late."

"Yeah. Maybe," Jason says. He looks discouraged. "We'll see."

They wait under the sign for a while, Jason and Dylan checking their messages every ten seconds while Alistair and Evie watch in concerned silence. They're standing a few feet apart, no longer touching, although she doesn't know if that's a deliberate choice on Alistair's part.

Ten more minutes go by. Evie approaches her brother. "You texting her again?"

"Duh," Dylan replies irritably. "She's not answering. Yet."

Evie frowns, but doesn't comment.

The four of them wait, shuffling from foot to foot and growing more frustrated. At last Alistair speaks up. "C'mon guys. She's clearly not gonna show, and we're wasting a beautiful day at the beach standing around waiting. Let's go grab some food up on the pier and try to have some fun. I'm sure Dylan will hear from her soon, and you can arrange another time to meet."

Jason and Dylan glance at each other, then back at Alistair and Evie. "Actually," Jason says, "I think we're gonna try to track down my dad. I looked up the address of one of his buddies out here this morning. We'll just take the bus and meet you guys back at the hotel later."

Evie opens her mouth to protest. She's responsible for her brother during this trip; she can't just let him roam the city without her. But before she can get the words out, Dylan holds up his palm.

"I know what you're gonna say. But I'm fine. *We're* fine. Jason and I'll stick together, and we'll text if we find out anything. And if by some chance we get lost, we'll just call a cab to take us back to the hotel."

Alistair pulls his wallet from his pocket, withdraws several twenties, and hands them to Jason. "This should take care of your lunch and cab fare. Skip the bus. It's easier—not to mention safer—to just cab or Uber."

"Alistair, no," Evie protests. "We should go with them."

"And what would that really accomplish, other than to ease your worry? They don't need us for this. Jason's an adult. Let them go play detective. We all have phones, so they can reach us anytime."

She bites her lower lip, her eyes darting to each of them in turn. Finally she sighs. "Okay. Dyl, promise you'll check in with me at least once an hour?"

Dylan rolls his eyes at her for what feels like the hundredth time. "Jesus, Evie. You're not my goddamn mother, you know."

She cringes. Over the past two years, she's tried her best to step into the hole losing their mom has left, but she knows those sensible shoes are impossible to fill. Her brother misses her as much as Evie does. She may not deserve his snark, but she has to admit, Dylan's both careful and capable. Of course, Dad wouldn't approve of them separating even for just a few hours—but maybe this is one little adventure he doesn't need to know about.

Bracing her hands on her hips, Evie attempts to look strict. "Dad told you you had to listen to me, remember?"

The glare Dylan shoots her almost makes her wince again, but she manages to maintain her stern expression.

With yet another eye-roll, he spits, "Fine. I'll text ya."

"Great." Evie forces a smile. "We'll see you guys back at the hotel tonight, then."

Her brother pulls the brim of his baseball cap lower and stalks toward the road. With a snort and a shake of his head, Jason glances at Evie, mutters "Later," and hurries after him.

Evie turns to Alistair. Her brow is furrowed, and she looks like she's considering going after them.

"Don't worry. They'll be fine," Alistair assures her, sliding an arm around her and pulling her against his side. "You're so parental with him. It's kinda cute, although it clearly makes him salty as hell." He grins. "You'll make a great mom someday."

"You think?" She looks up at him in surprise.

He kisses the top of her head. "I'm sure of it."

With a smile, she asks, "Now what? Want to go on some rides?"

"I think we should save that until later. The whole pier lights up at sunset. It also gets more crowded, but in my opinion, it's worth the wait."

"So what do you want to do between now and then? Can we swim in the ocean?"

He tilts his head to look up at the cloudless blue sky as if he's thinking hard. "Hmm. I think that can be arranged. Let's walk down the beach toward Venice and see if we can find a good place to get some lunch. Then a swim."

"I thought you weren't supposed to go swimming right after eating?" Evie laughs.

"I'm pretty sure that's just an old wives' tale. You're welcome to sit on the sand if you like, but I intend to jump into those waves first chance I get."

They continue along the boardwalk in the opposite direction from before. For almost half an hour they stroll hand in hand, the beach-side scenery changing from hotels and expensive oceanfront condos to brightly colored shops blaring loud music with their wares spread on tables along the sidewalk.

"This is Venice Beach," Alistair tells her, indicating the much busier area around them.

Before Evie can comment, he pulls her aside as two teenage boys on skateboards whiz by. Although she's shocked, instead of being annoyed, she laughs. "Guess I'd better pay more attention to where I'm going instead of gawking at stuff."

"Why don't we get off the boardwalk for a bit? We could head over there and get something to eat." Alistair indicates a row of stalls selling every type of food imaginable. The intoxicating aromas of sizzling meat and vegetables mixed with exotic spices fill her nostrils and her stomach rumbles in anticipation.

"Best idea yet."

After eating, they put on their swimsuits at the beach changing station, dump their stuff in a pile on the sand and, hand in hand, run into the surf. Evie took swimming lessons as a kid at the community pool, so although she isn't a strong swimmer, she isn't afraid of the water. It's a bit cold, but they splash and play in the waves until both are panting and covered in goosebumps. When Alistair notices Evie shivering, he insists they go ashore and dry off.

She spreads across her towel and the hot sun warms her up in no time. It's just like how she'd imagined a California day at the beach. Reaching into her bag, she pulls out her sunscreen and rubs the lotion over all exposed skin. It smells of coconut, and brings back childhood memories of eating freeze pops with her mom and Dylan outside the coffee shop on a hot day.

As Evie begins massaging a dollop into her shoulders, she feels Alistair's fingers on her arm. "Let me do that for you," he says, taking the bottle. His strong hands glide over her skin; they're warm and firm, and his touch brings back vivid memories of last night that chase away any lingering chill. She has a sudden urge to spin around and kiss him. Instead, she closes her eyes and tries to remember the sensation of his lips on hers.

They relax for a while, chatting softly and dozing in the sun for almost an hour, but eventually not only is Evie overheated, she's also getting restless. She's never been the kind of girl who sunbathes all day; she'd rather be up doing things. At her urging, they change into their clothes and head back toward the Santa Monica Pier.

A few blocks from the car, Evie realizes she hasn't heard a word from her brother since they left. She pauses in the shade of a copse of palms to pull out her phone. There are no new texts, but that doesn't surprise her. She types: *Did you hear from Charlie yet?*

A few minutes later, her brother replies: *No. But we have another address to check.*

Evie relays this to Alistair, who asks where it is. She texts Dylan his question and gets a quick reply: *247 Bianca Cres. Why?*

Alistair leans over to read her phone. Then he pulls out his own and plugs in the address. He frowns. "Shit. That's a pretty sketchy part of town, and it'll be sundown soon. Tell him not to go right now." He pauses, adding, "Say I'll drive us there in the morning."

With a worried frown, Evie taps out the message. "I'd rather they didn't run around the city alone anyway. Dad'd kill me if he knew I let Dylan go off without us. We have to stay with him tomorrow. I feel guilty enough about today."

Alistair slides an arm around her shoulder. "They're fine. Tell them to head back to the hotel and we'll meet them there in a couple hours."

"A couple hours? Why?"

"We haven't gone on the Ferris Wheel yet. And once they're back in their room, they'll probably end up playing *Mobile Strike* for hours. Nothing to worry about."

Her brow furrows as she contemplates his words. "I guess you're right."

"I usually am," he chuckles, leaning in to kiss her still-pursed lips. This elicits a small smile, which had been his goal all along.

The view from the Ferris wheel as the setting sun paints the sky purple, pink, and orange over the ocean is possibly the most beautiful thing Evie has ever seen. But no matter how stunning the scenery is, she's unable to fully enjoy it. She's far too distracted by the man in whose arms she's wrapped, and what their future holds.

It's not just how she feels about him, but how he makes her feel about herself. How she's become more confident since she met him. How she feels more like the woman she's turning into than the child she once was. And how all too soon she will be alone again. These tumultuous thoughts distract her from the magnificent sunset.

Instead of admiring the view, Evie keeps turning back to Alistair. She nuzzles her nose into his neck and plants soft kisses along his jawline. He groans softly in response, and the sound sends shivers up her spine. She grows bolder. Snuggling closer, she closes her eyes and presses her lips to his.

When they break apart, Evie is caught in his gaze as he stares at her, running his fingers gently down her cheek. His expression is intense, yet soft at the same time, like he's trying to peer deep inside her. She's never had any guy look at her like that before, and for a moment she wonders if he could be feeling the same thing she's feeling.

If only. If only he loved me, too, then maybe we could figure out some way to make this—us—work. She sighs, soft and nearly inaudible, and kisses him again so he doesn't glimpse the sadness she's sure has seeped into her eyes.

A few minutes later, as they watch the sun flare its dying breath before extinguishing itself in the Pacific, she laces her fingers through Alistair's and makes a wish—a futile, childish wish, but an honest one just the same.

With everything in her, Evie wishes this never has to end.

Chapter 23

A loud rap at the hotel room door jolts Alistair from an uneasy sleep. With a soft sigh, he sits up. He'd been dreaming of Paul and Michelle's betrayal again—a dream that used to plague him almost every night, but over the past month has barely made an appearance. Looking down at the disheveled blonde hair and sun-kissed cheek of the sleeping girl beside him, he smiles. He has a pretty good idea why the reoccurring nightmare went away.

Running his fingers through his hair, he retrieves his bathrobe from the floor and shuffles over to answer the door.

It's Dylan. He is pale, with dark circles shadowing his eyes. Clearly the boy didn't get much sleep. Seeing Alistair, Dylan frowns. "Where's Evie? You guys not up yet?"

Alistair snorts. "What was your first clue? Your sister's still out, so maybe try to keep your voice down."

"Well, time for her to wake up then." Dylan pushes past Alistair into the room. Alistair quickly moves to block his view of the bed in case Evie isn't decent.

"Evie! Get your lazy ass outta bed! We need to go get Charlie," Dylan calls around him.

Hearing a muffled yawn from behind, Alistair glances over his shoulder to see Evie sit up and drag on a matching robe.

"I'm up," she mutters, her voice full of just-awoke roughness. Alistair can't hold back a grin. He hopes her brother will soon get the hell out of their room so he can drag her back into bed for another twenty minutes or so.

Dylan steps around Alistair to face her. "Good."

"What's the big hurry?" Evie asks, stifling another yawn with the back of her hand.

Squaring his jaw, Dylan replies, "Get dressed. We need to go. Alistair said he'd drive."

With a sigh, she relents, "Fine. We'll meet you downstairs in ten minutes."

"Whatever." Dylan walks out, leaving the door wide open to drift slowly closed.

Forty-five minutes later, they pull up alongside the curb in front of a shabby, gray stucco three-storey apartment building. The lawn—if you can call it that—is mainly comprised of tall weeds and crabgrass, pock-marked here and there with bare dirt patches. Even the broken bits of wood, rusty bicycle parts, and garbage strewn about can't hide the fact that it hasn't had even the most basic tending in a very long time.

Evie frowns as she scans the property. There are no signs of life, not even a barking dog or stalking cat. "You sure this is the right place?" she asks, swiveling to regard Jason and Dylan doubtfully.

Her brother gives her a grim nod. "It's the address she gave me."

Jason and Dylan jump from the car. Evie swings her door open to join them, but before she can step out, Jason turns back to her with a raised hand. "You two better wait here. We won't be long."

Evie's eyes dart to Alistair. He frowns, but nods, so she waves the boys on. "Text if you want us to come in," she calls as they stride up the overgrown walkway to the front steps.

Dylan barely glances back at her and they both seem to be laughing as they go inside. The glass set into the front door is spider webbed with cracks. It's so discolored the guys disappear from view the moment it swings shut behind them.

Evie locks her door. In this part of town it makes her feel safer. She tries to distract her anxiety by playing with the radio and chatting with Alistair about *The Great Gatsby*, but nothing helps. This morning not even his usual ability to relax her works. She's fidgety and on edge, staring out the window at the grubby front door as if they'll reappear by her sheer will alone.

Evie sighs with relief when she at last sees Dylan and Jason step out into the sunshine twenty minutes later. Charlie isn't with them. "Well?" she asks the moment they get in the car.

Jason smiles, the first genuine grin she's seen on his face in days. "She's there. We talked to her. I think she'll agree to come home with us tomorrow."

The weight that had been sitting in the pit of Evie's stomach vanishes, and she straightens up in her seat. "Awesome! What did she say? And why didn't she come out with you?"

Shrugging, Jason replies, "She wants to talk to Dad first, says he's coming back tonight. I gave her my phone so she can reach us." His smile has fallen away, but he still looks hopeful.

"The place is a total dump," Dylan says. "Probably crawlin' with roaches." He shudders, eyeing the apartment building with revulsion. "She needs to get outta there. We're coming back to get her tomorrow morning either way, aren't we, Jase?"

Jason nods. Evie's eyebrows arch at the 'either way' comment, but she decides not to question him about it. Hopefully one of them will hear from Charlie, and when they return tomorrow it will be to pick her up willingly, not to attempt to force her to come home.

"How did she look?" Evie asks instead.

Dylan and Jason glance at each other.

"She seemed glad to see us," Jason says, "and I think she *was*, but I also think she was kinda faking it. Her good mood, I mean. I could tell she wasn't really happy—not with Dad, not with living in that place, not with anything, really. I think she'll come home with us even if he does try to talk her into staying. Which he'd better not."

"Hopefully not," Evie agrees. She shifts to face forward again. Alistair has opted to keep his thoughts to himself. He catches her eye, arching a brow. When she nods that she's ready to go, he starts the engine.

As they drive back toward the hotel along a busy boulevard, Evie's stomach rumbles. Loudly. Alistair grins, glancing over at her. "Hungry?"

"I am," Dylan interjects before his sister can reply.

Jason pipes up. "Me, too."

"Okay," Alistair says. "What do you guys want to eat, then?"

"Anything's fine," Evie replies. Her eyes land on a statue of a huge cartoon taco on top of a building and her belly gurgles again. She points out the window. "How about Mexican? That place you took me to in Lake Placid was really good."

With a quick turn of the wheel, Alistair slides into an empty spot not far past the taco stand. He puts the car in park and turns to face them. "I have an idea."

"Other than eating tacos, you mean?" Dylan asks sarcastically, but Evie notes his smile as he says it. Her brother's mood has definitely improved since seeing Charlie.

Alistair ignores him. "How about we grab take-out, and I drive us up by the Hollywood sign? There's a park below it where we can sit and eat and take in the view. What do you say?'

Evie's face lights up. "That'd be awesome!"

Dylan and Jason agree, and a few minutes later they're back in the car clutching two large paper bags while Alistair programs their new destination into the GPS. Mouth-watering aromas fill the vehicle as they start the winding drive up to the Hollywood Hills where the famous white sign stands sentinel over the city.

At last, Alistair pulls over to the shoulder along a curve in the road, parking behind a long row of vehicles. Tourists armed with cameras and phones are snapping photos of both the panoramic view of the city below and the huge Hollywood sign on the side of the hill above.

Evie walks to the barrier. Below her is a sprawling vista of mountains, valleys, tiny homes, undulating roads, and behind them, heat waves make the air ripple over the busy city. Far in the distance, haze shimmers over the ocean. A dark strip of an island rises in the distance.

"Wow," she breathes.

Alistair's arms slide around her waist from behind. "Yep."

She twists her head to look up at him. He's gazing down at the view, a wistful gleam in his eyes, and Evie wonders what he's thinking about.

Before she can ask, he seems to re-gather himself, straightening and turning back to the road. "The park's over there," he points. "Let's go find a good place to eat."

They luck upon an empty picnic table in the shade of some trees and unpack their food. Evie is quiet as she eats, listening to the others and taking in their surroundings: locals strolling with their dogs, packs of chattering tourists, birds calling each other as they fly from treetop to treetop. In the playground on the far side of the field, children run about, alternately shrieking in glee or howling in agony. She's enraptured by it all.

After lunch, Jason and Dylan once again opt to walk around and explore to give Alistair and Evie some alone time. Although Jason's attitude has been more upbeat since seeing his sister, it's still a small relief for Evie when the boys stroll away. She wants to cherish every second with Alistair before they're forced back to reality and certain separation.

He tosses out their garbage, then returns to sit with her. Reaching for her fingers across the table, he squeezes them. "Want to go for a walk, too?"

Alistair takes her hand in his as they get up. Again she marvels at how natural it feels holding hands with the man she loves. Her chest tightens with another regretful pang. Steeling herself, she pushes her sadness aside and tries to focus on the here and now as they make their way back to the road.

They walk around the bend and stop at the wide lookout, sliding into a gap at the wall between two groups of tourists. Raising a hand to shield her eyes from the sun, Evie takes in the city below.

For a while they just stand there, hip to hip, in silence, Alistair's hand resting lightly on top of hers on the ledge.

"My father brought us out here on vacation the summer after Mom died," he says quietly, his gaze fixed on the distant ocean. "My aunt and uncle used to live here, and we always stayed with them. I think Dad thought it would be a good distraction. To take our mind off stuff, you know?"

Though Evie's own dad had neither the money nor the time to take them away and distract them, she gets it all too well. "Yeah. But it didn't work, did it?"

"Nope. Not at all."

Evie glances up at him again. He still seems lost in thought. She flips the hand beneath his palm and laces her fingers through his.

"All my memories of L.A. were as a family. So being at my aunt and uncle's house, or eating at their favorite restaurant, or going to Disneyland—those were all things we'd done with Mom. Visiting those places without her just felt so..." He pauses, sighing. "So *wrong*. Her absence was more noticeable than ever. It was *brutal*. I think for Paul, too. But Dad just didn't get it."

Evie's squeezes his hand. She frowns as something else occurs to her. "So does being here now, with me...?"

At last Alistair looks down at her. With his free hand, he pushes a loose strand of hair off her cheek and tucks it behind her ear. A small smile curves his lips as he says, "Yes. It makes me miss her. For sure. But I don't mind bringing you here. Not at all. Thanks to you, I'm making new, happy memories to help alleviate the sad ones."

He leans in and kisses her, and as he does, a chunk of her worry ebbs away.

When they return to their hotel room, Evie's eyes land on her knapsack in the corner, the edge of her laptop just visible through the gap in the half-closed zipper. *Crap!* Isn't she supposed to be working on homework and, if possible, her column while she's here? She promised her dad she'd keep on top of everything, and knows it's a big part of the reason he'd agreed to let her come. Sighing, she turns to Alistair. "What time did you tell the guys we'd head out for dinner?"

"Two more hours. I figured we were in no rush to eat again soon." He grins, coming closer and setting his hands on her hips. "Why? What did you have in mind?"

Evie braces a palm against his chest and steps out of his grasp. "Not that," she says with a chuckle. Seeing his face fall, she adds, "At least not right now. I really need to finish up the last of my homework, like I promised Dad. We've been so busy running around I haven't looked at it since the day before we left."

He laughs, holding up both hands in mock submission. "Far be it from me to disturb your studies. I'll just head down to the gym for an hour. That enough time for you?"

"Better give me an hour and a half."

Alistair changes into a t-shirt and running shorts. When he looks back at Evie, she's lying on her stomach on the bed, her feet kicked up behind her, staring at her laptop screen. He grins, leaning down kiss her cheek. "Maybe you'll have time to let me distract you a little when I get back?"

Evie lifts her eyes to his and smiles back. "Count on it."

He gives her a wink, and a moment later she hears the door click shut.

She looks over the files she'd last been working on and is happy to realize she's further along on her assignment than she'd thought. In less than an hour, she manages to finish the rest of it. Standing up to stretch, she wanders over to the window to look outside.

Their room faces west, and Evie can make out the blue line of the ocean between far off buildings. The sun is getting low on the horizon and the light over the water has warmed to the pale orange she knows will soon darken to pink. It brings to mind the sunset she and Alistair watched from the Ferris Wheel last night, and how content she'd felt snuggled in his arms.

Her previous melancholy returns in a flood. Tomorrow they're flying home, which means there won't be any more sweet moments like that one. By the time she watches another sunset, her relationship with Alistair will be over.

Evie wishes more than anything that it doesn't have to end, but she won't delude herself into thinking this can last. It can't. And it won't. She'd promised to tell him if she grew too attached, and though she's delayed honoring that promise until they're home, she intends to be honest with him. Then that will be it. End of story. Back to being single, back to focusing on her plans for her future. Back to living her old life until she's able to start her new one. As she really should be, anyway. But still. Ending things with him is going to be brutal.

Exhaling a deep sigh, she returns to the bed and flops across it. Alistair will be back in a half-hour. What should she do in the meantime? She pulls her laptop toward her and opens Miss Lonely Love's inbox. There are four new emails waiting; not a lot, but enough for her to scan to see if any would be a good fit for her column.

The first two questions are similar to ones she's answered recently, so she files them away. The third is from a teen wanting advice about whether she should bring a new boyfriend home to meet her strict father. Evie copies and pastes this letter into a Word document and starts typing a reply urging the writer to be honest with both the boyfriend and her parents, and encouraging her to introduce them.

Just as she finishes up her response, her phone buzzes on the nightstand. Grabbing it, she sees a text from Dylan: *Come here.*

Why? she replies.

A few seconds later, two new texts come in: *Just get down here.* And right after*: Now.*

Coming, Evie sends back with a frown. What's going on? Has he heard from Charlie? Maybe she's changed her mind about coming home with them?

Tucking her phone into the pocket of her hoodie, Evie grabs her key and heads out the door.

Alistair whistles softly to himself as he gets off the elevator. He'd done weight resistance for thirty minutes, ran on the treadmill for another thirty, and now hopes to distract Evie with a different kind of workout, although one he's sure will get both their hearts pumping.

As he steps into their room, he calls, "You done your homework yet?"

He gets no reply. Walking further in, he realizes Evie isn't here. He pulls out his phone to see if she's texted, but there are no new messages.

Huh. He'd hoped she'd wait for him, but she must have finished up, grown bored, and gone down to check on the boys.

Alistair's gaze falls on her laptop sitting open in the middle of their bed. *That's weird,* he thinks with a frown. It isn't like Evie to just leave it out like that. He sits on the edge of the bed and reaches to close the lid, planning to move it safely over to the dresser. The sudden shift of the mattress revives the darkened screen.

He doesn't mean to look. It wasn't his intention. But there it is, right in front of him. His eyes flare; his mouth falling open in shock.

On the screen is an open document. A letter. And not just any letter, a letter signed *Miss Lonely Love.*

No fucking way. It can't be. Not possible.

As he stares at it, something clicks, nearly audible in his brain, and suddenly everything makes sense. His gut drops and a deep wave of disappointment flows over him. It seems

290

Evie isn't the girl he'd thought she was after all. She's been keeping secrets from him, too.

Just like Michelle.

Just like his brother.

God! So many fucking lies! Why does everyone he cares about always lie to him? What had he ever done to deserve this? His stomach is roiling, bile rising. He feels like he's about to puke.

Alistair stands, backing away from the bed and the computer, but his eyes remain fixed on the evidence on the screen. His heart races. A fire ignites in his chest and spreads in waves until his entire body feels like it's bathed in flames. Sweat trickles down his temples and between his shoulder blades.

I'm such a fool! Such a massive motherfucking idiot!

Again.

Tearing away his eyes at last, he squeezes them shut and tries to breathe, just breathe.

Will I never learn my goddamned lesson?

Chapter 24

Evie's still shaking her head in amusement as she unlocks her hotel room door. Dylan had called her down to their room to demand she make a judgment call in a disagreement over a video game he and Jason were playing. Leave it to her brother to let her think there was some big emergency and freak her out for nothing.

Boys!

Inside, she finds Alistair lying on his back on the unused bed, her suitcase and various other items now on the floor. His arms are crossed behind his head, his gaze fixed on the ceiling.

"Hey. I was just down in the guys' room helping them settle some stupid argument..." She trails off, frowning. Alistair hasn't turned to her; he hasn't even moved. "What's up?" she asks, suddenly wary.

"Have a seat." He gestures toward the other bed, the one they've shared the past two nights. As her eyes slide to it, she notices her laptop still sitting, lid raised, in the middle of the bedspread. Right where she'd left it.

Oh crap! I didn't put it away. Did he see what I was working on. How could I be so dumb?

The screen is dark, allowing her some small hope he hadn't noticed the *Miss Lonely Love* letter she'd left open. She perches on the bed to face him, trying to hide her mounting alarm. Sliding one hand behind her, she casually closes the computer.

"Let me tell you a little story," Alistair says. His voice is strange. She's never heard him sound like this before. "Feel free to stop me if you think you've heard it before."

A soft exhalation slips through Evie's parted lips. It's almost, but not quite, a sigh. She braces her palms on the edge of the mattress and straightens her spine. With no small amount of trepidation, she says, "Okay."

For a few moments he stays silent, still staring straight up. Just as she's about to ask him what this is about, he starts, his tone controlled and even. "I was with my ex for a little over two years. She was pretty much my whole world. I'd never met anyone like her before. I'd never been in love. But Michelle wasn't like other girls. She was in a whole different league, and I fell hard. Looking back, it seems stupid, I guess, but at the time I was over the moon. I had no clue what she saw in me. I was just happy as hell she saw anything at all."

Evie frowns, wracking her brain. Why does this sound so familiar?

"By last fall, she was basically living with me. My brother Paul was away at college, and Dad was always working or schmoozing clients, so we had the house to ourselves most of the time.

"One day I got called downtown for a particularly stressful meeting with my father, leaving her alone at home. Which wasn't all that unusual. I didn't even think twice about it. And after the meeting, I was pretty upset, to say the least—"

"Why? What did he say to you?"

Alistair waves off her question. "Doesn't matter. As I was saying, I was upset. All I wanted was to get back to her. I'd bought a ring a few weeks earlier, and I decided I was going to propose as soon as I saw her."

Evie sucks in a breath. He was going to *propose*? It had been *that* serious?

"I wanted to get out of my dad's house and start a life with her as far away from him as possible.

"When I got home, I ran upstairs to find her. But before I could head to my room, I heard laughter from the other side of the house. From Paul's room."

Her mouth falls open, her gut clenching as the pieces begin to click into place.

Alistair lifts his head to finally look her in the eyes. "Do you know what I found, Evie? Can you guess?"

She doesn't reply. She just stares at him in shock.

"No? Still doesn't ring a bell?"

Words escape her. It's like she's frozen in place.

A pause. Then: "I found the love of my life in bed with my brother. But I think you already knew that."

She closes her eyes. She can't stand to look at him. There is no playfulness, no kindness, no affection whatsoever in his eyes anymore. They're just empty.

"I didn't know JAI was you," she strangles out. "I should have. But I didn't."

After what feels like hours pass, he speaks again, softer now. "Why didn't you tell me? That's the bit I can't quite wrap my head around. What possible reason could you have for lying to me about this?"

A soft sigh slips from her lips. "I…I was gonna tell you. I was, but—"

"You should have told me from the start," he says firmly. "That's why you wanted me to teach you about sex, wasn't it? So you'd have more experience to write your column? You were just using me?"

"No! I wasn't using you!" Her heart is sprinting. *This can't be happening!* "I did want more experience to answer questions, that much is true, but I also…I just wanted to be with you. I still do."

He laughs. It's cold and merciless.

"I can't deal with any more people lying to me. I just can't. It's a deal-breaker. Once we get back, I don't think we should see each other anymore."

Tears well up in the corners of her eyes. The last thing she wants is to cry in front of him, but the waterworks are about to start and she doesn't think she can stop them.

"I'm so sorry." She manages to get those three words out without her voice breaking, but it's close. Alistair is staring at the ceiling again, and in a way she's relieved. She doesn't have to see that empty expression. That look hurts more than any words he could say to her.

"I don't feel much like eating," he says. "Why don't you go have dinner with the guys? Just charge it to the room."

Evie doesn't feel much like dinner, either, let alone being social, but she isn't so dumb that she doesn't understand this is his way of asking her to leave him alone.

So she goes.

Instead of heading to her brother's room, Evie takes the elevator down to the lobby and slips into the ladies' washroom, locking herself into the stall furthest from the door. She needs some privacy to analyze what just happened and there's nowhere else she can think to go.

Alistair is JAI.

JAI is Alistair.

How much of an idiot am I that I didn't make the connection?

She tries to remember the content of JAI's letters. In the first few, he'd made it abundantly clear that he never wanted to fall in love again, never wanted to be in a relationship again. But she also recalls the way Alistair had looked at her at the lookout earlier, and yesterday on the Ferris Wheel, and a few weeks ago when they'd been walking in Lake Placid. No one has ever looked at her the way he does. Well, how he used to anyway. Could he have started to fall for her as well? Not that it matters anymore. Any feelings that might have been growing are out the window now.

Evie knows that JAI's attitude in his letters had improved over time. In his most recent one, he'd said he was considering forgiving his brother. And that he was no longer in love with his ex.

Michelle, her name is Michelle.

Both of which are *huge* for him. And the letter before that one? What had he said?

Oh God, he told Miss LL about me!

Her hands are shaking. She sits on the toilet seat and grips her shoulders to still them. He'd written that he thought she was honest. And that he trusted her. And now she's gone and blown that fragile trust all to hell. Just because she'd been too proud to share her secret identity with him. Or…maybe she'd just been ashamed? Had she thought he might laugh at her, that he'd ridicule the idea of someone as naïve as herself offering love advice?

Closing her eyes, she sighs into the crook of her elbow, long and deep and full of remorse. Yes, that's exactly it. She'd been ashamed. And now she's paying the price for it.

A huge lump forms in her throat. She can barely swallow. It's difficult to breathe. With a gasp of surrender, her tears begin to flow.

When Evie returns to the hotel room hours later, no lights are on. She can see well enough to know Alistair is under the blankets in the bed he'd been lying on earlier. His back is to her.

She had texted her brother from the lobby washroom to say she and Alistair wouldn't be joining them for dinner. Then she'd sat in there stewing for over an hour. She hadn't known what to do. She couldn't go back up to the room. She wasn't hungry. And she definitely didn't feel like talking to anyone. So, she'd left the hotel and just started walking.

She doesn't really know where she went, but she'd walked for a couple of hours, stopping only once to sit for a few minutes when she'd spotted an empty bench under a tree. She hadn't looked at her phone, so she has no idea what time she got back. She just knows her leg muscles ache and her feet are sore.

The clock on the nightstand reads 11:34. It's not even midnight, yet she is exhausted. She doesn't change into pajamas. She doesn't even brush her teeth. She just climbs into the cold, empty bed and huddles beneath the covers.

Though she's tired, sleep refuses to take her. Tossing and turning, never finding just the right position, she grows ever more frustrated. She can see the outline of Alistair's body in the other bed, just visible in the sliver of moonlight through the curtains. From the sound of his even breathing, he's deeply asleep. She's jealous. Her mind plays their last conversation on a loop, over and over until she wonders if she might go insane.

The worst part is that, for the first time, she's in love. Not with just any boy from school, but with someone who seems like he's perfect for her. Though they'd agreed they wouldn't fall for each other, Evie fell hard anyway. And she suspects there's a chance he might have felt the same. Well, there *was*, anyway, before she went and screwed it all up.

If only she'd figured out he was JAI before they'd crossed the friendship line.

If only she'd been honest with him about her column from the start.

If only she'd never fallen in love with him.

Gah! If only she had a damn time machine to go back and fix this! But she doesn't. And she can't.

Tears well up again, and she rolls away from him. Though she's sure sleep won't come at all, after a while she cries herself into an uneasy slumber.

When Evie wakes the next morning, she can hear the shower running, and through sticky eyes sees the other bed is empty. With a deep sigh, she pushes back the covers and swings her legs to the floor. They still ache from her long walk last night. And her head throbs. It feels like a hangover. As she remembers all that happened, she supposes it is. Just not the kind you get from drinking.

Realizing she's still wearing yesterday's clothes, she hurries to change before Alistair returns. They soon have to leave to get Charlie and go to the airport, so she begins packing her bag. Evie hopes Jason's sister will agree to come with them, because she's not sure she can handle any more drama right now.

She grabs her phone to check her messages. There's a text from Grace: *So, how's Cali? Everything amazing? Find C yet?*

Evie texts back: *Yes, going to see her soon & hopefully bring her home. Tell you the rest later.*

She knows that last bit will drive her friend crazy, but she can't bear to explain what's happened yet. And definitely not over text.

The bathroom door opens and Alistair emerges. Evie's surprised to see he's already fully dressed. With an edge of hesitation in her voice, she says, "G'morning."

He gives her only the briefest of glances. "Morning." Grabbing his duffel off the floor, he starts throwing his stuff into it. He doesn't fold anything or organize, just haphazardly tosses it all in.

She frowns at the unusual behavior, but just goes into the bathroom to pee and brush her teeth. As she wipes the steam from the mirror, she's surprised as she catches sight of herself. The face staring back is pale, with puffy purple circles under each eye. The eyes themselves are ringed with red, sore skin. Limp hair hangs against drawn cheeks. She looks a mess. She feels it, too.

When she comes out a few minutes later, Alistair's bag is by the door and he's standing by the window. Without turning to her, he says, "You ready?"

A lump rises in her throat, and she feels those damn tears rise again. She picks up her knapsack and suitcase from the bed they'd made love in, takes a last look around the room where so many memories, both wonderful and horrible, had been made, and heads for the door.

Alistair is quiet on the way back to the apartment where Charlie is staying. Evie doesn't think her brother or Jason notice though, as they spend the drive squabbling over how they plan to convince her to come home.

Her fingers twist in her lap. She stares unseeing out the window, growing more stressed by the minute. Alistair won't look at her, and so far has only spoken to her when absolutely necessary. It stings much more than Jason's coldness had.

When they pull up in front of the run-down building, Evie decides she can't handle the tense silence of waiting in the car with Alistair. She swings open the door and gets out with the guys. They look at her in surprise, but before either can question her, she says firmly, "I'm coming with you."

Dylan glances through the car window at Alistair, then back at Evie, but thankfully doesn't comment. She assumes he has more important things to worry about right now than his sister and her boyfriend. Or rather, ex-boyfriend.

She follows them inside and up the narrow stairwell. They exit on the third floor, stopping in front of a faded green door. Darker shapes on the paint show where the number 302 used to be, before it fell or was pried off. Inside, music is blasting.

Jason steps up and knocks. When no one answers after a minute, he pounds again, harder, calling Charlie's name.

Finally, the door opens a crack, and a familiar heavily mascaraed blue eye peers out. Not waiting for an invite; Jason pushes the door open and walks inside. After an uncertain look at each other, Evie and Dylan follow.

"Turn it down!" Charlie yells at someone in the other room. Two seconds later, the music's volume lowers.

"Well?" Jason asks her.

"Well what?"

"You coming home with us?"

Before she can reply, a tall, balding man walks up behind her. "Jase!" he exclaims. "Great to see ya, buddy!"

Jason stiffens. He doesn't reply.

"So you're in college now?" Mitch Lancaster claps him on the shoulder. "How's that going?"

Evie and Dylan exchange glances again. Charlie hadn't told them her father would be here.

"Fine," Jason replies tersely. "We're here to bring Char home. Mom's freakin' out." He turns to his sister. "The whole county was searching the woods for you, you know."

Charlie's eyes go wide, but she can't help a little smile. "Really?"

"You had the entire town worried. Half of them think you're dead in a ditch somewhere."

"Sorry," she mutters. "I just couldn't stand it any longer. I needed to bail, like, stat."

Evie can see Jason biting his lip, wanting to tell her off for her thoughtlessness, but restraining himself. It can wait until later. Charlie will get lectured plenty once she gets home, something which Evie knows the younger girl is fully aware.

Mitch's former smile is now a frown. He slides a protective arm around his daughter's shoulders. "You don't have to go back if you don't wanna," he tells her.

Charlie looks up at him, then back to the rest of them. "Let me talk to Dad alone for a few minutes, okay?"

Jason's face is grim, but he concedes. "We'll wait for you out in the hall. Don't be long, okay? We've got a flight to catch."

They step out and Jason and Dylan take up sentinel on either side of the apartment door. Murmured voices can be heard from inside at first, but then the music is turned back up, obscuring all else.

Evie glances out the landing window to confirm Alistair is still out front. She knows no matter how upset he is, he'd never abandon her in a strange city, but she feels a bit better seeing he's there. Part of her wants to go down to him right now, to try to talk this through and fix things, but she knows he's not ready for that conversation yet. The last thing she wants is to make things worse.

The door opens and Charlie comes out, a small knapsack over her shoulder. She looks like she's holding back tears.

"That all you've got?" Jason asks her, eyeing it.

She shrugs. "Don't have much out here. Let's go."

Mitch follows her into the hallway. "You need anything?" he asks. Evie can't tell if he's asking Charlie, Jason, or both of his kids.

Jason looks at his father, his eyes hard. "Nope. We're good."

"I'll call you, then," Mitch says, attempting a smile.

"Whatever." Jason dismisses him, clearly fed up with empty promises. He starts down the stairs.

Charlie sighs. She gives her dad a parting hug, and they follow.

The drive to the rental agency is noisy, but all conversation comes from the back seat. Alistair drives in silence. He glances over at Evie. Her face is turned away, watching the city pass outside her window. He wonders what she's thinking about, is even tempted to reach over and touch her leg, but he resists. They are over. Not just their 'benefits,' but their friendship, too. He knew the former would end sooner or later, but now he knows he needs to cut all ties. It wasn't easy for him to trust her after all he's been through, and now that fragile trust has been shattered.

It might not seem like a big deal to someone else, what he found out, but honesty is vital to him. She knew that, and yet she continued to deceive him. Hell, maybe she knew he was JAI all along and decided to keep up the ruse for some twisted reason he can't comprehend. Right now he just needs this trip to be over.

When they get to LAX, Alistair purchases a ticket for Charlie. He asks the agent to give him the single seat by himself, and sit the others in the four original seats. She assigns him a seat five rows behind them.

Evie doesn't realize this until they board. After she sits down, she sees him walk past, and looks confused. "Where are you going?" she asks.

He waves toward the rows further down. "Back here."

"What? Why?"

He can hear the hurt in her voice, but he chooses not to answer. Continuing along until he finds his row, he tosses his bag into the overhead bin and slides into the seat by the window. He sees Jason take the empty seat beside Evie. She'd been watching Alistair to see where he would end up, and when Jason sits, she turns to him and says something with a frown, gesturing toward Alistair. Alistair smiles grimly as he buckles his seatbelt, sure Jason will be happy to hear things are finished between them. As far as he's concerned, Jason is welcome to her, although he knows damn well Evie can do much better than that guy.

A few minutes later, two girls around his age take the seats beside him. The one sitting next to him has long sandy hair and a pretty, pouty smile. After she settles in, she turns to him, batting her lashes.

"Hey there. I'm Kim. And this here's my BFF, Marcy."

He gives her a polite smile. "Alistair."

"Flyin' alone?" Marcy asks, leaning forward to look him over. She has curly red hair, most of which is pinned to the top of her head. Both girls are wearing low cut tops and skinny jeans, with lots of jewelry.

"No. The rest of my group is up there." He points forward."

"Aw, so you're the odd man out?" Kim says. He assumes she thinks the others are coupled up.

Always am, he thinks, but he replies, "Not really." He looks them over and drops Kim a wink. "I clearly lucked out sitting here." The three of them are stuck on a plane together for the next several hours. He'd assumed it would be a boring flight, but since the opportunity has arisen for a little entertainment along the way, he figures he might as well take it.

"Are they your friends?"

He glances up at Evie again, before returning his attention to the new arrivals. "Truth is, I hardly know them."

Marcy giggles. "You from L.A.?"

"Nope." Alistair settles back in his seat and angles his body toward them. "So, ladies, why don't we sit back and relax, and you can tell me all about yourselves?"

Evie shifts around in her seat, but she can't seem to get comfortable. Twice, Jason has asked if she's okay.

"I'm fine," she answers, the second time a bit tersely. She's anything but fine. Though they are several seats behind her, she can overhear snippets of Alistair's conversation with the two girls beside him, and the flirting makes her want to punch something.

Maybe he knows she can hear, and is deliberately trying to drive her nuts? It's a possibility, she decides. But either way, she doesn't think she can handle having to listen to them for the entire flight home.

She glances behind her again. He's smiling at them, and the blonde next to him is laughing at something he said. *She's pretty*, Evie thinks. *A lot prettier than me, anyway.*

She taps her brother on the shoulder.

He swivels to peer over his seat at her. "What?"

"Do you have a second pair of headphones? Something noise canceling?"

Without replying, Dylan turns around and digs in his knapsack on the floor. A moment later, he tosses a set to her.

"Thanks."

"Why's Alistair back there?"

She sees Jason watching them, and knows he's curious, too. With a sigh, she says, "We broke up last night." Then she puts on the headphones, leans her head against the window, and closes her eyes, not the least bit interested in their reactions.

It's past eleven when Alistair walks in the front door of his uncle's house. It had been an awkward last few hours in the Jeep, and an even more awkward goodbye at Evie's. She had just looked so damn sad as she'd said goodnight before he drove away. He knows her sadness is no longer his concern, but a part of him still winced inside knowing he was the cause of it.

Right now he is exhausted and cranky, and all he wants is to fall into bed and pass out. Possibly with a shot or two of thought-obliviating bourbon in his belly.

He climbs the stairs wearily, noting the empty library as he passes. Max must have already gone to bed. That's okay; Alistair can talk to him in the morning. It's not really a conversation he's up for tonight anyway, as he knows his uncle won't be pleased. Max has been good to him, and he hates to let him down, but Alistair knows it's time to put Sutterton behind him.

Chapter 25

On his way downstairs for coffee, Alistair hears Max call his name and makes a detour into the library. "Hey."

Setting down his own steaming mug, Max says, "Morning. So, how was your trip?"

Alistair shrugs.

"Not great?"

"It was okay. Listen, I need to tell you something." He takes a chair near his uncle.

"Oh yeah? What's that?"

Alistair isn't quite sure how to start, but he needs to be sure Max understands this is not because of him. "You know I appreciate everything you've done for me, right?"

His uncle frowns. "Yes."

"Good. Because I really do. You've been there for me when no one else was, and I'll never forget it. But...I think I'm ready to move on."

Max's eyebrows rise. He's quiet for a moment. Then he asks: "Going home?"

With a small sigh, Alistair says, "No. Somewhere new. Maybe Memphis. Or New Orleans."

"Know anyone there?"

"Nope. That's kind of the point."

Another frown. "I thought you and Paul were working things out?"

"We are. Sort of. Our presumable reconciliation is, at best, a work in progress. But no need to worry. I'll text you both once in a while, so you'll know I'm still kicking."

Max shakes his head, smiling wryly. "So, when're you thinking?"

"Tomorrow, actually."

Now his uncle is visibly taken aback. "Why the rush?"

Alistair shrugs. "It's nothing personal." He gets to his feet and starts toward the door, but Max's next question brings him to a halt.

"Does this sudden need to hit the road have anything to do with Evie Colville?"

Heat floods Alistair's cheeks as he turns back. He's neither embarrassed nor angry, but her name stirs up a rush of complex emotions. "It's just time for me to go."

Max holds his gaze, his face full of compassion. "You sure?" he asks quietly.

"I'm sure."

At lunch, Evie and Grace once again head up to the turret. It's chilly today; no sun shines through the windows to warm the small room. Evie shivers, wishing she'd thought to bring her coat with her. Across the road, the river roils and churns in the wind. Dark clouds building on the horizon promise rain.

"So, what happened?" Grace asks, sitting on the bench beside her. "You're all Miss Sad Panda today. Tell me."

Evie looks down at her hands. "I did something stupid. Well, several somethings."

"You got Charlie back. That's a win in my book."

"Yeah, I know. But I mean with Alistair. I never told him I was Miss Lonely Love. I know you said I should, but…I guess I just never got around to it. And I was working on my column in our hotel room and Dylan texted me and it sounded urgent so I just left. I left my screen open.

She hears Grace suck in a breath. "He saw it?"

Evie looks up at her. "Yeah. And it gets worse. He and I have been corresponding through Miss LL for a couple months now, and neither of us even knew it."

"*What*? You're shitting me!"

She shakes her head. "I'm not. I got a letter from a guy whose girlfriend had cheated on him with his brother. I didn't have space in the column, so I wrote back personally. Then he wrote back to me, and it just kind of continued. I can't believe I never put two and two together, but I didn't. I'm an idiot."

"You're not." She gives Evie's hand a squeeze. "This doesn't sound like that big a thing, though. I'm sure you apologized for not telling him. Can't you guys move past it?"

"You don't understand. His trust was broken by his brother and his ex. Honesty is *huge* for Alistair, and we promised each other complete honesty when we agreed to the FWB thing. I kept this from him. He thinks I was just using him to further my column. I said that wasn't true, that I was with him because I wanted to be, but he wouldn't listen. He won't even talk to me anymore." Tears start trickling down her cheeks. It feels like crying is all she ever does anymore.

"Oh honey." Grace hugs her.

"That's not even all of it." Evie swipes the moisture from her face. "There's something else I haven't told him that's even bigger, and I was going to once we got back, but now I guess there's no point."

"That you're in love with him?" Grace asks in a soft voice.

Evie meets her eyes once more. "How did you know?"

"Because I'm your best friend. And I've been waiting for weeks now for you to figure it out on your own."

"It doesn't matter now. He's probably packing his bags to leave town as we speak."

"Listen. Evie? You promised him you'd be honest with him, right?"

Evie nods, sniffling.

"So be honest. Get your ass over there tonight and tell him how you feel. You owe him that much."

"What if…what if he won't see me?"

"Then write a text if you have to! Just tell him."

Write a…Oh my God! She'd forgotten her last letter to JAI, the one she'd mailed from the airport. *Crap!* Hopefully it wouldn't arrive until after she could talk to Alistair in person. "You're right," she says. "I'll ask my brother to take my shift tonight, and I'll head to his place as soon as my dad gets home."

"Forget about Dylan. I'll take your shift. You'll owe me big, though." Grace smiles at her. "And I expect you to tell me how it went ASAP."

Alistair hasn't even unpacked his duffel bag from Los Angeles. It sits open on his mattress as he crams in more books and clothing.

Trying to recall where he stashed his suitcase after unpacking his things a few months ago, he drops to his knees to look under the bed. He pauses, hearing footsteps in the hall. A second later, there's a knock on the door. "Come in," he calls, dragging out the dusty case.

"This came for you," Max says, tossing a letter on the nightstand.

Alistair's brows narrow as he looks at it in surprise. "Uh, thanks."

"Guess you'd better tell her you're leaving. No point in sending any more mail here, right?"

"If you get more, you can just toss them," Alistair tells him. "It's nothing important."

His uncle shrugs. "If you say so." He heads back downstairs.

Alistair brushes cobwebs from the suitcase and opens it. Turning to grab another stack of books from the shelf below the nightstand, he frowns as his eyes land back on the envelope, Evie's handwriting looping across the front. How did

308

he never recognize that handwriting? He's seen it so many times. With a sigh, he picks it up and tears it open.

Dear JAI,

I'm SO proud of you! It sounds like a huge weight has begun the slow, painful, yet hopeful process of rolling off your shoulders. Fixing things with your brother is definitely the first step to moving on, and I have great faith in your ability to heal and go forward.

You will find love again—I'm sure of it It tends to show up when you least expect it, and it doesn't give a crap whether you want it or not. It takes you over and you're helpless to try to fight it.

Personally, I didn't even know what love was for a long time. I'd had a few schoolgirl crushes, gone on dates, had a boyfriend or two, but similar to you before you met your ex, I never loved any of them.

When I first met him, I was intrigued, but I wasn't looking for a relationship. Neither was he, as he'd just come out of an ugly break-up. We became friends, although I knew we had a connection early on. Our friendship grew, and along with it our attraction to one another. We got to know each other better, shared private moments that we couldn't with anyone else, and before long we became intimate. But even then, I refused to consider the possibility of falling in love with him. I told myself I wasn't at the right place in my life for love. He claimed he wasn't either.

But I was deceiving myself.

For a long time, I kept up the self-delusion, convincing myself that although we cared about each other, it wasn't love, and when the time came for us to part (which I believed it inevitably would) I'd be able to let him go. I was wrong.

Okay, brace yourself. Here comes the sappy part.

When I'm in his arms, I feel like I'd be perfectly happy if time just stopped and we stayed that way forever. Being with him makes me feel like I'm a different person, a stronger, happier, more confident person. Don't get me wrong—I haven't lost myself—I'm still me. I'm just a better version of me. Loving him has changed me, and no matter what the future brings, I know I'll never regret falling for him.

And THIS is what I want for you. I want you to find the kind of love I've found, because even though it means putting your heart out there and risking it being handed back to you, or worse, squished, I truly believe that real love is worth it, just to feel the way it changes you. It makes you better for having experienced it.

Best of luck,

Miss LL

The letter falls from his hand back to the table. As his eyes drift to his overflowing bag, he spots his tattered copy of *The Great Gatsby*. Gatsby had let his past keep him from moving on with his life. He'd let it control him until it took him over and ate him alive.

Holy shit. His eyes flare as he drags his fingers through his hair. *Am I doing the same?*

Evie is not Michelle. So why has he been acting like her secret is as bad as Michelle's betrayal? Maybe she had a good reason for not telling him about her column? It's not like he'd even let her explain. And let's not forget she wrote this letter before she knew he was JAI, which means she has another secret. This one he kind of gets, though. They'd promised to end their 'benefits' if either of them started to fall for the other. Maybe she hadn't wanted things to end yet?

Maybe he's blowing all this out of proportion as an excuse to run away from his own feelings? Feelings that, if he's being honest with himself, have grown far beyond mere friendship. He's not sure if he's in love with her, exactly—what he feels for Evie isn't the same as what he used to feel for Michelle, but that kind of oblivious, obsessive love isn't healthy anyway he knows now. And look how it turned out? No, he doesn't love Evie like that, but…he could love her. Maybe he does love her?

And maybe, just maybe, the time has come to stop running away. Maybe it's time to just live.

His fingers tremble as he overturns his bag and dumps it out.

It's still daytime when Evie knocks on the door, but you wouldn't know it. The rain started just before she left home and picked up intensity during her drive. She's been going over what she wants to say for hours though, and no amount of rain is going to stop her.

Max pulls open the door. He doesn't look surprised to see her. "Evenin' Evie." Thunder rumbles in the distance, and he glances over her head at the clouds. "Gonna be a doozy."

"Yep." She pushes back her dripping hood. "Is Alistair here? I won't stay long."

"He's up in his room packing. You know he's leaving in the morning?"

Evie sighs. "I kinda figured. Can I go up?"

"Go ahead. See if you can talk some sense into him."

"I'll do my best," she says, kicking off her sneakers and heading for the stairs.

Her heart is pounding almost as hard as the rain on the roof as she stands in front of Alistair's door.

I can do this. It's my last chance.

He pulls it open a mere second after she knocks. The surprise in his eyes tells her he'd been expecting his uncle.

"Hey," she says, attempting a smile.

"What're you doing here?" He wears a peculiar expression, one she's never seen before. He steps aside so she can enter, giving her a tinge of hope he might at last be willing to listen.

As she closes the door behind her, she notices a large suitcase against the wall. *He's already ready to go*, she thinks. "I need to talk to you before you leave."

"So talk." He gestures to the chair by the fire.

Evie chooses to remain standing. "I spoke to Jason earlier. He said to tell you he and his mom are beyond grateful for everything you did to help get Charlie back."

Alistair waves this off. "Is that why you stopped by? Because that seems like something you could've just texted."

She presses her lips together. "No. There's more."

Arms crossed, he sits on the edge of his bed. "Why don't you start by explaining why you didn't tell me about your column?"

"I was…ashamed," Evie confesses with a sigh. "I thought you might laugh at the idea of someone as young and inexperienced as me giving love advice."

"I have to admit, it's pretty crazy."

"I know it is! I told my editor that, too, when she asked me to write it. She said all she cared about was getting readers' attention, that I'd be fine if I just used common sense. But when the first letter showed up from a girl my age asking about sex stuff, I knew I wasn't qualified to help her. As I guess you know, sometimes I reply personally, and it didn't seem right to ignore the girls who needed advice. And then I met you, and I liked you, and one thing just kinda led to another." She pauses, frowning. "I'm really sorry. I should've told you from the start. I let my insecurity stop me."

He nods. "I guess I get that."

"The only reason I suggested Friends With Benefits in the first place is 'cause I convinced myself a *real* boyfriend would distract me too much. I've been working so hard to keep my grades up."

"I know."

Another soft sigh. "People around here think they know everything about everyone. But I know better. This town is *full* of secrets. I know the mayor has been sleeping with the high school principal's wife for years, though he plays golf with her husband. I know Jason's mom would've had her house repossessed long ago if she didn't, uh, do 'favors' for Dr. Cardiff. I know who loads of my classmates have crushes on. I know you never wanted to risk another relationship after what your ex did. And finally…I…I…" She stops, noticing the letter on the nightstand, and her heart sinks. He's already read it. Which means he already knows. The question is: does it change anything?

"You what, Evie?" Alistair stands and takes a step closer.

She bites her bottom lip. But she came here with a speech all prepared, so she decides to go with it. "There's something else I haven't told you, but in my defense I only just figured it out. Sometimes stuff just happens, stuff we never intended. Some of it's horrible, like losing a parent, but sometimes…sometimes it can be wonderful. And there's nothing we can do to stop it." She pauses again. Saying this to his face is so much harder than she expected. "This might be the last time I ever see you." With a deep breath, Evie blurts, "I don't want you to go. Because I'm in love with you."

His face softens. Lightning flashes through the windows and she thinks she sees a hint of a smile. In a quiet voice he asks, "What about not wanting any distractions? And what happens when you leave for school? What then?"

A warm rush of hope blooms. "College is a priority for me for sure, but…so are you. If we want to be together, we'll find a way to make it work. If you decide to stay, I promise I'll never lie to you again. I can't promise a happily ever after, though. Only time will tell. And I know you've been hurt, but the way I see it, falling in love is always a risk. You just need to decide if what we have is worth it."

He stares at her. She can't tell what he's thinking. After a few more moments, she whispers, "Alistair? Do you want me to go?"

He shakes his head ever so slightly, but still doesn't speak.

"I know how hard this must be for you. You don't have to tell me—"

A sharp thunder crack rattles the windows and they both jump. Before she can laugh, before she can react at all, Alistair closes the space between them and kisses her, pulling her against him. This time his kisses are not sweet and gentle; they're passionate and demanding, full of unspoken emotions. Evie doesn't mind. She gives it right back to him. This is what they need now. Sweet and gentle can wait for another time.

Spinning her around, he walks her backward and lowers them both onto his bed. They are near frantic in their need for each other, breaking apart just long enough to pull shirts over heads, to toss his glasses on the nightstand. Then they crash right back together. Hands roam. Remaining clothing is stripped off and tossed aside. Fumbling and gasping, they kiss and tumble and join together like they haven't seen each other in months, years even. His thrusts are desperate, nearly panicky, and she clings to him, rising to meet every one, needing this just as much as he does.

They cannot sustain this intense level of passion. He flips her on top, but it's too late. He's too close. A minute later he groans loud and long and primal, like something wild, previously caged, now broken free. With a final shudder, his head falls against the pillow. Evie rolls to the side, facing him, a small smile dancing on her lips.

"Holy crap," she gasps as thunder rumbles and another flash of lightning illuminates his face. She reaches up to stroke his sweaty jawbone.

Alistair chuckles. He covers her hand with his and looks into her eyes. "You proved me wrong."

She doesn't answer, just stares at him, afraid to do anything that might shatter the moment.

"I thought my heart was black and dead, but you proved me wrong." He shakes his head, incredulous. Cupping her face in his hands, he kisses her softly. "To answer your question, yes, it's worth it. *You're* worth it. And I...I..." He stops, gulping.

Evie's heart leaps. At that moment she knows. She knows without a shadow of a doubt by the way he's looking at her, by the expression in those incredible green eyes, that he feels the same way she does. And she also knows Alistair well enough to understand that if he isn't quite ready to say it out loud yet, that's okay. There's no rush. They have plenty of time.

"I'm sorry for being such a jackass," he whispers. "I should've trusted you." He knows he trusts her now. For him trust is, and will always be, the most important thing. Trust comes first. And you can't have love—at least not real, lasting love—without trust.

314

He kisses her again, no longer desperate or frantic, but confident now that there will be many more moments like this in their future.

"I'm all yours."

Epilogue

Five Months Later

Alistair comes down the stairs and sets his bags by the front door. He can hear water running in the kitchen. "I'm about ready to head out," he calls to his uncle.

Max comes into the entranceway, a damp dish towel thrown over one shoulder. "Hey College Dude. That time already? Seems like only yesterday you showed up at my door."

"I know, right? Feels like both just the other day and a lifetime ago. If that makes any sense."

"Yeah, it does. You're not the same guy you were back then." His uncle smiles. "I'll miss you around here. Remember, you're only gonna be a few hours away. Don't be a stranger."

Alistair returns his smile. In March, he'd applied to the English Lit program and had been lucky enough to get accepted to the same college as where Evie had earned a full ride. "You know I'll be back all the time. Knowing Evie, she'll probably want to visit her family every weekend." He thrusts out a hand. "Thanks again. For everything. Your offer to stay here really saved my life, you know?"

Max chuckles. "I dunno about that. But you're more than welcome." Grabbing his nephew's hand, he pulls him into a hug and claps him on the back. "I'm happy for ya, buddy. Take care of yourself. And take extra care of Tom's daughter, okay? I won't hear the end of it if you piss her off."

Laughing, Alistair says, "I'll do my best."

He loads his bags into the back of the Jeep and drives into town to Evie's house. Her father answers the door. When he sees who it is, Tom shakes his head with a grin.

"Morning, Tom. What's up?" Alistair asks. "Where's Evie?"

"Oh, just running around like a chicken with its head cut off, sure she's forgetting something important." He gestures towards the hallway. "See if you can talk her down, would ya?"

Dylan doesn't seem to be home. Alistair assumes he already said his goodbyes to his sister and is off somewhere with Charlie. The two have been nearly inseparable for the past several months, much to Evie's delight.

Her door is wide open, and he finds her standing on tiptoes in her closet, trying to reach something on the shelf. He knocks on her door jamb, and she whips around, ponytail flying. "Crap! Is it time to go already?"

Laughing, he comes over and sets his hands on her waist to give her a quick kiss. She's so distracted she barely kisses him back. One of her arms still stretches up, patting the shelf above her head.

"Can I help you find something?"

Evie heaves an exasperated sigh. "Is my mom's shawl up there in the back? The black knit one I wore to the Valentine's Party? Can you see it?"

He peers into the dimly lit shelf and spots the elusive shawl crumpled in the corner. "Yep. I've got it." Pulling it down, he brushes the dust off and hands it to her.

"Thanks. I couldn't go without it." Evie folds it carefully and tucks it into a shopping bag beside the overflowing suitcase on her bed.

"You almost ready?"

She sighs again. "I don't know. I said goodbye to Grace earlier. She's taking some of my shifts at the shop to help Dad and Dyl out, did I tell you that?"

Alistair nods. Grace decided to stay in Sutterton for another year to save up more money for college, and he knows how much Evie will miss her. Grace is also going to take over the Miss Lonely Love column, with Evie's help, so he assumes the two will continue to text or Skype daily.

"I still feel like I'm forgetting something." She braces one hand on her hip, her eyes sweeping around the room.

"Evie, look at me, please."

Pushing a flyaway piece of hair off her forehead, she turns back to him. "What?"

She looks so damn cute when she's frustrated. But now is not a great time to tell her that, so he stifles his grin. "I know an impending freak out when I see one. Relax, babe. We've got everything under control."

"But—"

Stepping closer, he kisses her again. "If you need something, I'll buy it for you. If it's irreplaceable, we'll come back next weekend so you can get it."

Her eyebrows draw tight, vertical lines appearing between them. He can see the argument forming—the past six months have taught him well—so he stops her before she can get started. "Yes, I will buy you things. Yes, I will drive you home when you want to see your family. No, you're not an inconvenience. And yes, I love you, too. Now zip up your suitcase and let's hit the road. Deal?"

Evie can't suppress a wide smile. She slides her arms around his neck and stares into those mesmerizing green eyes that she will get to see every day as they start the rest of their lives together.

"Deal."

318

About the Author

J.S. Eades lives in southwestern Ontario, Canada, with her family. An avid traveler and scuba enthusiast, she can often be found under the warm waters of the Caribbean.

She is currently working on the *Forever Twenty-One* supernatural series.

Contact
Website: www.jseades.com
Facebook: AuthorJSEades
Twitter: @JS_Eades
Instagram: @jseadesauthor

Dear Readers
Thank you so much for reading my novel. If you enjoyed it, would you please take a moment to write an honest review on Amazon or Goodreads.com so other readers can find and hopefully enjoy it, too? Even just a few sentences would mean a lot to me.

Thanks!
J.S. Eades

Other Books by J.S. Eades

DEATH DEFYING
(Forever Twenty-One book 1)

What happens when you discover nothing you'd believed about yourself is true?

All Genny Dupont wants for her 21st birthday is to sleep in, eat a great breakfast, and go out dancing with her best friend. At first, it seems like her day goes exactly to plan. She even meets a cute guy at the club. But when they get together for coffee the next afternoon, she realizes she's made a huge mistake.

Because the story JP tells her, that she and her sister are the only remaining descendants of a family of immortal vampire slayers, is completely insane. He's obviously a lunatic. Disappointed, she walks out, but Genny can't quite shake the idea he's planted. Could he possibly have been telling the truth?

Learning about her family and how they died opens the door to a world she'd thought only existed in fiction. Sure, this world includes enemies that want her dead, but it's not all doom and gloom. As Genny starts to embrace her legacy, she and JP grow closer.

She's a slayer. JP insists vampires are evil. But when she strikes up an unlikely friendship with Quinn, a vampire who risked his own life to save her, she comes to understand that not everything—or everyone—is how it seems.

MORE THAN JUST BLOOD
(Forever Twenty-One book 2)

Genny Dupont has a lot on her plate. Between working full time, training to be the best vampire slayer she can be, and preparing for her first trip, she hasn't had much chance to come to terms with the recent attempt on her and her sister Chloe's lives. She should be planning how to defeat their enemies. She should be helping Chloe manage her trauma. She should also be trying to mend her friendship with her ex-boyfriend JP, especially since he's accompanying her to France to testify at his uncle's murder trial. She should be doing a lot of things she isn't.

But the one thing Genny cannot do, the thing she shoves from her mind, although it never stays away long, is admit her feelings for Quinn. Acting on them would only complicate her life further, and undoubtedly drive a permanent wedge between her and JP. But even more concerning, Quinn is a vampire, one who has suffered more in his 139 years than she can imagine.

It's weird enough that a slayer and a vampire have grown so close. Anything more could only end in tragedy. At least that's what she's been told by other immortals. It's best if they just stay friends.

That's what she keeps reminding herself, but these feelings aren't going away. If anything they're growing. And they terrify her a lot more than the Vampire Assembly who still wants her dead.

PROMISES AND OTHER BROKEN THINGS
(Amelia and Declan book 1)

Amelia York seems to have it all: a great career, good friends, and she's married to her high school sweetheart. Starting a promising new job is just another step in the life she has all figured out. The intense connection she develops with a handsome co-worker, however, threatens to derail all her well thought-out plans.

Declan Kavanaugh's whole world revolves around his daughter. Overworked and under-appreciated both by his wife at home and his colleagues at his family's firm, the stress is starting to get to him. Making friends with the pretty new accountant comes as a surprise, but he finds time spent with Amelia is like the breath of fresh air he so desperately needs.

Neither of them wants any complications in their lives—and the last thing they want is to fall in love.

But as they discover, sometimes no matter how much you fight it, life has other ideas.

Read Chapter 1 of PROMISES AND OTHER BROKEN THINGS for free, starting on the next page.

THE FINE ART OF FORGIVENESS
(Amelia and Declan book 2)

You don't always get what you want.

Amelia York knows this all too well. Her entire life has been torn apart and she's lost nearly everything that matters: her job, two of her closest friends, her father, and most devastating of all, the man she loves. Though she's gotten good at pretending she's fine, inside she's still shattered. All she wants is to move on and rebuild. She never thought it would be easy, but she didn't expect it to be this hard. And an impulsive decision at a friend's wedding throws a surprise wrench into her life that makes it even harder.

Declan Kavanaugh considers himself a damn good salesman, but he's got no pitch capable of convincing himself the choice he made was the right one. He promised to be there for his family, but he's hurting. And he misses *her* more than he's willing to admit. Can a miracle give him the second chance at happiness he craves? Or is he doomed to always destroy everything he cares about?

Things never turn out quite the way you think they will. But sometimes you might just get what you need.

Available at most online retailers.

Promises and Other Broken Things

Chapter 1

Amelia

Let me make one thing clear right off the bat. This is not a story about two people who met and fell in love, and of course had hurdles to overcome, but they loved each other enough that nothing was insurmountable. You know the ones—the kind where in the end true love always conquers all. This is a story about real life, and real love, and it may not be a fairytale, but it is ours.

Some people will tell you that, looking back, they can pinpoint the precise moment when their entire world changed, when their lives were suddenly and abruptly shifted down a different path. I'd heard stories like this before of course, lots of times, but I hadn't really understood just what having a moment like that meant. Most of these same people will also tell you that you don't know it when it happens, you only realize the incredible impact that moment had when you look back later.

I knew the instant it happened to me.

It was just after eleven on my first day of work at Baker, Wright and Kavanaugh. My new boss, Diana Sharpe, was finishing up giving me an office tour and, though it was still morning, I'd already reached information overload. Fatigue had settled over my mind.

I glanced up over her shoulder and saw a man walking down the hallway toward us. He was about medium height, with broad shoulders and unkempt dark brown hair. He wore a black button-up dress shirt with the top couple of buttons undone, and black dress pants that clung to his slim hips like they were custom tailored.

He saw me and held my gaze with the most intense pale blue eyes, and something happened deep inside me, something that almost physically hurt as I looked at him. I forgot everything Diana had just told me. I forgot who I was. I forgot how to breathe. And I know it sounds ridiculous, but I swear we both froze for what felt like an eternity, although it was probably only a second or two.

Then Ryan Kavanaugh, to whom I'd just been introduced, popped his head out of his office and said something to the dark-haired guy. He startled, breaking our strange connection and disappearing inside.

You know the phrase 'my heart dropped'? I'd never experienced that feeling before. But at that moment? When he vanished from my sight? I swear it felt like my heart actually fell a few inches.

Closing my eyes for a second, I took a much-needed breath, desperately hoping neither Diana nor anyone else had noticed my strange reaction. What the heck was that about? I wasn't a schoolgirl anymore. So a good-looking guy caught my eye? So what?

Well for starters, *good-looking* didn't even begin to cover it. He'd caused me to react in a way I didn't think was even possible in real life. I'd turned into some embarrassing romance novel cliché for a moment there. And, second, I firmly didn't believe in the silly myth of love at first sight that popular culture and some of my more naïve friends spouted. I was married. And this was my new workplace. So it didn't matter. Couldn't matter.

Except deep down in the pit of my stomach, I knew it did.

I started off the day—the day that would change everything, though I didn't know it yet—by showing up early.

It was silly of me, in hindsight. Just as my husband, Scott, had predicted as I'd rushed around our house that morning, all being early accomplished was gaining me more time sitting and waiting.

So I sat, and I waited. The red second hand of the retro-style clock on the wall behind the reception desk seemed to be defective. I was sure it was moving far too slowly. Pushing a stray lock of hair behind one ear, I glanced up at it again

I took a deep breath, smoothed down the fabric of my skirt and tried to relax. I was bound and determined to make a good first impression. Just like I always did.

I was a Good Girl. It was the category I'd been slotted into from an early age, bestowed upon me by my parents, teachers, and nearly every other adult who'd ever met me. Because of this, I had always seen myself through their filters: The Good Girl, The Smart Girl, The Girl Who Did the Right Thing.

When I walked into the office to start my first day at Baker, Wright and Kavanaugh, I was nervous, but confident. They had approached *me* with the job offer, after all, so I knew they had high expectations. I'd worked at Bellmore & Sons Advertising since graduating from college with my accounting diploma proudly in hand. After seven years and my chances of advancement looking slimmer and slimmer at the large firm, I started exploring other opportunities. When BWK began wooing me, I knew it was the right time to spread my proverbial wings and leave the bosom of Known and Comfortable.

In her most recent e-mail, my new boss had requested I arrive at nine o'clock instead of the earlier eight I would have preferred. Of course, I showed up at 8:45 and not a minute later. So there I sat on a very sleek, modern, and therefore predictably hard chair in the reception area checking messages on my phone and glancing frequently toward the large glass doors which swung inward into the office proper.

At 9:04, I began to fidget and tap my toe against the gleaming hardwood.

At 9:08, I couldn't sit on that uncomfortable chair a moment longer, and got up to peruse the company's framed awards bragging audaciously from an otherwise stark white wall. The receptionist cast an uninterested glance my way before returning her attention to her monitor.

At 9:12, one of the glass doors opened, and the most stunning woman I'd ever seen stepped into the lobby.

"Amelia York?" she asked politely. Her voice was kind of raspy—it brought to mind images of long nights spent drinking whiskey in smoky dive bars. Tall and shapely, she had shoulder-length black hair, a flawless complexion and full plum-stained lips. Thick lashes framed almond-shaped dark eyes. She imparted an immediate sense of charisma that I couldn't help admiring.

I smiled, sticking out my hand. "I'm Amelia."

She gave me a quick once-over. Her face was carefully composed, betraying no hint of what her initial impression of me was.

It seemed like she looked down at the neatly trimmed nails of my outstretched hand for just a beat too long before taking it and shaking it firmly, once. I got a fleeting sense she hadn't really wanted to touch me, but forced herself to anyway.

"Diana Sharpe. Right this way." She turned and went back through the door without waiting to see if I would follow, her pointy-toed stilettos clicking along the floor.

I walked a few steps behind Diana along a hall lined with opaque glass-doored offices, then turned left and found myself staring at rows of beige cubicles. A small black sign stating we'd reached the Accounting department was affixed to the side of one padded half-wall. This cubicle-farm in front of me housed my new workspace. My new co-workers. My new life.

A few people looked up from their monitors as I followed Diana down the center aisle, no doubt anxious for their first glimpse of the New Girl. Conscious of their curious stares, I returned the smile of a pretty dark-haired young woman as we passed.

Diana stopped abruptly at an empty cubicle about halfway down the row and waved a hand toward the desk. "This one's yours. You can leave your personal belongings here, and we'll go into my office to discuss your role."

I draped my jacket over the back of the chair and resumed following her. Once inside Diana's office, I took a seat across from a large and messy desk. A print of one of Degas' ballerinas adorned the wall behind her chair, but no personal photos were displayed. Wasting no time, she launched into a description of what the company did, the corporate structure, and what would be expected of me.

The three partners, Robert Baker, Lucas Wright and Patrick Kavanaugh, founded this advertising agency thirty-two years ago. The department I'd be working most closely with was Sales, as it would be my job to price out advertising for new business, suggestions for add-ons, and any changes the clients decided to make down the line. I would have regular contact with the Account Managers and their administrative assistants. Diana began listing names and roles of some of the people I'd be working with, both here and in their satellite offices across the country, while I jotted notes in the back of my day planner.

I was surprised to find myself feeling a little intimidated by my new boss. Women didn't usually intimidate me. Actually, I'd found that other women were often intimidated *by* me. Diana Sharpe, however, was not intimidated by me in the slightest. In fact, I was willing to hedge a guess that Diana Sharpe was *never* intimidated. By anyone.

Declan

Goddamn it!

I was running late. Again. I'd had an early morning client meeting in Richmond, and ended up stuck in rush-hour traffic trying to escape the city to get back to the office. Christ, I'd be lucky if I got into work by *eleven.* Too much to do and too little fucking time to do it in. As usual.

I sped down the highway toward Lynchburg, hoping like hell I wouldn't pass any cops along the way. Impatiently, I punched buttons on the radio until loud rock music filled my Mustang, but the throbbing beat only incited me to hit the pedal harder. The aforementioned client, The Happy Tomato restaurant, was proving to be a pain in my ass. They wanted to advertise, sure; they just didn't really want to pay for it. Everybody wanted everything for damn-near free these days. Which meant more meetings, more wooing, more cajoling, more of my precious time spent holding their hands and coddling them, when what I really should've be spending my valuable time on was seducing bigger, richer, higher-profile clients. I had my own bills to pay, after all.

Running a hand through my hair, I sighed in frustration. I'd always been able to sweet talk my clients, turn on the charm and make the sale. It's what I excelled at. But to be honest, lately I'd been feeling a little off my game. My mind just wasn't as focused as it used to be. Other things insisted on vying for my attention. Work things. Home things. My brother's crap. My ability to compartmentalize all these aspects of my life and just focus on the task at hand had been wavering lately, and all these different worries had begun bleeding through. Sometimes at the most inopportune times.

Which pissed me off, because I was *always* focused, always in control, always got shit done.

Fucking Ryan. Keeping my brother's secrets while trying to rein him in and clean up his messes was what had been throwing me off the most lately. And the little shit didn't even appreciate it. Hell, he wouldn't even admit he *had* a problem. And it wasn't like I could go to Daddy Dearest for any help in the matter. First of all, Ryan would deny it, and then probably kill me for ratting him out. Second, Patrick Kavanaugh would never believe his youngest son could have an addiction problem. Even if I did manage to convince him, he'd somehow find a way to make it all *my* fault, like he'd been doing for the past twenty-nine years. In his eyes, Ryan could do no wrong. I was the one who always fucked everything up. So, no, telling our father was not an option. I had to deal with Ryan myself.

The simple truth was no matter how much it bit me in the ass some days, I loved my baby brother, and wanted more for him than the hell he was currently creating for himself. It might be a thankless task, helping family, but you just do it anyway. Cause they're *family*. Enough said.

When I pulled into the BWK parking lot at 11:04, I sighed again. My day had started out shitty, and I couldn't help but imagine the ways in which it might invariably get worse. What further torments awaited me inside? Another argument with Ryan? A dressing down from my father? A confrontation with the Bitch From Hell, Diana? All of the above?

Most days I loved being out on the road, meeting my clients, addressing their concerns, and making them happy. I enjoyed it, and I was damn good at it. Being in the office, however, was a different story. A lot of my co-workers didn't like me very much. They still judged me for my past, and refused to consider the possibility that I might have changed. Eventually I just stopped caring or bothering even attempting to be anything beyond civil to most of them.

There were a few notable exceptions. My admin assistant, Colleen, was a godsend. Somehow, she managed to put up with all my demands and fluctuating moods. I didn't know what I'd do if she ever decided to leave BWK.

And then there was Josh in Accounting. While hiding out at the bar during the fresh hell known as our Corporate Christmas Party a few years back, I'd discovered that Joshua Marshall not only preferred the same brand of whiskey I did, but that he was also sort of a kindred spirit. And those were few and far between in my life. Josh was more than just a co-worker—I respected the hell out of him and considered him my closest friend.

But most of the people in the office thought I was an ass, only still employed not because I was skilled at my job, but because my father was a partner. So the chances of the remainder of my day passing without further annoyance were pretty damned unlikely. It was just a matter of how much shit I'd have to endure before it was over.

Then the cherubic face of my sweet little girl, Alexis, popped into my head. I imagined how happy she'd be when I walked in the door later and swung her up into my arms. How her huge blue eyes would light up, and how she would smile her gap-toothed grin just for me. With that thought, most of my tension drained away.

Taking a deep breath, I squared my shoulders and walked into the office.

If I'd known then what I know now, would I have done anything different? Would I have turned around, gotten back into my car and left? I've wondered that hundreds of times, and ultimately I still don't think I'd have changed a thing. Everything happens for a reason, and you just never know when change is going to grab you by the balls and squeeze.

Plus, how the hell was I to know that in a few minutes my life was about to be forever altered?

Amelia

A low headache had started to creep its tendrils up from the base of my skull to wrap around my brain. I'd tossed and turned much of the previous night in anticipation of starting my new job in the morning, and so far had been running mostly on adrenaline. But now my mind was overloaded with so much information that the inevitable exhaustion had begun to set in. How would I ever remember my way around this maze of a building? How could I possibly recall which name belonged with each of these new faces?

Diana's voice interrupted my thoughts. The undertone of boredom that had subtly infiltrated all her comments and introductions during the office tour was suddenly gone. "This is the Sales department. As I mentioned earlier, you'll be working closely with everyone here, as they rely on Accounting to get them the figures they need to present to our clients."

We stopped beside a cubicle where a pretty blonde woman was chattering into a headset as she frantically typed away. She looked up and saw Diana, widened her hazel eyes, and began to end her phone call. Tugging off the headset, she swung her chair around to face us.

"You must be Amelia, the new accountant," she chirped with a wide grin as she stuck out a hand. "I'm Sam Upshaw, administrative assistant to Ryan Kavanaugh."

Kavanaugh? As in one of the partners, Kavanaugh? I made a mental note to ask later. Taking Sam's outstretched hand, I returned her smile. The other woman's bubbly personality was contagious, and I felt my spirits perk up a bit. "Yes, I am. Great to meet you."

"Sam will be your main liaison with Ryan's block of business," Diana explained. "Most of his requests for pricing will come directly from her. She's worked here for five years and should be able to help you with any questions you have about either Ryan's clients or this department in general." Sam nodded in agreement.

"Great!" I said, trying my best to appear enthusiastic. "I'm sure I'm going to need to take you up on that."

"I remember how overwhelming it can be at the start. Don't worry—you'll be up to speed in no time. Hey, if you don't already have lunch plans, would you like to join Kaitlyn and me?"

Kaitlyn? I recalled Diana introducing me to someone named Kaitlyn earlier. Lunch with a couple of co-workers around my own age sounded like a perfect opportunity to begin making friends here. I smiled at Sam gratefully. "Kaitlyn from my department? That'd be great. Thank you."

Diana wore an impatient look. Brusquely, she asked Sam, "Is Ryan in his office?"

"You're in luck," she replied. "He got in about twenty minutes ago."

I frowned in confusion. Only twenty minutes ago? He got to work at 10:30 in the morning? Diana must have noticed my expression because she clarified, "Ryan is an Account Manager, so he has to meet with clients a lot outside the office. Come on, I want you to meet him." She started walking toward an office with the door slightly ajar. The nameplate on the wall beside it read, *Ryan Kavanaugh*.

"Talk to you later, Sam. Thanks again," I said as I followed after my boss.

"See you at lunch!"

Diana knocked once on the door, then pushed it open and stepped inside. I heard a sigh and an irritated male voice say, "What do you w—" It cut off sharply when I came into the office behind her.

A man of around thirty sat behind another large cluttered desk. He was handsome in an athletic kind of way, with a thick jawline and short brown hair that curled above a broad forehead. When he stood to greet us, I realized he had to be over to six feet tall. "Oh," he said, flushing. "I didn't realize you had someone with you."

"I've brought Amelia York, my new accountant. I told you she was starting today, remember?" Diana turned back to me. "Amelia, this is Ryan Kavanaugh."

Ryan gave me an appraising scan, and seemed impressed by what he saw. Sticking out a hand, he said, "Pleased to meet you, Amelia. Welcome to Baker, Wright and Kavanaugh." He smiled brightly, and his eyes smiled along with him.

"Thank you, Mr. Kavanaugh. If you don't mind me asking, would you happen to be related to the Kavanaugh whose name is on the side of the building?" His face seemed open enough, so I figured I might as well get the question out of the way.

"My father, Patrick. Nepotism has not gone out of style around here, as you'll see," he said with a wry grin. "You'll likely meet him soon enough, although he's semi-retired now and spends as much time as he can on the golf course. And please call me Ryan. Did you meet my assistant, Sam, on your way in?"

"She did," Diana replied for me, and he glanced over at her almost as if he'd forgotten she was standing there. "They're having lunch together today. I'm sure she'll fill Amelia in on all the goings-on around here," she added pointedly.

Ryan frowned for a split second, but looked back at me and quickly replaced it with a smile. "Good. She's pretty much my right arm. I'd be lost without her." I noticed Diana's eyes narrow a little at that. "Well, if you need anything, Amelia, don't hesitate to ask Sam or myself. We'll be happy to help you out."

"Thank you. Everyone seems so nice so far. I can't wait to get settled in."

"We won't take up any more of your valuable time this morning, Ryan," Diana interjected. "I *would* like to speak with you about the Tuscan Airlines campaign later though if you can spare a few minutes." She seemed just a little strained, although she was clearly trying hard to hide it. I heard the miniscule quaver in her voice on the last few words, and it surprised me. I wondered if the two had some sort of history. Sam would likely know. I guessed if there was a back-story, before long I'd hear about it. Not that I was really one for office gossip, but I'd found in the past that understanding the personal relationships between people in my direct working circle could sometimes be helpful in knowing how to react to situations.

"Come on, Amelia, there are more people to meet in this department," Diana said as she guided me out of Ryan's office.

"There are two other Account Managers who work out of this office. I know Marilyn Silver isn't in this week—she's in New York—but Declan might be around." We walked down the hallway to another office. The nameplate outside the open door read, *Declan Kavanaugh*.

Diana saw me eyeing it. "Ryan's brother," she explained. "I see he's not in. Well, maybe that's for the best today. You'll meet him soon enough." She turned up a row of cubicles.

I couldn't help but steal a glance inside the other Kavanaugh's office as I passed. It was impeccably neat: chair pushed into the desk, file folders and mail stacked in a tray in one corner, even the man's pens were lined up neatly beside his keyboard. Beside the computer monitor sat a hinged photo frame displaying a wedding photo on the left, and a portrait of a smiling child on the right.

Diana's voice interrupted my perusal. "His wife is Laura Logan, from the evening news in Swann's Landing," she said. "Small town minor celebrity. You probably know of her?"

My eyes widened as I clicked in. I knew exactly who Laura Logan was. Scott watched the local news almost every night over dinner, and he'd admitted a few times that he thought she was hot. Laura had gone to Swann's Landing High with us years ago.

"Oh yes, we actually went to the same high school." Though we'd never run in the same social circles, I seemed to recall that we'd had a few classes together at one point. How weird that now I would soon be working with Laura's husband.

A woman with curly dark hair stood to greet us, and Diana led me over to her. "This is Colleen Talbot, Declan's admin assistant," she explained. I smiled graciously, faking alertness, and shook her hand.

So many faces. So many names. They all seemed very nice, and I was sure after a few days I'd remember most of them. But right now, all this information and all these people were beginning to blur together. We'd gone through five departments before this one. All I could think about was that this tour was nearly over, and I couldn't wait to get back to my desk and take a few moments to regroup.

Seconds later, although the extent wasn't fully grasped at the time, the universe threw me a gigantic curveball. It wasn't until late that night as I tossed and turned in my bed, unable to sleep, unable to get the face of the blue-eyed man out of my head, that I got some idea how much potential this had to become a problem if I wasn't careful.

www.ingramcontent.com/pod-product-compliance
Lightning Source LLC
Chambersburg PA
CBHW072123250626
47159CB00007B/2548